Lightbreakers

ALSO BY AJA GABEL

The Ensemble

Lightbreakers

AJA GABEL

FLEET

FLEET

First published in the United States in 2025 by Riverhead Books,
an imprint of Penguin Random House LLC
First published in Great Britain in 2025 by Fleet

1 3 5 7 9 10 8 6 4 2

A CIP catalogue record for this book
is available from the British Library.

ISBN 978-0-349-72543-7

Book design by Meighan Cavanaugh
Printed and bound in Great Britain by
Clays Ltd, Elcograf S.p.A

Papers used by Fleet are from well-managed forests
and other responsible sources.

FSC
www.fsc.org

MIX
Paper | Supporting
responsible forestry
FSC® C104740

Fleet
An imprint of
Little, Brown Book Group
Carmelite House
50 Victoria Embankment
London EC4Y 0DZ

The authorised representative
in the EEA is
Hachette Ireland
8 Castlecourt Centre
Dublin 15, D15 XTP3, Ireland
(email: info@hbgi.ie)

An Hachette UK Company
www.hachette.co.uk

www.littlebrown.co.uk

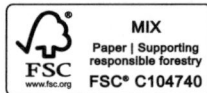

For David,
who helps me believe.

And we begin to see that we are time. We are this space, this clearing opened by the traces of memory inside the connections between our neurons. We are memory. We are nostalgia. We are longing for a future that will not come. The clearing that is opened up in this way, by memory and by anticipation, is time: a source of anguish sometimes, but in the end a tremendous gift.

—Carlo Rovelli, *The Order of Time*

I

The Beginning

Maya

In the beginning, there was happiness.

Maya remembered how nervous Noah had been when they met, clenching and unclenching his hands and repeatedly brushing a single dark curl off his forehead. The curl always fell right back, the act fruitless. At first this disoriented Maya, seeing how nervous he was despite being attractive. And though she was an artist who believed the very idea of objective beauty was suspect, she had to admit he *was* objectively beautiful. In the years to come, she often caught people staring at his aristocrat cheekbones, his flop of dark hair, his broad and perfectly articulated shoulders. But when he spoke to her that first time, he stammered, tripping over the academic phrases she'd used from her training in art history, and almost immediately he confessed, "I'm sorry, I only really know science."

He had wandered into her student symposium talk, which wasn't technically public, but the way he carefully crept in and took a seat behind the professors made it seem like he'd been invited. She'd been presenting on a Japanese photographer she admired, who had been a major inspiration for her own painting practice. When the talk was over and the congratulations offered, the professors dispersed. The stranger hung around, waiting to speak to her.

"That's all right," Maya said. "Art is for everyone." She felt stupid for blurting out a trite aphorism, but he gulped it right up. She felt like taking it back would be taking it from him. Her offhand thought was that she was safe.

She asked what kind of science he studied, assuming he was a graduate student, if an older one. He was white and had the same look of the intense white guys in the math department who had a nearby seminar at the same time as hers. He mumbled that he actually worked for JPL, the NASA research lab, as a physicist. *Oh*, she thought, *so he's smart, I'm in trouble.* As the room emptied, they remained talking. At one point, when neither of them moved for a spell, the motion-sensor lights flicked off.

"Oh no," Maya said, but Noah didn't seem fazed. In the darkness, he asked her to go out with him. When she laughed, delighted, the lights came back on.

They went to dinner right then, to a nearby taco stand, where they sat on folding chairs on the sidewalk. She told him that her talk was for her nearly completed master's in modern and contemporary art, focusing on the intersection of photography and painting, but that she wasn't sure if she wanted to continue on the doctoral track. She had a BFA in painting, and sometimes that was what she really wanted to do, paint. She told him some people said painting was dead, which she strongly disagreed with. That was like saying handwriting was dead.

"But handwriting *is* dead," he said, and this made her laugh again, at how plainly and earnestly he said it.

She was giddy with happiness. Any awkwardness fizzled away. They lingered with empty plates and shouted conversation at each other over the roar of passing motorcycles.

Now, looking back, she understood that Noah's earnestness was a kind of hope that she—and this taco night, this electricity between them—could propel him away from his sadness. But no, at that point, she didn't know about the sadness. She wouldn't know about it until their fourth date and two sleepovers later, when she found a picture of a baby at the bottom of a drawer, beneath a bottle of Tylenol and a box of Band-Aids. All she knew on that first night, as he dropped her off in front of her apartment, was that something in him was splayed out, something that she could put back together if she could only gather it all up in her hands.

Later, she would understand this as her impulse toward caretaking: Noah harboring a wound, Maya desperate to mend it. And even later than that, she would understand that his sadness was a sediment layer, never far away, waiting beneath everything in him.

"Wait," he said through the car window. "Will you come out with me tomorrow?"

The way he'd asked her, "will you" instead of "do you want to," implied he needed her to come out. *Will you, do you have the will inside you to be with me.* She would and she did, for years after, even when she began to realize that being with him was not the simple answer they'd both thought it might be.

Someone had asked Maya this question—"How did you meet your husband?"—at the museum where she worked. It was the kickoff cocktail party for the fundraising campaign she had organized herself. She knew she should have felt pride, but standing in the airy gallery surrounded by the wealthiest people on the museum's roster, she was only itchy with boredom. The woman standing in front of her was wearing trousers and a silk blouse that Maya recognized as Gucci, the kind of matching that was curated at a shop on Rodeo Drive, an on-the-nose pairing that indicated the person had no actual personal style.

But Maya had to be vivacious and interesting to this woman. It was her job as development manager, as someone in charge of extracting money from wealthy dilettantes.

The question—"How did you meet your husband?"—was not uncommon, especially after people found out Maya was married to a scientist, as though science and art were incompatible. But today she hesitated before answering. This woman was staring at her, her expression expectant beneath a smear of gold eyeshadow. Caroline, Maya's boss and good friend, appeared before them, her smile tight.

"Maya?" Caroline said, laughing a little. "What, did you forget how you met your husband?"

What Maya was trying to describe was a delicate balance between what it had felt like then and what it felt like now. Then: lightness, the promise of the unknown. Now: Even though so much was known, there remained an unknown slice. But this slice was not light, not a promise. Only gray space on a map, unexplorable land.

Maya blushed. "Oh, sorry. I was just remembering it. He wandered into a talk I was giving to my graduate professors," she said, making it simple. But then she said, "When we got to talking, it felt like there was so much potential for happiness. Like we were two sides of a convoluted math equation. And once you solved for everything, all the variables or imaginary numbers or whatever, there we were. My flaws and needs accounted for in his strengths, and vice versa."

Caroline and the woman continued to stare at her, uncomprehending.

"He's a physicist but he mostly works in mathematical modeling," Maya said.

"Ah," the woman said. "One forgets math is the basis of everything."

"I don't know," Maya said. "The ancient cave paintings in France might have you believe otherwise."

Caroline shot her the quickest look—*What are you doing?*—before turning back to the woman. "Susan, that reminds me, have you read that essay in the Alexander Calder exhibition book? About his use of the Fibonacci sequence and geometry principles? It's honestly very fascinating. Here, Sam can grab you a copy. Come this way."

And like that, Caroline had saved her. Holding her flute of warm champagne, Maya scanned the party. Attendees were eating the passed mini-quiches and standing an appropriate distance from the art on the walls. Every now and then someone would uproariously laugh over the mellow sounds of the live jazz trio playing in the corner. Maya spotted the museum's wealthiest targets, the couple with property in both the Beverly Hills flats and the actual hills, being charmed by the young ceramicist she'd invited, a long-haired Korean American man in loose carpenter pants and a threadbare T-shirt. She tried to catch his eye, to share a glance that would say, *Both of us Asians in this sea of white wealth, huh?* But he didn't meet her eye, and she realized with an uneasy pang that to him, she wasn't a peer. He was the artist, while she was the establishment, the suit.

Later, after donations had been taken or at least promised, and the crowd began to thin, Caroline found Maya once more. They'd been in college together, both art majors, but Caroline was more levelheaded and ambitious, always lining up internships and informational interviews. After school, she had dated around a couple of years before meeting Vincent, and then, like clockwork, she went to business school, bought a house in Los Angeles, and had a baby. Caroline had always been more grown-up than Maya, and Maya should have known that one day Caroline would hire her, which was exactly what happened when Maya's painting career stagnated and she was desperate for a change. Maya had been unqualified for this job, but she learned InDesign and the donor database and how to ask people for money without actually asking them, and the art she loved, always. They had a Robert Irwin at the museum, installed outdoors, and she was lucky to eat lunch some days while staring at it.

"You and Noah are *math equations?*" Caroline said, bumping Maya with her hip.

"No, we're one equation. Two sides."

"Okay," Caroline said. "Maybe the champagne is going to your head."

"She asked the question!" Maya protested.

"She didn't want a real answer."

Caroline took a napkin to a damp stain on Maya's silk shift. "You need soda water."

"I need . . ." Maya started to say. *A new job. Something to paint.*

But Caroline knew her. She knew what Maya wanted even when Maya didn't know how to express it. Their junior year they'd gone to Montreal for spring break and closed down a cheesy club that played French house music. Afterward, Maya had drunkenly dragged them toward the tiny convertible of the two beautiful Italian men they'd met on the dance floor, but Caroline seamlessly and believably made up the excuse that they *actually* had to go to the bathroom, and led Maya away from the strangers. From a terrace, they'd watched as the men drunkenly drove their car into a pole, crunching the hood and setting off the airbags. The men were okay, but Maya was shaken into sobriety.

"You knew the future," she had whispered.

"I knew the present," Caroline had replied. "You didn't want to go with them."

And Caroline was right, as she always was. Maya had gotten caught up. She tended to do that.

Which is why when Caroline said, "You need to quit?" Maya wasn't at all surprised that her friend had sensed what she was too afraid to say. This job was only supposed to be temporary, and here she was, caught up in it.

Maya smiled and said, "I don't know. I can't quit. I need the money." She added quickly, "And of course, I'm so grateful that you hired me at all."

Caroline nodded. "Always."

"I need to know if anything I did was the right thing," Maya said, sounding a little funny but also a little desperate.

"Anything you did?"

"Noah's whole deal, what he was coming out of, what we were going to do together, it was so hopeful in the beginning. We were both so hopeful. But explaining all that to her just now, I thought maybe I was wrong. Maybe it was only me who was hopeful."

Caroline laughed. "Right now is when you discovered Noah's baggage?"

Of course Noah had baggage. Everyone had locked away parts of themselves. But lately Maya had been wondering if that locked-away part of Noah was what drove him to her, and if keeping her away from it was necessary to maintain the careful balance of their union. She hadn't thought of his sadness that way before, and now she couldn't see it any other way.

"You and Noah are perfectly matched," Caroline said. She linked her arm with Maya's. "Let the crew you so expertly hired clean this up. Paperwork can wait until the morning."

Caroline walked Maya to the parking garage and told her that if she wanted, she could take some time off after the fundraising campaign was over. A week or so. "See if you want to paint again—you know, regularly." Maya shrugged. Was that what was bothering her? Not painting?

When Maya got in her car and started the drive home, she couldn't stop thinking. She thought about her and Noah's second, third, and fourth dates, and she thought about when they first brought up marriage, and then their actual marriage, now three years old, the age that most marriages decide to try to add a child or do without. Three was also the age Noah's child had been when she died. Almost four, Noah would say. Almost.

She replayed what she'd said to Caroline and the donor, that Noah accounted for her gaps and she accounted for his. It had felt like that when they met. It had felt like that for a while. Years into their marriage, though, she wasn't so sure.

She turned the car onto their street, up a winding hill in the Mount Washington neighborhood. A good school district, the Realtor had told them. Maya thought she wanted a kid, and Noah was not opposed to the idea. "Not opposed" were the exact words he'd used when she brought it up, in the toys section of Target, where she'd had to buy a baby shower gift. "I think I want it," he'd said, refusing to use a real noun, like *baby* or *child*. Of course, he'd already had it, long ago, with his first wife.

She wound around a blind corner and then into the steep driveway of their Craftsman. Noah's car wasn't there. It was 9:42 p.m., and he should have been home, even on a day he worked late. Maya walked into the house and set her boots neatly by the front door. She went straight to the kitchen, where she pulled from the fridge a cold bottle of pinot gris.

She poured a glass. What did she want? To know what to want, how to want it.

When she turned around, Noah's silhouetted figure in the doorway startled her backward, sending the wineglass stuttering across the counter. Miraculously, it didn't break.

"The door's wide open," he said.

"I just got home." She must have forgotten to close the door behind her. "God, you scared the shit out of me."

He turned on the lamp by the door, and she saw that his face wore a look she recognized, the same anxious, energized expression he'd had when he first suggested they get married.

"What's going on?" Maya asked.

On the couch, with Maya three sips into her wine and his untouched, he told her about Klein Michaels, the invisible clock, and a person he used to be, years before she knew him.

Noah

It started with the invitation to dinner.

No, it started with the paper.

Years ago, a lifetime ago, when Eileen was pregnant, before Serena was born, Noah published a paper. It wasn't his first paper, but it was the most controversial. No one in the academic community was willing to touch it, so he put it up on an open-access platform as a preprint, thinking it wouldn't be noticed but at least it'd be out there. But people *had* seen it, because they'd laughed about it, and soon Noah's name started popping up on chat boards where his peers and people he'd met at conferences shared anecdotes about how they always knew he was sloppy with his data (he wasn't!) or how he was not a rigorous student (he was as rigorous as one could be) or how one time at a dinner he'd been too sympathetic to the visiting fringe theoretical physicists who were clearly off base (this one was true).

All because his paper, "Quantum Tunneling and Electromagnetic Fields in the Brain," had dared to make the case that human consciousness arose from quantum mechanics. Almost everyone in neuroscience agreed that consciousness is a product of classical physics—complex neural activity in the brain. The problem, however, was that scientists hadn't determined exactly *what* activity produced consciousness, because the brain's neural network was the most advanced computing system on earth. But if that was the case, then why couldn't a very powerful computer reproduce consciousness? So, in that vacuum of provability, a fringe idea from quantum physics emerged: The brain didn't operate like a classical computer, and instead, on the smallest scale of the brain, the scale of particles and fields, a quantum phenomenon must be taking place, resulting in consciousness.

The theory was unpopular and disorganized, but it had appealed to Noah. His paper looked at the role of electromagnetic fields in the neural encoding of memories, involving particle entanglement. Entanglement, that strange idea in quantum physics that two entangled particles can be connected even when separated by vast distances. What Einstein called "spooky action at a distance." For Noah, the spookiness was exciting, a place to posit theories, to explore the edges of possibility, to practice believing. But with his paper, that excitement had exposed something laughable, a tendency toward an unprovable faith in quantum physics.

So, embarrassed and shamed in certain corners of his field, Noah had left theoretical physics and taken refuge in experimental physics instead. He'd taken a job at JPL, a scientific organization that was decidedly *not* sloppy with data—the steady, safe world of creating math justifications for labs across disciplines, and designing models to answer questions about what would happen or had happened in experiments. There was always a solution to be found in math. This was what he loved most about what he did. He answered small questions in the field of physics, where so many larger questions remained unanswered for generations.

And then Eileen had Serena, and Noah didn't think about his paper anymore, or the assumptions and implications of entanglement. And then Serena died, and not even math solved that problem. Now he tried not to think about any of it—his paper, his daughter, and his last marriage.

Until now. He'd received a call at the lab from someone claiming to work for Klein Michaels. Noah had thought he was being scammed. But then the executive gave an address, and a quick online search showed that the Klein Michaels Foundation had recently bought a compound in the exact part of the Hollywood Hills that the executive had named. Klein Michaels was a billionaire who had fallen out of public favor when Noah was younger, after a series of investments turned out to be flops. Noah scanned Klein Michaels's Wikipedia: American-born. Unmarried. Oxford-educated. Liked to call Cyprus home. Partial to mid-century properties. Passionate about a pescatarian diet. Heavily invested in areas that seemed generally bad for the world: oil, fracking, viscose factories, data centers. Largely reclusive for the past two decades, but his money still made money.

"You'll come for dinner tonight," the executive said. "Dress casually. Klein doesn't like suits. And he won't be eating, as he begins his fast every day at five p.m., which we realize is much earlier than most people begin their fasts."

Was Noah supposed to be fasting? He said, "How do I know this isn't a prank?"

The executive laughed a little. "You don't, of course. You'll have to believe. Which, given your background, shouldn't be hard."

Given your background. The rest of the day Noah wondered what this meant. His background in physics? Physicists are notorious non-believers. As a divorcé? Also a faith-crumbling exercise. As a Californian? As a younger brother? The only other background of note he had was as the father of a deceased child. During lunch, sitting in his car eating an unsatisfying salad that cost eighteen dollars, he allowed himself to think about that classification. There had been so many people in those months after Serena died who invoked God as a salve. Near-strangers from his past, preschool parents, an HR person from an old job he'd held for mere months, reaching out to say they were praying or that God has a plan or that in the absence of a plan, God soothes, God saves. None of it soothed or saved.

People thought losing a child would make you believe. No, it could only make you desperate to believe, and sure you could never.

So Noah drove up Mulholland and into canyons he didn't know existed, arriving at an intimidating bronze gate bearing the Klein Michaels Foundation logo. He gave his name and license to the security guard and was directed up a winding, eucalyptus-lined road to a compound that rivaled the Getty Museum. It had the stark, chrome veneer of an institution. Klein lived here? Noah briefly wondered if he should have texted Maya to tell her about this strange dinner, but she had her fundraising event tonight, anyway.

A young man in an impeccably tailored suit emerged and introduced himself as Oliver, the executive Noah had spoken with earlier. Noah looked down at his own light-wash jeans and checked button-down, irritated that Oliver had told him to dress casually.

"It's okay," Oliver said. "I prefer suits. But when Klein meets people—you know, real people—he likes them to come as they are."

"I'm real people," Noah said, though it came out like a question. He realized the walls weren't stark white, but textured, made of some kind of opulent, crinkled fabric.

"Yes," Oliver said curtly, and he spun on his heels. "This way."

They passed through a massive English garden to reach what Oliver called a cottage, but which looked to Noah like an art deco spaceship on stilts. Inside, Oliver led Noah along a curved hallway past several closed doors, finally stopping in a carpeted dining room that held a massive table. Noah sat in a deeply uncomfortable angular wooden chair.

"Nine minutes," Oliver said without further explication, and left Noah alone in the room. Somewhere an invisible clock ticked, ticked, ticked. Noah wondered if this was a test, *where is that clock*, and just as he was about to get up from his chair and take a look around, Klein Michaels entered.

He was, of course, much shorter than Noah had expected. But he had an incredible head of brown hair and the world's firmest handshake. Noah had to hold back a wince. Klein was immediately affable, offering an easy smile. He was wearing a suit.

When they both sat down, Klein nodded at an open door, and almost instantly a waiter in whites appeared holding a dome-covered silver tray. Noah's dinner. Salmon with dill, perfectly crisped potatoes, and asparagus, exactly as Noah had approved in the email that followed Oliver's call.

"I caught that salmon myself. Yesterday. In Alaska," Klein said.

Noah's eyes widened. "Really? Wow, thank you."

Klein smiled. "I always wanted to be the sort of guy who fished. My father didn't fish, and never took us. And then one day, I was twenty-seven years old, fresh off the sale of my second company, and it occurred to me. I could take *myself* fishing. Of course, now I have a team of expert fishermen in Alaska, Scotland, even Russia, and a semi-monthly heli-fishing date during the season, but back then, it was only me and a pole in Montana, Wyoming, Idaho. It's good for the soul. To be alone out there, outside of any context, just me, my brain, my spirit. And man, I love fresh salmon. I tried veganism but I missed this fish too much. Plenty of research shows that eating salmon as a primary source of protein contributes to a longer life expectancy. Do you believe in that, anyway?"

Noah understood Klein's speech as a performance—the cowboy philosopher billionaire going on a tangent about fishing, something a regular guy like Noah might understand—but he liked the performance. It felt fluent and easy.

"I haven't read that salmon data," Noah said. "But I believe you."

"Not about the salmon. The soul."

Noah looked at him. "Sorry, what are you asking?"

"Please, dig in." And then when Noah began to eat the fish: "The soul. I'm asking if you believe in a soul."

Noah laughed. The fish was buttery, tender, the freshest he'd ever tasted. He had to slow himself down. The drive had been long, and he was starving. "I think there is no evidence that a soul doesn't exist. Hard to prove either way."

"Mm," Klein said. "Do you want to know what I think?"

"I didn't know I was allowed to ask you questions."

Klein laughed at this. "Of course you are."

"Okay. Do you believe in a soul?"

"It's as reasonable to believe that quantum mechanics is responsible for human consciousness as it is to believe that there is a classical physics justification, which has yet to be proven. It stands to reason that electromagnetic fields could amplify quantum effects in the brain's neurons on a macro level, concerning coherence across consciousness levels."

Noah put his fork down. Klein was parroting back to him, word for word, the final paragraph of Noah's forgotten, laughed-at paper. Klein continued: "But I leave such expansive proposals to be examined by future scientists."

Noah spoke aloud the paper's next sentence, the part that everyone seemed to forget, which was his disclaimer: "Who am I to say?"

"Ah," Klein said. "So hello. This is the future, Noah. You are the future scientists."

"I wasn't talking about the soul in that paper."

"You were talking about consciousness, something more than synapses and neurons."

"But I didn't name it the soul."

"You didn't say it outright, but you were talking about it."

Okay. Noah would give in a little. "What I think is that consciousness has to be more than classical mechanics. Otherwise we'd be able to replicate consciousness with a complex machine."

"But we haven't yet made a machine as complex as the human brain."

"Are you arguing against me now?"

Klein smiled warmly. "For argument's sake."

"Okay, then. Your argument doesn't make what I'm saying untrue, necessarily. If we could make a machine as complex as the human brain, all I'm saying is that we'd likely have to replicate quantum processes in that complex machine to produce consciousness."

"To produce a soul."

"To produce the ability to know who we are, to understand past and future, to have moral quandaries, to desire and want, to regret."

"To believe in something."

"Yes."

"Which is what a soul is, isn't it?"

"The part of us that believes," Noah said.

Klein slapped the table, excited. "That's why you're here."

"You made a machine with a soul?"

"No, of course not." Klein laughed a little. "I made a machine that can transport a soul."

What Klein went on to describe, he did so without pause, without letting Noah interject or ask questions, which meant the whole of Klein's argument descended on Noah like a slow-rolling boulder.

He said that Noah's work was accurate, and that Noah was right, the findings were applicable to larger, more expansive quantum effects.

With the help of a team of neuroscientists, engineers, and physicists, Klein had done what others had been laughed at for even suggesting. He'd found a way to prove not only that human consciousness was indeed a quantum phenomenon but also that human consciousness was a cohered system that could participate in entanglement, enabling information to travel across time and space, however briefly.

When Klein finished speaking, Noah coughed, suddenly parched. Klein nodded again toward the door, and a waiter appeared with a fresh glass of water. Noah drank the whole thing.

"That's . . ." Noah trailed off. The sun had dipped below the canyon perimeter and the light in the room changed. Now, without the blast of sunlight, he saw an embedded clock on the wall behind Klein's head, the source of the ticking. How was the clock attached to the wall? Had it been built into it?

"Information travel," Noah said. "In consciousness. Proven by quantum mechanics."

Klein bowed his head, a single nod.

Noah continued, almost laughing. "You mean to say that driven by quantum processes in the brain, you've made possible what some people might call *time travel*."

This time, Klein didn't bow his head. He looked at Noah straight on, like what Noah was saying was deeply interesting and amusing.

"In rats?" Noah asked. "Mice? As a proxy for human consciousness?"

Klein clasped his hands together on the table, a gesture of finality, though there had been no offer or proposal. Instinctively, Noah stood. But Klein remained seated.

"You think I'm ridiculous, don't you?" Klein asked.

Noah shrugged. "I think you're rich."

Klein laughed again. "I didn't think you'd be funny. Considering."

"I'd like to stop by this lab," Noah said. "And see what you've done. Perhaps JPL could partner with you in—"

"God, no," Klein said. "I'm not looking for a JPL partnership. This is self-funded. The only way to assure we stay on track, no need for red tape, regulatory bureaucracy, et cetera. But you're welcome to come by the lab. In fact, that's why you're here. Please, sit down. Your wife is at her museum event. She won't be expecting you home anytime soon."

A cold shot ran down Noah's sternum. He hadn't told Klein or Oliver about Maya or her plans tonight. But Klein was a billionaire, and of course he had done his research on Noah. Noah had to assume he would not be inside Klein's personal home if Klein didn't already know everything about him. He relaxed into this thought, the intimacy of Klein knowing everything about him. A burden relieved.

And that's when Klein invited Noah to Marfa, Texas, to a parcel of undeveloped land right outside town, where Klein had built a lab. More than invited—he offered Noah a job at the lab. Then he named a salary figure so high Noah initially thought he'd misheard him.

"Look, I know how it sounds," Klein said. "But you have to come see it. You'll get it then. Are you an extravagant guy, Noah?"

"I think I live pretty modestly, actually," Noah said.

"Yes, but I think you're extravagant in your ability to believe. Don't you believe me? Don't you want to?"

Tick, tick. Noah had already decided he'd go, he realized. He hadn't even tried to come up with an argument against it. For the second time that dinner, he said, "I believe you."

Maya

"Klein named it the Janus Project," Noah told Maya. "The lab has taken their work as far as it can go and now they need me. At least that's what Klein said. Who knows if it's true?" As Noah spoke, Maya saw that he was wired; he was barely blinking.

"Klein knows. If he said that, it's true," she said.

He shrugged, but he was grinning. "Yeah."

"What did he smell like, Klein?"

Still smiling, Noah said, "Like nothing at all. The whole place had no scent, it was pristine."

"Incredible," Maya said.

He had recounted the entire meeting for her, including the mention Klein made of her fundraising event at the museum. Maya privately wondered whether one of Klein's people had followed her, and she thought back to her conversation about Noah with Caroline. Had she said anything incriminating? *Noah is sad, Noah has baggage.* She finished her glass of wine and put her hand on Noah's leg, high enough to claim him, his body, his mind, his breath, hers. "This is important to you, right?"

"Maya, it's important to the entire scientific community. If what they're saying is possible, then I was right."

"Let's do it," she said. "Let's move to Texas." Once she said it, she felt like the train had already left and she'd barely grabbed on, wind in her hair, her life zipping by. A thrill coursed through her.

"Time off would be good for you, too," Noah said. "You've been wanting to reconnect with your art practice for forever. Maybe you'll be inspired there. Or maybe something entirely different will occur to you, an idea we haven't thought of because we've been trapped here, in the slog."

The slog. Noah hadn't been anything but calmly supportive when Maya took the museum job from Caroline two years ago. They'd needed the money. But she could tell he felt like the job was a step backward. When they met, she'd been an intellectual, an academic, an artist. She completed her master's, sold a few pieces, got representation at a minor gallery, but then, just as their relationship took off, her artistic promise stalled. She'd stopped selling, and she'd stopped painting, and now she made far less than someone should make in this city, mastering spreadsheets and mailings and party planning.

The hope on Noah's face she hadn't seen in a long time. This was the Noah who had stood before her at her symposium talk, enthralled by her brain and her promise. He said, "I think the possibilities are endless, and you'll never know if you don't feel free."

He spoke this line like he'd planned out what he was going to say, Maya could tell. She could have found this irritating, knowing he had practiced on the drive home how to convince her to agree to his proposition. But she found it endearing. It had been so long since he'd been in this position, asking her to believe.

So she said that she wanted to believe, too. That she *did* believe. "It'll be good for us."

He moved his leg away from her hand. She initially took this as a rejection, but then he pulled her at the waist, and his hands were in her hair and he was kissing her hungrily. There on the couch, he wordlessly guided her into lovemaking that was far from the measured and efficient way of having sex they'd fallen into recently. Breathlessly, she tried to keep up. It was wonderful in that way that required no thinking, only doing. He pinned her wrists against the cushions and moved inside her such that by the time they finished, the couch was on a diagonal, all the dust bunnies on the floor exposed.

After, they lay across each other like leopards or gazelles—Maya couldn't decide which animal exactly. The porch light was still on, bleeding through the curtains. Two years ago a mountain lion had strolled the neighborhood and Maya had watched it on a compilation of neighbors' security cameras, moving deftly around the Priuses with muscly disregard. She watched those curtains every night for a week, waiting to see it cross their driveway, but it never did.

Noah's head lay on her torso. They were content.

"You never told me about the paper," Maya said, breaking the silence.

"It was so long ago," he answered, the movement of his throat rocking her belly. "And it was embarrassing. I tried to forget it."

"But I didn't know *that's* why you went to JPL. I asked you how you got into doing models and you said your mentor told you it was an interesting area for people who wanted to work in cross-discipline physics."

"He did."

"Can I read your paper?"

"It would be so tedious, I promise you. I explained anything relevant to you already."

She couldn't see his face but she could feel him sighing hot air, his warning sign: He didn't want to talk about this.

But then he said something she didn't expect.

"Eileen always made a big deal out of it. It was annoying."

Her name, *Eileen*, like a dull dagger pressing against Maya's chest.

"She did?" Maya asked, treading carefully. He almost never spoke of his ex-wife.

She felt Noah shrug against her body. He was done, but she wasn't. An electric bubble formed in her throat.

"So this professionally embarrassing thing happened to you and made you abandon a whole sector of physics, and you never thought I should know about it?"

At this, Noah sat up, ungluing his skin from hers. He pulled his boxers back on. "You're making this into too big a deal."

"But Eileen knew all about it."

"What does that have to do with anything?"

Eileen has to do with everything, she wanted to say. Eileen held the other half of the sadness boulder Noah carried around. But Maya didn't say that. Noah was irritated and she knew if she pushed, the irritation would turn to anger. Instead, she sat back and listened to his steps upstairs as he readied himself for bed. He'd fall asleep, she'd follow, and they'd wake up new, happy, and ready to move to Texas.

But first. Maya pulled out her phone and typed in the search terms her browser had stored: "Eileen Merrick" and "Eileen Merrick Byatt." It had taken Eileen a couple of years to expunge Noah's last name, Byatt, from her online presence, but she was listed without it at the university up north where she was a professor. Maya checked all the usual spots—Eileen's sparse LinkedIn, her private Instagram, an unused Facebook page, the university website, Eileen's face smiling out from all of them. She was blond with broad features, big wide-set eyes, a stately nose, a warm and open smile, but she was plain, really. Or she seemed plain in the photos; nothing in them was afire with secrets about Noah.

Tonight she was in search of a different kind of information. There was a public photo storage account under Eileen's married name, so old that Maya was shocked it hadn't been deleted. It held an album of three photos. Maya had visited these photos many times. One was a blurry picture of Noah with layers of filters that were trendy at the time, and another was a mirror selfie in which Eileen's whole face was covered by the phone. Maya figured the bathroom Eileen was standing in belonged to the Los Feliz house Noah had shared with her, only because his green plaid robe hung on a hook next to her head. He still had the robe, and now it hung in their bathroom.

But the third photo, Noah had taken. Noah, Maya was sure. It was of Eileen, pregnant, maybe late second trimester, her stomach perfectly round. She was standing in profile, holding the bottom of her bump, and behind her was the giant luscious green lawn of the palm garden at the Huntington Library in Pasadena. In the far distance were sixty-foot-tall palm trees, but the camera wasn't concerned with those. Eileen was what shone in the picture. She wore a light blue smocked maxi dress, and her hair was half-up. Her head was tilted down toward her stomach but her eyes cut up, at the camera. She had a look that was part mischief and part invitation, part open and part closed. The kind of double look you can only give the person who knows you the best in the world, and whose heart you own without reservation.

There was a secret in the photo. If Maya had to pull from it a thesis, the way she'd been taught to talk about her art in school, she would say: *This image is about the future.*

"Moving to Marfa will be good for you," Caroline said.

Maya and Caroline were using all their hand strength to pipe hard icing onto gluten-free low-sugar cupcakes. It was Caroline's son Jasper's fourth birthday party. Outside, in Caroline's tiered backyard, children stood precariously on ledges and jumped into the garden plots.

"I know, I've been to Joshua Tree for a long weekend. Change of scenery. A little remote," Maya said. "Crystals. Sunsets."

"Except you're going for more than a long weekend. Klein told Noah six months to a year? That's like, when you come back, all the wine bars will be different."

"That actually puts it into perspective."

"Okay, so what I'm saying is, it will be good for you, to focus on your own art." Caroline leaned across the counter and whispered, "But also you'll have time for a Jasper."

"Time for Jasper?"

As if on cue, Jasper shrieked outside. Someone turned on a hose, and the spray thunked against the side of the house.

"Goddammit," Caroline said. "Vince!" she called out the open window. "They're four years old! Don't give them a hose!"

When Caroline turned back to the icing, she said, "Not Jasper. *A* Jasper. A baby."

Maya could feel her face flushing. She looked around for Noah, and found him holding a beer and talking to a woman with an infant strapped to her chest. He bent down slightly to say hello to the baby, but kept a healthy distance.

"Are you blushing?" Caroline asked. "Can you be bashful and also pipe icing at the same time?"

Maya tightened her grip on the piping bag. "I'm not bashful. I don't know. It's exciting. But I haven't talked to him about it yet."

"You guys have talked about having a baby," Caroline said.

"We've talked about it, but we haven't agreed on exactly what or when."

"I'm telling you, Marfa is when. Imagine when that money starts depositing in your bank account, and you start painting sunsets or Georgia O'Keeffe flowers—"

"Stop it," Maya said, laughing.

"—which is to say, perfectly primed ovaries. Desert air, full bank accounts, can't lose."

Caroline had seamlessly known she wanted a baby and then seamlessly conceived. It was so easy for some women, the knowing, the making. But Maya felt like she lived in a place of permanent ambivalence about having children, which wasn't helped by Noah's situation.

"Well, I'll have to talk to him about it."

"Of course. Only you and Noah know about your future. In Marfa you'll have lots of time and space for Noah to come around."

"I don't want him to come around, though. I can't be the one carrying the enthusiasm for both of us."

Yes, Noah had lost a child. But that meant he knew how transformative it was to love a child. He'd said so himself, in the early days of their relationship, how he often thought of things as *before Serena* and *after Serena*. But with Maya he wouldn't be making a decision about another Serena. Not everything was about Serena. The decision Noah had to make was a specific one, about a different child with a different woman.

"I'll tell you one thing now," Caroline said. "As a mother, you carry a lot for other people that you don't want to. Now let's carry these cupcakes."

Noah popped his head in the sliding glass door. "You talking about me?" But he was smiling, and the front of his button-down was dripping. "We need Mom. The hose is broken and we can't turn it off."

Outside, once Maya and Caroline handed out all the towels and Caroline had taken pliers to the hose, she presented the cupcakes. Maya and Noah stood in the back, one of only two couples without children. The other couple, Vincent's retired aunt and uncle, sat in beach chairs on the edge of the patio.

Maya and Noah put their arms around each other and started to sing "Happy Birthday." Jasper, with wild black hair and an equally wild grin, took it all in, the praise, the attention, the treats, the fire of the candles. Maya felt Noah's arm go limp on her shoulders, and she started to hunch under the weight of it.

"Noah," she said into his ear.

He didn't look at her.

"Noah," she said again. "Are you okay?"

She saw Caroline cut a cupcake in half and hand a portion to Vince. They smiled at each other over Jasper's head.

"Do you want to sit?" Maya asked, but this time she moved around to face Noah, and saw that his eyes were shining wet and his cheeks were streaked. He smiled at her, as if nothing were out of order. "Oh," she said. "What's wrong?"

He didn't stop smiling the whole time, as if he could smile through it and make it all fine. But he said, in a half voice that wobbled, "Four years old. It's quite an age."

Oh, Maya understood now. Jasper was older than Serena ever would be. Now she knew the wobble in his voice belonged to Serena, halfway in this world and halfway in the world of his loss. She had been wrong. Everything was about Serena. Caroline had said that only Maya and Noah knew about their future, but looking at her husband, swallowing a sob from a world she'd never see, she realized that only Noah knew.

Noah

The house was rented out and the car was heavy with their life, but Noah felt light. He and Maya drove along a strip of highway in the New Mexico lonesome, heading toward an overnight stop in Las Cruces. With each *thwomp* of the road under the tires, Noah felt lighter. He wasn't sure what exactly he was leaving behind—everything but what was necessary—and he couldn't name what he was heading toward except to say something in him felt locked up, and he had the feeling that in Marfa he could make a key.

"There's a turkey vulture," Maya said.

She rolled the window down and a burst of warm air filled the car. "Look. Don't normally see them this close."

Noah couldn't see the bird from the driver's seat, but he enjoyed Maya's astonishment. She was always astonished by things. Not in a childlike way, not wild and unfocused, but deeply focused, and curious about what the astonishment could lead to.

"Anyway." She tucked her head back in the car and rolled the window up, sealing them in. "This one girl I went to school with did her entire thesis on ways of looking at a vulture. Art school loves a pretentious symbol."

"Nothing more pretentious than a bird of death," Noah said.

"You could say it's also a bird of rebirth. Part of their job is to carry stuff on to the next phase of the life cycle."

He warmed. Maya, sitting next to him, was similar to how she was when he met her. Unexpected, a little askew, tall, long dark bangs, a loosely knit sweater hanging off one shoulder, eyes bright, with a look on her face like she'd never get tired of asking questions. She had kinetic energy, even when she was still, when his stillness made her so.

She'd asked him a few hours earlier when he first knew that he loved her. When he really *knew*. She liked to do this on road trips, ask a loaded question and then riff on it for the entire drive. It made Noah feel a little loopy, but she liked being an investigator, of memory, of experience. She said she learned it from art school, that following a line of questioning as long as it continued to provide interesting answers was part of a studio practice.

Noah wondered where to begin. Three years married, five years together, Maya entering his life like a warm steady light after years of darkness, pain, and grief. He couldn't say that, not without invoking the darkness, pain, and grief. Or other people. He didn't want to weave Maya into all that. She deserved more.

So he said, "The cactus garden. That's when I knew I loved you."

"Obvious choice. I already knew you loved me by then."

"What? How?"

It had been early in their relationship, and he'd shown up at her tiny Silver Lake apartment on a clear April morning, thinking they'd get brunch, fool around, see a movie. But Maya knew the plants in the cactus garden at the Huntington Library were superblooming. The rains had been unusually heavy that winter, she said, and cacti that suck up water during a rainy winter explode in spring. Noah was over-

whelmed by the experience. The plants all looked like they were trans-
forming into aliens, flowers bursting out of their bodies messy and vibrant and neon. They came across one patch of tall, skinny cacti that
carried massive white blossoms at their heads. The flowers, mature
now, grew heavy, and one by one, the cacti had been toppling, breaking clear in half, their gooey white centers bursting out.

"Oh no." Noah had knelt down. He tried to pick one up, but it
pricked him and he withdrew his hand. Maya knelt down and put her
arm around him, placing her head on his sweaty back. They looked at
the broken plants, overwatered, weighed down with their new selves.

Now, in the car, she asked, "Okay, then why? Why there?" and Noah
made his argument.

He changed lanes, and in the back seat, a picture frame jangled out
of the mess of cargo and fell onto the center console. Maya picked it
up. She'd thrown it in the car at the very last minute. It was a selfie of
the two of them on the day she moved into his house. He'd been living
there for only a couple of years, having purchased it way over market
value in a rush after he and Eileen sold their Los Feliz home. The cash
felt like a physical reminder of the divorce, and he was happy to immediately shuttle it into a new, unfamiliar home. One of the rooms
was entirely empty and remained that way until Maya moved in. She
made it her art studio, eventually, and the photo was of the two of
them standing in that empty room. In the photo he was looking at the
camera but Maya was looking at him lovingly.

"I still don't get why we need a picture of our faces with us," Noah
said.

Maya wiped some dust from the frame. "It's for you to take to work,
in case any of those Klein Michaels women get the wrong idea."

"You think Klein hires many women?"

"Good point." She held the photo up in front of her. "But this is
how we know where home is. West Texas or wherever."

"Nonlocal," Noah said. Maya had looked up his paper even after he asked her not to, and he'd had to spend some time trying to explain what he meant by "nonlocal." Eventually he'd settled on saying that scientific truths were not necessarily local to one particle in one place in time. Instead, nonlocality indicated that it was possible for particles to be entangled with other ones, for one particle to know information about another particle, across great distances and spans of time. That phenomenon was possible for everything in the universe, meaning everything in the universe was connected. Maya had said, "Of course it is."

"Home is nonlocal," she said now.

He knew that she was a little sad to leave the house, to rent it out to that Australian couple with two young kids, to pack up her art studio. But she never made him feel guilty about it. She told him she was eager to go, that it would be good to have a new beginning. And then she said maybe they'd find answers about whether they should have a child.

She'd caught him off guard. It had been months since they'd talked about having a baby, and the last time they discussed it, Noah felt he'd indicated that he needed some more time.

"You think?" he had asked. They were sitting on the floor of the upstairs hallway, meticulously folding the contents of the linen closet so it would look nice for the renters.

"I think it would be a good time to try," Maya said. "To take it seriously."

"I'm taking it seriously." He had been slightly offended.

"Oh, I know," she said, immediately retreating. "Sorry, I meant, I guess, getting clarity."

Clarity felt slippery for Noah. There were times when he thought he'd never have another child. That he couldn't bear it. To love someone like that meant risking, once again, the loss. It was so much easier in every way to stay childless with Maya. But there were other times when his desire to have another child, to create a being that generated love and more love, felt like a burgeoning thing tucked deep inside him, a desire gestating.

He'd said, "I agree," which wasn't an answer, and both of them knew it.

Perhaps the answer was nonlocal, vibrating somewhere, and he only had to find the coordinating element. This was easier than believing an answer was something he had to create. No, an answer already existed, if he could locate it.

Of course, there were secrets. In any marriage there were, reasoned Noah. There were the forgivable, unimportant secrets: staying an extra hour at a work happy hour, reporting back that he had three drinks instead of four, the time he slept in the car in the parking lot of the gym instead of actually going inside the gym, the fact that he actually hated that reality dating show she made him watch—well, he enjoyed watching it, but he hated the way it made him feel after. He never said anything. Noah was sure Maya kept those same kinds of secrets from him.

And then what he thought of as medium secrets, harmless but which might hurt Maya if she knew. One such secret was the way that Eileen had surfaced in his brain after his meeting with Klein. Eileen had loved his paper. When he put the preprint up on arXiv he knew he was being a little risky, but she had admired that he'd made those intellectual leaps, that he'd devoted his time and effort to the edges of possibility. "I love you when you're like this," she'd said, and he'd basked in the compliment. But when the paper was poorly received, his instinct was to cower, and hers was to be indignant. She talked so often about how Noah had been wronged in the court of public opinion that eventually he had to ask her to stop.

What would she think now, Noah wondered. He wished he could call her. A medium secret.

But then there were weightier secrets, secrets so heavy he didn't ever let them rise to the surface, their presence more like a creeping iceberg in his chest. Occasionally, the secrets iced through him. The secret of loneliness, of withheld desire, of divorce. The secret of great pain, one Noah was afraid he'd never be able to unload, a burden that would never melt away.

In the beginning of their relationship, he had told Maya everything. Everything that was acceptable to say, at least. He and Eileen had met young, in college, dated a long time, then married, then remained without a child for another long time, until Serena was born. Serena lived for three years and nine months, and those years were glorious, and Noah would have said that even before Serena died. He loved being a father. He didn't feel constricted, only expanded. And then one night, Serena cried out in her sleep, and Noah woke, and when he ran to Serena's room she was unconscious, and by the time the ambulance came, she was gone. A rare form of pediatric cardiomyopathy for which Serena had no exaggerated symptoms. She'd never had a chest x-ray, a shortness of breath complaint. But there inside her, a heart was swelling. Within the year, his marriage crumbled and Eileen moved away. A year and a half later he wandered into Maya's talk.

But there were, of course, things Noah had never told Maya. Answers to questions no one asked: What was the worst part, when do you forget her, does grief have a half-life. All of that was a lifetime ago, though. An actual lifetime.

As he drove forward, toward their new home in Marfa, a new home with his new wife, the car quieted. Maya fell asleep with her head against the window. Her forehead rocked back and forth across the glass. Suddenly Noah sensed that he might cry, his eyes hot, the road blurring. But in the next instant it faded. It was only the heat leaving the pavement at the end of the day, seeping through the crack in the window.

Maya

They stopped in Las Cruces for the night, one last night together before their new lives started. They got a cheap room in a fluorescent motel. The sheets were scratchy and the AC wouldn't turn off, but they'd bought the most expensive red wine from the gas station and dropped ice cubes into it before turning on the TV.

"It's what we'd do if we were young and scrappy," Maya said. "Rough it."

"Romantic," Noah said and laughed.

But they weren't all that young, and now they were further from scrappy than before Noah had met Klein Michaels. They could have sprung for a luxury hotel, now that the first wave of Klein's money had hit their bank account, but they weren't used to it yet. Maya had stared at the alert on her phone, then her banking app, for minutes, in shock. She called Noah over and they sat together, looking at the number in their joint account like it might disappear. She thought of what she most wanted to buy, a mid-century mustard Eames chair for the living room window and a vintage bench for the entryway. But it would be silly to buy new furniture right when they rented their house out.

So she took herself to the Century City mall and bought various frivolous things she didn't need—a leather jacket, a rust-colored silk caftan, Chanel skin tint. But the purchases felt unsatisfying. What she wanted to buy was something she couldn't name, some feeling inside her that had gone missing.

Entwined with her on the motel bed, Noah turned and kissed her. A house-flipping show played in the background and they made out like teenagers, while a couple on television decided what they wanted more: money or a home with a beautiful deck where they could grow old. When the episode finished, they turned off the TV and lay in the dark.

"You said yes," Noah said.

"To what?"

"To coming here, with me. On some blind mission run by a guy who only eats one meal a day and believes in ozone therapy."

He threw his leg over hers, and the heaviness felt good. "A guy *billionaire*," she corrected. "The billionaire part is important."

"Right."

"It does make me a little weirded out that it's privately funded and it's this lab out in the middle of nowhere. There's no recourse if—" She couldn't finish the sentence.

"If something goes wrong? In that case, we'll have billions to pull from in the civil suit."

Maya smiled in the dark. "I'd be a widow, but a rich one."

"Now I'm dying in this scenario? Shit." Noah removed his leg and rolled over to face the window. "Publicly funded projects are no better. Eileen used to say all her federally funded research grants had crazy safety and morality loopholes that most people don't know to look for."

And as Noah slipped into sleep, Maya heard it: *Eileen used to say, Eileen used to say.* He hadn't mentioned her name in years, and now, twice in the span of a few weeks. A specter, a living wound, an ex-wife coming back to life.

Maya never told Noah she found that photo of Serena at the bottom of his nightstand beneath the Tylenol. In it, Serena was young, still a baby, with wispy blond bits of hair, large blue saucer eyes, an angelic pout, and puffy red cheeks. The baby was sitting up, a woman's hand at her back for support.

Maya put the picture back in the nightstand and never dug it out again. Serena was an unsolvable problem, gone, locked up in tragedy. There was a part of Maya that was afraid the more she knew about her, the more unsolvable Noah would become.

Of course, there had been other photos of Serena here and there, a night when she'd asked to see pictures, but Noah never showed her that particular photo from the nightstand. Instead he pulled up a couple on his phone, buried deep in an album many swipes away. When Maya moved in, Noah got rid of those nightstands, and she never saw the picture floating anywhere else. She didn't look too hard.

And now she lay awake in Las Cruces, thinking that Eileen was also an unsolvable problem. Yes, she'd found those photos of Eileen online, saw where she worked, what city she lived in, her various likes and follows on social media platforms, but none of that seemed like enough. And until recently, Noah had kept Eileen's name out of conversation.

Maya got out of the motel bed and pulled a sketchbook and some pens from her travel bag. This was a sketchbook she used only for mindless, embarrassing drawings, not the real stuff she'd use as studies for a painting. She flipped to a blank page and started moving her pen. After several strokes, Maya realized she was drawing the vulture from the drive, the substantial body, black velvet feathers, neck curved and thick, the shape of a land animal, sky-bound. For the first time in a long time, she felt the peculiar calm of art.

Sketching like this always cleared the noise for her. What she was drawing didn't look exactly like the vulture, but instead recalled the bird's movements. That was the key. That she could represent an idea without knowing everything about it. That, in fact, knowing the details of the vulture's anatomy wasn't crucial. Knowing the vulture was knowing the way it moved, the articulation of its circular search, the shape it made in the moment between leaping off the ground and gaining air.

When she was the most in touch with an artistic practice, she'd felt the thrill of creation every day, a lightning bolt of healthy desperation to make something, to love something, to risk something.

So then, like the thick roll of thunder following a lightning bolt, she thought of Ren.

Her last major relationship before Noah, back in Portland. A wrenching breakup that she had run from instead of healed from. When she was with Ren, they'd made art every day. They would have done this. Taken off for an unknown place, stayed in cheap motels, lived on hope and a hundred dollars for as long as they could. She dated Ren off and on, but mostly on, for five crucial years. Right up until he was selected for the Whitney Biennial and moved to New York without her. Before that, they'd been inseparable, beauty-obsessed, proudly bohemian, on the same track toward artistic success.

But to really describe what it had been between her and Ren, she'd have to go back to the beginning, to how their relationship originated with their parents. Both she and Ren had grown up in Japan with one American parent and one Japanese parent, and both of them had gone to international school (she in Tokyo, he in Kagoshima), both of them had left Japan for college (she for Stanford, he for NYU), and neither of them had returned to Japan to live afterward. They shared the combination of guilt and thrill that came with leaving your homeland and family and trying to weave the bigger, flashier world into your life. The guilt part is what they were both tending to by going on the blind date set up by their respective retired mothers, who were scheming their union back in Tokyo. But what originally felt like a favor to their families soon seemed like an inevitability. They stayed out all night.

They had twin aspirations, wild artistic ambitions. They understood that being young and poor in Portland was their time to be incendiary, before they transitioned into the comfortable life of art-making that surely would come. On that first date, they drank shochu over ice and then Ren took Maya to his warehouse studio to show her his work. Back then he worked primarily in multimedia photography and sculpture, creating layered images that felt dirty, that were limited in color and almost suffocated by their progressive erasure. His work was a little violent and ugly, if interesting. That old work was how Maya remembered him best. In his cold and damp studio, he kissed her and she didn't leave for days.

Together, they were a sort of homecoming without going home. Not expats, not immigrants, but people of many places, with a composite identity. They missed and despised the same things about Japan, and sometimes, rarely, they spoke to each other in Japanese. Those times felt like the most intimate they could be with anyone, a tiny tunnel to their most private selves. Most of those times were in Japanese restaurants on the outskirts of Portland toward closing times, slurping the dregs of bowls and convincing the owners to pour one more beer, just one more. Ren would think it was funny she married a white guy who couldn't pronounce the "r" sound in Japanese to save his life.

Eventually, they moved into a one-room apartment beneath a loud bridge, and used his neighboring warehouse space to make art together. They scraped together money: He assisted wedding photogra-

40

phy gigs in Oregon wine country and fabricated other people's art, and she was an assistant at an architecture office, pretending to be interested in the architects' thoughts on design-build. They read poetry books simultaneously, they showed up to dance parties in unmarked loading docks, they camped on the coast in low tide and woke up, soaking, at high tide. They shattered phones and didn't replace them for months. They hopped every fence they saw, they never had money, and they spent what they did have frivolously. They were busy and tired and social and energetic and always wanting, and it was difficult and romantic. They never once went back to Japan together. They didn't have to. Together they belonged to their village of two, people who carried everywhere they'd been inside them.

And then Ren started to have an actual career, getting high-level gallery representation and fawning press, taking long residencies and doing campus talks, and then he was selected for the Biennial, and he moved to New York, and it was over for them. The breakup was as painful as peeling back all her skin, exposing her guts to the chill. Maya had planted herself with someone who felt like both her past *and* her future, and it had all disappeared.

So it made sense that here, in the dark of a Las Cruces hotel room, on the bridge to another big change, as a man she'd tethered herself to was stretching the fibers of that tether, she was reminded of Ren, of the way they'd lived—carefree, alive. Maya felt that she and Noah were on the verge of catching air, of having a new life, of pulling their past into a great and buoyant present. But she wanted that for herself, too.

The vulture was done. Maya closed the sketchbook and crawled back into bed. Under the sheets she grabbed Noah's hand and held on until she fell asleep.

Noah

He had expected it to take some time to adjust to their new place, but once they arrived, he found the opposite to be true. When he walked in, it was as clear as day: Their new home felt like his old home. Not his and Maya's old home, but the Los Feliz house he shared with Eileen. Warm, light-filled, terra-cotta tiled floors, aubergine cabinets trimmed in yellow, a coved white ceiling, and a kiva-style fireplace. A window above the kitchen sink was open, the late sunlight filtering through lace curtains. A weathered Spanish revival. Empty and beautiful as the day he had moved out of it.

Oliver had met them and was walking them through the place. Noah worried Maya might suspect it somehow, but all she said was, "This looks like a classic L.A. house."

Relief washed through Noah, but the unease remained.

"Klein wanted you to feel like you hadn't gone very far," Oliver said. "It's your place now. Maya, you can put your own stamp on it with some decorating."

Noah didn't even have to look at Maya; he felt her bristle at Oliver's suggestion that she was a decorating kind of wife.

"Ah," Oliver said, welcoming in a thin man with a slash of blond hair, dressed in denim on denim. He smiled a slightly too-big smile, his expression working hard to be casual, like his outfit.

"Nils Olsson," the man said, holding out his hand. "Nice to meet you, brother." He had a faint accent. He turned to Maya. "And you must be—"

"Maya," she said.

"The wife," Oliver confirmed, smiling. "Maya is helping out the new gallery in town. You'll be . . ."

"Putting together an exhibition, a show, a talk. We're not sure yet. This all happened so fast," Maya said. Noah could hear the edge in her voice, trying to counter Oliver's use of "the wife."

But neither Oliver nor Nils seemed to be listening to Maya.

"Nils is head of the Klein Michaels Lab and the one personally overseeing the Janus Project."

"I'm more in the trenches than overseeing, don't you think?" Nils said, turning back to Noah with a wink. "Glad to have you, brother. We're going to do something amazing."

Noah nodded. "So I hear."

Nils stepped to the big window opposite the couch and looked out. "I live in town, but you've got a nice vantage point here of the whole campus."

The window framed the courtyard and the squat mint green buildings surrounding it. Nils and Oliver pointed out the buildings' various uses—administrative offices, Klein's dwelling, another guest suite, Nils's labs—but one stood out, larger than the others. It was windowless, at least two stories high, and spread out wide. The big steel door at its front was vaultlike. Building D, Nils told them. Noah would see it tomorrow.

Noah felt a little desperate, breathless, being back in a space so familiar, so similar to his old life. He reached for Maya's hand and held it. She looked up at him, curious. He squeezed her hand and shrugged.

"It's not much to look at," Nils said. "But we like it that way. Doesn't draw any attention. All the buildings with sensitive material are locked with retina scan security, even if someone got past the gate."

"Are people trying to get past the gate a lot?" Maya asked.

Nils laughed, as if her question weren't serious. "Anyway. Tomorrow morning. Nine a.m.? At my office. We'll leave you to settle in."

When Oliver and Nils left, Maya plopped down on the navy suede couch and sighed. One leg bent under her, one leg hanging off, her head back and eyes closed. Noah had to fight a sinking feeling in his stomach, a slippage, an image of Serena bent over with hysterical laughter. Her toddler laugh was infectious, often unlocking a silliness that Noah and Eileen joined in on. Once, Serena laughed so hard she drooled, right onto the blue suede fabric of this same couch.

Maya yawned. "Weird that they made it so L.A. in here."

Noah didn't say anything. He was caught up in staring at the blue couch, both now and then.

"Are you okay?"

He sat down next to her, carefully, as if skirting a memory. "It'll be fine."

He didn't ask her if she was okay, though. Later he would regret that.

Maya

When Maya woke, she found the other side of the bed empty. Noah was sitting on the bench outside their house, and he told her he'd been there for an hour, watching the sunrise. He was nervous, and she'd never seen him nervous about work before. She liked seeing him this way, proof that it was possible to show new facets to each other, that there was new ground to be broken.

They had breakfast and avoided discussing how big this day was for Noah, for both of them. Maya tried to make it feel normal, and Noah played along. But there was an undercurrent of trepidation shot through everything.

"You're going to be great today," Maya said, kissing him at the door. "I know it. My mom always used to say, if you're nervous, you know you're alive. Something like that."

Noah laughed. "Wow, I don't know if I want to adopt that idiom."

She watched him walk across the courtyard and try the door of Nils's office, discover it was locked, and stare into a keypad on the wall until Nils came out and ushered him in. Protected by retina scans, of course. Then the courtyard was empty, and Maya was alone.

. . .

Maya drove into town to meet the owner of the gallery that Klein had set her up with. Leaving the compound was easy enough. She used the personal code given to her to open the gate and watched it automatically latch behind her in the rearview. Nils was right. The place looked completely nondescript from the road, nothing announcing Klein's name or that anything groundbreaking was happening inside its walls.

She wasn't sure how she felt about Klein bartering this connection for her, but she wanted to be open to the possibility. The gallery was not as prestigious as Marfa's Chinati Foundation, made famous by Donald Judd, but it carried the prestige of its original location in Chelsea. Justine Koppelman of the Koppelman Gallery had so far been very nice to Maya in their correspondence. She wanted Maya to propose either a curated show or an artist talk. Maya wanted to show the Japanese photographers she had featured in her thesis, but Justine had asked her to defend "the why." Why this concept, now.

On the drive, Maya should have been practicing an answer to that question, but her mother called. It was late in Tokyo, but her mother liked to stay up long after her father went to bed, to revel in some alone time. Maya answered, "Mama," using the word she was too embarrassed to use around anyone else. She started to use "Mama" when she was very young, thinking all Westerners called their mothers that, until she realized, too late, that it was a baby word.

"Maya," her mother said. "You're in Texas."

"Unn," Maya said back, reverting to a Japanese conversational interjection.

Maya didn't see her parents very often, an ocean away, but her absence didn't seem to affect her and her mother's closeness. They were used to having a relationship at this distance.

"And what's it like?" she asked. "Cowboys?"

Maya's mother was American-born Japanese. She'd left Northern California at seventeen, the same age Maya had been when she left Japan. And so in her mother's memory, the whole of America had been flattened to the easiest, most entertaining stereotypes. It was only fair, Maya knew, since Americans did that flattening to Japan all the time.

"For the most part, scientists," she said. "So far."

Her mother quickly pivoted to gossip, stories of people Maya had never met, grandchildren of the neighbors she didn't know. Her mother loved gossip, but her stories were never tedious or mean, always full of kindnesses masked as sharp observations. She seemed to possess the best of both of her worlds: her American drive and swagger tempered by her Japanese appreciation for slowness and beauty.

Her mother had gone to college in Japan and then stayed after graduation to work in Japanese TV, first as a host, then as a producer. She met Maya's father on an empty street in Daikanyama in the middle of the night after the bars finally closed, and shocked him with her fluent Japanese and her American clothes. She always said she was wooed by the life of travel and adventure Maya's father promised. But to Maya, her father seemed like a regular salaryman with an administrative job who worked insane hours, even if he did travel a lot. She wondered if her mother felt like she got the life that was promised.

When her mother paused at the end of the story about the pharmacy owner getting drunk and handing out free pimple patches to those who needed it, Maya spoke up. "There's a phrase you used to say about being nervous. What was it again? Like, if you're alive, you're nervous. *Sowa sowa*," Maya said, using the Japanese word she knew for "nervous."

Now her mother laughed, just as Noah had. "What a horrible saying. That's not it at all. How could you misremember?"

Maya sighed. "Just tell me, please."

"No good life is free from unease, because unease is the start of exploration." Her mother laughed. "My father used to say that. It's what he told me when I left California for Tokyo. I was so scared. But I knew there was something else out there for me."

Maya told her mother about Noah's nerves, how he seemed apprehensive about this mysterious work at the Janus Project.

"Should I be nervous about him being nervous?" Maya asked.

"Well, you were always the one more comfortable being in motion. He's not that way. You have to assure him that whatever's outside of work is a constant."

Maya could picture her mother in Tokyo, sitting in her favorite lounger, a constant in her father's life. She probably had the remote tucked into the arm of the chair and a book tucked on the other side. A small bowl of rice and furikake, a boiled egg. Maya had left this life, run away to America, not wanting to be some man's wife but to be an artist. And now she was talking to her mother, who herself had once run away from home, asking for advice on how to be some man's wife.

"I think the word you're looking for isn't *sowa sowa*, but actually *kitai*, to be expectant or to anticipate what's to come. That's probably a better way to describe it to Noah."

"Thanks," Maya said.

"You lose your Japanese. I don't mean only vocabulary. You lose your Japanese when you go away, and then the farther away you get, the more is lost. It's fine, I suppose. But you like to stay away."

"Is this your way of saying I should come to Japan?"

"You're doing a good thing by being there for Noah now. But we would always love to see you."

Maya pulled into the parking lot of the gallery. "Hey, have you seen any of your friends from the old days?" She tried to keep her voice light. "Like Ren Hayashi's mother?"

"I ran into her just last month. Ren's here now, you know. He has a place in Ebisu. He owns it. A car, too."

Maya nodded, but she was too embarrassed to reply, too worried whatever she said would reveal what she couldn't even say to herself. That she was thinking about Ren. That she didn't know why. That she wondered what it meant.

"Will Ren be one of the artists you bring over?" her mother asked. "For the gallery?"

Maya blushed. "Well, he's big-time now, you know."

"Too big-time for you?"

She didn't know Ren had left New York. Or that he was living in both places, the way she was currently living in two places, Marfa and L.A. Somehow he seemed closer in Tokyo, just on the other side of her mother's voice.

"Why not call him and see?" Her mother had a way of cutting right to the point. "I'm sure he'd love to hear from you. I can ask his mother."

"We don't talk much anymore."

"Don't be silly. Not talking doesn't mean the line is broken," her mother said. "People have a way of getting inside each other and staying there, no matter what."

Maya was early to the appointment. Justine was tied up—"putting out a curatorial fire"—so her assistant handed Maya a badge to show to the guards next door to get into Chinati for free. She recommended the concrete Donald Judd sculptures out in the brush.

"It's very peaceful over there," the assistant said. "Meditative. Like nothing exists."

Maya had worn an expensive black wrap dress knotted at her waist, hoping to signify to New York–bred Justine that she, too, was cosmopolitan and serious, despite not knowing the why of her gallery proposal. Now, tromping into the fields behind the building where the famous Judd cubes were, the expensive dress seemed stupid, coming untied with each big step.

Maya saw what Justine's assistant had meant about this part of the Chinati being peaceful—there was quietude. Only the sound of dried grass and dirt crunching underfoot, and the thick air of a warm day building up. But the closer Maya got to the cubes, the more she realized the quiet wasn't at all desolate. It wasn't that nothing existed; it was that everything did. Everything felt alive. She reached the sculptures and stopped mere inches from one; the concrete slabs seemed almost vibrating with a cold thickness. And the land around it felt newly soft and pliant in response. She knew, of course, that the sculptures had been on this ground for decades, but she felt everything fresh, as if it had formed there now, for her.

That was how good artwork could rattle through you, she thought, make you not only look, but see. She thought she should take Noah here. An antidote to whatever algorithm or math problem he was staring at in the lab.

The Judd sculptures were concrete cubes about six feet high and six feet wide. There was a top and a bottom and two sides, but the inside was hollow, so you could look straight through them. The landscape on the other side, the golden scrub, the loose dirt, the gentle breeze blowing, was perfectly framed, and it felt to Maya like she was looking into a mirror in which she didn't exist.

She felt an urge to crawl inside, though she knew that wasn't allowed. She glanced back at where the guard had been standing watch, but he was no longer there. There was only sun blasting off the glass of the building. She turned back to the box and did something she had been trained her entire life not to do: She touched the art. She entered it.

Inside was a whole new climate. The day was sunny, but inside the

Judd cube it was icy, pricking Maya's skin. Everything was steely gray, clean. Maya had seen so many photos of this installation, but never considered what the tactile experience would be. She'd never imagined the cold could be enlivening.

She walked across the inside of the cube, trailing her hand against the stone. She slowed a bit, not wanting to reach the other edge. There was a feeling she couldn't quite articulate, dread mixed with the inevitable. The knot in her dress came loose and she pulled it tight, and then, when she looked up, she saw.

A face. An animal standing there. A dark stripe down its long pointy nose, the eyelashes of a fawn. For a moment, truly a moment, not more than two seconds, Maya met its eyes. She swore that she could see herself reflected in the animal's pupils. But the moment slipped away; the animal raged. It rushed against the wide edge of the opening with a violent snort, then reared back and rushed again, and this time, when it pulled back, blood speckled the snout. Bits of white foam like bubbles around the lips. Maya noticed two horns, impossibly curved back like hair frozen in place, inky black. Then the sound of those horns cracking against the concrete.

"Ma'am, you can't be inside here."

Maya swiveled. The guard was on the other end, squinting at her. She pointed to the animal. "But something's wrong."

By the time the guard walked around the box to the other side, the animal was on the ground, its face a mess, eyes open and lashes still, one horn askew.

"Well, shit," the guard said, bending down. "Not again."

From far away, Maya heard her name. She looked back, at Justine's assistant standing outside the building, waving her arms, *come here*, come back, come back, come back.

"I didn't . . . I didn't do anything," Maya said to the guard, who was now radioing someone on his walkie.

He nodded at her. "It's not your fault, yeah. This has been happening with the pronghorn."

He kept talking, and the assistant kept calling her name, but it all faded into the background and Maya felt—in the same way she'd felt the ground soften around the sculpture—alive but unnameable, something beautiful emerging from something horrific. And a desire to record it, to tell what she'd seen, and to tell it to Ren.

Noah

When Noah had first transitioned to experimental physics, a colleague told him he "lacked physical intuition," which is what he repeated to Nils during his medical exam on his first day.

"As if physical intuition had anything to do with what we were working on," Noah said, trying to catch his breath. He was completing a treadmill stress test, a little confused as to why he was undergoing a physical exam in the first place; he'd already submitted a drug test as part of his paperwork, and all he'd be doing for the Janus Project would be sitting in front of a computer. But Nils said it was standard, that he wanted to get a sense of his overall stamina.

"When did you realize your colleague was wrong about your intuition?" Nils asked.

Noah paused. He had realized they were wrong when he first held Serena. When she was placed in his arms, he felt like someone had poured molten light inside the most delicate casing and said, *Here, you take care of this*. At the time, he'd been working with superposition—quantum superfluids, observing phase states that were simultaneously at rest and moving. Holding Serena felt like that concept realized, a perfect stillness and the greatest explosion, a superposition of impossibility.

Yet he knew how to hold her. It was his physical intuition. How to caress her fuzzy head, how to open her minuscule fingers to make room for his own.

"When my child was born," Noah said.

"Ah," Nils said, looking at the monitor. "I am sorry about that. Serena. Your heart rate is erratic. Stop walking."

Noah hit the red button on the treadmill and the belt slowed to a stop. Nils was silent, looking at his monitor. "All right. Your descension is normal."

"You know about Serena, then?"

"If it matters to you, brother, then we know about it," Nils said with the same disarming warmth he'd deployed when they first met the day before. "Is that a problem?"

"So, what, there's a dossier on me?"

"Back to walking, please," Nils said, and Noah obliged. "Did you think there was not a dossier on you? You've been invited to join the most secretive, cutting-edge laboratory in the world, run by an elusive, eccentric, and, by the way, *brilliant* billionaire—because, trust me, they're not all brilliant—in the middle of the desert. Did you think we'd take your word for it that you're not crazy?"

Nils was smiling, so Noah smiled back. "Well, when you put it like that."

Nils led him to a chair and told him to make a fist. It was time for a blood draw, another one. Nils was seamless with the needle, like he'd done it a million times.

"So, am I crazy?" Noah asked.

Nils smiled. "Data shows you're just crazy enough, brother."

. . .

Nils's office was haphazard. He had three desks and somehow all of them were covered in yellowing stacks of paper. He had one ancient computer turned off and a brand-new one turned on but in sleep mode. A diamond shape pinged around the screen, daring Noah to disturb it. Next to the computer was what looked like an old picture frame, but which still held the shiny stock image inside it, a man with sandy hair and a perfect jawline holding hands with a boy with sandy hair and an almost perfect jawline, walking on the beach.

That's funny, Noah thought, and picked up the frame. When he did, a small business card fell out of it. He retrieved the card and turned it over. It was soft and frayed from age.

Talia Bolson, PhD // Associate Professor, Researcher
Department of Physics // University of California, Berkeley

An email, a phone number, and a fax number followed. Talia Bolson, was she supposed to be familiar to him? He took out his phone to look her up, but the door to the lab burst open, startling him. He dropped the business card.

It was Oliver, in a linen suit, whipping off his Ray-Bans and carrying a tray of food. He nodded at Noah.

"Get out of this depressing office. Only Nils can stand to be in this box all day long. We're having Thai, Klein's favorite. You'll love it."

Behind Oliver the afternoon light streamed into the open door and there, cutting through the light, was Klein Michaels. Noah had still only met him the one time, and the effect of seeing the billionaire in the flesh was still striking. He had wealth and composure and a directness in his energy that was wholly intimidating.

"Oh, hi," Noah said, caught off guard. Why had Klein come all the way out here for Noah's first day?

"Conference room," Klein said, a command. "The only place not an absolute mess."

Noah, Klein, Oliver, and Nils gathered around a shiny conference table to choose from seven Thai dishes displayed with formal precision in porcelain serving dishes.

"I haven't been able to try any Marfa restaurants yet," Noah said, piling on his plate. "I'm surprised there's a Thai place."

Klein laughed. "Oh, no. This is Anthony's special."

Noah looked at him blankly.

"Klein's chef," Oliver said quietly, as if Noah should be embarrassed to not know Klein traveled with a chef.

Nils seemed to be as comfortable with Klein as Oliver was, and the three of them small-talked with ease. Noah couldn't find a place to jump in, and they offered no doors to the conversation. Soon he began to feel anxious, unsure why he was here, what he had to offer. Plus, the food was not very good, confusingly bland, lacking the spice and bite of his favorite place in Thai Town back home.

"With flying colors," Nils said, catching Noah's eye. "Noah, I said you passed the physical with flying colors."

"You're forty-two," Klein said.

"Forty-three," Noah corrected, but Klein didn't seem to register it.

"It's clear you've preserved your mind, which is what we want. We find that most mathematicians have done that well. Physicists not so much. It's easy for them to get caught up in the absence of answers." Klein sat back in his chair. He'd barely touched his food. "But I find that when you have a framework with which to look at the problem, the absence of answers becomes merely an empty corridor for you to walk down and populate. How thrilling."

Noah nodded, but was unsure what Klein was getting at.

"And your wife, Noah. How is she getting on?"

"Thank you for setting her up with the Koppelman place. She's there right now, I think."

"Yes, I know that, but I mean, well, how is she getting on with all of this?" Klein gestured at the table of Thai food. Noah was confused.

Oliver stepped in. "What have you told her about what we are doing here?"

It had been hard for Noah to explain it to Maya. Layman's terms slipped into technicalities pretty quickly. He told her this: The Janus Project had found a way to consistently prove Noah's shaky proposal, that consciousness emanated from quantum processes. And once they'd done that, they'd reliably held conditions for neuron-directed entanglement across time and space. How exactly they'd done this, Noah wasn't sure. But he knew that Klein had hired him to arrange the unruly principles of quantum mechanics into mathematical models so they could find a path toward publishing their research. Mathematical models would make it all make sense. The reasoning behind the phenomenon would be explicable—not absent, but hidden. Noah's job would be to find it.

"I told her you'd found a way to prove what my paper failed to prove," Noah said.

"Good," Oliver said. "But what we're doing here is actually much more interesting than that."

"And what did he tell JPL?" Klein asked Oliver, as though Noah were not right there.

"An unpaid yearlong leave to explore private sector work, no mention of your name," Oliver said.

This seemed to please Klein, and he nodded.

Oliver stood up and flipped off the overhead lights in the conference room.

"I assume you looked over the work we gave you, how we use nanoparticles to record the exact neural activity of a memory and then re-play it in a person's brain."

"Yes," Noah said. "At a resolution no one thought was possible."

"But it's not only that. The memory isn't just replayed. It's relived."

"Well sure, if the neural activity is exactly the same then it would feel exactly as if it was happening again," Noah said.

Klein shook his head. "Not as if. It is."

"What do you mean?"

"The quantum phenomenon of neurons actually enables your current consciousness to cohere with your past consciousness, the one that produced the memory, wherever that past consciousness was in time and space."

Noah's breath fell out of him in a burst. He wasn't confused, exactly, but resistant. "What?"

Nils leaned in so close that Noah could smell fresh bar soap and the beginning of sweat.

"It stands to reason that electromagnetic fields could amplify quantum effects in the brain's neurons on a macro level, concerning coherence across consciousness levels."

Nils was quoting Noah's paper back to him, as Klein had done on their first visit.

"I didn't mean—" Noah stopped himself. He didn't want to say it. "I didn't mean you could *think* yourself back to the past."

"But why not?" Klein asked.

"I meant maybe, *possibly*, hypothetically, if neural encoding arises from a quantum process, we could imagine a world where the smallest quanta of neurons could entangle. Not a whole person's entire consciousness."

"If consciousness is a quantum system, why can't it entangle with a past version of itself?"

Noah shook his head. He couldn't begin to know where to ask

questions, so scientifically illogical was their reasoning. "How would you sustain the coherence of such a large system? How would you document that? How would you—"

Klein slapped his hand on the table, which made Noah jump. But Klein was excited. "Let's go to Building D. It's best to just show him."

Nils nodded. "Noah, you're about to walk into a room you can't ever walk out of. Of course you can leave it, but you won't ever unknow it. Do you understand?"

Noah nodded, though he did not understand.

Building D was shockingly cold, a sensation that was somehow amplified by the shiny white floors.

As if reading his mind, Oliver said, "We keep this place as sterile as possible. And cooled, of course."

"The cooling costs a pretty penny," Klein said proudly.

The building was dark and hangar-like, filled with massive computing power, which glowed and blinked in the darkness like an intelligent entity. They led Noah through a maze of machine storage until they reached the far corner, where he saw through a big window a pristine, bright white room. Inside the room were two identical, shiny, black coffin-shaped structures. On this side of the window was a large computer and a panel of complex controls.

"The time baths," Nils said, following Noah's gaze through the window. "An electromagnetic transportation envelope for what we call Episodic Folding. There's nothing else like them in existence."

Another retina scan opened the door to the room and Noah followed Nils and Klein inside. Oliver stayed behind by the computer, looking through the window.

Inside felt churchlike. Calm, quiet, away from the hum of the computers outside.

Nils gestured to the two baths. "That one is decommissioned, not quite as powerful as this one, the latest iteration. Almost a thousand pounds of salt in here. You'll float like you're dead."

"Or like before you were born," Klein said, smiling.

Nils pushed an indentation in the lower left corner of what they were calling a "time bath" and the top popped open with a wheeze. At first, Noah couldn't recognize what was in it. But then, like a camera lens focusing, he saw gently undulating liquid, the same deep black of the machine. An actual bath. About five feet across and eight feet in length. Slightly larger than human-size. Attached to the head of the bath was a black helmet, the inside of which glowed.

A professor once told Noah that when an experiment was yielding wild results or overwhelming information, go into record mode, and tell the story later. Get it all down, the professor said. That is your job during the experiment. Later, your job is to arrange the details so that they tell a story.

So in Building D, Noah recorded the unlikely, astonishing details Klein and Nils gave to him. And later, lying awake at night, he would try to tell himself a story. A story of impossible things made possible.

The first incredible thing they had done was map a memory down to individual neurons. Not only had no one ever done this before, but with some eighty-six billion neurons in the brain, most thought it impossible. They had developed something called an Echo Injection—an injection of nanorepeaters into the bloodstream that targeted brain neurons. When someone was wearing the mapping helmet and recalling a memory, nanorepeaters near active neurons would echo (or repeat) a path into the helmet. The mapping helmet would read an almost perfect neural picture of the memory.

The second incredible thing they had done was use the sensory-deprivation bath to replay that memory. A person would only have to climb into the bath and settle their head into the attached reignition helmet, which would then reignite—or write—the exact neural activity of the mapped memory. The person in the bath would be reliving the memory, reexperiencing it as if it were happening now.

If they had stopped there, it would have been enough. It would have been groundbreaking. They would have won prizes. Everyone—brain researchers and Alzheimer's experts and medical device developers—would have been clamoring for their tech. The story would have been perfect and triumphant.

But they didn't stop there.

The third incredible thing they'd done was make the sensory-deprivation bath into a "time bath," with a core that promoted an electromagnetic field that enabled quantum coherence. Inside the time bath, a person would not only reexperience the memory, but would fold space and time to inhabit that past consciousness. This part was Episodic Folding.

Episodic Folding required two things: a psychoactive compound called a Fold Cocktail, and the core of the time bath. The Fold Cocktail was derived from the same elements in ayahuasca that light up the hippocampus and neural connections. Once injected, it enabled the person's present consciousness to entangle with the past consciousness of the memory. The core, with its resonance program, prepared those entangled states so that they could cohere longer. Long enough for a person to travel back into his memories, to move and talk and make decisions as the past self, *in the past*, but with all his present self's knowledge.

This begged the question of the fallibility of memory. But the core only needed to find a 25 percent resonance to cohere; so as long as the person was able to reconstruct a mostly accurate memory, folding could occur.

This also begged the question of causality—does what happens during the fold in the past affect the present? Klein and Nils assured Noah that causality was not an issue here. You had to assume that the moment the fold occurred, whatever you did in the past created a new branch of time. And when you left the fold? *It's impossible to know*, Klein said, *but those branches aren't our responsibility.*

But all of this, the whole story, should have been impossible. The questions were outlandish, the results were unlikely, and the processes were uncharted. But the Noah who recorded what they were telling him in Building D was not in the business of belief or disbelief. It was later Noah, telling himself a story, who would have to choose to believe or not. And at the center of that belief was his experience inside the time bath.

"You want proof it works? Get inside," Klein said.

"Klein," Nils said. "He's not ready."

They had continued talking in Building D, but Noah, in record mode, had stopped participating. Klein had taken Noah's silence for disbelief.

"Sorry, what?" Noah said.

"Just for a minute," Klein said. "Take the Echo Injection and we'll map a memory and then reignite it. If you get in and you don't think there's something there—something happening—you're free to go. Of course, our contract stipulates our initial deposit is paid back with interest, but I can't imagine you've spent all that already. As you said when we met, you're a modest guy."

Klein's thinly veiled threat cut a small sliver inside Noah. He had no choice.

Nils gave Noah the injection with such expertise that Noah didn't even feel it. He waited to feel different, his blood heavier somehow, but he felt exactly the same. Nils said it only took a few minutes for the nanoparticles to travel, so by the time Noah stripped down and put on a robe, everything was ready. Klein and Nils joined Oliver at the computer outside the room, where they watched Noah. Nozzles in the ceiling performed a quick atomic sanitization.

They instructed Noah to put on the mapping helmet and to sit, get comfortable. The helmet was stiff and awkward, but manageable. Nils's voice came through the helmet as though he were inside Noah's head.

"Relax, Noah. Think of a very accessible memory."

Noah didn't take time deciding on a memory; it simply blossomed inside him.

Serena, the night before her first birthday, when Noah and Eileen had tucked her in. They were being sappy about it, like they were saying goodbye to a baby and tomorrow she'd wake up a toddler. Noah was prompting her to say "Dada," to add it to her limited repertoire of words like *wawa* and *up* and *no*. But instead of saying "Dada," Serena had smiled like she knew what she was doing and said her favorite word: "Mama."

Noah felt angry when Nils's voice filtered back in. "Beautiful. Now we'll reignite the memory for you. Please take off the mapping helmet and enter the bath."

Noah felt a wave of embarrassment climbing naked into what was essentially a saltwater sensory deprivation tank, and then a wave of claustrophobia as he settled his head into the reignition helmet, larger and more oppressive than the mapping helmet. The top of the bath slowly closed over him and Noah was engulfed in darkness.

Noah knew it was due to the amount of salt in the bath, but he felt like he was levitating. Like he didn't have a body, like he was only his brain, which was powerful and substantial. First it was smoke clearing, vague fog slowly resolving. And then, with sudden clarity: the sound of Serena's voice, "Mama," as real as the sound of his breath in the time bath.

As real as. Real.

He's there. Leaning over her crib, feeling Eileen's sweater against his arm. The smell of baby detergent. Laughter so bright it cracks through his brain like lightning. He isn't remembering Serena's voice. He's hearing it. Her high pitch, her voice still unsure—like a tiny daisy in a field of grass, or the first noise a piano ever made in the history of music. They'd laughed, all three of them. They'd laughed so much and Noah thought, *This is happiness, it's so easy*. Then they'd said good night.

He felt now, where the brick had been in his throat, a ball of nausea. He felt helplessly choked. He thought about speaking, calling out, responding, but he couldn't tell where he was making sound—then or now—and he thought, *I'm dying*, and he thought that for a stretch of time that was unmeasurable, until a pale hand reached for him.

It was Nils, shaking his shoulder. His voice came closer, and Noah realized his eyes were squeezed shut. Noah, Noah, Noah. In time, Noah recognized his name.

He rolled and stumbled. He didn't remember getting out of the bath. On his hands and knees, soaking, aching, he took a moment. *I am Noah Byatt. I am a physicist. I live in Los Angeles. No, Marfa*. And also: *With my wife and child*. And then: *No, with my wife*.

Noah stood and looked at Klein and Nils. Nils handed him a towel. "What the hell?"

Nils put his hands together in prayer. "I'm sorry, brother. I should have prepped you more. It can be oppressive, I suppose, the first time. Claustrophobics need not apply."

"I'm not claustrophobic," Noah protested.

"You can't become an astronaut if you're claustrophobic," Klein said. Now he'd come striding into the room, looking out of place in his crisp suit jacket and newly shaven face. "You wanted to be one, right? When you were younger? That's why you were at the Europa launch."

"Um, yes," Noah said, heart pounding. He knew he hadn't told them about seeing Europa.

"I am truly sorry about that," Nils said. "You won't endure that sort of vertigo again. I'll be sure of it. But wow. You only did memory reignition. You didn't even have the Fold Cocktail."

"I need to see."

"See what?" Nils asked.

"What happened in there. To my body. I need video footage and the data, both. We're adding thermal and barometric monitors, I assume—"

"Oh, we have to be careful what sort of data monitoring devices we put inside the bath. Certain mediums could interfere with the process. We've only tested this exact iteration."

"The process."

"Yes, the process. The fold."

Noah considered this. "When do I get to meet them?"

"Who?" Nils asked.

"The team."

"There isn't a team, per se."

"How do you mean?" Noah asked.

Klein looked at Oliver, and Oliver looked at Nils. Nils looked down at the time bath. He ran his hand along the top of it. "You'll find it's quite something, what we've done here. But the circle must remain small at the moment. You understand that, of course."

"You said you had a team of engineers and neuroscientists and, I assume, physicists, too. Beyond me."

Klein cleared his throat. He spoke plainly, which was a warning, a threat. "We did. They were exceedingly helpful. Now they've been released. Nothing to worry about."

They've been released. Like captives, Noah thought, like animals. Now his brain scrambled to find a way that any of this made sense.

"But where's the data on why this works?"

A lightness came over Klein's face, like he'd been waiting for Noah to ask this question. "What's the most powerful quantum machine on earth? The brain."

Then he stepped closer to Noah, who was still dripping.

"And what's the most mysterious quantum machine on earth?"

Noah felt like he was shaking. Was it the injection, the salt? Had he not eaten enough? Quietly, he answered. "The brain."

"See? The reason you're here is because we believe you knew it first."

"I didn't, though. My paper was about—"

"Oh, but you did," Klein said. "You have to accept that. It was all there, in your paper. And now, now we're ready for a real test subject. Someone who understands how this all works, where it was born, and where it could go."

Nils put his hand on Noah's wet, bare shoulder. "A transport subject."

Klein nodded. "A human one."

Now Noah understood. He hadn't been brought here to make mathematical sense of the Janus Project. He had been chosen. He would be the lab rat, a man going back into memory to live another time.

The room smelled both new and old, a mix of plastic and salt water and the arid scent of emptiness. Noah thought of the byline, the awards, the big ones, and the brand-new field of science they were breaking, and what they might discover, how it could help NASA and JPL, or organizations and enterprises he couldn't possibly predict. It felt dangerous, but he supposed all paradigm-shifting enterprises did. And then he thought of Serena. How it felt dangerous to have children, how no one told you that. Your life, all of it, on the line. But also that he wouldn't take it back for anything.

"You'll add my retina scan on the door," Noah said.

"Of course," Nils said.

"And I'm serious about the barometric monitoring."

"So this means you're with us? Because it's you, you know."

"The transport subject," Noah said. "Yes, me."

Maya

Maya had hoped to talk to Noah about seeing the pronghorn die, but when he got home from work, he went straight to bed, citing exhaustion. She couldn't remember the last time he'd done that. But she felt tired, too. The pronghorn had disturbed her. The animal, feral, mad, bleeding, dead. And yes, it had been strange that no one else seemed as alarmed as she was. During her meeting with Justine Koppelman, she'd explained what she'd seen, but all Justine had said was that the Judd sculptures were "a breeze to clean," missing the point of Maya's concern entirely. When Maya pushed back, Justine tried to assuage her by saying there had been several other pronghorn deaths in recent months, but not to worry, a wildlife biologist was investigating. After all, she'd joked, they were one of the fastest land animals on earth, they could outrun whatever this was.

Back home, with Noah bypassing her for bed, Maya felt herself growing anxious, and went to the bathroom to splash water on her face. She looked at herself in the mirror, and then her stomach fell out. Her face was replaced by Eileen's. The mirror selfie Maya had found online, of Eileen in their old house. Behind her, here in Marfa, was the same checkerboard tiling and mauve tub that was in the selfie. How had she not noticed this before?

Maya thought of going to the bedroom to wake Noah and tell him this, but he must have already noticed, and decided not to say anything to her. She left the bathroom and looked at the bedroom door, still and dead. So she walked outside.

The sky was less violet now, settling into the pattern of endless stars she couldn't believe existed out here. She had no destination in mind, but she found herself walking down the long dirt road off campus until she reached the edge of the two-lane highway that cut west out of Marfa. It was carless, and the night was a desert-dark so thick you had to use other senses: hear the crunch of gravel, smell the manure from the neighboring ranch, taste the woodsmoke from a distant campfire.

The meeting with Justine had been frustrating, for reasons other than her lack of answers about the pronghorn. Justine had thought Maya's curatorial idea, bringing in artists who could speak to climate change and land use in the desert, lacked a contemporary justification. If Noah had stayed up and had dinner with her, she knew what he would say to that. He liked to say that what he did, science, was "toward the promise of answers," and that what Maya did, art, was "in spite of answers."

But if they had been able to have that conversation, if Noah had delivered that line to her once again, Maya would have told him no, he was wrong, they *both* looked for provable answers. In Noah's profession they came through math and logic. In Maya's they came through penumbra, outlining the part of the gesture that wasn't quite visible. Noah would have resisted this, Maya knew. For him, a statement was not true until proven true through math; reality was suspicious until it had a corresponding equation.

She thought of an artist she loved, Ruth Asawa, and how she'd once said that the art object itself didn't matter as much as the process of making it, that the process of making the art should reveal you to yourself, as each moment is a decision, and each decision a chipping away at your mask.

Maya wanted to make a decision. She didn't want to push Noah, but she wanted to discuss having a baby. Caroline said they'd have all the time and space in the world once they got to Marfa, but so far, the conditions had not been ideal. What decisions were they making with their bodies now—his in the bedroom, hers out here? How could they reveal themselves if they were living in this limbo? She wanted to reveal herself. The alarm bell ringing when the pronghorn's dead face appeared to her: She wanted to feel alive.

In the dark, she pulled out her phone, which was heavy in her pocket. She looked at the time and did the math. Tokyo was awake. She went to her email and found a message with the subject DO NOT OPEN. She copied the numbers in that message and dialed.

Ren's voice as he answered, "Hi, Maya," like a decision already made, from a future that the two of them were catching up to.

Noah

For as long as Noah could remember, he'd wanted to be part of something big. When he was a child, he dressed up as an astronaut every year for Halloween, and he slept in the costume until it was more torn holes than suit. But when he watched a video on astronaut training, he was immediately heartbroken. It seemed similar to military training, and he knew he'd never be athletic enough to qualify. He'd been scientifically minded always, analytical and inquisitive, logical, in search of certainty in everything he did. So as he grew, he thought of astronomy and the stars as his mistress, and focused on the more practical sciences, excelling in chemistry and biology, seriously looking at neuroscience as a concentration when he went to college. Quantum physics hadn't occurred to him, a science the younger Noah thought was an option only for dilettantes and philosophers.

But all that changed when he was twenty and a private company launched a cutting-edge rover from a newly built launch center in Florida. It was the first mission to Jupiter's exotic moon, a moon that scientists speculated might hold life similar to Earth's, in a long-buried frozen ocean. Against the advice of every reputable scientific organi-zation, the company caved to a pushy investor, the brother of a conser-vative publishing magnate, and let him man the mission onboard. He made several convoluted speeches about his decision, about both his deluded belief in the untested cryosleep he'd have to be in as well as his willingness to die for the cause, in the name of exploration. The mar-keting campaign around the launch was a circus. All those missions to Mars and no one had gotten up early to watch the live stream, and yet people pilgrimaged in droves to the remote landscape to squint at the sky in hopes of witnessing an event that could mean something, or that would render them irrelevant or even exceedingly relevant. Of course Noah and his friends went. It was spring break, and they were in love with the power of science, most of all.

Noah remembered more clearly than Maya, who was only twelve and saw news coverage. They'd flown the cheapest flights to Florida and gotten tickets to sit on a flat-topped hill a few miles inland from the site. The crowds were thick, and the rocket launch was bright and loud, adrenaline-inducing. The stagger of noise—mechanical, human, spark—was communal, rippling through the beach crowds. The ex-plosion happened forty-four seconds in, but it felt like longer. At first, they only saw smoke spread high in the sky, and they heard the disappearance of sound. There was no other way to describe it. The sound that had filled the air moments before, emanating purely and ferociously from the Goliath force of energy it took to launch the rocket and rover and all its requisite engines, had vacated. Where had it gone? A downside of privately funded space travel run by the wealthy was a lack of oversight. One small piece, a valve in the second combustion chamber, was refurbished from Russia to cut costs, and it turned out to be faulty from overuse. The man onboard was instantly incinerated in the explosion, and the mission that stood for so much was now in violent pieces. Tears filled Noah's eyes long before any facts came in. What it looked like to watch such vacancy, to hear it and feel it.

Noah and his friends sat on the hill for a long time that afternoon, long after most of the crowds had dispersed. While fire trucks sped up and down the streets with no ground fire to put out and news crews roamed the site, they talked about anything but what they'd seen, what was being rapidly and inaccurately reported. Girls, novels, films, comics, fathers. When they finally did get up, sun-worn, salt-throated, and irrevocably changed, one of Noah's friends ran into someone he knew. There was a group of young people sitting on a blanket a few yards away, a contingent of chemistry majors from Berkeley, one of whom eyed Noah's crimson Stanford sweatshirt. A blond girl, tall and athletic, an almost masculine face, a wit and daring that were immediately apparent to Noah. It frightened him and it attracted him.

By the end of the night they'd all ended up at a touristy beach bar, where they became instantly drunk on frozen daiquiris, enervated by the proximity to tragedy. They closed the space between them to counteract the mourning expanding in the world. She was so substantial. Smarter than him. More beautiful and sure, so sure. The sureness he'd hoped a pursuit of science would bring him, here, in this woman, already predicting what the day's tragedy would do to privately funded space travel and exploration in general. In bed, in the extra room he'd paid cash for at the cheap motel he was sharing with his friends, she'd been directive and hot-breathed, and he'd thought, *That should be me, I should be like that.*

It had been Eileen who eventually drove him to physics. She had pointed out that it was truly what he'd been interested in, understanding how things worked. He'd assumed it would be biology that would tell him about life, or chemistry that would give him the building-block knowledge, but Eileen told him that the sort of thinking he was looking for lay in physics. "You want to get in on quantum physics," she'd said in bed that first night. "You can linger in the uncertainty there. It's the only thing that really looks at the invisible and the macro at once. Like you."

"How do you know what I'm like?" he asked.

"I can tell what you're made of," she said, poking his chest.

The very next morning the media took to calling it the "Europa disaster." He sat at the airport bar eating gluey eggs, flipping through a Stephen Hawking book he'd bought at Hudson News. The TV behind the bar replayed what he'd seen with his own young eyes the day before. "What you're watching," the crisp-voiced newswoman said, "is footage from yesterday's Europa disaster." *No they're not*, Noah thought. In the video there was none of the emptying absence of sound, the absence that long shuttles grief through life. It didn't occur to Noah—or Eileen—for a very long time that the Europa disaster itself was a shortcut phrase; it wasn't even the name of the mission, or of the rover that was supposed to comb the icy surface. The rover had been called Possibility.

When Noah left Building D, dizzy with information—Echo Injection, Fold Cocktail, the core, the bath itself—and also the lack of it, the Europa disaster was what he thought of. The disaster that had brought him and Eileen together. Then he thought about the disaster that had torn them apart, Serena's death like an explosion in their hands. They'd shattered into pieces, landed the way debris did, far apart from each other and telling a story only when put back together. But they were impossible to put back together.

For a long time, Noah should have known better. He should have known that day the rocket exploded that one day he and Eileen would, too. Or he should have known, from all the years they'd waited to have children, that they weren't meant to have children. Or he should have known that Serena would be born with a heart condition, he should have asked for a fetal echocardiogram, or he should have pressed for an ECG; he shouldn't have thought himself exempt from anything, from the worst thing. The idea that *he should have known* paralyzed him for a long time. The paralysis worked for a little while, because after your child dies, no one requires anything from you. For months he coexisted with Eileen in the house, immobilized, afraid to make any sudden movements. He barely ate—he felt ill all the time, couldn't stomach food. The house lost color, became the nothing shade of cobwebs. They played no music and there was no sound except the cars driving too fast down Griffith Park Boulevard. A cactus they never tended to in the front yard teetered over on a hot day, clear juices running from the jagged stump onto the sidewalk, a warning.

But he didn't know the marriage was over, not for sure, until one day in mid-July, the dead of summer when interminable things often give out. They were sitting in the backyard, on dried-out patio furniture that was poking into Noah's thighs. Eileen was drinking wine, like she often did then, and she said, "Remember the Europa disaster?"

They'd told the story many times of how they met, but in recent years, they'd stopped. It had started to feel cynical, romanticizing their meeting in a tragedy. Noah often took a shortcut and said they met during college on a spring break trip.

"I do," Noah said. "Clearly."

"Remember, right after?"

"The absence of sound?"

"No, not the sound. The authorities."

"There were no authorities," Noah said, confused.

But Eileen went on as though not hearing him. "Trying to calm everyone in a panic. But no one was in a panic. They had these stations where you could get information, or help. Spiritual counseling. But everyone just sat there."

"I remember everyone sitting there," he said.

"This feels like that."

"What do you mean?" He looked out at the backyard, still in the heat.

Eileen finally looked at him. "Everyone should be panicking, but no one is. Even you, you just sit there. But"—and here her voice was wet, a whisper—"this is a fucking emergency."

Noah's face went white. She was spitting the words at him. They hadn't ventured toward this kind of emotion in months. It was too dangerous, too explosive.

"When Serena was born, you just sat there, too," Eileen went on.

"What?" Noah said, his voice wobbling. "What are you talking about?"

"They put us in that room, and you fell right asleep, and she was asleep in that clear bassinet, and I was there, awake, like *What the fuck is going on, someone help me.* And you slept while I was crying."

Noah leaned forward in his chair. "I'm sorry, Eileen, I didn't know. I remember Serena stayed up for a while. She didn't sleep right away. She was opening her eyes and crying a little, and we held her. We watched the sunset. Don't you remember that?"

She was shaking her head. "No. You're wrong. She was born in the middle of the night. Four thirty-six a.m. The whole place was asleep."

He felt choked. How could he misremember? He left Eileen in the backyard and ran up to the tiny office where he kept important papers and dug through a file until he found Serena's birth certificate, tucked right next to an envelope that contained her death certificate, an envelope they'd never opened. Right there, 4:36 a.m. Eileen was right, of course.

He sat on the floor of the office and wept. Hot tears and weeping that burned his throat. At some point, Eileen came in and put the birth certificate away. At another point, she was sitting on the floor with him, and she was crying instead of him, then. They took turns. They knew it was over. She wanted him to rage—it would allow her to rage. But he wouldn't, and so she had to leave.

And now, Noah was in this strange little Marfa home that looked like that old L.A. home, sitting on an impractical blue suede couch, the throw pillows the same mustard yellow color Eileen liked. The whole place—both the home and him in it—becoming awash in the past. And then, as he always did when he allowed himself to remember, he *heard*.

He heard Serena's voice, three years old, the sound of sunshine, the way she asked a question by saying his name three times, "Dada, Dada, Dada," and then a perfectly formed question, even with her inability to pronounce *f*'s. She had questions about everything—the definitions of words, the words for parts of furniture he'd never considered, the reason why a person shouted or didn't, why a person left or stayed, why an animal existed, why a different animal didn't exist. She was endlessly curious, or endlessly loving, knowing that questions made Noah and Eileen engage with her, and what she wanted more than answers was love.

Thinking of Serena like this, memory following memory, was too much. A ball of thread unraveling, choking on string. The clarity of her presence against the reality of her absence. When this happened to him, he had to move, make the movement of his body match the movement of his memories. He went out, crossed the courtyard, and stood in front of Building D. The retina scan wouldn't work for him, not yet, so Noah stared at the door, behind which was something that was momentous in a way he couldn't quite name.

He closed his eyes and heard Serena, her voice as real and close as it had been when he'd heard it inside the bath: "Mama."

The sound shuddered through him and before he consciously thought to do it, he pulled his phone out and called her. Mama, Eileen. To his surprise, she picked up.

"Hey," she said. A little husky, grounded, Eileen's voice in his ear, in his brain.

"Hey," he said.

They didn't ask each other "How are you?" They didn't say "Nice to hear from you." The last time he'd called, or she'd called, it had been to do with the property they'd sold, the last of the mounds of paperwork it took to separate a life. They never called to catch up. Catching up would require acknowledging the separation, which would require acknowledging the union, which would require the summoning of Serena's memory.

He turned and leaned against the door to Building D. The sun had dipped low behind the lab and now long shadows sliced through the pale walls and divided up the perfectly landscaped courtyard, the economy of light and dark suddenly revealed.

Why had he called? To summon that memory they'd implicitly agreed to bury. To rouse the only other person who also knew the incantation.

"Do you ever . . ." Noah said, not sure what the end of the sentence would be. "Do you ever see her?"

On the other end of the line, he heard a shudder pass through Eileen's breath. He wouldn't have been surprised if she hung up on him, if she yelled at him, if she never even answered.

"All the time," she said, finally.

II

The Choice

Eileen

Leaving a life was more difficult than a life leaving you. When Eileen was younger, she, like most people, had abandoned former selves to make something new. She'd left her childhood in Massachusetts to become a star student at UC Berkeley, then left the amateur life for the placid hills of Stanford, where she became consumed by science and its promise. When she finally left the Bay Area for the scorch of Southern California to become a real, full adult, a professor, a scientist, she thought that was it, but then there was the way motherhood slowly and almost pleasantly throttled the version of her who didn't have a child, until what remained felt permanent. Noah, Serena, Eileen. But it was only when she'd done her ultimate disassembly, the transition from a mother into a childless mother, and then into a lone woman once again, that she found out what could happen when you simply let life abrade you.

Abrasions: the discordant stuffed animal in the back of the dark closet. A child lock on the junk drawer that she'd forgotten how to open. The alien sounds of her own sobbing in the clean, sunny kitchen, unreturned by an awoken baby. She wondered if she was still a mother if what made her a mother was gone, but she found no answer to that wondering. Eventually, it was less horrible to stop wondering.

Noah was painfully present. He was there when she came back from the airport, having nailed her campus interview up at Sonoma State, and there when she packed her things up, and there when she signed the paperwork removing herself from the car lease. He was still there, so she had to leave, not just across town, but halfway up the state, until there were four hundred miles between them. It wasn't fair that he remained, while Serena didn't.

Now, eight years later, Eileen had sloughed off evidence of that old life. She must have seemed complete, confidently so. Unmarried and childless in her forties, a professor of undergraduate biology and chemistry at a non-R1 university, and the owner of a small one-bedroom bungalow in the old part of town. Life abraded; she remade. But the acuteness of the loss remained. No matter how many coffees taken on porches, or new leases signed, or nice divorced men met at wine bars, her former life pulsed inside her. It often felt like an illness, this one a confusion of time, the logic inside her no longer aligned with what was happening outside her body. Other times, it felt like a blessing. How lucky, to live two lives at once. And so she lived like that, an ecstatic sickness churning the water of her days.

"All the time" is what she said to Noah when he called about the Janus Project, but that wasn't quite true. She didn't see Serena all the time, but she had the option to see Serena anytime she wanted. If she willed it, she could see her daughter as she last was, running down the hallway to hide, giggling at the possibility of disappearing. Photos helped, but the great cache of photos and videos from her phone had been pulled onto a hard drive that she didn't power up these days, not unless she felt like a cathartic cry.

But when Noah called, she hadn't been seeing Serena at all. She was about to go on her sixth date with Prem, a chemistry professor at the junior college. She was about to go on the kind of date after which you stopped counting dates and were simply "dating." Prem stood in the living room while she took the phone call in the bedroom, unable to mask the shock at seeing Noah's name pop up on her phone.

"I have trouble seeing her," Noah said. "Even looking back at photos and videos, they feel outside of me, somehow. But I can hear her voice all the time, usually."

They were both hushed.

"All the time," he said, repeating what Eileen had said. "In all the time."

"Noah," she said, a warning, a question.

"But what if it was another way?"

She listened to him explain the lab to her with awe tinging his voice and nausea swirling in her gut.

"Oh," she said. "That sounds unrealistic."

"Just because it doesn't resemble the reality you know doesn't mean it can't be real," Noah said. To Eileen, he sounded like he had in the early years of their marriage, like a young scientist who didn't yet know what parts of his speculation to keep private.

"Should you even be telling me this? Aren't you under an NDA?"

"I thought you'd want to know. I *know* you want to know."

"Klein isn't a scientist. So who exactly is in charge here? I mean, if JPL knew—"

But he cut her off. "Think about the implications for neuroscience, repairing memory structures for people with dementia or Alzheimer's. Or even simply understanding the physics of the brain, on the smallest level, what we could unlock in brain research."

Eileen didn't speak, but her silence said a lot, because even formerly married people could still read each other's silences.

Noah sighed. "I thought you of all people would understand."

"Noah, stop," she said, raising her voice a little, surprising them both. At the end of their marriage, there'd been no strife or big outbursts. Their last physical contact was a limp hug before Eileen pulled away from the house for the last time, both of them brittle, dry. The dull ache of the love they once had, and the absent child that love had produced. She'd wanted to cry. No, she'd wanted to *want* to cry. But nothing came. And in that nothing they were fused, and then parted.

"What does this have to do with . . ." Eileen trailed off, not wanting to use Serena's name.

"What if you could see her again?" Noah said. "For real?"

Grief melted through her, hot and liquid. *How could you?* she wanted to say. The darkening bedroom blurred. Wasn't it enough, what they had been through already? Wasn't it enough?

Prem came into the bedroom, as if sensing her discomfort. "You all right?"

"Who's that?" Noah asked in her ear.

"I'm so sorry," she said, her voice cracking. "I have to go."

She hung up to the sound of Noah's voice protesting.

Prem put his hand on Eileen's back and she turned to him. "My ex," she said, producing a smile from somewhere. "I'll tell you in the car."

She didn't tell him in the car, not exactly. She left out the time bath and made it all seem theoretical. She told Prem how insane the whole thing sounded, and then he expressed concern at Noah's mental state, and Eileen got defensive. It was the project that was insane, not Noah. Noah was just Noah, living on a razor's edge of hope, even when it was obviously ill-fated.

Prem changed the subject and chatted away, discussing his chemistry students, whom he loved, the rescue dog he'd been thinking of adopting, but all the while Eileen was thinking about the way Noah had been after Serena died, soaked in sadness and lingering there.

Nothing left of his constant search for something to hold his foolish hope. She was angry at him for that, unfairly, she knew, but they'd needed his hope. Now here he was again, sounding like old Noah.

After dinner, Prem dropped Eileen at her doorstep. He looked down at his feet in a way that indicated he wanted to be invited in, but she told him she had a stomachache. Prem, always decent and kind, kissed her on the cheek and got back in his car.

While she lay in bed that night, she held her phone inches from her face and looked up everything she could about Klein Michaels, whom she'd always taken to be a charlatan with too much money. Her searches proved her hunches correct, so she changed tack and looked up Maya. She'd never googled Maya before. Part of the silent contract she'd made with herself when she left L.A. and Noah and the house where she'd brought her baby home and where her baby died was to never look back. She couldn't envision Noah's parallel life. To do that would be to remember a truth that was too painful to bear.

She knew her name was Maya from an email Noah had sent her once he'd gotten engaged, and now Eileen quickly found an article in the *L.A. Times* about the florist who transformed weddings into art events, including the wedding of local physicist Noah Byatt and artist Maya Tanaka. Eileen felt comforted the more she read about Maya, who had higher degrees in art, who was younger and beautiful and lively, and who was skilled in both painting and photography. It was good to know that Maya was different from Eileen, that Noah wasn't trying to do over his old life. *It's good that Maya's with him in Marfa,* she thought. Maybe Maya could talk some sense into him.

Being awake in the half dark made her feel more open, closer to the part of her that tugged when Noah called. Hearing his voice on the phone, how it shook and broke at the end of "hey" and hers did, too. She'd been so far from the source for so long that it was easy to convince herself the old grief was finally retired, hibernating, quieted. But

then his old grief recognized hers. That connection had fired up between them, electricity igniting a wire, running back and forth, back
and forth.

A dream but it's real.

Serena is eighteen months old, tottering and talking unintelligibly.
She's two years and three months away from dying suddenly, alone, in
her sleep. Eileen is in the backyard, letting Serena fall on the spiky
grass, the grass they need to get rid of because the upkeep is too much
and it's not environmentally responsible. Serena's chunky legs wobble
as she walks, and every so often a mound of dirt upends her. Eileen
resists running over to help; Serena seems determined to get up by
herself and continue walking. She's headed toward a large bed of dai-
sies the former owners planted, many of which have withered with
neglect. Eileen can't garden, but Noah can.

Where is Noah?

There he is. She can't quite see him, but she senses him coming
near, a new warmth approaching through the front door, spilling out
the open back door to where she sits, watching their daughter fall,
laugh, get up, fall.

Did this happen?

Noah is smiling to himself. He's grinning, actually. What's he thinking about? Where's he been? He'd told her something . . . he was going
for a walk.

And now, Serena's gone. It's later, more than two years and three
months later. Noah is still behind her, smiling happily. *He's happy.* She
doesn't know why. He shouldn't be happy, even for a moment. And
she turns and sees him, and his smile fades. There he is, paralyzed
again, a sadness come rushing back into him with her gaze.

What she had done when it was real: She'd gone inside and walked right past him and upstairs. She'd cried with no apparent source until she fell asleep.

What she does now: She walks in the door that was open, and she walks toward him. She's angry and happy and sad, devastatingly sad, all of it like pool balls spinning around inside her, and if she touches Noah, if she puts her hand on him, maybe all of them will slip nicely into pockets, maybe it will all land somewhere, they'll be somewhere together, even if that somewhere is impossible.

She walks toward him. Behind him, the front door is still open. They're not home, but in a tunnel, with two exits. They'll meet in the middle.

She walks toward him, and then she wakes.

Maya

Ren thought Maya should do some kind of exhibit about the pronghorn. She walked up and down the edge of the two-lane highway in
the pitch-black, hoping she didn't blindly step on a snake or a scorpion
or get sideswiped by a pickup truck going too fast toward the closest
town, an hour away, but her mind wasn't on those dangers. The call
felt dangerous enough. She told him as much, how his numbers had
been stashed in an email she had instructed herself never to open. He
laughed.

"I hope all that can be safely in the past," Ren said.

When he'd gone to New York to become a well-known artist, it had
been over, but that wasn't the last time she'd seen Ren. A few months
later she'd flown to New York to try to convince him to get back together. She was in her late twenties, when she still believed love could
be convinced out of someone. He was a star coming out of the Whitney
Biennial and was exponentially busy, and he'd said no, as gently as he
could. They were standing outside his apartment in Cobble Hill. He
wasn't in love with anyone else, he said, but he needed to move on to
the next phase of his life, and that was here, without her. She couldn't

understand it, how he couldn't evolve with her. Where did that leave her? She'd cried guttural, breath-stopping sobs. Her face ached. People were spilling out of the tiki bar around the corner from his apartment, smelling like rancid sweetness. He held her hand. Then he let her go. It took years, but eventually she let him go, too. Though her letting go didn't come from healing. It was simply time.

"It's in the past," Maya said, but a thin thread of hurt crept back into her the more they spoke, pleasant in its familiarity. She felt alive. She hadn't known she was starting to feel not so alive.

Ren had lots of thoughts on Marfa, on the way the art tourism was both good and bad for artists—good to bring money to abstract art of any kind, of course, but he wasn't so sure that Judd and Flavin and all those mid-century minimalists had paved the road for people to appreciate contemporary art. Ren had made a career out of his aggressive collages. He rejected color, working in neutrals and browns, and treated photography like painting and painting like photography. He thought he highlighted the absurdity of the categories, his photos smeared and his paintings eerily grainy. Maya didn't like how angry the paintings seemed. New York thought differently. He'd had lots of success. Men could find success in anger, she thought.

"You're back in Tokyo now?" Maya asked.

"I needed a break. My work isn't as popular as it used to be. I thought I had to change it up, so I came back here."

"And is it working? Going home?"

"Is this home?"

"Isn't it?"

"I don't know," Ren said. On the edge of his voice, inside his uncertainty, was an invitation.

Maya told Ren about the Donald Judd cubes, and the pronghorn. She could tell he was interested, his voice animated, and he suggested she do a project around the pronghorn. They talked a little about how

to do it without being gauche or violent. They didn't really get anywhere. It would take time to figure out, she decided.

Ren had to go because it was daytime in Tokyo. He wavered. Maya
sensed another suggestion he wouldn't name. She said, "I'll call you
again," and he said, "I'd like that," and she hung up and walked the
long dark road back to her bed with Noah, her insides sparking.

Days later, Noah asked Maya on a date. He'd come home early from the
lab. Most nights he seemed exhausted at the end of his lab days, but
on this day he'd bounded in with energy. He'd dressed up, put on a
cotton blazer and his nice jeans, product in his hair. She pulled out a
curling iron and applied makeup, choosing a long, flowy printed maxi
dress she'd never worn, but that felt very much like something an artist in Marfa would wear. When she emerged from the bedroom, Noah
smiled a grateful smile. He reached out his hand and she took it.

They drove to the nicest restaurant in town and discovered the wait
was an hour. The host directed them to a local bar down the street
where they could wait to be called for a table. On their walk in the
dusk, Maya saw the town more alive than when they'd arrived. There
were young people drinking beers on the patio of the hotel. A group
of high schoolers in purple jerseys giggling at something concealed in
their hands. A small bookstore was buzzing with customers. The line
between visitors and locals was so clear. The people who lived here
were ruddy with years of high-desert sun, dressed for functionality—
for a ranch (mud-splattered Levi's), for their art (paint-splattered
button-down), or for their serving job (food-splattered black apron).
The visitors were everyone else, wearing cowboy hats that were too
pristine, shoes that weren't yet dusty, or a perfect wrap dress, like Maya
had worn earlier that day.

The bar had a big cowboy boot over the door. A few old men stood outside with a horse tied to a post, scowling at tourists who wanted to pet it. Inside was a whole world. Grizzled, unfriendly-looking white men, wearing plaid shirts and baseball caps. A small clump of young kids playing pool, bursting out in hysterical laughter. A table of ranch hands eating tacos they'd brought in from somewhere else. A lone Latino man wearing a cowboy hat and his border patrol uniform.

Maya and Noah chose an empty spot on the far side of the bar, and as he settled in, she pulled out her old Pentax camera. Noah groaned. "No, it'll flash."

In the early days of their relationship, Maya had taken this camera everywhere, trying to get better at photography. When she developed the film, she had stacks of slightly blurred photos of Noah standing in various forms of light. Now it had been more than a year since she'd brought it out.

"One millisecond of your time," Maya said and held the camera up, framing him perfectly. "Don't smile or anything. Look at me." She watched for his eyes to shift from the lens to her, for his face to soften, and then she snapped. Waiting for a lightness to come to the subject, that was the key, she remembered. In photography, timing was everything.

A few of the grizzled men looked at her after the flash and Maya waved. Noah looked around nervously. "Don't invite them over. I know you like to do that."

"Do what?"

"Get in with the locals."

"What else is there to do?" Maya said. One of the men was already coming over. "Here we go." And then, "Hello, sir!"

The man was large, round, and bald. He glanced at Noah but focused his attention on Maya. "My friend and I, we were wondering if you could take a picture of us. We want a real photo, like a printout."

Maya beamed at Noah as she answered the man. "Why, of course!"

She hopped up from the stool and arranged the men under a hanging light. They'd gotten new sleeves tattooed and wanted them photographed, even though they were still raw and a little wet. She'd misjudged their unfriendliness. They were bashful and appreciative of her time and her posing suggestions, and she got an address to send them the scans. When she returned to the barstool, Noah gave her a look, but he was smiling.

"This is how I like you," he said. He'd ordered them two Lone Stars, crisp and cold.

"What does that mean?"

"You're exactly like you were when I met you."

"How's that? Surprised by the handsome stranger who barged into my symposium?"

"Amused. Open. Open to being amused."

Maya felt warmed by this. Noah did understand her.

"Am I the same?" he asked.

Maya considered this. When she met Noah, she thought he was delicate, like he was trying out new legs. But that wasn't what attracted her to him; it was his curiosity. Everything she said, he wanted to know why, what, how. Yes, he'd go to that weird art event she was sure would be terrible, but he wanted to see for himself *why* it was terrible. What was a talent she secretly thought she possessed? Did she have any ideas for movies? If she wanted to disappear, where would she go? After Ren, and after the series of terrible men she dated for a few months at a time who were painfully incurious, she'd found Noah. Noah was always curious.

Maya worried now that he was different—she felt a change, amorphous. So what she said was, "You're still in search of something greater."

"Because of you."

"Because of me?"

"Yeah. Before you, I leaned on that search all the time, wanting there to be something good. And then, suddenly, nothing was." A shadow passed across Noah's face, but it was brief. "But then, there you were. Something good."

Maya laughed. "Did I miss our anniversary? What's happening? I mean, I like it, say more, but what's happening?"

Noah shook his head. "No, but I've been thinking. About how we are. Then and now."

"Ah," she said. "You're curious. About us."

"Yeah, sure. Among other things. What are you curious about?"

"These pronghorn deaths. There have been a dozen at least, you know? That's what the wildlife guy told me."

"You talked to a wildlife guy?"

Maya realized she hadn't told Noah. He'd been so tired and she'd been so in her head that they'd stopped eating dinner together, instead scavenging in the kitchen and turning in early. He didn't know what she was up to, and she hadn't thought to fill him in.

"It's been suggested I do a project around the dying pronghorn." The passive voice, *it's been suggested*. But the suggestion was all Ren's. A flash of guilt that she was keeping this from Noah, and then righteousness. Noah could ask the right questions and get to the answer of Ren, if he really wanted.

"I thought you said Justine brushed the whole thing off."

Justine didn't actually know yet, but Maya wouldn't tell him that. "Sure, it could be a little gross, but there's a way to make it appealing. I think. I don't know. I'm still figuring it out."

"Dead animals make great art. Consider the turkey vulture," Noah said, smiling. "I'm sure it'll turn out. Let me know if you want me to ask Klein about the pronghorn."

They were quiet for a few moments, the din of the bar swaying around them. Klein was a bridge to a topic they didn't discuss: what happened at the lab. Yes, he was under an NDA, but she didn't expect trade secrets.

"Should we play pool?" Noah asked. He nodded toward the teenagers rolling the eight ball around the felt with their hands. "I think I can take 'em."

There was a lightness with him that Maya enjoyed, even if it concealed a subterranean layer, denser and darker. That night they were easy, as they hadn't been in months. They were called for dinner, and indulged in local goat cheese and rabbit confit and lavender cake, and the manager had to ask them to leave because they were closing the restaurant down. They tried to walk home but it was so dark and way too far on this much wine and Lone Star. They made it halfway and then turned around, sobering up on the walk back to the restaurant to retrieve their car.

At home, they pulled the shades and didn't make it to the bedroom before Maya had her hand on Noah's belt, and he sighed. They dropped to their knees and shed their clothes, the poplin of her maxi dress dampening under Noah's grip. They made love like they were dating, which is to say they treated each other's bodies as brand-new, exciting, full of erotic potential. At one point, Maya crawled away and ran to the bedroom, and Noah followed, and they finished on the bed, both of them half hanging off the mattress, and by the end she was laughing, tears pricking the corners of her eyes. Noah let out a huge exhale. They lay there, pulsing. The lightness she'd felt at the bar sustained through dinner, through home, through this. It was possible to get back to who they were.

Some time passed. The gray light in the room seemed to change, lighten a bit. They were still naked, lying on top of the sheets, but Maya was cold now.

She said, "Maybe now is the time to start trying to get pregnant."

"Now? Right now?"

"Here in Marfa. Why not?"

"Maya, there are a million reasons why not. I just started this new thing, we have no idea how long we'll be here, we have no idea of anything about the future."

She sat up on her elbows and turned to look at him. "We don't know about the future? What does that even mean?"

Then Noah said, "I have to tell you something."

Ren had said the exact same thing to her when he told her he got the Biennial. Never in the history of that sentence had what followed been good.

"Okay," she said, turning on her side.

He spoke without turning on his side. He stayed on his back, speaking to the ceiling, the open skylight, the sky, the stars. He told her about what Nils and Klein were up to, what the Janus Project had achieved. There were phrases that stood out, that she knew would come to have meaning in her life the way they seemed to have meaning in Noah's life now: *Echo Injection, memory mapping, Episodic Folding, time bath, nanorepeaters*. With each term, a piece of the buoy keeping her afloat fell away. *Okay, okay*, she thought, quelling any rising panic in her. There was no rising panic. There was no panic. She would survive. They would be okay.

"And it's me," he said. "They want me to do it."

To do what?

"To be the transport subject. To fold."

It was as if the gears of her body suddenly jammed. She felt a colder chill wash over her, a breeze from above. She grabbed the blanket that had fallen on the ground and pulled it up over her shoulders.

"I know you probably have questions," Noah said. "I don't have many answers. Not right now."

She asked them anyway. Was it dangerous? How long would he be back in his memories? How would he come back? Where would he go?

His answers were vague: *Maybe, it depends, the way I left, wherever they want.*

"Oh, Maya," Noah said, his mouth fixed into a sympathetic frown, which is how she knew she was crying. She tried to talk, but her throat was tingling and wet.

She retreated. Not physically. Physically she remained right there on the bed. But in her memory, she fell away, back to a night with Ren. They'd been at some party in a Portland warehouse, they'd taken MDMA and maybe a bump of coke, and it was raining, lightly, the way it rains in Portland, so light you could almost not realize it, the air suddenly wet, and that's how Maya was, standing in the dark outside a loading dock, alone, looking for Ren, getting damp until she was shivering. It had been a mistake—Ren was taking a piss somewhere in the dark—but for those ten minutes, she was sure she was alone. Time slowed down the way drugs stretch a moment into an eternity, and she felt herself growing more alone as she grew more damp, and then reaching a horizon where she was okay with it, being alone, being left.

Now here on the bed with Noah, the blanket she grabbed did nothing. She felt heavy, sinking into this mattress, it was closing up around her, the mattress and time—how long had she been lying here? She wanted to say, *Are you crazy, Noah? Or am I?* It seemed one of them was, at least one.

"No, no," he was saying, a response to she didn't know what.

He curled around her, held her. They looked up at the window to the night until eventually Maya stood up on the bed and pulled the skylight glass closed.

Noah

His days were spent practicing memory mapping with Nils, in preparation for his first official fold. Of course, he'd already sort of folded, for a moment, when Klein had him try out the bath in his orientation. But that had been too much too fast. The first step before attempting to fold, Nils explained, was simply having a clear map of a memory. So in Noah's training, they focused on mapping something easily accessible: the morning Noah had just had. He would put on the mapping helmet, meditate on his morning for as long as he could, and Nils would attempt to get a clear read of his neurons. One day Nils left the controls for lunch, and Noah declined to join as he normally did, saying he wanted to stick around by himself and get a little more meditation practice in. He needed to be able to stay in a memory longer, to make the details more vibrant and contoured.

It was there, alone, that Noah first really mapped a memory of Serena.

He'd already had his weekly dose of the Echo Injection, and he was accustomed to using the helmet. The hard part was lingering on the kind of memory he'd neatly packed away, a Serena memory. But after his conversation with Eileen, even though it had gone badly, he felt armed with clearheadedness, as if her reticence emboldened his determination. So he kneeled on the meditation pillow on the floor next to the bath, put the helmet on, and created a neurological map of his dead daughter.

This is the memory he first mapped: a chilly morning in December, waking Serena up. At first, as he'd been taught, Noah pictured himself in blackness, floating as in space. And then he made that image of himself walk, and then jump. Being physical helped conjure the rest of the scene. And slowly but surely the imagined ground of his and Eileen's Los Feliz home assembled beneath him. Quickly after that, as if being scribbled into focus, the rest of the environment: the couch, the chair, the counter, or the smell of jasmine hanging off the shade trellis on the patio. Being able to conjure that so completely filled Noah with an even greater sense of power. Details from the life that he'd buried came pouring back into his present brain: the robin's egg shade of the accent wall in the downstairs bathroom, the way the rug in the living room shed fibers he found between his toes, and the gray spots along the windowsill in Serena's room where they both liked to rest their chins to watch the bird feeder outside.

He walked into the room and touched the night-light sensor, a gentle blue to help her wake. This morning she was still asleep—she often slept in on cold mornings. He padded across the thick mauve rug to her bed on the far side of the room. He sat on the little stool where he read her bedtime stories, and where his knees bumped the bed's side panel. Smooth, slick wood, worn away by their constant presence.

There was a smell, too, a little floral, a little sweaty, detergent mixed with Serena. And she was there. Her body an S shape on her side, the tip of her thumb in her mouth, her blond hair fanned out on her favorite rainbow pillow. Blue light was creeping through the pulled shades. Christmas lights at the perimeter of her ceiling were turned off, waiting to be illuminated. When she woke, Noah would tell her how many days from Christmas they were, how many days from Santa and reindeer and toys. When she woke, he would know again that she was perfect.

But this was only memory mapping, the helmet reading the neurons. Reigniting the memory—the helmet inside the bath writing that memory back into the brain—was a whole other thing.

"Consistency is key," Nils had said. "We need to make sure the memory map is as perfect as it can be."

Step one in his training was what they had been doing for days, Noah with his weekly doses of the Echo Injection, wearing the mapping helmet, practicing meditating on a memory while Nils mapped it. Step two was memory reignition—Noah getting in the bath and using the reignition helmet to rewrite the memory back into his brain. This was what he'd quickly and clumsily done during orientation, what had been so overwhelming. Step three in his training was to take the Fold Cocktail during the memory reignition, inducing the fold. But he wouldn't do that for a while, not until the rewriting went off without a hitch.

But there were hitches. The first time they tried memory reignition in the bath, he panicked and the session was aborted. Even without the Fold Cocktail, the intensity of having a memory so vividly replayed in his brain felt claustrophobic.

"Claustrophobia is normal," Nils had said. "I felt it when I tried it, I mean. You'll get there."

Noah did get there, eventually, but it required a certain amount of giving in, of letting his brain not belong to him for a moment, that moment right when the memory was reignited. In those milliseconds, he felt all the parts of himself: his body, his mind, his not-mind. Was that his spirit? His soul? It felt like a gasp of air, *himself.*

And then the memory flooded back in, whole, real. It was difficult to keep that separation and let the memory play out, and he could only last ten seconds in the memory before the habits of his brain rejected it. But those ten seconds were as real as living it the first time. He felt the memory in every part of him.

So once Nils had shown him how to do it, how to program the helmet, how to operate the bath, Noah waited until Nils was gone again and wrote the memory of Serena back into himself. Again, no Fold Cocktail, but he wanted to feel what it was like to have Serena lit up again in his brain.

What happened then was different from recalling a memory. He wasn't remembering it, he wasn't *telling* himself about the December morning; every part of him was in that morning. The feeling, it didn't originate in his brain, either. It was born in a warmth spilling over the top of his lungs, electrifying his heart, then up his neck. This was happening. He felt tired. He felt anticipation. He felt close to his daughter. Impossible.

Then the experience started to wobble, as it always did. Noah felt the time-bath water on his arms, but smelled Serena's damp hair. His heart pumped with the tightening desire to hold his daughter again, but in the memory, he held her. Pain lingered at the periphery, heartbreak waiting to join, waiting to take this away.

Wake up, present Noah told memory Noah to say. But memory Noah didn't say it. The mouth opened, the words at the back of the tongue, but he couldn't. The expulsion from the past into the present didn't come, not yet. Serena remained sleeping. Everything as it was.

Noah's eyes snapped open.

A voice, Nils. Far away at first, and then there, in his ears, coming through the bath. Noah gasped and pressed the release on the top of the bath.

"Memory igniting without me?" Nils said through the mic, but he was smiling.

Carefully, Noah climbed out and grabbed a robe hanging on the wall. "It's difficult to stay in it," Noah said. "But it's exhilarating."

"Isn't it, brother?" Nils said. "Tell me."

Not looking at Nils, Noah said, as if speaking to himself, "She was wrong."

"Who was wrong?"

"Eileen. She said it was unrealistic, but she's wrong. It's exactly like reality. It *is* reality."

Noah realized in a flash that he'd accidentally confessed he'd told Eileen about the project.

But all Nils said was, "Back to work, then. Let's prove her wrong."

So they continued. Practicing memory mapping. Practicing having that memory written back into his brain. The first goal was to take the Fold Cocktail and complete his first fold. After that, they'd work on increasing the time in which he could stay in the fold, and the volition with which he could move around. When Nils was present, he did this, was the perfect transport subject. Without Nils, he visited his private past.

The hardest part was not telling Maya that he saw Serena in his sessions. It wasn't the right time, not with the baby conversation still on the table, and Maya still seemed to be struggling to adjust to Marfa. She was putting on a happy face for him, with constantly raised eyebrows and a too-high voice, asking questions without tracking his answers. He knew Maya well enough to know that she thought she was pulling off the act of happiness. But he could see beneath it.

A shift had occurred between them since the night they'd gone out and he'd told her what was going on in the lab. He thought he'd expressed himself well in telling her about the project, but afterward, there was a thick layer of silence between them. As though there were no more questions to ask, no more answers to seek, at least not to-gether. He sensed that she thought he was losing his mind. He some-times wondered if he was.

A week after he first began the memory sessions, a Saturday, his day off, Maya interrupted his long post-lunch nap. He'd been sleeping deeply since training started. The second his head hit the pillow he'd fall into blackout, a long dreamless sleep, his subconscious all used up.

But Maya had energy and wanted to go see some art. There was so *much* art here, so many installations and strange little galleries, but if Noah was being honest, seeing art didn't relax him the way it relaxed Maya. He often felt her loosening when they went to museums, and her opinions came so easily and articulated, whereas he often stood in front of a work of art absolutely bewildered.

He said as much when she suggested they go see a building-size in-stallation by the artist Robert Irwin. Maya had already purchased tick-ets and confirmed they could go on a self-guided tour.

"Oh, so you want to see me bewildered," Noah said.

"Bewilderment is a useful, valid reaction to art," Maya said, already in the bathroom applying mascara. He was still in bed. "Five minutes enough for you to get ready?"

She wanted to get there around sunset, because she heard it was the best time to view the piece. On the short drive into town, Maya told Noah about Robert Irwin. "Irwin was from the Light and Space movement, in the sixties and seventies. A very California thing."

"So his medium is . . . light and space?" Noah guessed.

"Exactly. Like you."

"Eh." He tilted his head, as if to say maybe yes, maybe no.

"So what's your medium, then?"

"Math?" he said, but it was still a question. Technically, now his medium was the time bath. Or his neurons. His memories. Was that space? Space and time? Time was sometimes measured by the speed of light, so possibly his medium was light and space. But he didn't say this to Maya.

When they arrived, Maya was still chattering on about the way Irwin's work had evolved and the way it had stayed the same. From the outside, the U-shaped building was plain and unadorned. The heat was fading, a chill cutting through. There were two entry points and each seemed equally weighted, no arrows or signage, and no one else there to direct them. It had a frightening, destabilizing effect. But Maya walked confidently into the left entry point, and Noah followed.

Inside was a strange darkness. The wide hallway was bisected by black scrims. In the silence Noah felt nervous, unsure how to interact with this art. Tinted windows on one side muted the desert view, and on the other side, the dark scrim filtered everything into leftover light—a hint of golden, but greatly diminished. He stayed a few steps behind Maya, procession-like and reverent. They turned in to a hallway where scrims were set up like doorways, portals to the next paradigm of light. He walked through the first scrim, charcoal, and then each one after progressively lighter—gray, amber, honey—each portal delivering them out of the darkness, shepherding in more light, until it was blinding. This time the light was not leftover; this felt like the very source of light itself. Warmth like he'd swallowed it and absorbed it, all the way through his skin and tissues and tendons and bones.

Everything here was the inverse of the beginning: white scrim, clear windows, light walls. Noah wanted to turn away, a feeling caught in his throat. They'd begun at a diminished light, and now they were meeting this almost unbearable brightness, and Noah was suddenly sure what this art was about. It was about dying. Beginning in the dim world, only to end at the crushing light of death. He'd never been so sure what a piece of art was trying to say before. He wanted to run and tell Maya, but she disappeared down the hallway. Then he stopped walking. The building felt churchlike. He felt weak. And he knelt.

And in that kneeling, with clarity, he remembered what Maya had said in the car on the way here. *It used to be a hospital,* she'd said. The statement landed on him now: of course. Of course the building had been a hospital.

"It's not a choice."

That's what the doctor in green scrubs had said to him and Eileen in the hospital hallway after they'd brought in Serena. An autopsy would be done, as was standard when a child died unexpectedly at home. *It's not a choice.* Eileen said no, but that was all she said, the only word left in her body that day and for many days. It was Noah who'd spoken, who said, "All right," who allowed some doctors he'd never met to turn their daughter into an investigation. Maybe there'd be someone or something to blame, besides themselves.

"No," Eileen said. "No, no, no." She said it in different intonations, as if that simple, powerful thought could deny their reality.

He and Eileen sat in the hallway of the hospital—it was too wide, too slick and clean, too empty. After a while, they were moved from the hallway to a private room. Everywhere the feeling was unwell, clouded, vague. It was the middle of the night at the children's hospital. There should have been more emergencies, but there was only theirs. The light of the room was unbearable. They were alone in it. And then they weren't even together in that aloneness. That feeling would last for years. Until he met Maya.

Here in Marfa, kneeling, he remembered that other hospital, he saw it, felt it. A gentle swaying moved through his body, as the hallway back then and this hallway now formed a tenuous link in his brain.

He was having a hard time seeing clearly. Someone was walking toward him. A girl, a woman. Then his vision settled, and he saw the figure was Maya, and she wasn't walking toward him. She hadn't even turned around and seen him kneeling. She was walking away, continuing down the hall, into the light.

Eileen

There was a bright crispness to fall days in Northern California, but the darkness came early. Eileen noticed that her students were sleepier as the semester waned on, but she let it slide. Eileen herself became more relaxed in the classroom the closer they got to winter. She was known to let a student or two call her "Ms. Merrick" instead of "Dr. Merrick." One student wouldn't stop calling her "Dr. Eileen," and though she always corrected this student, Prem used the name playfully on their dates. "Dr. Eileen," he whispered to wake her up in the morning, and sometimes in class she blushed, thinking of it.

She was qualified for more prestigious jobs. In her former life, Eileen had a large lab at USC, and she didn't have to teach. But this job had exactly the stakes she wanted. She had TAs and graduate assistants to help her in her research on neural responses in the brain as they related to schizophrenia, but the college didn't put a lot of pressure on her to publish or teach graduate seminars, and they were okay when her lab went dormant because of lackluster funding or ill-suited grad students. She taught two classes per semester, with one remitted every third semester. This semester she was stuck with Biology 105, which felt like a place AP chemistry students came to decide they wanted to be religion majors.

The morning after her dream that felt so real—walking toward Noah in their old house—the students gave their end-of-unit presentations. Rather than grading tedious papers, Eileen liked tasking the students with presenting on "a defining moment in science" and seeing what they had to say. A young woman named Alice was set to go today. She was painfully shy when called on, and in one-on-ones her shyness played as disinterest. Eileen tried to be gentle with Alice, but she sometimes became annoyed, and then felt guilty. Why couldn't she be more like Prem, who cared and thought so much about his students?

Alice lugged a giant posterboard up to the front of the room. When she opened it, Eileen raised her eyebrows. Other presentations used PowerPoint or Keynote to depict flow charts and complex tables above their comprehension, but Alice's posterboard glowed with aesthetic DIY chaos, various shades of blue and green, exacting handmade illustrations, and long captions in tiny handwriting. It was art, actually art.

Alice began to speak. She explained scientific discoveries as they related to artistic and cultural expression in moments throughout history. She said, "Science bolstered the way we understood the world and the way we saw beauty, which explained why we were alive." She drew a line from the Big Bang to French cave paintings, and connected it all to Copernicus's understanding of sunrise and sunset. She used an exploded image of DNA to explain Seurat's pointillism. Somehow, and Eileen wouldn't be able to explain it later, Alice showed how Marie Curie's discovery of radium made Andy Warhol possible. Eileen hadn't even considered those lives overlapped. Alice went beyond the twenty-minute allotment, but she had the entire room's rapt attention. She ended with a physics breakthrough, describing atomic entanglement, Noah's original area of study.

For this piece, Alice showed a photograph of a nude body. A woman standing on a ledge, from behind, a cityscape before her. But Alice showed that on closer inspection the cityscape was a mirror, indicated by its cutoff edges and the shadow of a reflection in the bottom corners. The subject was in a studio, a painted landscape behind the camera. It looked like the photographer had tried to scrub out the reflection of her front side, but a ghost outline remained, a blurry face and a tangle of pubic hair, as though photocopied or far away. "This is a representation of coherence," Alice finished, using a physics term Eileen was sure no student in the room had heard.

Eileen was struck by this presentation, because of its bold difference. The other student presentations had been cold and small and, Eileen would never say this to anyone, boring. But Alice's was raw and impassioned, and attempted to tell the story not of a single moment, but of the entire endeavor of science in the context of the world. Eileen wasn't sure if it was entirely successful, but it was admirable. She was so rarely surprised these days, and Alice's way of thinking surprised her.

As class ended, Eileen reminded the students of their homework defending evolution, due Thursday. She caught Alice on the way out. "Nice work," she said. "I've never seen a presentation like that. How did you come up with that?"

Alice set the posterboard down and hiked up her backpack. "I was reading that book you gave us," she said. "It talked about Stephen Hawking so I looked up Stephen Hawking and started reading more and more, and it's funny, you know, that phrase they use? 'A unified theory of everything.' It seems silly. Like, isn't there a more scientific term for that?"

Eileen smiled. "I guess I never thought of it that way."

"Well, that's how I thought of this presentation. I thought, so, if they actually want a unified theory of everything, then they should think about *everything*. Science ignores people, you know? Living their lives, making stuff, movies, painting. What about the people?"

"Yes," Eileen said. "You're right."

"I hope you aren't offended, Dr. Merrick."

"Oh, no. Why would I be offended?"

"Because," Alice said. "You're a scientist. That's your religion. And I feel like I blasphemed all over it."

"No, no," Eileen said. "You're right. We should think about everything. That's sort of what I was trying to get at with the prompt about choosing a defining moment in science, but you did me one better. Everything is the defining moment."

Alice shrugged, but Eileen saw a small smile creep across her face. "Thank you. I'm majoring in poetry, anyway." Alice picked up the posterboard and started out the door, but she paused at the threshold. "Thank you for seeing more, Dr. Merrick."

Thank you for seeing more, Dr. Merrick, Eileen replayed in her head on the drive home. Said with the profundity only an undergrad could muster. Refreshing. Because yes, what about people? What was science describing if not people, our existence here?

On Saturday, Prem came over and watched Eileen botch a meat lasagna. She'd decided to cook for him just this once, to prove she couldn't do it. He needed to know what he was getting into. The lasagna smelled good when it came out of the oven but it crunched under their forks when they ate, burnt, and Prem laughed generously. She felt drawn to him. He was not as quick as her, but he was kind, and his affection was uncomplicated. She'd decided that was enough for companionship. Besides, he was busy. Junior college work kept you a different kind of busy, managing student lives or trying desperately not to manage them. When Prem talked about his students, Eileen was struck by how tenderly he felt toward them, these people who probably wouldn't remember his class in five years. He seemed to be drawn to teaching because of the student interaction, whereas Eileen taught despite that. When he kissed her on the couch, she idly wondered if she would be found out by him, her indifference exposed.

He wanted to kiss her more, but she stopped him.

"Are you okay?" he asked.

Eileen nodded at the wall behind his head, above the couch. When she'd moved, she'd left a lot of furniture with Noah, not wanting any of that life to carry over. So she'd put together a new desk, and while trying to get a leg into position she'd backed the blunt end into the wall with a crunch. The indentation it left was the size of a marble, three cracks branching out from the center. On the wall behind Prem's head.

"I hate looking at that," Eileen said.

"So fix it."

She laughed, not because she wasn't able to fix it—she could have figured it out—but because fixing it hadn't occurred to her. She imagined calling someone, a vague faceless someone, to come repair the wall, and the idea of it, of finding the someone, of calling them, of arranging it all, exhausted her.

"I guess I should," Eileen said, her voice trailing off as she realized she definitely would not fix it.

"Want me to?" Prem asked. He looked at her, his face genuine, his question honest.

She was startled by his quick, serious offer, and stared at him, waiting for an answer to come to her.

But he didn't wait. Prem got up from the couch and disappeared into the small garage off the kitchen. He came back with spackle and a tiny tub of paint.

"They always leave this stuff behind," he said, holding the tubs up to her.

Then he got to work. Eileen continued to not say anything, watching him fix her wall, until Prem finally said, "What, have you never seen anyone fix anything before?"

"No, but the time between deciding to fix it and fixing it, it was so swift."

"My mom always said, 'Do it, don't list it.' She hated lists of tiny things to do. She said she didn't immigrate to do errands."

Eileen hadn't heard Prem talk much about his family. Only that his retired parents lived in Modesto, where his father had also been a chemistry professor.

"What did she do, your mom?" Eileen asked.

"She owned a home goods store. So, errands, in a way. But back in Pakistan she went to school for nursing."

"She didn't want to do nursing here?"

"She said she wanted to take care of us, me and my brother. Not strangers in Modesto," Prem said a little wistfully. "She had a harder time than my dad, coming over. That's what she told me once, at least. I don't know."

Eileen wanted to say, *I'd like to meet them*, but doing so would thrust them into a different, more intense level of relationship. But the sight of Prem, fixing her wall, talking about his parents, had placed him squarely in context, his own context, with a history full of complex branches, family members, locations. He wasn't only a guy with whom she had the basics in common: science professor, midforties, an affinity for alien invasion movies. Eileen was trying to keep Prem blurry, a light presence with little domino effect. But he was a person, solid and real, present, and if he was there, she must be, too.

He finished spackling. "Paint tomorrow. This paint won't match perfectly right away. It'll match when it dries," he said. "I promise."

"Thank you," Eileen said, almost shyly.

Prem stood with the spackle. "I'm going to put this back, and then I'm going to make out with you some more."

"Oh, wait, I haven't cleaned up." She made a move to go to the kitchen.

He lightly held her wrist. "We can leave it for the morning. I'll do it."

She followed him to her bedroom, where he looked at her hungrily. They'd done this many times, but Eileen felt off. She thought about how the food was disappointing, the weather strangely overcast, and the mess left in the sink. Prem was handsome and he was touching her, and she closed her eyes and tried to be there, in that bed, being undressed by him, but instead of feeling the desire, she felt his hands willing it. Eileen wanted more in one direction or the other, to be held down or freed.

She cried out before she felt the urge to cry, her body doing so before her brain recognized the need. Prem backed away immediately; her cry wasn't one of pleasure. This relationship between mind and body was one Eileen recognized from labor and delivery. The insistent action of her body a beat ahead of her mind's understanding. She felt a primal sadness, invisible grief tearing through her abdomen. Prem did not know her body that way. He never would. Only Noah, only Serena.

"I'm so sorry," Prem said. "Did I hurt you? Tell me."

Eileen clapped her hand over her mouth to stanch the crying. She shook her head. The world blurred. "What is it?" He put his arms around her and held her. Her mind raced, while her body went on below her. She was a match that had gone out, the hissing memory of burning. Finally, she succumbed to Prem's embrace. She quieted. *I wasn't here*, she didn't say.

In the morning, she left Prem in bed and dug out her ancient, thick-soled running shoes from the hall closet.

In her past life she'd run every Wednesday after work and every

Sunday before breakfast. A few miles, five tops if she was feeling exceptional. After she moved away, she'd stopped running. Simply surviving felt like enough, calorie-burning, and she had new routines in her new life. The gym at school, long solo walks to the farmers market, endless time to herself. She didn't have to *make time* for herself by running.

But now she felt the urge to get some distance under her feet. She started slowly, admiring her little neighborhood that was still asleep, but it wasn't long before her pace quickened and she felt that familiar ease, when rhythm took over and time receded. There was control there: She was passing time, time wasn't passing her.

As a rule, Eileen didn't look back. Of course, a part of her was always back there with Serena, but she wouldn't live in that place. That was what Noah did.

But it was becoming clear to her now that she was also unable to look forward. Though Prem hadn't explicitly asked her to; he was a good man, gentle and caring. Prem was the future, or at least *a* future. To be with him, she had to gesture toward that possibility. And then Noah's call, a voice from so many years ago, his simple question that tossed her into impossible depths.

She should turn around, get back to Prem, who would wonder where she was. Make breakfast, apologize for her breakdown, explain that her ex's phone call had made her feel weird. That was what normal people would do, that was what Eileen's idea of herself would do. But when she tried to picture doing it, she resisted. She didn't belong in that version of events. She struggled to find a version of events where she did belong.

Up ahead, a tree wept little white wisps. Eileen slowed, unsure. But as she got closer, she saw the tree branches were hung with messy toilet paper strips, a victim of a midnight prank. She smiled. She and Noah had done that once, on their joint bachelor and bachelorette trips. They'd gone to a little archaic island off the Georgia coast where a friend had a house, and everyone got drunk and loopy, a state of mind in which light vandalism seemed like a silly, life-affirming thing to do. They'd had so much fun. Not only then, but together, always. Late at night, when it was just the two of them on the strip of humid beach, fireflies lighting up and dying all around them, he'd slurred into her ear, "You'll never get rid of me." Here, years after, at least one tragedy later, he was right.

Now, on her run, if she turned the corner, she'd be headed back home. Instead, she jogged in place, looking at the tree. Her feet bounced up and down, but she didn't move one way or the other.

Maya

Pronghorn weren't antelope. That was the first thing Maya learned in her research. Even though they were often mistaken for antelope, they were the last of their kind, the only surviving members of a family of animals called Antilocapridae, more closely related to giraffes. Maya had to agree, their faces were strangely long and beautiful, giraffe-like. An employee at the wildlife authority told her they used to number in the tens of thousands, at least in the region, though the population had dwindled to a few thousand at best, due to drought and malnourishment. In all Maya's searching she found no reports of pronghorn going mad, bashing their heads in on minimalist art.

With Ren's words ringing in her ears, she decided to paint the pronghorn. There was a screened-in mudroom off the kitchen that led out to a field of scrub grass and a fence that marked the property line. One morning she had seen three pronghorn bound through. They were fast and graceful, like strong, lithe ballet dancers, and they cleared the fence with no problem at all. Before the image fizzled out of her brain, she grabbed a pen and started to sketch. It had cooled down outside, and while she worked Maya listened to the sounds of birds chittering and horses stomping across the nearest property.

Her pronghorn sketches were fine, she thought. They were very literal, though, and she found them lacking in communicating the animals' speed and ease. They wouldn't do.

Maya found an art supply store in a town over an hour's desolate drive away, but the distance didn't bother her. Noah was still in training, coming home exhausted and woozy, as if permanently in that meditative dimension, and they were no longer spending their evenings together. She had nothing to do but paint. She acquired a few massive canvases and started planning out larger, more abstract paintings. It occurred to her that she would need a bolder color logic to turn her sketches into large paintings. She started mixing her own colors to create tonality.

Weeks later, when she was done with the first large painting, she was pleased. In shades of magenta, purple, and pink, she'd encapsulated the idea of fast, precise movement, of a strange presence that felt both alien and familiar. There was the scrub, the sunset, the fence, the three pronghorn, but it was gesture and color that told the story. The quality of the tones and brushstroke made the painting appear viscous, as if the image were bleeding out from the canvas. The brushstrokes were fine, and if otherwise arranged might have seemed chaotic, but here they were indicating urgency. That was it, she thought. The painting felt urgent.

When Maya had asked Justine from the gallery about the pronghorn deaths, Justine had been vague in her answers—she wasn't sure, that wasn't her department. Maya knew Justine was a gallery girl, concerned with bringing buzzy art to town, and nothing was less buzzy than animals beating themselves to death on the sculptures.

But this painting was so alive and dynamic that Maya felt sure

Justine would react positively to it. So, she invited Justine over, said she had something interesting to show her. Justine showed up at the door on a Wednesday afternoon, dressed in a pleated jumpsuit Maya recognized as Issey Miyake. Maya wore jeans and an old Stanford shirt of Noah's. She wished they were a little dirtier, so she could look more like the kind of artist she knew Justine wanted.

"Oh, I'm so delighted to be here," Justine said, letting herself in the front door. "I've always wondered what it was like inside the Klein Michaels compound. Didn't even know exactly where it was. He attends our gala every year, you know, but he hasn't extended an invite here, even though we'd be dying to do some sort of collaboration."

Maya smiled, but as Justine walked around the small living room, touching the furniture and trim, it occurred to her suddenly what was happening here. Justine wanted to collaborate with Maya as a way to collaborate with Klein, to get closer to his faucet of money. *Of course*, Maya thought. *It's not like I'm some established artist or critic or anything. I'm a spouse.*

Her smile waned. Justine turned around. "Curious decor, isn't it? It's not typical for the region. More California or New Mexico, if you ask me."

"Yeah," Maya murmured. "I think they wanted to make us feel at home? Or less jarred by the transition. The effect is kind of strange, though."

"Let's see it, then," Justine said brightly.

Maya led her through the galley kitchen to the mudroom. She'd tidied up a bit before Justine arrived, and now wished she hadn't. She should have shown the labor, the progress of the mess, had Justine over for a real studio visit. Justine walked back and forth, taking in the painting from different angles. She was painfully silent. The expensive soles of her loafers clicked on the floor. Maya felt like she should get ahead of the disappointment, disavow the work, insist she could do better. She could, probably. With time. But the truth was the act of painting the pronghorn was the closest she'd felt to a real flow state in a long time.

Finally, after ages, Justine spun around. Her face was inscrutable. She said, "It's brilliant."

Maya breathed out relief and realized the tips of her fingers and toes were tingling. She hadn't even shown the painting to Noah yet.

"No, really, Maya. It's beautiful. The way you've worked with color, it's gorgeous, wild but very controlled. The gesture here. Now tell me, where did this begin?"

Maya told Justine about the pronghorn that had swept through the backyard one day, and where she envisioned the project going: two more large paintings, perhaps a few small studies, to do with their death and madness, whatever was killing them, the way their other-worldly speed and grace so quickly translated to destruction. And against the art, of all things.

"It would be about the question of what is beautiful. Does something have to die to make itself beautiful in its life?"

Justine laughed softly. "Look, Maya. I love this painting, but for the other paintings, can we do them without the death part?"

Now it was Maya's turn to laugh. The death part was the whole point. But she realized what Justine was asking. She wanted to neuter the piece, so it didn't offend. She said as much to Justine.

"It's not that it's offensive to *me*," Justine said. "I get what you're after. But you have to understand, we can't go making commerce out of the vandalism of Donald Judd's work."

"It's not vandalism," Maya said. "They're dying. And why can't we make art of it? No one's even talking about these deaths."

Justine turned toward Maya with sharpness. Maya regretted the exasperated tone she'd taken. If she wanted to show, she needed Justine on her side. But did she want to show if she couldn't make art about what seemed most vital, that animal who'd sputtered to death in front of her?

"We have relationships with the foundation to think of, with estates, with the community," Justine said. "With Klein Michaels." She was cold and calm now. She began to walk past Maya, toward the kitchen, toward the front door. "Why don't you take a beat. Think about what you actually want to say, the question you're asking. I'm sure you can do it in a tasteful way."

"Oh, fuck her, for sure," was what Ren said when Maya called him an hour later. Justine was long gone and Maya had driven into town. She needed to be away from the compound, so she had parked in a neighborhood and was walking up and down the side streets in the purple dusk. Ren's cursing activated Maya's insides. "*Tasteful*, gross," he said. "And, like, what the fuck does this have to do with Klein Michaels? What the hell would he care?"

"I have no idea," Maya said. "I'm having a hard time tracking any of that guy's logic."

"Is his job going okay?" Ren asked, not using Noah's name.

She made a sound like a shrug. She didn't want to talk about Noah with Ren. "It's more like this place is weird and the weirdness is confusing. Like this place is an in-between place."

"Now you're speaking Judd."

The asphalt was crumbly beneath her feet. Next to her was a deep, grassy trench, which sloped back up to meet a rickety fence. She passed an entry to the property that had wide, rusty cow grates dug into the ground. A smell wafted, organic, pungent.

"It's not fair to blame the place," Maya said. "Lots of people live here, ranch here, immigrate here. It's the art scene that is confusing. You can be askew but it has to be in the right way."

"So change it up," Ren said.

He was using vague language on purpose. It would have to be Maya who would push. "Ren, this is changing it up. We live in Marfa, for fuck's sake. On an unmarked compound-slash-lab owned by a billionaire who apparently gets to say what I can and can't paint."

He laughed. He had a low, husky laugh that you had to earn. Noah's laugh was wide and generous, but Ren's was elite. You always had to earn things with Ren.

"It sounds like Justine is trying to make you forget that the painting isn't just about the image. You only find out what the image means through process. If you don't go through the process with intentionality, the image is empty."

Maya sighed. Ren was right and she knew it, and she didn't love being told something very obvious by him, but it was what she needed to hear. He had always known what she needed to hear when it came to art. It was what had made their relationship so vibrant.

"Maybe I could stand a change of scenery, too," Maya said, her voice low. She almost didn't want to say what she meant, what she wanted.

"The scenery's nice here," Ren said.

The line crackled with silence. She could see it, Ren lying back on a lounge chair, an expensive one bought in Omotesandō, eating one of those squishy egg salad sandwiches from Lawson. He was probably smiling an eggy smile, knowing he had her, he had Maya. She knew this because even in her trepidation, she felt the same, like she'd found herself, even if it was the version of herself that was tethered to Ren.

Maya found that she was standing in front of the bar she and Noah had been to several weeks before. The cowboy boot sign glowed green on her arms.

"I think I've walked myself to a decent night," she said before Ren could say anything more. "I better go."

Inside it was the same. The sound of billiard balls clicking on the edge of the pool table, Fleetwood Mac on the digital jukebox, boys huddled around baskets of greasy food. She took a seat at the bar and nodded to one of the men she'd taken a photo of that night with Noah. She'd had to drive forever to get the film developed, but she made good on her promise and emailed the photo scans to the man—Albert was his name—and he'd thanked her with a series of emojis. People were so unexpected, she thought.

In her purse, her phone lit up, and her heart leapt for a moment thinking it was Ren. But it was a text from Caroline, a photo of her son, Jasper, with broken lipstick bits all over his face. Caroline had written: *pregnant yet?*

She tucked her phone away and vowed not to take it out. She'd be with herself and her thoughts. She'd have more clarity after one to three Lone Stars.

She was halfway through one beer when a man sat down next to her with a huff that gave off the faint scent of rubbing alcohol. She turned to see that it was Nils. Maya and Nils had passed each other a handful of times at the lab, but their conversations had been brief and superficial. She wondered about this man with whom Noah spent all his time, but he never seemed too interested in her. She recalled the way Oliver had referred to her as "the wife" when they arrived. Perhaps she had unfairly attributed that same attitude to Nils.

"Long day at the office?" Maya said.

Nils sighed. "They all are. And you? Are you enjoying the house? We tried to make it homey." He had a slight accent, flattened ends of words. He was born in Sweden but raised in Seattle, that much she had gleaned from his bio online.

"Not like any home we've lived in," Maya said.

"Homey for Noah, at least."

She studied him. She knew Nils was younger than Noah, in his thirties, but his seriousness and his Scandinavian reticence made him appear older, more lived-in. He possessed an authority that made it easy to believe him.

Nils swallowed the last of his whiskey soda and held the glass up to the bartender for another. "It's quite tiring, what Noah and I are doing. I'm sure you understand."

"I see that."

"Sometimes that can be frustrating for the spouses. I've seen it in various labs I've worked in. It's hard to understand if you're not there, but of course, you aren't allowed to be there, and if you were, you wouldn't quite get it."

Maya bristled. "I'm not frustrated," she said, but it was the wrong retort. Anyone could see she was unhappy. Anyone but Noah, she guessed. "I think I would get it. I do get it."

"So he's told you, then?"

Maya paused. The NDA, had she signed it? She couldn't remember, and she didn't know if Noah had signed a different one, or what he was allowed to tell her. "The gist," she said. "It's not rocket science."

Nils laughed a little. "Sure. Speaking of, I know how much Noah wanted to go to space. He'd have been a terrible astronaut, don't you think?"

Noah had wanted to be an astronaut? What was Nils talking about? She wouldn't ask him, though. She nodded. "As long as what you're doing is safe. It's safe, right?"

The bartender delivered another whiskey to Nils, another beer to Maya. Someone started playing nostalgic emo on the jukebox.

"We know what we're doing," Nils said.

"But I asked if it was safe."

He took a long drink. "The first lab I ever worked in, in Houston, we were trying to understand the specific neurobiology of autism. We used mice. Cute ones, little guys. I won't get too much into the process, but it involved repeating the same sequence of events over and over again. So every few days we'd have to put the mouse down. After the outcomes were recorded, we'd grab a new one. You get the idea. I worked there two years. We put down hundreds of mice. And after I left, who knows. So what I'm saying is safety is relative."

Maya gripped her beer. This guy. "I'm not asking about mice." She heard a tremor in her voice. "I'm asking about my husband."

Nils looked at her, concern wrinkling his face. "Perhaps you should take it easy. The pool at the old hotel is gorgeous, you know. But the pool at the new hotel has amenities."

"You want me to check into a hotel in town?"

"Or out of town." He shrugged. "You have options. Choices."

"My choice was to come here with my husband."

"And it's an admirable one. Especially when Eileen thought it so ill-advised. It can be hard on partners, to be here alone, while the researchers are off having experiences."

It was as if the floor fell away from beneath her stool, and she was floating in the bar. Eileen. He'd said Eileen had thoughts on what Noah was doing here at the lab. Eileen knew.

"Are you all right?" Nils asked.

Maya dug a twenty out of her purse and put it on the bar. "I've got to go." She stood and accidentally swiped her beer glass, sending a mess across her lap and the floor. The glass broke cleanly into three shards.

She should stay to clean it up, she knew, but everything in her was screaming to leave Nils, to leave this information. Thankfully, a barkeep appeared at her shoulder with a broom, and Maya backed away.

As she walked off, she heard Nils behind her. "The good thing about you is you believe in Noah. But it can be tiring. That's all I was trying to say."

On the walk back to the car, Maya kicked at the crumbling asphalt with her boots, trying to dampen her rage at Nils, at his suggestion that she leave, that she was a bored housewife, that she couldn't understand what Noah was doing, at the fact that he knew that Noah had wanted to be an astronaut and she didn't, and at his casual mention of Noah's ex-wife. Beneath all that, sadness and fear that Noah hadn't told her he'd spoken to Eileen, and anxiety over what that meant.

At home, Noah was asleep on his right side as he always slept, snoring softly. In deep REM, that snore would turn walloping, irregular. This was what it was to know someone, knowing the rhythms of their sleep. But this was also what it was to not know someone, to not know where they went when they dreamed.

There was so much she hadn't asked Noah about the Janus Project, so many answers she was afraid to know. She'd thought it meant she was trusting him to make the right choices, to do the right thing not only for his career but also for their marriage. But now she wondered if not asking him meant that she couldn't trust him to know the difference, or trust herself to withstand the answers.

The questions felt stuck inside her like a broken zipper. She crouched down next to the bed, next to Noah's face. Still handsome, with curls of dark, almost black hair, his chiseled face gone soft with sleep.

She shook him awake.

"Ahhh, what?" he said, rousing.

Maya sat next to him. She couldn't do it, she couldn't say Eileen's name, ask why he'd talked to her, and when, and how. If he answered honestly, there was a possibility she could never go back to the time before his answer.

So she said, "I want to have a baby with you."

"Maya," Noah said, his tone a warning.

"It's been weeks."

"Can we not do this right now?"

"Then when, Noah? You're gone longer and longer each day. When you come home you're practically already asleep. We barely talk about anything. This project is like a parasite."

He looked at her without comprehension.

How could she explain what she was feeling? She would have to start with Nils, or Ren, or Eileen, or Serena, or the baby they hadn't yet agreed to have. She began to cry from the futility.

He embraced her, which felt good. He was still there. She smelled him, felt his body, warm with sleep. She heard her own cries, airless and desperate.

"It's going to be okay," he said.

But she didn't believe him. She wasn't sure he believed himself, either. Eventually, after her crying dried up and his grip on her had loosened, she rolled over and undressed. She pulled the covers up over her. Noah was already asleep again, his face slack.

She touched the softness.

"Noah," she whispered.

His eyes fluttered but didn't open. "Mmm," he said.

"Noah, I have a question."

He raised his eyebrows, but his eyes remained closed.

"When did you want to go to space?"

The question sounded stupid in the darkness. How could she not know? How could she ask?

"Did you want to be an astronaut? Did you want to go to space, Noah?"

He didn't answer. His face still now, descended back into sleep. Maya got close to him, her face centimeters from his.

"Did you want to go? Did you want to leave?"

She kept asking, even as he slept.

Noah

They set a date to attempt the first fold, in ten days' time. A simple fold, back only a couple of hours. Nils told Noah he'd run it by Klein, and Klein agreed they were ready, but he wanted to talk to Noah first. Noah hadn't seen Klein since the first few days of training. He'd been told Klein was back in California overseeing a new build on his property, or in the Arctic tracking beluga whales, or in the Maldives researching a climate change initiative he was funding.

"Is talking to Klein a test?" Noah asked Nils at the end of their last day of official training. Noah was tired but his body felt like a live wire, keen to attach itself to a memory, an idea, anything but the present. He'd lost weight during the past few weeks, his eating and sleeping schedule adjusted. He felt whittled down, essential. He admitted to no one that it felt nice, this new way of existing. He was simpler, his purpose—to inhabit memory, to fold—physically represented, mind and body connected.

"It's not a test," Nils said in an equivocating tone that indicated the meeting was some kind of test. "Klein likes to have a finger in the pie as we transition to the next stage."

"If it's a test, you should prepare me. Tell me what it is."

Noah had dressed and joined Nils at the controls. When he was on this side of the time bath, he felt nervous, like he was being watched by a presence in the dark maze of servers and drives behind him. He started to say as much to Nils, but Nils glanced at his fitness tracker on his wrist and started walking away, toward his office next door. Nils was a man driven by efficiency, step count, numbers. Noah followed.

"I've told Klein you're ready, that your readings are stable and consistent, that you understand what's required, and that you've devoted your days and even some nights to memory reading and writing. Your meditations are clear, and your ability to withstand memory reignition has only gotten better. He trusts what I say. But he wants to see for himself."

"So he'll run a session, then?"

"No. He has no idea how to do that." Nils smiled a little as they exited Building D. The orange sunset lasered through the courtyard. "You'll talk. Just be yourself. Tell him what it's been like for you. He chose you. He knows what you're made of."

The labs in Building C were as much a mess as Noah remembered them. He'd been here so infrequently the past few weeks, because Nils wanted to remove clutter from Noah's brain and avoid taking him to spaces that were literally cluttered. He didn't ask why Nils didn't simply clean up the labs. Now he understood the detritus to be the remainders of a team of scientists who'd been "released."

Noah followed Nils to his office, where Nils stood behind his desk and started sorting through stacks of files.

"Ancient design schematics," Nils muttered. "Klein prefers hard copies even as I upload them to the shared server. A mess."

Noah watched him as he crumpled pieces of paper and tossed them in a wire wastebasket under his desk. Nils seemed to have forgotten Noah was there.

Next to the tossed paper, wedged against the side of the waste-basket: a business card. A last name visible. *Bolson.* Noah remembered now, Talia Bolson, associate professor of physics, UC Berkeley. Who was she? Shouldn't he ask Nils now? His instinct told him not to, that Nils even noticing the business card would invite some bad news.

"You all right?" Nils asked. "Are you judging me for not recycling?"

Noah snapped his eyes up, caught. "Oh, yes. I mean, no, sorry. You should recycle."

Nils shrugged and looked back down at his stack. "Klein does more for the good of the planet than recycling does. Trust me. You can ask him his thoughts on recycling tomorrow afternoon."

"Okay, then," Noah said. "Tomorrow afternoon. Got it. Oh, and I had a question."

Nils looked up at him, a piece of paper balled in his fist. "Yes?"

"About the pronghorn?"

"What about them?"

"Maya wanted me to ask you," Noah said, lying. Maya hadn't wanted any such thing. But Noah felt curious, and he'd seen what she was painting in that room off the kitchen, though he hadn't asked her about it. "They're dying?"

Nils raised his eyebrows. "Is there a question there?"

"I mean, are they dying? She says they seem to be dying of some disease, and I thought, since you've spent so much time here, you might know."

Nils laughed. "She could have asked me herself. At the bar the other night."

"She was at the bar? You saw her?"

"I did. I don't think she was very happy with me. You didn't know?"

Noah shook his head. "I've been busy. You know. Tired. I haven't seen her very much."

"I know as much as you do, brother," Nils said. "Or as much as she does. They seem to be dying in some horrific way that no one quite understands. Wouldn't be the first time something like that has happened. I'm not a biologist or a zoologist. Perhaps she could find a researcher in El Paso to talk to."

Researcher. That's what Talia Bolson's card had said. *Associate professor, researcher.*

Nils stacked a sheaf of papers with a cutting sound that told Noah the conversation was over. Noah nodded. He turned and started to walk away, but Nils called out after him.

"And hey," Nils said, tapping his temple. "Try to keep it clear up here. There are lots of disasters everywhere, right? All around us. I want you concerned with the world in here, though. That's where you live."

That was where Noah lived. That was how he forgave himself for the distance that had grown between him and Maya since they'd come here. At first, he thought it was nice, both of them consumed by their work, for once. Maya had been so excited to come here, and then she'd thrown herself into the gallery gig, right as he'd thrown himself into work at the lab. This was how it was supposed to be, he'd thought.

But it wasn't long before the distance stopped feeling healthy and started feeling, well, far. The deeper Noah got into training, the more Maya felt unreachable. Part of it was simply time—he stayed late, she woke early, he was exhausted, she was out in town, looking for supplies or a certain kind of light or some inspiration. But part of it, he knew, was that he'd created this bubble around himself, to protect that pristine landscape of the mind that Nils wanted, that the project required. The effort was physical and it was mental. He hadn't explicitly instructed Maya to leave him alone, but she had.

The morning after she'd come home late and cried herself to sleep, they carried on as if nothing had happened. She made breakfast, he said he wasn't hungry, they shared a brief kiss, and each left to spend their day doing things they wouldn't get to tell the other at the end of the night. Normally, back in L.A., Maya would have been unable to move on without talking it out. Noah wouldn't have been able to stand the idea of her being mad at him, and he would talk it out with her until she felt better. But here, they were missing the intimacy those interactions required.

After Noah left Nils in his office, he came home and found Maya in the living room. She was wearing painting clothes, loose jeans with streaks of paint on them, and a button-down she'd cut the sleeves off of. She wasn't painting, though. She was sitting on the couch, looking out the window that pointed to the courtyard. It was where he liked to sit. It reminded him of sitting in the backyard of the Los Feliz house.

"It was the last day of training," he told her, sitting next to her. She smelled like sweat and her acrylic paints. He liked it. He missed it, though it was right here.

"Oh, really?"

"We have about a week off. Then . . ."

"Then . . ."

He found her hand on the couch cushion and held it. She squeezed back. She was still there. They were still here. When did it become so hard to say the honest thing, he wondered. Why couldn't he talk to her about it, the distance between them? It was because of the distance, he thought. He had to close it. But not now. He couldn't now.

"Aren't you tired of looking out at this courtyard?" Maya said. "Like a reflection. Nothing ever happens out there. Nils walking by, the groundskeeper. That little Oliver running around sometimes."

"It's comforting, nothing changing."

Maya sighed. "I prefer looking out the back better. There are animals back there, at least."

"I never go back there," he said.

"Does this place . . . seem familiar to you?" Maya asked.

Of course. So much of it, exactly like the Los Feliz house. "It does," he said.

"The bathroom," Maya said. "I recognized it."

"You did?"

"There's a photo of Eileen standing in the bathroom. It's almost exactly the same color, the same tiles."

The mention of Eileen's name made his shoulders tighten. He hadn't told Maya he'd spoken to Eileen. And he didn't remember this photo Maya was talking about. It was possible he'd forgotten, as so much had slipped out of his mind the past few weeks.

She turned her body to face him. He turned his to face her. "This place, they made it feel like home to you, but not to me."

"What do you mean?"

"They made it to recall your life with Eileen."

He shook his head. "That's ridiculous. More likely they found some old picture and wanted to make us feel like—"

"That's why you called her."

"Who?"

Maya looked at him, her eyes low, her expression broken with hurt. He knew who she meant.

"Eileen," she said.

Of course this time had come, Maya finding out. It was the kind of explicit secret that couldn't be hidden, that existed, big and plain.

"She's a biologist," Noah said in a small voice. He knew that was not an excuse.

"You didn't tell me," Maya said. She didn't ask why. It was a statement.

He didn't tell her because she wasn't part of it. It would crush her to hear him say that out loud, but it was true. She was not a part of the world of Serena, or the world of his grief.

"I'm sorry," he said, because he was, even if he didn't know how to change the situation.

Maya looked straight into his eyes, like she was about to confess. "I called an old friend, too," she was saying, but his brain was wandering, something he hadn't allowed it to do for a while. He retreated into a memory and didn't hear her.

Remember, he wanted to say, *the fires two Octobers ago?* Fire season had always been bad in L.A., but this one was relentless and close. The flames had leapt over the freeway and then over another freeway, like they were sentient, and though their house was far from danger, it was so high up on a hill they could see it, the smolder hovering over a ridge of orange fire. They stood on the tiny deck off their bedroom and watched cars move like funeral processions through walls of burning brush. This was before the smoke got so bad they had to lock themselves inside. He said to her on the deck that the fires would one day come for them and their home. It was inevitable, the earth reshaping itself. Maya laughed and said that would be their grandchildren's problem. Both of them blushed and quieted when she mentioned grandchildren. Then they wore face masks for days and stuffed towels into the window crevices. They lay in a windowless bathroom and read books and played card games and imagined what they'd do once the smoke cleared.

Outside in the courtyard, the light was fading. It was blue light, gray light, the color of smoke, of a memory.

"So, he's helping me," Maya was saying. "Figure out what's what."

The thing was, Noah had been holding at bay so much in his brain: the project, its assumptions and implications, the place, Marfa, the strangeness and desolation, the facility and how little he really knew about it, all in service to the vast emptiness he was able to create in his mind that he could then fill with memories. To do what Nils and Klein wanted him to do, what Noah now wanted to do, he had to blur some tenets of quantum mechanics and general relativity. He liked to think of it as putting those ideas in little packages, boxed up in a corner of his mind. They were still there, he reasoned. In a way, it was a testament to quantum theory itself, everything true at once, until something had to give. That you could live in conditional truth, a negotiated reality. He clung to the uncertainty principle, the concept in physics that allows for the unknown.

"What's next?" Noah asked, but he was only repeating what Maya had said.

She shrugged. Her eyes were shining, but with sadness or delight, he couldn't tell. "I don't know," she said, and left him there, staring at his reflection in the window.

"Do you take mushrooms?" Oliver asked.

Noah had walked into the big cement block building on campus where Klein stayed, and was immediately taken aback. The ceiling seemed impossibly high. The living room space with couches and a coffee table was sunken a few feet. And now Oliver was asking about mushrooms.

"Lion's mane? Reishi? We can make a latte."

Ah, so Klein didn't want to do psychedelics with Noah right now, though Noah wouldn't have been all that surprised if that was the gauntlet before him.

"Sure," Noah said. "Whatever you recommend."

"Chaga it is," Oliver said and disappeared down a hallway to the kitchen.

Everything inside was gray and neutral, polished cement, thick white rugs, jute baskets, tan bouclé couches. Noah stopped in front of a painting on the textured wall, which was textured in the same manner as Klein's Hollywood compound. The painting was white on white, with a thin eggshell line running through the center. Would Maya hate this or love it?

"I like to keep things minimal when I'm traveling."

Noah turned and saw Klein standing at what he previously thought was a cement wall, but which turned out to be a corner. Everything felt so seamless in here, it was hard to tell where the edges were.

"I'm just back from India, and I like to keep my places simple to reduce transition noise." Klein approached Noah and looked at the painting. "I hope you don't think it's boring," he said, gripping Noah's hand in a firm handshake.

"Oh, well, you should see the inside of my mind now. Spotless," Noah said. He'd meant it as a joke, but Klein didn't laugh.

Oliver delivered the mushroom lattes to the quartz coffee table in the sunken area, and Klein sat cross-legged on the ground to begin drinking his. Noah did the same.

"So, tell me," Klein said. Noah waited, but no noun followed.

Noah told him what training had been like, settling his heart rate and blood pressure to accurately create a neurological picture of a memory. And then clearing his brain of thoughts in order to write the memory back in, in the bath. The way he quieted the reflex anxiety. He told Klein it had been tiring but rewarding, that he'd never had such control over his body and brain. He expressed awe at what Klein had built, how it worked, why it worked, at the level of daring Klein and Nils had to have to even attempt building it.

"Due in large part to your paper," Klein said, nodding.

Noah had begun to doubt that part. His paper was fine, middling, somewhat interesting for a young scientist, and somewhat embarrassing. Sure, its thinking was mirrored in the philosophy of Janus, but it was in no way the bedrock for what the project's aims were. Best not to question Klein now, though.

"We've set a fold date," Noah said, telling Klein what he surely already knew. "And I tested well with the Fold Cocktail. I understand the aims, the locked-box test."

"All of this sounds exactly as Nils described in his reports. But what I'm curious about is why you want to do it. Fold."

"Why do I want to do it?"

"Yes, why."

To stall, Noah took a big gulp of the latte, and it was so earthy and thick that he almost spit it out. Why did he want to time travel? An impossible question.

"Who wouldn't?" he said.

"Oh, many people," Klein said. "Trust me on that one."

Noah looked around at the windowless block, the clean, neutral palace, this place that had the audacity and hubris to invent time travel, to do something impossible, and now to ask impossible questions. What Noah wanted to say to Klein was so much: because I miss everything, because I forgot to live for several years, because years were stolen from me, because there's much to fix, losses to untangle, people I could have become, so many possibilities. All of it was so far away, but when he was in the time bath, distance collapsed. He was everything, everywhere.

He was reminded of the evening his brother, Colin, came to visit. It was early in his marriage to Maya. Colin and his wife had three-year-old twins, who were born so quickly after Serena's death that it caused a rift in the brothers' already tenuous relationship. They'd had little in common before Colin had kids, and now they had too much in common, Colin's children a constant reminder of what Noah used to have. But once Noah remarried, Colin seemed to think it was safe to reenter his brother's life. He invited himself and the brood over for dinner, argued about wave function collapse with Noah the way only someone who made too much money at Deloitte could do, and then whisked away without offering to help clean up. Afterward, Noah had retreated to his office and plugged in an old thumb drive of pictures and recordings of Serena and quietly sobbed. He felt feelings he'd stuffed down for a long time—pain and grief and despair—but also new feelings, like anger, revenge, and rage. There'd been so much to grieve, so much to be angry at, all the time between his life's trajectory and Colin's, all the squandered and stolen possibilities. What he wanted was to never feel that way again.

So what he said to Klein was, "I think if we can get a handle on time, the result could be a reduction in suffering in the world. And that's a good thing I can do, a good thing I can help do."

Klein seemed pleased by this, in that he finished his cup of mushrooms and stood. He gestured for Noah to follow him. He led Noah to the corner that looked like an optical illusion, and then he disappeared behind it. When Noah followed Klein around, he was blinded. The place looked windowless from the outside, but he'd been wrong. This entire side of the building was one floor-to-ceiling window, overlooking a massive piece of land and bright blue sky. Louvered steel slats served as shutters. Noah watched Klein pull them into wall pockets, revealing the unencumbered view.

"It's a beautiful country out here, even if nothing grows. Did you know there are scientists using CRISPR to try to re-create woolly mammoths that can redirect the Arctic ecosystem that's now purging CO_2? Can you believe that? An ancient behemoth could be walking our tundras, resurrected as if by God? Incredible what we can do. We're studying immortal jellyfish to figure out what in the genome could transfer over to us, to make us live longer. And I hear chatter in the private space exploration area that there's renewed interest in the Europa mission. After all this time. Even tragedy and failure don't deter us."

Klein was talking as if he were addressing the landscape. Noah felt mesmerized by the scope of the desert, how it was massive and didn't seem to change at all, how it was a living painting.

"Humans tame animals, reanimate entire species, explore the seas, rocket to space. And the last frontier, the thing we haven't tried to tame, to even understand, to *master*, is right up here." He tapped his temple. "The quantum phenomenon of our brain."

"So that's your goal, then?" Noah asked.

For a moment they stood in silence, looking out over the desert. Then Klein spoke. "You know what my father did? He trained as a plumber, but fancied himself an entrepreneur. His parents didn't have enough money to send him to college, so he went to trade school and worked in shit. He made okay money, enough to raise a middle-class family at the time, but he was never satisfied. He tried to start his own plumbing business, but it tanked after he failed to market himself. Then he tried to start a home improvement business with a contractor friend, but he wasn't trained in people management, and everyone he hired quit. Before I went to college on a scholarship he tried to get his real estate license, but he didn't have the stamina for all the studying. He died a plumber, working for someone else."

Klein paused, gathering himself. "There was a moment he told me about once, a memory he had, of trying to tell his dad that there was a financial aid application they could fill out for university, but his dad didn't think the paperwork was worth the hassle. His mom could barely read. So he never filled it out. He tore it up and put it in the trash. But my father said he wished he hadn't. He wished he'd filled it out. He wished he'd sent it off and seen if they'd give him enough money for school. He wished he'd gone to school and learned how to study. And then after that he'd have gotten a white-collar job that would have helped him apply to business school, where he'd learn how to market himself, how to manage employees, how to come up with a business plan. He wished a lot of things, but it started there, by not taking no for an answer. By finding his own answer."

Klein turned to look at Noah now, and pulled by his magnetism, Noah turned, too.

"What if my father had been allowed to go back and live that moment and make a different choice?"

"No causality. It wouldn't have changed anything," Noah said.

"But what if it could?"

Out in the scrub, things shifted almost imperceptibly. Animals leaping through grass in the distance, field mice ducking into holes, scorpions lifting their tails. Noah felt sure that was happening, if only he could see it.

"So that's why you're doing this," he said. "Causality."

"You're saying you didn't know?" Klein cut a wry smile up at Noah.

Noah shook his head. He'd been foolish, but he'd believed.

"We're on the brink, I think, of effecting causal change. Imagine what we could do to prevent climate change, genocides, dictatorships. It's only that we've had trouble sustaining a fold long enough to really be able to test it. But I think you're the one to do it."

Noah had a million questions and a million concerns. But the way Klein was talking to him, how sure he was, indicated to Noah that there was no room for questions. Klein had hired him because he didn't ask questions; he believed.

"Why didn't you tell me earlier?" Noah asked.

"Ah, well, you had to see it to know what was possible, didn't you?" Klein looked directly at him, his gaze leveling. "You, of all people, have the hunger to look backward, a vivid connection to your past. Now you see, don't you?"

He knew, of course. Klein knew what Noah would have tried to do, where he would try to fold back to, who he'd try to see. It was unbearable to be seen like that, his wound splayed open. There was nothing Noah could say to protest his vulnerability. Klein knew what Noah would do, and Noah would do it.

"All for your father," Noah said quietly.

"Oh, no, no," Klein said. "My father was an asshole. But you, you're exactly right."

The stillness outside was painting-like, but then a wisp of a cloud began to move, to travel across the sky with a speed that meant a storm was coming this way. Noah's breath caught.

Klein nudged his shoulder.

"Don't worry. We're about to do something huge. It'll solve everything. Even that little glitch I just saw in you."

Then Klein walked away, leaving Noah with the answerless world.

Eileen

Eileen hadn't spoken to Noah again, but his presence only seemed to grow bigger in her life. She found herself wondering how he was doing in Marfa, what Maya knew about the Janus Project, what she knew about Serena, what Noah had said—*What if you could see her again?* He'd said *for real*, but what did that even mean? The only real thing now was that she had died.

She tried instead to will herself to be present for Prem. There had been men before him, of course, but none quite like Prem. It was easy enough to pick up someone in a bar if you didn't care about anything other than the obliteration of sex. You had to look a little hopeful and a little dumb, like what you wanted was clear and simple. Men liked that, she'd learned. To see that what you wanted had an answer. She only had one-night stands a handful of times, in neighboring towns where there were lots of wine-country tourists—lonely, tipsy men on ill-conceived bachelor party trips. Afterward she always felt disgusted, not with herself, but with the men. That they wanted so little. She had an excuse. She was a grieving mother, a divorcée, utterly alone. Them? They had no excuses.

Prem, though, he didn't do excuses. He wasn't interested in Eileen's, either. As she spent more time with him, she realized what she had previously thought was dull was him being plain and direct. There was no veil between inner Prem and outer Prem, she learned, no mediating process in which he decided how he would appear. If she asked him a question, he considered it and then answered honestly. If he didn't know the answer, he simply said he didn't know at the moment. In this way, wide and open, Prem began to shrink the space between the persona Eileen was trying to maintain and who she had become.

One day, the afternoon almost saturated into dusk, Prem took her into the city, to the zoo. She hadn't wanted to go. Zoos are for kids, she'd said. But he'd insisted, and in the parking lot he pulled a weed pen out, and after a few puffs she was giggling furiously.

"I'm glad we came," she said in front of the giraffes. A giraffe with a bump in its neck loudly chewed on leaves, unbothered.

It was one of those crisp days, the season fully changed over, the air bright and sharp.

"You remind me so much of the guys in the math labs in college," Eileen said.

"You've said that." Prem squeezed her hand. "So I have to assume the labs were full of nerdy hunks."

"Something like that."

They reached the ape enclosure. "I mean that the answers for you are always very accessible," Eileen said. "Even if they're not apparent, you know there's a way toward them."

Prem considered this. "I'll take that as a compliment."

"Oh, you should! For real."

"I wouldn't want to mansplain or anything."

"It's the opposite. It's like you're not bothered by not having the answer. You trust that you'll find it, or someone will find it. But you don't perform an answer where there is none."

"All right. For a scientist, that's a little troubling, but okay."

"Trust me, my ex was a physicist. Not knowing the answer was *not* okay with him." The words *my ex* felt hot in her mouth.

A silence fell between them. She never talked about Noah to Prem beyond the fact that he existed, was the father of the child she'd lost. She expected Prem would ask more—what Noah had been like, where he was now. She'd prepared an answer: They had fallen in love when they were practically children, and they had that strength of love as a rod through the center of their life. Until. Until Serena's arrival, and then Serena was the rod, the core, and all the energy shifted there. And then when Serena was gone, everything fell in on itself, nothing to hold it up. Was that it? Was that what she would say happened? A collapse?

But he hadn't asked, not yet. What he asked instead was, "Did you ever take Serena to a zoo?"

Eileen and Noah had tried to take Serena to the Los Angeles Zoo when she was fourteen months old, which they knew was too young to enjoy much, but it was something to do, and parents were supposed to provide experiences, make lasting impressions. Maybe Serena was an animal baby, and zoos would make her come alive. They arrived bearing diaper bags and backup toys and pretzel snacks and cheese snacks and changes of clothes for everyone. But they barely made it past the flamingo enclosure before Serena had a total meltdown, mysterious in origin. She had cried so maniacally on the way home that Eileen cried, too, though her crying was silent, and Noah drove clutching the steering wheel in a panic. They hadn't tried to take Serena to the zoo again.

"She never got to do the zoo," Eileen said simply. It was too much, too complicated to explain, too sad.

Prem leaned into her, solid and warm. An ape came lumbering out of a black cave, a rust-colored orangutan. Its perpetually old face looked right at Eileen and Prem, and Eileen lifted her hand and gave a little wave. The orangutan tilted its head, then turned away and began to climb some rocks.

Eileen looked at Prem, afraid she might cry, but instead he started to laugh, and so she laughed, too.

"I'm even bumming out the ape," she said.

"Do you want to talk about what that was like, losing her?"

There were, in grief, two separate hallways to walk down. One was darkness. The hallway wasn't empty, but there was no light. And without the light, there was so much to run into, old furniture and broken glass, many things to hurt you. That was what it was like to talk about losing Serena. The other hallway was separate, all perfect late-afternoon light and soft music to soothe you and the smell of sweet flowers that made you feel gently alive. Most of the time, Eileen stood at the precipice of these two hallways, entering neither. She told Prem no, she did not want to walk down the dark hallway. But she would go down the light one, if he wanted.

He did.

Neither Eileen nor Noah could have predicted what it was like to have Serena. Part of why they'd put off having children for so long was because they suspected what they were in for—sleepless nights, sacrificed fun, physical exhaustion, emotional erosion. It turned out those elements weren't even close to representing the experience of parenthood. No one had really told them what having a child was like because it was impossible to relate to until you were in it. But Eileen tried with Prem.

She skipped over the delirious parts, those newborn months when everything was both horror and joy. She skipped over how watching Noah become a father felt like digging a cool, shady canyon into their romantic relationship, a depth and darkness only the two of them could access, which would remain mysterious and magnificent forever. Instead, she told him a story about when the three of them had driven out to San Gabriel for a food festival, which was ill-advised in the heavy

August heat, but an event that felt organized enough and stimulating enough for a toddler. More than an errand and less than a museum. Serena's language abilities had recently exploded, and in addition to her endless questions, she offered endless answers, pulled from the neon corners of her three-year-old imagination. She chattered on in her car seat the whole way there, and Eileen remembered feeling a dizzying sense of luck, that the future she had hoped for—a beautiful child saying magical, nonsensical things in the back seat—had become her present.

She looked at Noah with an expression that said *Can you believe this child?* "Unreal," she said.

He got it. "Super-real."

"And then I went back before I came in and went all the way back," Serena was saying. "There was a unicorn going twinkle and a baby bear and a car going fast."

"Wow," Eileen said.

"Wow," Noah said.

"And stars," Serena said.

At the festival, they walked slowly and sweated down their backs and ate hot, melting crepes. Serena's eyes widened at the powdered sugar. They hadn't brought a stroller because Serena had started to hate it, so Eileen held her hand and took small steps. In Serena's other hand she clutched a fistful of churros and then a low-sugar juice box and then finally a pink plastic frog key chain advertising a bar booth, where Noah had bought a pilsner.

"Mommy and Daddy, Mommy and Daddy, Mommy and Daddy," sang Serena.

Eileen loved it when she did that, put them both in a unit together, in her mouth, in language. Serena had recently transitioned from "Mama and Dada" to "Mommy and Daddy," further signifying her growing up, and Eileen preferred these monikers. She felt they were a family, of course, but hearing Serena say it, knowing that their daughter understood they were a unit, her protectors, her guardians, the people she loved, well, it was intoxicating. A family, what a strange, messy, animal thing to make.

There was a booth selling farmers market fruit, and Eileen could never resist. She loaded up her arms with an oversize basket of strawberries and a handful of magenta dragon fruit. She loved dragon fruit— not too sweet, very soft, and aesthetically pleasing. She weighed them at the register, vaguely aware of Noah's tall presence near the entrance, standing over some kiwi.

Dragon fruit. She'd eat one right then, she thought.

As soon as she turned around and saw Noah, she knew Serena was lost. He was standing there looking at Eileen expectantly, like Serena was supposed to be with *her*. But she'd been buying fruit! What had Noah been doing?

"You took off with her!" Noah said.

But she didn't bother to answer. She thrust out into the crowd and spun around, scanning for Serena, thirty-eight inches tall, blondish hair down to her shoulders, and she realized that in her head she was already describing Serena to the police. It was already an emergency. The worst had already happened.

Noah bumped up against her, and he held on to her forearm, like he was afraid to lose her, too. They said things in hushed and panicked voices, but in a way that didn't feel quite present: *I don't see her, where is she, do you see anything.* Eileen had a hard time remembering exactly how long it lasted. That time felt refracted, in two directions at once, hurtling toward disaster and pushing toward air. She had to remind herself that it was possible to find her, just as the counter-thought—it was possible she was gone—rushed in. What she later remembered thinking was "Mommy, Daddy, Serena," like an incantation, a reminder of the mysterious magic of blood bonds, as if it could conjure her family, complete.

And then a cluster of people parted and there was Serena, in a dragon-fruit-pink dress, her hair not loose as Eileen had thought but in a braid, which Serena had demanded because she'd seen it on a cartoon character. She was standing at the corner of a booth crowded with adults who were trying to order sliders, people who were not paying any attention to the child who'd sidled up to the patch of plastic grass decoration lining the table. Serena was hopping the frog on the plastic grass, and when Noah and Eileen rushed up to her, she looked up and said, "The frog needed water." She hadn't even noticed they'd gone away. She didn't know about being lost. Mommy and Daddy were ever present, crucial to her sense of existing.

That was it, Eileen thought to tell Prem. Having Serena, becoming a parent made real the abstract idea that life could be both sturdy and delicate, willful and mutable, here and then gone. You had to hold on to it, but not too tight or it would slip away, and not too loose or it would fall away, and learning how to love that life properly was learning how to remake yourself around it, a person with the empty shape of another person inside them. You made a family and then you kept making it. Family was in a constant state of taking form, of realizing, of pulsing. Until it wasn't.

Of course, she didn't say all that to Prem. What she said was, "Having Serena made me feel real."

Prem nodded, though Eileen knew he didn't understand, couldn't. She wasn't upset that he didn't understand; that's how it went with most people, other than Noah. Noah in her mind again. Prem put his arm around her and she accepted. They'd been walking, and she looked up to see where they'd landed. They were at the flamingos, squawking and stinking in the dirt, flapping their wings with the threat of flight, standing on one needle leg like a question permanently asked, a thin wire between the earth and its unlikely creation.

Maya

Midway through the drive to view the Marfa mystery lights, Noah told Maya he didn't believe in the mystery part of it.

"It's pseudoscience," he said. He was driving, looking straight ahead. "Like astrology."

Maya tried to hide her hurt. Inviting him to do this felt like a last-ditch effort to close the gap between them, to try to reestablish the intimacy and optimism with which they'd come to Marfa.

"Spoken like a true Aries," she said, but Noah didn't laugh.

Everyone said they had to see the Marfa Lights. Even Caroline back in L.A. knew about them. No one could pinpoint where they came from, and they weren't always visible. You just had to go to the lookout spot and hope. A location-specific phenomenon made into a tourist destination, which sold T-shirts and mugs and key chains. She thought it would be exactly the kind of thing Noah would want to do, that they could only do here.

He kept going. "I read that scientists can now explain the lights. I can send you the article."

"You told me you wanted to come," Maya said, disappointed. "I thought you'd like it."

"I wanted to come because you wanted to come. And I'll like it if you like it," he said. "Doesn't mean it's real, though."

She didn't want him to go along for the ride. She wanted to see him marvel, the way he'd done when they first met, when he sat in on her art talk. She wanted to see him engage with something that didn't have to do with the Janus Project, but that had to do with her and their world.

"I could have come by myself," she said.

"Well, I'm here," he said, knuckles firm on the steering wheel.

"Can you try?" she asked. "Try to imagine you don't know all the answers."

"What's this?" he asked, gesturing toward the cup holder between them, where a strange Frankensteined cactus fit perfectly.

"I went to the plant store today while you were in training," Maya said.

He'd gone in to train alone, even though the official training phase was over. He wanted to stay sharp, he told her. Annoyed, Maya got in the car and drove in the direction of a cluster of shops almost an hour away, in hopes that when she got there she'd be less angry. There was a plant shop she'd seen, and when she entered, the owner's wise demeanor and long gray braid put her at ease.

"The shop owner grafted it for me," Maya said to Noah in the car, picking the plant up. She'd chosen a small bright red succulent, but the woman with the braid told her it was too finicky, likely to die, bad with photosynthesis. "She grafted the bright one on top of the one with the sturdier rootstock. Now I have to plant it."

The bright one was attached to the sturdier one with a rubber band. The owner had said when Maya planted it, eventually they'd grow together, if she was patient.

"It's nice," Noah said.

"It reminded me of the cactus garden."

"What cactus garden?"

In an instant, Maya felt her breath leave her. He didn't remember. "The one," she said. "The one where you knew you loved me."

"Ah," Noah said, lightly, trying to cover for the seriousness of his mistake. "Of course."

Maya looked out the window at the blue desert flying past. Driving out here, it never looked like you were going to arrive anywhere. There were miles of desolation until suddenly there was exactly what you were looking for, a mirage made real.

They passed a sign for the Marfa Lights Viewing Area and Noah slowed down. Maya was tense, pulled into herself. The center was a modest circular structure, the color of desert dirt, with walls and over-hangs framing benches on which to sit. The sun was already below the horizon, and the sky was quickly darkening. There were a few people huddled in groups, chattering quietly, but it felt mostly empty, like many things in Marfa, not much populating the brush and desert. A nearby sign read *Wait for it.*

"What are we even looking at?" Noah asked as they settled on a cold bench. A chilly wind started to blow.

It was hard to say. A whole bunch of nothing, a road in the distance, some power lines. Maya shrugged. "It said to wait."

The cold seeped upward from the bench through her butt. The side of Noah's thigh was pressed against hers, and she tried to glean some warmth from his body. The whole place had the feeling of a bus stop, a temporary space, everyone waiting for some night magic to whisk them away, or release them back to their warm cars, back to their ho-tels, and then back to their homes, jobs, families. But Maya and Noah were stuck in an in-between spot anyway. The place they'd go back to was neither home nor hotel, their jobs were imagined into being, and their status on expanding their family was still undetermined. She'd stopped tracking her ovulation because, well, she'd stopped seeing Noah enough for them to have regular sex. They'd had the one night, when they'd gone out and everything was perfect and light. She wanted this, tonight, to be like they used to be, though how they used to be was becoming hard to remember.

"So you're not even open to the possibility you'll see anything?"

"I'm open to it," Noah said. "But I won't think it's a mystery."

Maya thought of the times when Noah had embraced ambiguity, magic. One of those times had been when he proposed. They'd gone to the Broad art museum downtown to see a special installation by the famed Japanese artist Yayoi Kusama, an entire room of mirrors and water and hanging lights, with little walkways where two people were allowed to stand for forty-five seconds. Noah's impulse was to explain the installation, how the optical illusion worked. But while they waited in line for their turn in the exhibit, Maya told him to hold on to those thoughts.

"Let go of the why and experience the what," she'd said.

He'd agreed, and when they entered, it took Maya a moment for her eyes to adjust. They were in a black box, with small hanging lights illuminating the space, doubled and tripled in the mirrored walls. She was everywhere, on every surface, but also moving, shimmering in the water, like light. She was light. They stood on a walkway jutting out into shallow water, but they were suspended, floating with no up and no down.

She first spotted Noah on one knee in the mirror, and nearly fell off the walkway into the water trying to figure out where to locate him in all the reflections. He was holding open a box containing a small sapphire ring, his face scrunched up like newspaper, about to cry.

He knew she'd like being proposed to inside a piece of art, which was why he did it, but he later told her that he surprised himself with how moving it all was. He felt like they were floating out in space, the only people in the world, bound together on a little strip of land. He knew how the art piece worked, but it hadn't mattered; he was still swept away in the illusion.

"But it wasn't an illusion," Maya had said to him. "That was reality for us."

And now here, on this cold bench in the desert, waiting for mysterious lights to show up in the sky, it could be the same, she thought, but it wasn't. She felt no warmth from his body, no wonder in the desolation.

"Look to the horizon," Maya said. "That's where they appear."

"Aha, a likely place for refracted light to appear."

"Let go of the why and experience the what," she said, calling back in time, back to his proposal.

He didn't get it, though. "The what *is* the why."

Then Maya saw a shadow pass through her line of sight. "Look," she whispered and strained her eyes to clarify the darkness.

"Where?" Noah asked.

But as her eyes settled, she realized it was an animal—a pronghorn. Even in the dark, she recognized the soft stripes on the face, the black horns, the athletic perch of its body. No one around Maya seemed to notice it, camouflaged in the night, but she was attuned to the animal's shape and movement, having painted pronghorn for the past few weeks.

This, she should paint this. The animal, barely perceivable in the dark. She pulled out her phone and recorded, not knowing what was going to be visible in the video, if anything.

And then the pronghorn leapt away, bounding toward the lighter horizon, and Maya lost sight of it. She put her phone down.

She hadn't wanted to bring up Eileen again. She hadn't wanted to hear what he would say in response, because what if he said something he could never take back?

But Maya couldn't help herself.

"Do you think Eileen would know about the pronghorn dying thing?"

"Eileen?" Noah's voice was too high, caught off guard. "Why would she know about dying antelope?"

"They're not antelope. And because she's a biologist."

"She's a *neuro*biologist."

"Next time you talk to her," Maya said, feeling the words settle around them like cement, "you could ask her."

She felt Noah's whole body sigh beside her.

"Why . . ." he said, drawing out the word, ". . . am I not allowed to talk to my ex-wife?"

What had felt soft and generous in Maya began to sharpen. "You're allowed to do whatever you want." She gestured around the desert. "Obviously."

"Then why are you so mad?"

"I'm not mad," she said, but of course now she was. "I'm confused why you didn't tell me."

"You didn't tell me you were talking to your ex-boyfriend."

"I *did* tell you," Maya said. "That's how you know."

She felt people around them starting to glance as their voices rose.

"Yeah, but I also know because you have to be talking to someone, and you're sure as hell not talking to me."

Maya was hurt, not only by what he was saying, but because she knew he wasn't actually jealous. He was simply fighting her accusation with one of his own.

"If you want to talk about who's disappearing, then we can do that."

"I'm not disappearing, Maya. I'm working." Irritation coated his voice.

"You can do both," she said. "You are doing both."

"I haven't even folded yet," he said, lowering his voice, as if protecting Klein and the Janus Project was what he really valued.

"I don't understand," Maya said.

"I told you," Noah began to explain. "Folding happens after the cocktail—"

"Not about that, Noah, god." She swiveled her head and found his eyes, locked his gaze. "I don't understand why you confided in her about the project and not me. I'm your wife *now*."

There were so many things he could have said that Maya would have accepted. Eileen was a scientist, Nils had requested her input, Eileen had paperwork the project needed, Eileen had called him, Eileen had recommended him, Eileen had a question, Eileen had an answer.

Instead, he said, "Eileen knew Serena." A confession, or at least it sounded like one. "I wanted to talk to someone who knew her, and you never will."

He was giving her an answer to a question she hadn't explicitly asked. This was where he'd been, physically but also mentally. He didn't have room for Maya anymore, not with Eileen in his ear and Serena in his mind. She thought back to when she'd met Noah. He'd told her she was so full of life and he felt like the living dead. Maya mistook that to mean she'd brought him back to life. She'd been tending to him, patching up his potholes and paving over the scars. But now she understood he hadn't come forward, away from his past. He'd only stepped sideways toward her, leaving his grief, the death, his old life next to them, running parallel to their life this whole time. A ghost life. So real and easy that he could simply step back into it, leaving her here.

Nearby someone shouted and pointed to the horizon.

Maya's voice barely sounded. "I need you to believe. In us. Right now. While you do whatever else, you have to still believe in us."

It was dark, but she could swear she saw tears in Noah's eyes. There were tears in his voice. "I can't," he said. "There's too much else."

Then it happened. The Marfa Lights. Prism-filtered, the imprint of light bubbling up and down and then disappearing. What looked like a headlight where there were no cars. Maya's heart skipped a millisecond and then everything was back to the way it had been, phenomenon witnessed.

Noah was right. The lights weren't anything special, gone as quickly as they'd arrived. Everyone at the lookout slackened, disappointed. There was no mystery.

"I saw them," Maya said, looking to him, unable to make out the fine contours of his face in the dark. "Did you?"

Noah shook his head. He hadn't even been looking. "I missed it."

Back in the car, he reached for the gearshift and pricked himself on the plant in the cup holder. "Ouch," he said.

She said what he wouldn't. "You're leaving."

"I'm folding," he said.

"Time travel," she said, though she knew he didn't like her to say it. Maya knew she should have said, *I wish I could know Serena*. To carve out a space in her anger for his grief. But she had been doing that for years, carving space for his grief, and he'd never stepped into it.

"I'm leaving, too," she said.

Noah kept his eyes straight ahead on the empty road as it disappeared beneath the car.

"Where?" he asked.

"Home."

"Home where?"

"Home Japan. Tokyo. I haven't seen my parents in a couple years."

"That's not why you're going." Resentment in his tone. Maya felt strangely gratified. She wanted him to hurt, too.

"It's also Ren," she said.

There. That was it.

. . .

Later that night, in bed, Noah tried to poke holes in her logic for leaving. But what about her work with the gallery? There was no hard timeline there, she said. And anyway, wasn't it just something to entertain "the wife" while he worked? He insisted it was more than that, it was about her career, her art. Maya said going home was about her art. How, Noah wanted to know. You couldn't understand, she insisted. Ren had been there with her, back when she was actually an artist.

Ren, Noah said. Eileen, Maya said. Serena. All of it, everyone, everyone they'd entangled with, all the versions of themselves they'd left behind, never forgotten.

The night wore on and they didn't fall asleep. They both lay on their backs, looking up at the closed skylight. Light from unadulterated stars played softly on the other side of the glass. Unbearable.

The question was a long time coming, and then it came.

"Is this a break?" he asked.

She thought of Noah's surge of grief at the Robert Irwin building, his face breaking apart behind a pale scrim. The pronghorn's blank face, an animal relieved of his existence. Ren's voice over the phone, delivering electricity into her veins, color into her mind. And Eileen, years and years ago, pregnant in a field, buoyed by love, practically levitating off the ground. And Noah, in his mind, racing back to Eileen, slipping backward.

"We're already broken," Maya said.

Noah

The mission was simple. Exceedingly simple, which gave Noah some relief. Simplicity was easy to track, easy to manage. He liked knowing that the initial goals were within reach. So much of the project had felt just beyond reach, at the edge of comprehension.

The locked-box test. The plan was this: Early in the morning before Noah folded, Nils would write a message on a piece of paper and place it into a chrome box he'd outfitted with a time-sensitive lock. Nils would set the timer on the lock to open only between 9:15 a.m. and 9:30 a.m. on that specific day. But during that exact time period, from 9:15 a.m. to 9:30 a.m., Noah would be recorded on a monitor while Nils operated his memory reading. They would be mapping Noah's memory of that morning before he arrived at Building D, so that when he took the Fold Cocktail, he could fold back to then. Instead of going into Building D, though, he'd go find the box, open it sometime between 9:15 and 9:30, and read the message. When he folded back to the present, he would tell Nils what the message said, delivering information in the present that was only retrievable in the past.

There were questions and concerns, of course. Each time Noah folded and made a decision that his past self had not made, he would likely create a new branch of time. That was only a theory, but it had to be true, otherwise the fold would have already occurred in this timeline and both Nils and Noah would have a memory of it. But what happened after Noah abandoned the branch and folded back to this timeline, where his body was in the time bath? Nils said there were two possibilities: first, that those branched timelines temporally collapsed and blipped out of existence, or second, that they extended on as a branch, forever altered by whatever decisions *this* Noah had made in his brief visit to *that* Noah.

"Either way, it's none of our concern," Nils said. "Not in this timeline, anyway. Our priority is getting you back here safely."

The goalposts were clear: Fold successfully, many times, with controlled volition, for a sustained period of time. With each fold, the volition and duration would get easier to sustain, but Nils warned Noah to expect it to feel difficult at first.

"It will take many folds until you can easily move around in a memory, without falling out of it," Nils said.

"What does it feel like to *fall out* of a memory?" Noah asked.

"It feels like loss. Like you're losing that experience," Nils said. "But don't worry about anticipating that. I'd rather have you not anticipate anything."

For the past few days Noah and Maya had spoken only when necessary. She told him she was buying a plane ticket; he spent more time training on his own. On the night before the first fold, while Noah went to sleep, Maya went on one of her midnight walks around Marfa. Now he assumed she was talking to Ren on those walks, but Noah had trouble working himself into jealousy. Jealousy pivoted on what might happen, what betrayals might yet occur, but all the memory reading and writing had trained him to reserve strong emotions for the past. He had a hard time working himself up about the future.

So he and Maya were taking a break. Perhaps they'd heal from it, like a broken bone. Perhaps they'd move on from it, like a severed limb. He couldn't think that far ahead.

The morning of the first fold, as he got ready to leave for Building D, Maya remained asleep. He took her hand in bed and gently rubbed his thumb over her knuckles. He made promises to himself he knew he would not have to deliver on. If she woke, he would kiss her. If she kissed back, he would tell her he loved her. If she said it, too, he might not go, fold back to his dead daughter. But she didn't wake, and none of the ifs ever came to be.

Now, he crossed the courtyard and scanned his retinas at the entrance to Building D. He walked in, through the maze of humming servers, and paused at the controls, where Nils was standing, waiting.

"Ready when you are," Nils said. They'd agreed to say as little as necessary, so Noah could preserve the memory of each moment in order to map it.

Noah entered the room with the time bath. Without speaking or pausing, he sat on his meditation pillow and put the mapping helmet on. He began to meditate on the memory of the half hour prior, leaving a sleeping Maya, getting dressed, drinking a cup of tea, going to the bathroom, walking across the courtyard, coming here. He tried to remember every bit of it, every sensation, slowly and deliberately, to feel what it felt like, to create the neurological picture for nanorepeaters to communicate to the helmet.

At 9:31 a.m., Nils said, "Time to begin memory writing."

Noah stood, stripped off his clothes, and retrieved from a small fridge the syringe with the Fold Cocktail. He administered it into the good vein in his left elbow, almost painlessly. He was good at self-administering shots now, after the weekly Echo Injections. This was only the second time he'd taken the Fold Cocktail. The first time he'd taken it, Nils wanted to see how his body reacted. Noah felt like he'd gotten a little high, felt a burst of nonspecific joy, and then he fell asleep. Nils had explained that in the bath, with the machine engaged, it would feel slightly different and a little more intense, but Noah tried not to think of it now.

He pushed the button to open the time bath. The black liquid undulated. He carefully climbed in, resting his head in the bath's reignition helmet. He pushed a button on the inside of the bath and the top wheezed down, locking into place, leaving only a sliver of an opening. The top of the machine was several inches from his nose, and the bath was wide enough that Noah had plenty of room to attach the sensors and electrodes to his chest, the base of his skull, and his temples.

Floating in the bath, he felt the cocktail begin to take effect. From the nape of his neck upward, it was like a balloon being inflated, his mind getting both large and light. An intense pleasure, relief from thinking, from having to be so squarely in this world. Time passed without Noah being aware of it, and then Nils's voice came through the mic.

"Noah," he said, using a soft voice with an even cadence. "Are you all right?"

"Yes," Noah said, barely sure if he'd even said it.

"Do you feel the effects?"

"Yes," Noah said again.

"Then we'll begin."

Through the sliver opening in the bath, Noah saw that Nils cut the lights in the room.

"Engaging the core," Nils said.

Behind his head, Noah heard the core rumble. He saw a black void, but it was not cold or frightening. It was an invitation, warmth.

"Beginning the resonance program."

He was aloft in space, moving toward the void.

"Regulating the energy cycle."

Then he saw the black void he was moving toward was not darkness, but light. Or both at once. It was like dying, he thought, and then swept the thought away.

"Ten, nine, eight . . ."

Nils's voice faded. Noah was left alone.

An anchor sensation: the feel of the doorknob in his hand as he latches it behind him, a short metal pull, releasing it and hearing the click, the crisp morning air on his face. The ground beneath him is at first vague, as though scribbled in. Then the walls of the compound form. Then the pebbles, the plants, the walkway. The quickening scent of fall air fills every part of him, his lungs, his blood.

He folds. He halves. He knows he can never explain it. He is himself, but without himself. He forgets everything. He remembers.

• • • • • • •

For a brief moment he can't breathe. His throat is full of lead. Suffocation explodes over his body; he's sure he is dying—how long will it be this painful? Something bends like a snake writhing, the stem of a flower being snapped between two fingers, a seizure in time, and he's in the space between alive and dead, he is sure.

He gasps.

Look up.

His hands. He gasps.

Look up.

"Look up." The voice is coming from him.

Noah lifts his head and opens his eyes. He feels like he's soaking, but when he touches his chest, then the tops of his thighs, he's dry. He's clothed. He's trying to breathe.

He's standing in the courtyard, exactly as he was before he entered Building D.

He's here. He's done it.

He takes a few burning breaths and focuses his eyes. There is no one around, no sound. When he tries to walk, he feels like he's underwater or paralyzed. The stuck feeling fades, and he is now moving. He is walking. Each decision, each movement made and sustained with great effort.

Everything looks crass, the sun brighter, the succulents greener, the prickly pear thorns sharper. When he takes a few steps on the stone path, gravel crunches under his feet and the sound pierces his ears. His heart races. He tries to slow it, to calm himself. Nils will see back in the time bath that his vitals are going wonky. Noah doesn't want to be pulled out of the fold.

It's the same world, he tells himself. *Oh but it's not*, he reminds himself. *Not anymore.*

Look up.

Noah looks up. The sky is a light denim, cloudless. A small black bird with a white tail streaks across it. He's trained himself to remember to look up, to know he is physically in this world and it is going to be okay. The sky is not falling.

He turns to look at his and Maya's house, the morning light striking the window. He looks away. The mission is to spend as little time here as possible, to interact with no one in his pursuit of the locked message. Noah slips between Nils's office and Klein's house, into a narrow alley that leads to the back of the campus, ending in the field on the other side of Klein's vast floor-to-ceiling windows, from which he looked out the previous week. He and Nils chose this place for the lockbox because he's unlikely to run into anyone back here.

Noah spots the chrome box in the middle of the blond brush, an anomaly. He kneels and looks at his watch: 9:13 a.m., two minutes until the box unlocks. He sits back on his heels, and he tries to breathe. What was it he used to tell Serena when she would get red-faced with a tantrum? Inhale the beautiful flower, blow out the birthday candles,

In flower, out candles. He breathes. No, it was Eileen who came up with that, Eileen's method.

9:14 a.m. Eileen . . . he shouldn't have thought of her. She's in his brain now, sticking to his neurons. His breath catches as he tries to rid his mind of her, but the more he tries, the more she sticks. In flower, out candles. And then there's someone else there. Serena, her face flushed purple, tears streaking down her cheeks, shaking, trying to calm herself, in flower, out candles, and now Noah is shaking. They feel so close.

His watch ticks to 9:15 a.m., and he reaches for the chrome box. The lock clicks open, a perfect, clean sound. Noah tries, he does, he tries to open the box. But his trying comes from the deep recesses of his mind, a desire not met by his body, the distance between his hand and his thought so very far.

He looks up. He sees his own reflection in Klein's giant windows. He's a small man, crouched on the ground, supplicant to this box. His face is like a prism, a surface to bounce light.

His vision goes first, a gauze pulled in front of his face, smoke that won't clear. His eyes close. He is losing control of his legs, his face, his breath. And that's what it feels like to fold. If entering felt like death, leaving feels like a relief. Falling unconscious, passing out, or back in.

Noah.

Look up.

The violence of returning was the same as leaving. Noah choked for air. The liquid sloshed. He was back. He launched himself out of the time bath and onto the hard floor, banging his knees.

The first thing he said was, "I'm thirsty." He wrapped himself in a robe and drank two bottles of water. Then he described the physical sensations in as much detail as he could. He felt sick; it was his heart that hurt, like heartburn. Nils said that was likely a side effect of consciousness entanglement. The suspension between here and then, Noah suspended in the thick, magnetic blackness of the salt bath, had caused his heart and breath to slow, then speed, then slow. And now, suddenly here, his nervous system snapped back to this time.

"It's all right," Nils said. "This will take a while. You need to build stamina, get your body used to this. That's enough for today."

But Noah felt a separation inside him all afternoon, a gap that hung open like curtains letting in white light. He stayed to help Nils document the session, make notes, run some models. He stayed to clean up—he'd sloshed a lot of liquid from the bath onto the floor, after all. He stayed because he didn't want to go back to the house and see Maya leaving. And then Nils went home, finally, and Noah made excuses to stay in the building so that he could fold again, alone.

It was dangerous to fold alone, without a second person to man the control center, monitor his vitals, and bring him back if necessary. He would have to start the resonance program and then enter the bath, even though the program was only supposed to be initiated after the subject had entered the bath. If the subject wasn't clearly focused when the program began running, there were risks. While the subject's brain activity scattered, the machine would become overloaded trying to compensate. Nils hadn't been explicit about what exactly could happen, but Noah inferred that there was a small but nonzero possibility that his brain would be forever altered in coming back, but in what way, no one knew.

Then there was the matter of another Fold Cocktail injection, the second in one day. Nils advised twenty-four hours between shots to recover. Perhaps Noah could have done another fold without a second injection, but he wanted to make sure he was primed.

Folding solo would require sustained focus. Noah began by meditating for one hour. Then he went to the entrance of the building and switched off the retina scan. The building would now only be accessible with a physical key, buried somewhere deep in Nils's messy office. Noah approached the controls. He'd watched Nils do this many times, but doing it himself was oddly intoxicating. He felt godlike, beginning the sequence, watching the algorithm run. He saw the source code as the program started up—only pieces of code were available each fold, as a security measure—and he marveled at its complexity. He was careful not to let the excitement build in him too much, though. He tried to maintain equilibrium: his breath, his heartbeat, his mind, his goal.

Back in the room, he dimmed the lights and undressed. He administered the shot, climbed inside the bath, and began to go back.

Again, he's unable to breathe. He's drowning. And then he's not.

He lurches to standing. The swerve from lying in the time bath to being upright makes him instantly nauseated. He reaches out and touches a wall. It's his old hallway. It's where he wanted to be.

He walks, one foot in front of the other, and opens a door, Serena's door. The smell, old plushies, sweet detergent, plastic toys. His eyes brim. He touches the night-light and the room glows an alien blue. In the corner, in her bed, Serena doesn't stir. This is the same memory he's been meditating back to, a chilly December morning, before Serena woke up, when he sat by her bed, rested his chin on the railing, and watched her sleep.

He vows not to do anything different now. He doesn't want to inflict chaos on this timeline, whatever happens to it after he leaves. He won't change the flow of things here, not this time, not now.

Quietly, he pads to the little stool by her bed and sits on it. His eyes are adjusting, like a pixelated image resolving. Serena is a small mound under the pink-and-white quilt his mother had made her. Everything in Noah's body yearns to reach out and touch her, wake her, to relive this perfect morning moment, to feel her weight on him. Oh, to feel her weight.

The want is heavy, begging at his throat. His hands shake. He looks up and sees a black hole. There, on the ceiling above her bed, a cluster of glow-in-the-dark stars. She'd wanted them desperately, and Noah had picked out some expensive ones, with glue that wouldn't tear up the paint. But when it came time to put them up, Serena insisted she pick out every placement. He stood on a small ladder while she pointed. *There*, she said. *There. No, there.* And he did as she said. And the stars were as close to each other as they could be, an explosion of green-white light when the lights were off. *A clump*, Eileen had said when she walked in to see it. *A black hole*, Noah had said. So the stars could be close to each other, not lonely.

Eileen. The thought of her tears at the memory. Noah feels destabilized, his footing unsure, as if he's on a boat. He grips the railing of Serena's bed and she starts to shift under the quilt. *No*, he thinks, but Serena is vanishing; everything he sees is vanishing.

There is pounding. His heart in his ears. A fist on a door. Someone is saying his name, shouting it. He's pulled back into the world where everything has vanished.

* * *

He launched out of the time bath again, in survival mode. His knees once more crunched on the floor, and he cried out. Slick, he held his head, but the pounding didn't stop. In fact, it increased. It was outside him. Where was the pounding coming from?

It was Maya. Her voice calling his name, a question, loud and insistent through the outside intercom. The door to the building was locked. Noah pulled his boxers on and ran across the building to the door. He slipped in the dark, but caught himself, and then flipped open the keypad and turned the retina scan back on so he could let her in.

Maya was standing in the moonlight. He was surprised to see how long he'd been inside. Her mouth was half-open as she took in his semi-nakedness, his disheveled state.

"I'm sorry," he said, pulling her in. He quickly searched the courtyard to be sure no one had seen her.

Maya took in the space with a look of horror. The massive darkness of the interior full of machinery was alarming if you weren't used to it, Noah supposed. He took her hand and she followed him to the back corner, to the room containing the time bath. She walked around the bath slowly, stepping over puddles Noah had dripped on the floor.

"Here," she said, holding up the robe he hadn't grabbed. "Dry off."

There were no chairs in the room, so they had to sit cross-legged on the floor. Maya's eyes were rimmed with red, her mouth turned down. She was sad, and he didn't know how to fix it. Fixing her sadness was crossing a bridge he couldn't locate. He had his own sadness island.

She asked only two questions. First, she wanted to know if it was painful.

"Yes, in a way," Noah said. "But then it passes."

"And was it successful? Your fold?" She said the word *fold* tentatively, as if trying it out.

"I was able to fold," he said. "But I couldn't stay long. Not long enough, at least."

"Oh," she said, her voice a razor. "I wanted to say, I bought a ticket. I have to go to El Paso now. My flight leaves soon."

"When will you be back?"

Maya shook her head. There was no way to know.

"I love you," he said, but it wasn't enough.

They sat with their knees touching, their heads bowed. So he told a story. When he spoke, it was as if loosening a stuck marble in his diaphragm, his whole center splitting open.

"I never used to be afraid of dying. Not more than anyone else. But when Serena was born, I felt so strongly that I had to stay alive for her, and I began to fear dying. I'd never felt that way before. And when we lost her, I realized there was another, equal feeling—that the only other thing I had to do besides stay alive was die before her. And I'd failed. After Serena was gone, I didn't have to stay alive or die for anyone. Not even Eileen. There was an absence of the impulse to live and the impulse to die. So, that's when I knew."

"Knew what?" Maya asked.

"Knew that I loved you. You were sitting on the couch in the living room, reading some book, and I was making dinner, and I kept checking on you, making sure you were still there and content, and you were getting annoyed at me because I kept asking how you were. It wasn't a special night or anything. Just a night. You said I was making you anxious, so I went back to the kitchen, and there was this feeling then, not exactly the same, but close. That I wanted to stay alive for you. As long as possible."

Maya's hands trembled in her lap. He couldn't bring his eyes up to look at her, but he felt, on the backs of his own hands, warm tears. His own, hers, both.

"I felt alive with you," Noah said. "But there's a part of me that feels if she—if Serena—is somewhere, how do I stay alive here, if she exists there?"

Maya was nodding. But she didn't speak.

"I have to find out," he said. That was the end. He'd said everything he needed to say.

And finally, she spoke. "I know," she said. "We all have possible lives."

That statement seared through him. He felt it burning hot in his body, like a black hole, sucking everything in, all the light, every light he'd had in his life. He wanted her to stay the same, stay here, stay still, and wait for him. But she couldn't. They'd go in two directions at once. They'd stay and they'd leave. They had to.

Eileen

Eileen received a text from Noah, the first in years and years. *Come to Marfa. Let me show you.* She didn't reply. He texted again. *Please.* She ignored the text. He texted again. *I saw her.*

What made Noah special was what made him difficult and also a good physicist. He became stuck in cycles, obsessive and determined, myopic about *now*. Eileen had recognized it that first evening they met, at the Europa disaster. He'd wanted to understand all of it, right then. He'd talked about it, all the possibilities where things might have gone wrong in the engineering. But Eileen was different. Where Noah was demanding in his work, she was methodical. Where he immersed himself, she retreated to get a better view. It made sense that he was well suited for theoretical physics, the kind of science that changed you, that you had to live and breathe to understand. The way language changed thought patterns. Concepts in physics, some of them felt like a thought paradigm, a religion. She saw it in the Florida motel they'd stayed in the first night, the way he touched her, that he liked to fall into things, that he wanted to believe in something, but that he was also wedded to scientific thought. He thought he could own the world that way.

That tendency Noah had to fall hard was intoxicating in love. In her time with him, she always felt wanted and hungered for. His brain was alive, and it enlivened hers. But when Serena died, Eileen watched that part of him wither. He didn't want to be in the here and now, he couldn't, and she understood. Their marriage churned forward without anyone in it, until they called it. Divorce.

But now, whatever they'd had—a marriage, a family—was being repopulated. Noah was lost in that space again. She had to go find him. She decided to tell Prem.

"Come on," Prem said. "You, more than most, know how life and death work."

"Yes, yes, I know," she said, embarrassed.

"There's no way this is real."

She shrugged.

"Isn't emotional rescue the job of his wife?"

"That's not how it works," Eileen said. "We used to be married. We were together sixteen years. We had a child together. There are things that you do for people. I can't explain it."

"Eileen," Prem said. "You're a biologist. You know this is crazy."

He was standing just inside her home, his coat still on, one hand reaching back to touch the doorknob, then letting go, then reaching back.

"But it's not about biology," she said. "Noah works in this field, in quantum entanglement. Don't be deluded."

Prem scoffed. She hadn't seen him this outraged, not ever. "You're calling *me* deluded? You're talking about driving to nowhere Texas to go transcendentally meditate your way to your dead daughter."

His phrase, "dead daughter," turned off all the lights inside her. Eileen flashed to Serena's ashes, split up in separate urns, hers still in the funeral-home-issued plastic bag, in the back of a hall closet. Prem stuttered and stumbled, realizing the line he'd crossed, and tried to take her hand, to explain, but he didn't go far from the door, and then eventually he left the house. Eileen didn't hear what he said after that, or see him leave, but she knew when he was gone that she was alone.

What he couldn't know was how hurtful the phrase "dead daughter" was, implying total eradication, when what was gathering inside her was that love, that old love, for her daughter—completely alive love.

Talking to Noah again, revisiting the life that had included Serena, had her wanting to believe. She felt—against her better judgment, her education, and everything she'd spent her life knowing—that the past was actually alive again. It was true inside her. The memories of Serena had come back lucid and in Technicolor. Serena's serious demeanor with servers and grocery store clerks. The weird one-day trip they took all the way to Ojai for lunch, how Serena kept saying Mickey Mouse lived there. The unicorn toy Eileen couldn't figure out how to turn off, so she eventually cut a hole and tore the battery out of its core. Memories big and small, good and bad, things she'd stored away. Aging in a storage unit, out of sight, out of mind, as if they didn't exist at all, not until she needed them.

She hadn't bothered telling the school all the details, only that there was a family crisis. A colleague agreed to cover the few classes that were left in Eileen's semester.

She texted Noah that she'd be there in a few days and he texted back, *OK, Maya left*, which made her hurry more. She bought an expensive plane ticket to El Paso and when she got there, she rented a car and drove the whole way to Marfa with her heart leaping out of her chest, propelling her forward. She didn't know what she'd find there. A Noah who'd imagined it all, driven mad by grief, or a suspect billionaire lying to a vulnerable man, or a device that actually worked, an incredible machine matched to an incredible brain.

And then she thought about Maya. About what must have happened to spur her away, what betrayals she carried with her, wherever she'd gone. The Noah Eileen knew at the end of their marriage was hollow and far away, and it was hard to imagine how he'd found such a vibrant person, a beautiful artist. But she did feel a kinship with Maya. She must know the same Noah secrets Eileen did. Noah's inability to understand a grocery store and how to navigate it efficiently. His never-finished projects building tiny models. How he brushed his teeth after lunch, even if he'd only had soup. They were strangely connected, Eileen and Maya, points of light in a hard-to-see constellation.

She drove. The desolation of the West Texas desert reminded her of Joshua Tree, where she and Noah had been when they decided to divorce for good. Now that memories were so available to her, Eileen decided to slip into the ripe pain of that world.

The house in Joshua Tree was a beautiful rental, but it was wild. Strange beetles she'd never seen before slipped under the door and through the cracks in the walls. In the mornings the sun lashed the white stucco, and a snake wrapped itself around the base of a cholla in the backyard. At night coyotes screamed in the velvet blackness. They'd come out there for the stars, a billion of them in every direction, like being inside a snow globe at night. It was the one-year anniversary of Serena's death.

"It doesn't need celebrating," Eileen had said.

"Not celebrating," Noah said. "Marking."

He'd made the rental arrangements and planned everything. The hikes they'd do in the park, the new café they'd try on Highway 62, the hot tub on the property. She made herself heavy and agreed to be dragged along. In the end they did no hikes, no cafés, and only one hot tub, where they failed to argue.

The failure to argue was the thing. Eileen wore a bathing suit she hadn't fit into since before Serena was born. She'd had no appetite, and though everyone assured her it would come back, it hadn't yet. Everything tasted like old marshmallow, a memory of sickly sweetness. They sat on opposite ends of the hot tub, and Eileen looked at Noah. Noah looked at Eileen.

"Did you bring a cake?" she asked.

He was confused. "A cake?"

"My mom used to buy the cake my dad liked on his birthday after he died."

"On his birthday, Eileen. This is something else."

"Okay, so what will we do? To mark it?"

They sloshed around a bit.

Grief had moved through her that year like liquid metal in her veins, slow and heavy. Around eight months on, it settled in her feet, made everything a hard slog. And then suddenly, she felt empty. She took up running and cycling. She wanted to feel fast and light in her emptiness. Noah was still in the eddy of it, though, swirling and swirling and swirling.

"I'm trying to remember that night."

"Noah, there was nothing you could have—"

"I know, I know. I'm not talking about that part. I just want to remember it. Piece by piece."

"Why?"

"So it doesn't go away."

Eileen looked at him in the hot tub, the bubbles a low soundtrack to their silence, and couldn't find any of the blind energy she'd felt when they first met, under the charged tragedy of the Europa disaster, kids with their whole lives inside them, ready to unfurl. Now he was just a regular human, trying to stay afloat, like her. They'd both drown.

"Don't you want to talk about—"

Eileen shook her head. "No," she said. She didn't want to talk about Serena. There was nothing to say. Not even one year in. Where were they? The same, only more hollow, still lacking an outlet for the love that had shaped them.

"What are we doing?" she asked.

He looked up. They'd turned off all the lights on the outside patio and they could see every single star. She felt his foot graze hers on the bottom of the tub.

"This is beautiful," he said, but it was like a question. Beautiful?

She couldn't look up. She couldn't do it. She didn't want to, but she also didn't have the capacity to look up at the stars above them. She knew he wanted her to. His face craned to the sky, she saw his throat, the undulations there silent and sad.

That's how Eileen knew it was over. He wanted them to be the same as they always were, looking up, looking up at the sky when they first met, watching the terrible explosion in the near distance. But she was different. She wanted to be different.

When he brought his face back to hers, they both were crying. They wouldn't say it that night. In fact, they would have sex that night, moving against each other like they were apologizing. In the morning they would decide to leave a day early, and in the car, she would say it casually, "You know what, we should go ahead with the divorce," like it had already been on the table, which it had, in a way.

Back in the hot tub, with tears marking lines down his cheeks, he'd said, "What's wrong?"

Her face was hot with her own silent crying. "What's wrong with *you*? It's old light up there."

It was night when Eileen finally pulled into Marfa and navigated down a dark desert road to the lab. She used the code Noah had given her to open the gate. The grounds were dark, and only two unmarked black town cars were parked in the lot. Eileen wondered if Klein's driver was in one of them, always on call. The entire place felt cold and empty, with buildings encircling a courtyard and no light to speak of, except the stars. It was almost unbearably starry out here. She stood there at the precipice of the courtyard for a moment, her head craned up, looking at the expanse.

When Noah first told her that he could fold back to Serena, that he could not only imagine it but actually visit that time using quantum consciousness and a clever contraption to experience it again, she became angry. Not only had he opened up the cavern she'd long ago closed off, but now he was flooding it, bombarding her with the possibility that there was a life where her daughter had not died.

Now, though, standing here, her body was thrumming with anticipation. The feeling wasn't eroticism or terror or grief, but it was adjacent to all that. A feeling that her future was here.

She approached the building marked D and gently knocked. After a while with no answer, she knocked louder. Then she pounded. She saw a button that appeared to be for an intercom and she pushed it and called his name, Noah, Noah, Noah. If he didn't let her in, she would die here, coming all this way only to be locked out of her future.

Finally, a sound like a body being birthed, falling on the floor. And then the door beeped and the lock unlatched, and Noah, dripping wet in a robe, matched his eyes to hers. She hadn't seen him in years, but everything that had ever passed between them—love and sex and rage and grief and anger and finally, horribly, indifference—was suddenly present, too. Surrounding them, ghosts. None of it ever goes away.

"Come in," Noah said, and Eileen did.

III

The Fold

Maya

The evening Maya first met Noah, she had been talking about weight. Not pounds, not about dieting and body image, but about art, a photograph she'd loved since college, called *Weight*. The artist was Yuko Matsuda, and the work was old by the time Maya gave her symposium talk. Yuko herself was the subject. She stood nude before a massive rectangular mirror reflecting a painted backdrop behind the camera. Yuko's grandfather had painted backdrops for movies, and Yuko had re-created one of the Tokyo cityscape in the 1980s. It looked as if Yuko were standing on the edge of a building's rooftop. Just above her, out of reach, a cluster of colorful balloons. But she wasn't reaching for the balloons. That always struck Maya as sad, salvation a cheery possibility right beyond your fingertips. An image in which, if you looked closely enough, you saw that the void this body would fall into was a reflection of a re-creation of a representation of a city, the future having lost layers of meaning in the reproduction.

In Maya's symposium talk, she'd laid that out, her theory about the dynamic sadness of the photograph. She'd described how the composition asked you to look in the darkness and shadows, to search for what was almost seen. She'd outlined the many vectors of movement, the way Yuko's body tipped backward, implying an eventual tip forward, implying a fall. The way the balloons gestured up, while the body gestured down. The drama of the buildings reaching skyward, and the longing of the unseen ground.

After, when Noah approached her, that's what he wanted to talk about. How he appreciated her theory.

"You don't often see sadness presented that way," he'd said. "Usually it's so static. I didn't realize that until I heard you talk."

This had driven Maya for a long time, this idea that Noah truly got what she was trying to say. That was a large part of why their marriage worked, why she'd gone to Marfa with him. He believed her, and she believed him.

But now, as the plane she'd taken away from her husband landed at Narita Airport, as that sensation of being both lifted and pulled happened in the millisecond before the plane's wheels touched the runway, she realized she'd been wrong about *Weight*. The photograph wasn't about dynamic sadness. It was about relief. The subject, Yuko, was about to relieve herself of gravity, evidence of its push and pull everywhere. She was going to relieve herself of the weight of the past, its re-creations and reflections. She had let go of everything, even her clothes. No need for balloons or salvation. Everything was going to be all right. The photograph captured the moment just before great joy. Now Maya wished she'd brought the copy of the image she kept in her notebook, but she'd left the notebook in the painting mudroom in Marfa. She hadn't wanted to bring anything sketched there over here.

Maya loved the train ride into the city, the singsong recordings playing over the speaker in three languages, the orderly crowds, the machines spitting out tickets, the platform conductors in suits and hats and gloves. She took a window seat and settled in for a backward shuttle into a life she used to live. The low wooden homes grew denser and taller and less wooden the closer the train barreled toward Tokyo, the colors brighter and louder, the train more crowded. A young family with a small girl boarded the train and sat opposite Maya. She didn't verbally greet them, the way she might have in the same kind of intimate setting in America, but she did nod, and the little girl nodded back and then pulled out a coloring book.

Outside the window, Tokyo gathered itself. It was drizzling, but that didn't dampen the charm. Though Maya had moved around a lot as a young child, following her father's company transfers, Tokyo was where she spent those important, sweaty teenage years. She often took the train from her parents' house in suburban Chiba to gorge on sweet coffee drinks and ube croissants, and sometimes she conveniently missed the last train back, crashing in a women-only capsule hotel or on a futon in her friend's parents' living room. Though a romanticized longing for California loomed largest in her teenage heart—the California her mother had abandoned, the one she saw in movies and magazines—the smaller longing for Tokyo was close and fulfillable.

But now, as the train crawled through Ikebukero and Shinjuku, the stations alive with people moving politely about, dressed smartly, speaking a language that lay dormant in the base of Maya's skull, she wondered if this wasn't her true longing, always. To go home, to where she was from. For so long she could have belonged anywhere. Here, though, stepping out of the train into Shibuya Station, as a blur of businessmen and -women crisscrossed around her, she felt both cocooned by a community and also singular and bold. What was that combination of feelings if not belonging, she wondered.

When she exited the train onto the busy platform, the same young girl bumped into her. "Sumimasen," the girl said, and then offered her hand, which held a piece of white paper with a drawing on it. "Onegaishimasu," the girl said, nodding her head a little. *Take it.*

Maya looked at the girl's mother, sharply dressed in a trench coat, and the young father with movie star cheekbones. They smiled and nodded.

Maya took the paper. It was a drawing of a person wearing the same clothes she was wearing, black jeans and a blue sweater, and her hair was dark and messy like hers, and it took a moment for her to realize it was a drawing *of* her. She looked at the eyes. Though the child's drawing was straight on, the eyes were cocked left, toward where the train window might have been, if the girl had drawn the train. In the picture, Maya looked like a child. Like the girl.

"So sorry," the girl's father said in English, and Maya was momentarily wounded that they knew before she'd spoken that she was from America.

"Mondai nai," Maya said. *No problem.* She crouched down to the girl's level. She pointed to the drawing of herself and thanked her.

But this move was a touch too intimate for the parents, and the father gently tugged on the girl's hand. The family moved away, and Maya understood her mistake. Too close for a stranger. The girl was smiling, though, and she waved as her parents led her far from the American woman with the subtle accent.

Maya folded the paper and put it in her backpack. She made her way out of the station and snaked through the small streets away from the crowds, the famous crossing, the statue of Hachikō. The dense pack of tourists and Tokyo residents thinned out quickly. There was a hidden Shibuya on the edges of the neighborhood, a place where a certain demographic of old Japanese lived, the people who didn't want to live alone in a quiet village, who still wanted to walk to the market, gossip with shop owners, eat at ramen counters among the kids. Tourists would only find this Shibuya if they walked from the station to another neighborhood, like Nakameguro, which they never did, which afforded those outskirts privacy and quiet as well as priceless proximity.

Maya was proud that she didn't need a map to find her parents' street, but she struggled to find their particular building. After navigating the coded maze of Tokyo addresses, she finally found the beige nondescript complex they lived in, and once she was buzzed in, she walked the outside stairs slowly. It had been a few years since she'd been to Tokyo, since she'd stood in the same room as her parents. The last time she was here, she and Noah had come for a brief visit right after they eloped. When her father handed them an envelope with congratulations money in it, her mother had said, "So sorry you didn't invite people to your wedding so we couldn't see it."

Outside the door, Maya lifted her hand to knock, and hesitated. This place they lived in now had never been her home. She knocked.

Her mother's first words to her were "You brought no luggage, you silly girl!" but then she drew Maya in for a hug. "Welcome back," she said, her voice thick like she was holding in a cry. Maya descended into the hug.

"Are you hungry?" her mother asked, heading toward the kitchen before Maya had answered.

The apartment was familiarly cluttered, every corner decorated with a cute shelf or cabinet, stuffed with life detritus, reusable shopping bags, figurines, envelopes. Maya herself had inherited this tendency to fill living spaces. It was partly why the house at the Klein Michaels lab had bothered her so much. The place had been filled like they already lived there. She hadn't even put up the framed photo she'd brought of the two of them.

Maya slid off her shoes and her backpack, and the relief she'd felt upon landing at Narita surged. With her mother knocking around the kitchen, the opening and closing of the fridge, the smell of tea and tatami, she felt specifically somewhere, and this specificity loosened her muscles. She felt her eyes well up with tears and her neck flush. Her mother brought her brightly colored daikon and rice on a beautiful ceramic plate.

She didn't say that she noticed her daughter's tremble, but she guided Maya to the couch, sat her down, and grabbed her hand. "You're home now," her mother said. "It's okay."

Just then Maya's father emerged from the bedroom wearing his trademark formal weekend wear, a thick brown sweater over a collared shirt, slacks that had been pressed. Her father was not used to casual wear, having worn impeccable suits for most of his career, and he liked how his formality commanded attention and respect. Now, in retirement, he still looked like an off-duty businessman.

"Maya-chan," he said affectionately, holding out his arms, and she stood to hug him. Her relationship with her father had not been as close as the one with her mother, but that also meant it had not been as combative. There was an ease to their communication, and also a shallowness.

"And where is Noah-san?" her father asked once she was released from the hug. He looked around, as though Noah were hiding behind the couch or secreting sushi in the kitchen.

Maya's face reddened. She looked to her mother. Of course her mother hadn't told her father; of course she would save herself the embarrassment of having to explain it. What could Maya even say? That Noah was time-traveling with some crazies in the Texas desert? That he'd abandoned her emotionally so she'd abandoned him physically?

"Noah's back in America," she said.

A pause. "Oh," her father said. "I see."

"We're trying this out," Maya said.

"Ah," he said, not asking what "this" referred to. "Well, do you want to speak Japanese, then? Or shall we stick to English?"

Yes, this would be the foremost concern for her father: which language they would communicate in, the rules of engagement, how to proceed. Business. It was comforting, in a way.

"Whatever you want," Maya said, but she said it in English.

"Whatever you want, too," her father said in Japanese. "Both, then."

She'd first begun using English at home regularly when she announced her plan to attend an American university, to her father's dismay. As an adult, she went back and forth between the two languages, and they'd often use Japanese if her parents wanted to tell her something they didn't want Noah to hear. But now there was no Noah.

And then something happened that no one expected. Her parents sat down with her on the couch, and for the first time in a long time, the three of them had a conversation.

Maya asked about their plans—would they travel soon, did they miss living in a place with a yard, gardening, did they know any good places to get tonkatsu because it was hard to find that in L.A., good katsu that doesn't feel like a heart attack. And they asked her about Marfa, if it was hot there, and if she liked Texas, and did she miss Japan, and she could stay and even go skiing up north, not that any of them had skied ever, but they could try something new. They stopped short of asking about Noah, or his work, or what was keeping him there. They also didn't ask about her work, or her art practice. But the conversation moved through the three of them like a sound wave, a ripple, leaving their dynamic subtly changed.

Her mother popped up from the couch and disappeared into the hallway. She returned holding slippers and gave them to Maya. The slippers were red shiny fabric on the outside, with white shearling on the inside.

"They reminded me of you," her mother said. And then she took her daughter's feet and slid the slippers on.

Maya unfolded the child's drawing from the train and pointed to the feet of the person in the picture, wearing red shoes, which Maya had not been wearing on the train, a detail born in the girl's imagination. Her mother took the drawing in her hands.

"Look," Maya said, pointing to the slippers on her feet. "This little girl predicted the future."

Later, wide-awake from restless jet lag, Maya sat up in bed. She was on a futon laid out in the spare room, a room that was piled with her mother's sewing, her father's notebooks, and a few bins of Maya's old keepsakes, including stacks of manga she didn't know enough kanji to fully read. She scooted on her knees toward the window and looked out, fingertips on the sill. Through the endless stacks of apartment buildings and bars she saw a sliver of the lights of Shibuya. They flickered projections Maya couldn't quite make out, but that signified lives being led out there, a whole world. She stared at the lights, and the blue outlines where the tops of buildings met the gray night, until she was stripped of everything she'd shouldered on her journey over here, and light with possibility, she finally slept.

Noah

Noah and Eileen sat on the floor near the time bath for hours. He explained how it worked, what he'd seen and done. He answered every question Eileen had, even the ones she asked twice, unable to believe the answers. He opened the bath and showed it to her. He asked if she wanted to go inside and she declined. Somewhere, an invisible clock ticked. Noah realized it was Eileen's watch. She wore an ancient analog watch that had been her father's. Every couple of years she had to take it to a specialist to get the gears replaced.

"I still wear it," she said, noticing his glance.

"Some things don't change."

"Some things," Eileen said. Her face was gray, and she had bags under her eyes.

"Let's go to sleep," Noah said. Eileen's watch read 3:17 a.m. The same time he'd woken up the night Serena died, rushed to her room, found her unresponsive.

Eileen nodded. She followed him out of Building D and across the dark, silent courtyard to the house. When he opened the door, she put her hands to her mouth, shocked.

"I know," he said. "It's uncanny."

She shook her head. "No, it's creepy. Noah, did they do this on purpose? Try to make this look like our Los Feliz house? How would they even know?"

"Klein knows everything," Noah said, resigning himself to that truth. It would have been easy for Klein's people to find old Realtor photos, to source certain decor, to add a fireplace and a big picture window in the exact proportions as in the Los Feliz place.

Noah walked her to the bedroom. Maya had made the bed before she left. He wondered if she'd landed in Tokyo yet. He wondered if he should call her. They hadn't made any explicit arrangements about communication, but she hadn't texted him when she was at the airport, which she usually did, or when she got on the plane. He took this as a sign that there would be no communication, at least not for a while. It was only fair, he thought, that she cut him out. He had his ex-wife in their bedroom.

Eileen was not how he remembered her. At the end of their marriage she had been so thin, like a hanger. He didn't remember her eating much in that year after Serena died. Mostly she sat on the back porch, looking at the empty, dying backyard, her forearms tanned brown from sitting there. But here in the bedroom that was like a sparse version of their bedroom in the Los Feliz house, Eileen looked more substantial. She was still lean and muscular, but she'd filled out, tall and commanding in her posture.

She walked the perimeter of the room, examining the bed with its wrought iron frame, similar to the one they'd bought together, all those years before.

"Sleep here, please," Noah said. "I can sleep on the couch."

"No, I'll take the couch."

"You must be exhausted."

"I don't want to presume . . ." she started to say, but she didn't finish.

Noah approached her and held out his hand, the way he used to when she'd come back from a conference and her bags were still in the car. It was his job, bringing the luggage in. She reached into her pocket and pulled out her car keys. When she put them in his palm, their hands touched, and they lingered. It was enough, this touching, to tear right through a person.

Noah grabbed her small suitcase from the rental and when he brought it back into the bedroom, she was already lying on the bed, still in her long coat. He left the suitcase in the corner and went to make his own bed on the couch.

The moon was bright, making the night almost pale blue, cutting through Noah's eyelids as he lay on the couch. He lay there awake. He heard Eileen's voice, soft, a close speaking voice, like it was okay if he didn't hear it: "Noah?"

He snapped up and went to the bedroom. Eileen was lying on her side, turned away from him, under the covers now. He sat on the bed, on his side.

"You're not lying to me," she said. It was a question, but she didn't say it like one.

"No," Noah said. "I'm not. I can show you. I want to show you."

"I don't want you to lie to me."

"Okay."

"Because you think it might be easier for me to swallow."

"Okay."

"Because you've lied to me before."

Noah didn't reply. He lay down, on top of the covers. His body mirrored hers, on his side, facing the window. The distance between their bodies was the size of a small person. Eileen didn't express any desire for him to leave, so he didn't.

"I'm sorry," he said.

. . .

He would have thought it a secret, not a lie, but he had to lie to keep the secret.

In the months after Serena died, Noah and Eileen barely left the house. There was a big flurry of activity around the funeral, Eileen's mother always in the house, friends dropping off wet casseroles, work colleagues checking in with vague emails. But about two months later, all of that faded. They were no longer other people's emergency. And so, except for going to work, they stayed in the house, walking around like ghosts, watching procedurals on TV at the lowest volume, turning off anything with a dead child in it. They made meals separately and ate separately, Noah often at his desk in his office, Eileen alone at the dinner table. They spoke of mundane things—grocery lists, utility bills, unsubscribing from the preschool emails. They had sex five or six times that year, without speaking about it, each time in the middle of the night, in the middle of sleep, in the dark, so they didn't have to look at each other.

And then Eileen started spending a lot of time in the backyard. Now Noah understood this as the transition, when she began to think about leaving him. She needed to separate herself from the house and look at the outside world, to see if it could offer anything to her. Then he saw it was freedom from the heavy unspoken fog of grief inside the house's walls. So he left the house, too.

He told Eileen he was joining a gym, though she hadn't asked and didn't seem to care. He intended to join a gym, but he never did. At first he went on walks around the neighborhood, up into the rich parts, big hills and wide streets, houses set far back from the sidewalk. And then he walked down into the commercial area and noticed for the first time a small, windowless bar in a strip mall. It was open, menacingly, from seven a.m. until two a.m. The first time he went inside, he sat at the bar and ordered a Lagavulin and drank it slowly. It was so dark inside, and no one spoke to him.

But after that day, he made friends. He hadn't made friends in years. Not since he was living in Studio City, sharing an apartment with a college roommate, commuting up north to see Eileen at her grad program on weekends. Bars were like that, Noah guessed, places where people who didn't make friends could make friends. A conditional life once you stepped inside, a place where you were exactly who you said you were, and your connections never followed you outside the doors. Being there wasn't about drinking. He only ever had three drinks, maximum. He didn't like being drunk. It made him sad in those days. Being at the bar was about the friends.

There was Roman, a Russian washing machine repairman, large and funny. Stevie, a kid who worked crazy hours editing movie trailers. Bria, older, a receptionist at a hair salon and a smoker. Noah could still hear her raspy laugh to this day. And to them Noah was the clean-cut physicist with marriage troubles he never spoke of, the quiet guy, easy to be around. Inside the bar was one place where Serena not only didn't exist, but never had.

But mostly there was Guy. Guy was only a little older than Noah, and had been an actor, or so he said, and now he taught acting, but mostly he lived off not having any financial responsibilities. Divorced and without children, he'd inherited a small paid-off bungalow from his mother. He rented out the back house for Airbnb. You could make a killing, he told Noah, with the right decor.

A part of Noah recognized a part of Guy: They each had a little galaxy of sadness in their core, Noah thought. They often sat next to each other at the bar, and Guy would ask him about simple physics problems he'd learned in high school, and Noah would ask him about movies, and what it was like to audition. They never spoke about the real stuff.

When Noah would go home, he would find Eileen sitting on the back patio. Sometimes he'd sit out there with her, talk about work or the election, before going upstairs to bed. She would join him an hour or so later. They passed many months this way.

Grief didn't work the way people thought it did. Noah found that you didn't move through grief linearly, going through whatever stages therapists told you about, and you didn't come to this point where you accepted it and your new life could begin. You weren't deliriously happy and manic, and you weren't desperately sad and sobbing every day. You only survived, in whatever way you could, for as long as you could, until the wound scabbed over a little. Grief was about time, passing time.

Noah saw his new social life, private from his wife, as that—survival. A way to try out a world where he was healed, normal, unencumbered. It had to stay private to be functional. At the bar, Noah was just a guy. Fitting that his best friend there was named Guy.

Early one evening, on a Saturday in June, he returned home from the bar. They had all been there that day, Roman and Stevie and Bria. And Bria had gotten a little sloppy, and she was trying to coax Noah to play darts, and he didn't want to, but finally he relented, and when he did, she kissed him on the jaw, a weird place for a kiss, leaving a streak of magenta lipstick. Noah hadn't noticed. It was so dark in the bar. And when he came home, the door to the back was open, and Eileen was sitting out there. She turned around and looked at him. Then she did something she never did. She got up and walked toward him.

He saw it in her eyes, the lipstick. Not the lipstick exactly, but that Eileen recognized betrayal. She put a hand to his jaw and gently wiped. When she pulled her thumb away, it was magenta.

"It's not . . . it's this bar I was at," Noah said, fumbling.

But she wasn't full of rage, demanding answers. She spoke calmly. "You've been lying to me for months. I'm not stupid. You don't even own real gym clothes."

"But it's just these people," he said. "A bar I go to. I don't even drink that much."

"I smell it on you. Scotch is strong. Other people's perfume. Beer." And then, "I'm not mad. Not about this, whatever you're doing."

"Oh," Noah said. "Then what are you mad about?"

Eileen shook her head and went up to bed. He followed her. They wept next to each other. They hadn't cried together like this in months and months. They cried separately, or at least Noah did. That should have been a sign, he thought. There wasn't a lot of space in their life for the gravity of their combined grief. Lying beside her on the bed, he understood why Eileen was mad. What had happened to them was unfair and permanent. Some piece of their life had been ripped out and now there was a cavern between them. Life was cold and drafty, and also fine and stable. But it wasn't really life. Noah knew Eileen was mad that they had to be separate, that they had to survive at all.

He went back to the bar one more time, to say goodbye to everyone. He made up some reason why, he'd been transferred or was taking on a new project, some reason no one cared about. In the middle of his goodbye, the fire alarm went off. A deafening sound in such a small space. The bartender flipped all the lights on and made everyone go outside. Outside? They hadn't ever been outside together, not out front. But they all spilled out into the strip mall parking lot and squinted under the daylight.

He put his hand on Guy's shoulder. "Thanks, man," Noah said. "For being there for me."

Guy looked confused. "What do you mean?"

Noah didn't know why he said what he said next. He hadn't planned on saying it. "I had a kid, a little girl. She died. I was coming here to, I don't know, not be in that reality."

The look on Guy's face was one Noah had spent months running from, a look he would spend the rest of his life running from. That

crumbled look of pity on a person's face, the inability to relate, the refusal to relate because it was too dangerous.

"No, I mean, it's okay," Noah said. It wasn't okay, of course not.

"Wow" was all Guy said. "Condolences, man."

Then Noah saw that he'd hoped Guy would confess his sadness,
tell Noah he'd done something awful, or that he used to be in prison,
or that his dad had beat him up, or that he'd accidentally run over his
cat. Something unspeakable that would twin Noah's sadness, so Noah
would know there was kinship out there for him.

But Guy didn't say anything. He was just a guy at a bar. And Noah
walked home in the daylight, never to return. The official decision to
divorce didn't come until the fall, but it was all in motion already
then, even if Noah hadn't said it to himself yet. It had been in motion
for a long time. Maybe since the moment Eileen decided to go in the
backyard and Noah decided to go to the bar. Maybe since the second
Serena had died.

Now, in the dark in the bed in Marfa, Noah told Eileen about all of
them, Bria and Stevie and Roman. And also Guy. He had never elabo-
rated before. And now it was sort of funny, how boring and regular
Guy was.

"A struggling actor," Noah said. "A dime a dozen. And I thought he
was my best friend."

Eileen laughed a little. "I never thought you were cheating or anything."

"Why not?"

"I didn't know. But mostly I didn't care. It wouldn't have meant
anything, if you did." She turned over in the bed, facing him now. "I
wasn't thinking of marriage like that then, some sacred covenant you
had to uphold."

"It was all poisoned by then, anyway."

"Exactly."

Now she looked exactly like she had when they first met, the night they spent in that weird Florida motel, giddy from sex, from the idea that they might really like each other, from the tragedy of the explosion in the sky. He wondered if he looked the same to her, or if he felt the same, if it was even possible for her to go back to a time when she could feel how he used to feel.

"Let's go to sleep," Eileen said. "But stay here with me."

He did.

Eileen

In the morning, Eileen woke before Noah. For a few moments she watched him as he slept, a thin line of drool on his pillow, his face soft and slack, exactly like a sleeping Serena used to look. Noah's and Eileen's features had been constant reminders of Serena in that year after her death. Eileen's hair and eye color, Noah's heart-shaped face, the way Eileen frowned, the way Noah was suspicious of everyone until they proved themselves, the timbre of Eileen's laugh. All part of Serena's spirit. For Eileen, it was so much easier when she was not around Noah to let Serena be a person who had gone away. It was why she'd had to leave. And now they were back in a bed, and here was Serena, invisible between them.

Eileen got up and went to the bathroom. In daylight the similarities to the bathroom in their Los Feliz house were obvious. Old 1920s dimensions, a small pink bathtub, a modest pedestal sink, and black and white tiles. But there were a few differences: a modern, low-flush toilet, a narrow window running along the top of two walls. The lumber and paint smell, like it was newly built.

Noah slept soundly and she explored the place. She saw evidence of Maya everywhere. Things Noah never ate in the fridge, like kimchi and Nutella, a mason jar with wildflowers on the table, a shiny black puffer coat with an asymmetrical collar from a French brand, something Eileen pictured an artist wearing. In a room off the end of the galley kitchen she saw what she assumed was Maya's art space.

A massive canvas faced the backyard. Eileen opened the curtains to see it better, and in the early morning light, the painting glowed. It depicted a bright sunset, and everything was sunset-colored, animals that looked like deer or antelope, bounding across a field alive with electric shades of pink and purple. The painting felt sad, though, bright as it appeared. There was violence in the brushstrokes. Eileen reached out to touch it, the thickness of the paint at the end of the stroke, or the beginning.

She didn't notice Noah appear beside her and was startled when he said, "Hey."

She snapped her hand back. "Hey," she said. Noah didn't look well. He was pale in his face.

"Are you all right?" she asked, following him into the kitchen.

"I need coffee."

Eileen pulled herself up to sit on the kitchen counter and swung her legs back and forth. From the look on Noah's face, she knew that what he was seeing in her leg swinging was painful—their youthful past, or Serena. She went still.

"I'm sorry," she said.

He didn't ask for what. "It's weird," he said.

Even though they'd slept in the same bed, they hadn't touched each other, not even a hug. Eileen knew if they had touched each other, she would have started crying, and not stopped for a long time.

"You should meet Nils. And possibly Klein, if he's around. So we're not keeping secrets," Noah said.

"Okay," she said. "And I should stay somewhere else."

He nodded. "Why?"

"I don't know," she said. "There are a lot of ghosts in here."

Eileen stood outside Nils's closed door. She heard some low mumbling but couldn't make out what Noah and Nils were saying. Whatever case Noah was making for her presence, it didn't take long. The door swung open.

"Please, come out of that mess," Nils said, smiling. "Noah says you've wanted to see what we're about here, and I couldn't be more pleased."

She shook his hand. He pushed a stack of paper across the desk at her. "If you wouldn't mind, we'll need this NDA signed, and then we'd be more than happy to put you up here and show you around."

Eileen flipped through the papers, and when she looked back up she saw Nils staring at her, holding a pen out. So she was to sign it now. She took the pen. She didn't want to tell anyone what was happening here, anyway. Look how it had gone with Prem.

"I want to be there when Noah folds," she said. "I want to see it happen."

"Of course," Nils said. "I could use another set of hands. Klein will want to meet you first, but that'll be quick. I'm sure Oliver could arrange that today, actually. We're scheduled for our second fold tomorrow morning. For now, may I show you to the guest suite?"

Noah looked at Eileen, expectant. He hadn't said anything since she'd come into Nils's office. "I'll show you," he said. "It's right next to our place. My place."

Maya, that's what no one was talking about. One wife gone, another come to take her place. That's what Nils must think of her, Eileen thought. Just another woman to keep Noah company, to keep him in line, to keep him from losing his mind.

The guest suite was astonishing in its difference from Noah's living quarters. It was arranged like a hotel suite, with a high, plush bed, all white linens, blackout curtains, a large television, strange corporate carpet, and a bathroom with mini toiletries already provided.

Eileen sat on the bed and looked at Noah, who was inspecting the room. He seemed much more diminished than he had last night. His usually broad shoulders caved, and his face was foggy.

"Noah," she said.

He popped out of the bathroom. "Yeah?"

Yes, Eileen thought. The look in his eyes was fading. "You don't seem well. I'm worried about you."

Noah shrugged. "It's hard on the body. There's a certain amount of radiation exposure."

"Well, how much? I mean, you seem almost sick."

"I'm not sick. I'm tired. It's exhausting."

"So otherwise you feel fine?"

His face hardened. This, an echo of an old fight, one they used to have, one whose outcome was already known. Eileen trying to help Noah, Noah insisting he didn't need help, Eileen saying Noah was angry, Noah angrily insisting he wasn't. One would push, the other would retreat.

"I'm annoyed that you're not taking my word for it," he said.

"Because I'm looking at you and you don't seem well."

"You haven't actually looked at me in years."

"But I know you."

"Do you, Eileen? You used to."

"Oh, so you've completely changed since we were together? Because to me, you seem like you're still caught up in this idea that somehow there's an answer for Serena's death."

Eileen saw then how Noah's face closed up, but beneath the surface, rage boiled. He turned away from her, so she only saw his breath rise and fall in his back, animal-like. He lifted his fist and slammed it onto the wooden surface of the TV console, sending a horrifying crack through the air.

"Noah!" she shouted. She sprang up from the bed and went to him, inspecting the wood.

"It's not fair," he said, calmer now.

"What's not?"

"How easily you accepted it."

Eileen felt her eyes go hot and wet. She turned away. She didn't want him to see how deeply this cut. Moving forward from Serena's death without dying herself was the hardest thing she'd ever done, and it remained difficult every single day. It was also her greatest accomplishment, surviving. There was shame in that, too. Living was not the same as acceptance. And that refusal to accept it, Noah's cross, was just as awful as what he'd accused her of doing.

But something had come loose. From the console, that is. A photograph, face down on the carpet below where Noah had slammed his fist. Eileen picked it up. It was of a woman and a man, a woman with long red hair, mixed race, freckles across her nose. The man was white, dark hair, tall and thin, hugging the woman from behind. The faint outline of a frame's indent lined the photograph.

Noah took the photograph from Eileen's hands. Briefly their fingertips touched. She inhaled, expecting electricity, but she felt nothing.

"That's her," Noah said.

"Who?"

He took out his phone and furiously typed. Then he showed her a page of Google Images, all of a woman with long red hair and the same bright smile as in the photograph. The search words at the top, "Talia Bolson."

"Who's Talia Bolson?"

Noah looked around the room like it was listening to them. He ran his hands along the baseboards. He felt behind the TV.

"What are you doing?" Eileen said, hissing more than she wanted to.

She watched as Noah took out his wallet, dumped it on the bed, and snatched a penny from the pile. He used the penny to unscrew the light switch panel.

"Noah, please. Say something."

"Wait a second." The panel came off in his hands and behind it were two metal brackets and a series of wires, and behind that, a light glowing faintly red. "Look."

Eileen looked over his shoulder. "I don't know what I'm looking at."

Noah switched the light off. The faint red glow disappeared just as the recessed lights in the ceilings went out. "That light behind the switch, it's a camera, somehow wired to the lights. Or some kind of recording device. But it looks like a camera light. I noticed this when Klein's assistant turned off the light switch during a meeting, right before they told me what the Janus Project was about."

Eileen recoiled. "They're recording you? Us?"

Noah turned to her. "They must be. This woman is Talia Bolson. I found her business card in Nils's office, hidden in a picture frame. And now this photo. They've never mentioned her, but she clearly has to do with the Janus Project."

"Did you ask?"

Noah shook his head. "I don't know if they'd tell me, anyway. I think we should try to find her."

"You think she knows something?"

"They said an entire team of researchers were 'released' from their jobs before I got here. Many people must have helped make this lab, but they don't want me to know what happened to them."

Eileen felt disappointment heavy in her chest. Of course there had been an entire team, and of course there were secrets that Noah ignored in his quest to believe.

"How many secrets are they keeping from you?" she asked.

He shook his head. "I don't know. But if she's one of the secrets, I want to know why."

They might make you a secret, Eileen thought but didn't say. Noah looked so overwhelmed that she didn't want to pile more on him. "So, there *is* something going on," she said.

"I think so. With the project. But there's nothing going on with me, Eileen."

"You *are* the project, Noah."

He took his time screwing the panel back into the wall. Eileen sat on the bed, her knees up to her chest. She didn't want to stay here, but she couldn't leave Noah, not with him like this, looking like the gears inside him were slowly winding down, while he spun, frantic to stop it. This reminded her of how he'd been right after Serena's death, gutted and unable to accept that there might not be an answer for the problem of their tragedy.

Noah joined Eileen on the bed. "Keep the lights off," he said. "I have a lamp you can use."

She was pulled so tightly against herself that she was mouth-to-knees. "You know," she said, "it's not that I accepted it. I just kept going on. At some point, that's what you do."

Noah stared at the penny in his hands, turning it over and over.

Eileen kept speaking. "Sometimes it's like it happened yesterday. I could go to that reality every day if I wanted to. It's always there, in memory. Her death. But I chose to build a house around it, and make a key, and then put the key in a pocket, and I don't usually reach for that key. That's okay. I'm not a bad person. I'm just living."

Noah said what Eileen had already asserted: "I know." He did know.

A truth they shared, even if the way they dealt with that truth was so different. She felt his shoulder soften against her on the bed, a slight lean. He needed her. She'd follow him into the house he'd built, inside which was a black hole where he insisted there were answers. Then she'd walk him out. She put her hand over his, closing the penny beneath their fists.

Maya

Her mother wanted to make a big American breakfast for Maya when she woke, but Maya said she wasn't hungry, that her body was still on Marfa time. She had traveled so far, strapped into a plane as it crossed time zones and an ocean, and she was tired and wary of everything— the familiarity, the unfamiliarity, what it meant that she had come back here. She felt like she had to see Ren, the lit fuse that sparked her here in the first place, before she unraveled everything else.

She told her parents she needed to go for a walk, and texted Ren the moment she left the apartment.

I'll meet you in Nakameguro at the first bridge by the station.

In the text exchange before that, she'd told him she bought a ticket and he'd sent back a photo of the ramen he was eating, cloudy broth, jammy egg, a mound of green onion.

Nakameguro was neutral ground, neither her neighborhood nor his, a place they'd both have to journey to. Leaning against the first bridge closest to the station, she briefly wondered if she was setting herself up. If she'd convinced herself she was starring in a romantic comedy, waiting under these cherry trees at dusk for a wealthy, successful ex-boyfriend while thousands of miles away her estranged husband fell deeper into a project she couldn't explain. But when she turned and saw Ren, she knew, no, she hadn't set herself up at all. She'd stripped away all the bullshit, peeling back everything so that only the fuse remained, and she touched her finger to the spark.

And there he was. Maya wanted to memorize what he was wearing: a mid-length slate overcoat, a cobalt button-down, light Japanese denim pants, drawstring, a little loose, artist pants. His shoes were beige slip-ons with thick soles, his black hair with a little wave over the left side of his forehead. He looked expensive and he was still handsome, the kind of smooth-skinned-no-problems handsome that should have been a red flag from the beginning, the sign that he would be the one to break her heart and not the other way around. Men that handsome lived in a world just beyond.

They laughed before they embraced, and they embraced before they spoke.

"You've teleported," he said.

"Yes," she said.

"I didn't think you'd actually come. But I'm glad you did. Is this weird? It's weird we've never been in Japan together, right? I mean, it feels like we have."

He held out his bent elbow and she slid her arm through. They strolled, arms locked like a couple who had nowhere to be, and not like ex-lovers who hadn't touched since she'd sobbed at his doorstep halfway around the world.

"It does feel like we've been here together," she said. The main drag was full of shops carrying expensive draped clothes in one size only, bars with picture windows framing other people's dates. Café lights were strung up along the river that divided the street, and the spotlit cherry trees leaned over the sidewalk. In spring, this walk was something else, pink petals falling like snow. Now, in late fall seeping into early winter, it was emptier, chilly and damp in the after-rain.

"Let's pretend we've walked this street together already," he said.

"That sounds like a relief," she said.

"I haven't been down here in a very long time."

"Moves to Ebisu, forgets there are other cool neighborhoods."

"Oh, not at all. Ebisu is much hipper, which you of course know. This place, well, it's quaint. Nice choice."

"You have a touch of my mother's condescension, and frankly, it's impressive."

They talked like this for almost an hour, easy and light. She steered him to a yakitori place, where they ordered the strangest meat on the menu and all the dipping sauces. The place was full of men smoking, and their smoke coated her hair, and she knew it would take days to get that smell out, but she didn't even care. It wasn't that there was electricity between her and Ren, but a well-worn familiarity with each other, deep grooves they fit into without effort.

Ren liked living back in Tokyo, he said. And though they'd talked on the phone while she was in Marfa, he gave her a brief history of his life since they'd last seen each other. He recapped his rise to art stardom with refreshing self-awareness, how his work at the time—those angry masculine collages—was exactly the kind of dirty, messy aesthetic the art world wanted. How his multimedia approach—still images with sculptures growing out of them, or images that melted into video installation—was also a kind of pandering, calling out the medium while benefiting from it. All of that, he said, made him feel bad, but it had brought him so much success.

"You looked good on the cover of *Artforum*," Maya said, not without flirtation. He smiled: *Sure, that, too.* Anyway, after the Whitney he worked with a big pop singer for a while (no, they didn't sleep together), and then a hip-hop artist bought almost everything he made as soon as he made it, which was exciting but then became boring. And then there was his gallery owner's sexual harassment scandal, so Ren cut ties, and then his most recent trip to Art Basel was soul-crushing, with gallery girls and art dealers all acting like investment bankers and tech bros, which, he realized, was what the art world had become. What it always had been. He felt like a cad, a commodity, selling himself to the world's richest, becoming rich himself. A closed loop.

"I didn't want to do any of the stuff that *looked* easy anymore. I know I made it seem easy, and that was part of the point, but it wasn't easy, ultimately, and I'm not sure why I made it look that way. Do you know what I mean?" he asked, leaning over the steaming meat. "I want it to look as difficult as it is."

She nodded. "I know what you mean. I don't think it's bad to be in this transitional phase. You started making art when we were young and poor, and now you're neither, and it makes sense that your interests would change. That your source would have to be different."

"My source," he says. "Yeah. I don't know what that is right now, but I sure do like being somewhere where I think differently because I have to speak differently. My brain changes when I go to the grocery store. I say different phrases to the clerk, I get that agreeable, sing-songy thing, you know?"

"Oh, I know. Women have it worse here. I practically have to sing a lullaby to buy a train ticket."

He laughed. "So what about you? I know about the pronghorn paintings, but what about your work in general?"

When people asked her that question, she usually recoiled. But when Ren asked it, her whole body flushed. Not many people, not even Noah, knew her as Ren had known her, obsessive about making art and talking about art and being an artist. After their breakup, she felt like she grew up a little, saw who got to do art for a living (Ren) and who had to figure out some other way to live (her). But now, here, she got to be that twenty-six-year-old again, struggling and open and excited by everything. He still thought of her this way; she could hear it in his question, the possessive, *your* work. She tried, for several seconds, to think up a good answer. She stalled by chewing on some meat. But then she settled on telling the truth.

"The pronghorn paintings—that *is* my work. After you and I broke up, it was hard for me to go back to doing the sort of stuff I was doing when we were together. My belief system fell apart after we broke up. So I got sucked into a graduate program, which we always made fun of, so much talking about art instead of doing it. But I was good at it, actually. I liked it. But then I met Noah, and when we got married, my life, whatever trajectories were available to me, they narrowed. Not his fault, I don't think. When you have a life with someone, a grown-up life, it's hard to wander. I got a job that made sense, in development at a museum—I know, I know. I quit it, don't worry. But Noah's life is results-focused, and I never have results."

Ren was listening, kindly, attentively. "So that's what it's come down to, results?"

"Doesn't everything? I mean, you work on a piece, you show it to someone, a gallery hangs it, you sell it. That's a result. The piece itself is even a result. I don't have results. I have, like, vectors. Pointing toward ideas."

"I don't want to be oriented toward results anymore. That's why I'm here, removed from all that. I need to figure out what I do that isn't about external validation and money and write-ups."

"But making stuff is about sharing it with people."

"That's different. That's . . ." Ren searched for the word. "Well, I don't know what that is. I'll figure that out."

Maya looked down at her hands. "Do I sound pathetic? I still work on things, I do, but the obstacles start to become cumulative, instead of consecutive. When I was younger, I could slay dragons no problem. Now, I don't know. It's exhausting."

"Maya, I know," Ren said, reaching across the table to place his palm on top of her hand. "I remember everything."

After they'd broken up, she spent what felt like years diminishing all their memories. That was the real tragedy with a breakup like the one they'd had—one that felt earthquake-like in its change—there was so much between them, so many specific *things*, and yes, everyone had *things*, but now those things were Maya's alone to remember, to keep, to decide not to keep, to unremember. A short road trip they'd taken down the wild Oregon coast in winter, sandy and damp, feeling like vigilantes on the vast, empty beaches. How when she moved out of her studio to move in with him, he painted the outlines of their bodies on the walls. She'd repainted over it alone, slowly, sadly. That he called her "little chimp" because of the sounds she made while talking in her sleep. The time a woman in a grocery store overheard him calling her that and whispered, "Let me know if you need help." Years of small things, stupid things, embarrassing things. And the painful things, too. When he got word about the Whitney, and sat down on the floor of the kitchen, staring at his phone, speechless, and she'd had to plaster a smile on her face even though she knew—she knew it but wouldn't admit for months—that it was over then.

After the breakup, she'd remembered as many moments as she could first without trying, and then by trying, so as not to let go of him. And then she found she remembered them enough times that they lost their power, were just faint outlines etched on the walls of her brain, and though they were a part of her, they were not screaming inside her anymore. It took a while. It had never occurred to her that he was doing the same.

But the look on Ren's face now said so. It contained all that time, both the togetherness and the absence. She saw it flickering across his face, how he'd been sad, too. She hadn't been able to see that before. Maybe it had taken a while for him to understand the loss. Maybe it had taken her a while to be able to see it.

Maya felt dizzy, nauseated by the dislocation between parts of the past and here, now, a tiny, loud, smoky yakitori restaurant in a Tokyo neighborhood neither of them lived in, thousands of miles and an ocean away from her husband. It was overwhelming in her body, the multitude, all the selves she'd been, her failures and desires, the way she had loved Ren, the way she loved Noah now.

It was so much that it forced her from her seat, and she mumbled an apology and hurried outside.

A minute later Ren followed, holding her jacket. He placed it around her shoulders.

"I'm so sorry, the smoke in there," she said, and he nodded but didn't say anything.

They walked slowly, not touching, in the direction of the train station. At this hour, in this posh area, there was barely anyone out on the street, no din except for the sound of the river gurgling below them.

Finally, Ren said, "Your husband. Is he getting his results?"

"I don't know. Not in the way he expected, I don't think."

"Then in what way?"

"In a way that requires him to be alone, I guess."

"So this is his doing, the separation?"

"No. Not entirely."

"You needed to be alone, too."

"I needed to be apart from him to figure out what I need."

"Mm," Ren said, a sound of understanding.

Maya was sad then, describing the separation. It felt pathetic, in some way, to not know what she needed. But then she remembered what Ren had said, that he also didn't know. He was here in Tokyo trying to figure out his own path. Maybe that's why she'd come to Japan, to be around someone who was in a state of rearranging his life.

She did the thing their bodies had been moving toward all night. She grabbed Ren's hand and held it. He held hers back. It felt good, purely good, Maya thought. But only for a moment, until Noah's face came blaring back into her brain. She loved Noah. But she also loved the way she felt with Ren, reverting to a version of herself that was freer. More stupid, beautifully stupid.

She guessed it all came down to hope, being able to have hope for the future when you were young, before the world let you down in all sorts of ways.

Between their palms, a warm, dark space, tingling with atoms of possibility, like a star about to be born.

"We're walking toward Ebisu," Ren said. "Do you want to come see my place?"

Maya stopped walking. They turned to face each other. "Not yet," she said.

"Is seeing places allowed in the rules of your separation?"

She shrugged. "I think so. But still, not yet."

"Okay," he said.

"I want to stay in this part of things."

"I get it," he said.

He didn't ask which part of things, but if he had, she would have said the part where she didn't have to be someone's daughter, someone's employee, someone's wife. She wasn't even Ren's ex-girlfriend here. She was a person he knew, holding his hand, walking from nowhere to nowhere, landing nowhere. She could live in the prickling, swirling place of becoming.

Noah

Noah worried that having Eileen in Building D would be distracting, but when the time came for his second fold, he found it comforting. Seeing her through the window at the control panel with Nils, he was calm. Somehow it all made sense, a burden lifted from his shoulders.

"Echo Injection," Nils said into the microphone.

Noah slid the needle into his vein without a wince or a blink. Then he undressed mechanically, as he'd done many times in this room, with new awareness that Eileen was looking. He climbed into the black water without making eye contact. He closed the top and he was alone.

He heard Nils marking the session with the date and attempt number while he attached the electrodes. Then, "Engaging the core." Noah heard the core rumble behind his head, and then he felt warmth come through his neck, bloom through his body.

"Beginning the resonance program."

Noah dropped out of time.

"Regulating the energy cycle. Ten, nine, eight . . ."

Everything began to inscribe itself again, like a pencil drawing. He breathed in.

* *•* *•* *.*

Look up.

Noah lifts his head and opens his eyes. He's standing outside Building D, about to enter, no one else in sight. His heart starts to pound as the familiarity butts up against the strangeness, but he focuses on a spot on the floor to quiet it. Then he opens the door, and he's in this world. Not *his* world, but this one.

This time he walks more slowly than before. He turns toward Nils's office and looks up, the brilliant blue sky like a painting above him. He watches the sky, a bird slicing through the blue, until it becomes real. It is real. He slips through the space next to Klein's house and comes around the back.

The chrome box is in the brush and dirt, exactly where it was before, where Nils left it. He goes to the box, kneels, and looks at his watch: 9:07. He's gotten here earlier this time, having subdued the panic of his first fold. He looks down at the box, the lock, all of it shining in the sunlight. Then up at the wall of windows that is Klein's house. He sees his reflection again, crouched.

So he stands. He watches himself do it. Like being actualized in this new timeline, his body, his consciousness from another timeline inhabiting it. This is his body. No, this is his body somewhere else. No, some*time* else. The paradox sits comfortably inside him.

The window is a mirror with the low morning sun blasting the surface. He walks toward it. He can clearly see the reflection of his body, the specific movements of his long legs, the way his left foot pigeons slightly in. But when it comes to his face, it's just a black hole, shadowed.

He glances at his watch: 9:12, a few more minutes until the box unlocks. He approaches the window, until there are only a few inches between his nose and the glass. He can almost make out shapes on the other side. He should get back to the box, the lock, his mission, but instead he presses his nose against the glass, and a scene emerges. The huge inside wall of Klein's living room. Noah can see the speckles and veining on the quartz—it was quartz? He doesn't remember observing that before. And standing at the edge of the wall, Klein himself, dressed as if for a workout, in sweat-wicking shorts and a shirt, and beside him, Oliver, in a suit. They're looking right at him. Noah's heart jumps, but he doesn't move. Klein holds up a hand and gives a wave. Oliver ducks away.

They're watching him. Noah pulls his face away from the glass and it's like a seal closes up between him and the inside of Klein's place. What time is it? It's 9:15. He turns and starts toward the box, but then turns back. Klein was watching him. Why? Has that always been part of the process? Noah doesn't remember. It's hard to hold on to memories from the other timeline.

So he turns back, to look at the window, and this time Noah thinks he can see both scenes: the beautiful, wild outside, blue and blond and green and white; and the stark inside, a flicker of Klein's face coming through the mottle of a cloud reflection in the glass. Like seeing two ways at once.

And then, with a startle that feels like it ruptures through his torso, he sees in the glass a pronghorn. A long, thin face, streaked with black, velvet ears pointing up to the sky. The pronghorn lifts its head and looks right at Noah, the Noah in the glass, and somehow it is dizzying, being seen by the animal, being seen in two directions.

Noah turns his face back toward the box, the pronghorn, but it's as if it's happening in slow motion. A dizzying nausea filters up through his feet, his legs, his hips, and he looks down and the ground is no longer there. He thinks, *Oh, shit*, and then he's—

Coughing. He coughed water and slammed the button inside the bath and threw his body outside it, onto the hard floor, knees crunching yet again, choking water. On his hands and knees, he gagged, and his hands slipped, and his head hit the floor, and everything went black.

When he woke, he was outside the meditation room, propped up on the floor near the controls, wrapped in a robe, looking at the concerned faces of Eileen and Nils.

"Fuck, Noah," Eileen said.

"Perfectly normal," Nils said. "Not great, but normal. Soon you'll be able to stay in it longer."

"Water," Noah said, and Nils handed him a bottle. He drained it, and Nils handed him another. Noah was so thirsty, and the water felt like a lifeline to this timeline.

"Explain," Nils said. "Your vitals were unsteady for much of that fold."

Noah explained as best he could. He said he got there early, having moved much more calmly than last time, and so he walked around. But this time he saw a pronghorn next to the box, and it startled him, and he fell out. He omitted the part about seeing inside Klein's house.

"You fell out," Eileen repeated.

"Of time," Noah said. "I have to be on an even keel to be able to stay there. No sudden movements or unexpected emotions. The animal scared me."

Nils was frowning, but he said, "All good, brother. We'll try again day after tomorrow. Get some more memory training in, and we'll try again. The more unexpected events you can prepare for, the better."

How do I prepare for unexpected events? Noah wondered. But he nodded. He looked at Eileen, whose face was scrunched up with worry and suspicion. She knew he wasn't telling the full truth.

After they'd cleaned up, Noah walked Eileen back to her guest suite. Inside, he turned off the light switch and told her.

"They were watching you?" she said.

"Klein waved at me."

"Maybe he likes to observe his subjects."

"It's not that he was watching. It's that no one told me. It makes me think they're watching me always." Noah looked around the dimmed room. "How do they not know everything? How are they okay with you here? It's almost like Nils expected it, for you to come, for Maya to leave."

Eileen felt his forehead. He was clammy, but not hot. "You don't have a fever, but you're very pale."

"You saw how hard it is on my body."

She pressed her lips together. He recognized this, her move when she was trying not to say something. But she always said it, anyway. "I don't think it should be this hard on the body."

Noah shook his head. Eileen had no idea. "You need to try it. You have to."

"Not yet," she said, in a small voice. Her voice was rarely small. She was drawing back from him.

"What do you mean, not yet?"

"I mean, I don't know if I want to."

"Eileen, come on."

"Come on what? I'm here, aren't I? I left my life, my boyfriend, to come make sure you're okay—"

"You didn't come for just that. You came to see, you know you did. Because you miss her, too, and this way you can see her and hear her."

Eileen's body stiffened. He'd gone too far. He might as well go further, but he lowered his voice. "Do you think," he said. "Do you think if we went back and put one of those baby vitals monitoring devices in the room—"

"Noah," she said, a warning.

"—then we'd see if she was struggling to breathe in the night—"

"We wouldn't have seen. She wasn't displaying symptoms like that."

"—or just taken her to the goddamn doctor—"

"The doctor wouldn't have checked for this condition."

"But we could—"

"Noah!" Eileen shouted. "You said you can't effect change when you go back."

"But my consciousness is temporarily inside that timeline. If I planted the idea, if I wrote instructions down, if I told someone, maybe I could."

She sighed. "And then what? Those versions of ourselves would have her?"

"Yes, those versions."

"But if all of this is true, then doesn't some version of us have her? She lived, we stayed together. She lived, we didn't stay together. She lived, we stayed together, but were unhappy."

"She lived, we stayed together, and were happy," Noah said.

"Yeah, that version, too."

They didn't say anything for a while. The light from the windows was dimming and Eileen was becoming a shadow, backlit against the window of the suite.

"You would get to save her," Eileen said. "That's what you're saying. You'd get to do the thing you didn't get to do."

Noah's throat flushed hot. Yes, that was it. He squeezed his eyes shut and heard her, Serena, her voice, chattering away in her room, the door closed. She liked to narrate conversations between her dolls and her Legos, entities from two different universes. The dolls would have to teach the Lego people how to drive cars, and the Lego people would have to teach the dolls how to build houses. Both constructing their separate realities.

"Just say it's about you," Eileen said. "It's not about Serena. She's gone."

.   .   .

Later, in the middle of the night, when everyone else was asleep, Noah returned to Building D. But this time, again, he folded by himself.

Look up.

He gasps.

Look up.

"Hey, dummy, look up."

He looks up. Esther and Mike and Victor and Diane. He had a crush on Esther. He suddenly knows this, or re-knows this. A crush that evaporated the moment he met Eileen. Eileen. His eyes dart around, looking for her.

"You missed it," Esther says.

"What did I miss?" he asks. His own voice sounds different. Slower.

"The plane. Flying the sign? 'The end of this world,' it said."

He's on the hill for the rocket launch, the day the Europa disaster happened in front of his eyes, the day he met Eileen. But none of that has happened yet. He's with his friends from college, Stanford friends, all of them wildly smart and young. He must be young, too. He looks down at his hands, unlined.

Noah has the distinct sensation of being wet, especially on his back, and he reaches his hand back to check, bending his elbow awkwardly. Nothing. He has an itch on his neck, and when he touches it, he knows that if he scratches it, he will scratch all over his body, and it won't stop. He shakes his head, rolls out his shoulders.

"Hey," Esther says quietly, hand on his arm. "Are you okay?"

"I got hot," he says. He smiles at her. It is good to see her again, but he can't tell her that. "It's so hot."

"Here." She grabs a water bottle from the backpack next to her. "Stay hydrated, Noah. We have dinner reservations."

"That's not so bad, is it?" Mike says. "The end of *this* world."

Mike's trying to get Diane's attention, but Diane's deep in a textbook chapter on cell biology, cramming for when they get back. This he remembers. How Mike always pined for Diane, and Diane never seemed to notice. Where is Diane now? She works for the president, he heard.

No, that was not now. This is now.

"Shouldn't be too much longer," Victor says in a booming voice. He is behind Noah, and Noah jumps a little at the sound. "You zoned out there. Zone in instead. Try that."

Esther laughs. Victor is her boyfriend. The pieces falling into place, the memories of how they all fit, make a satisfying pop in Noah's brain.

"How'd that plane even get flying clearance?" Victor wonders.

Noah scans the area where he remembers Eileen and her friends sitting, but nothing stands out. Could it be a different spot he's remembering?

"Zone *in*, Noah," Esther says.

"I'm here, I'm here." Noah holds up his hands. He takes a swig from the water bottle. "Sorry."

Now Esther is leaning back into Victor, and Mike is trying to close Diane's textbook and she's fighting back, and then Noah sees her. Eileen. She's sitting in a different area, in the line of sight behind Mike and Diane. She throws her head back and laughs, yes, this all happened. Her hair is long and straight down her back, not up in a bun as he remembered. And she's wearing a blue shirt, gold Berkeley shorts, her long legs pulled up against her body.

He doesn't see her this early, though. That's not how it happens. He doesn't see her until after the explosion. This discordant thought throws him out of the fold.

He's back in it now, fighting the nausea working its way up his body. It's too much, he knows, to do consecutive folds like this, but there's something he wants to see.

The disaster has just happened. Some people scatter, but not Noah and his friends. And not Eileen and her friends. Some people take pictures. Some people cry a little. No one was injured, but it was sad, to watch a dream go up in flames. Esther narrates the whole experience. She was always unable to sit in silence. Noah nods and smiles at her. Mike wonders if they should go to a bar instead of dinner. He and Victor start looking at a paper map. Diane calls her mother to tell her she's okay. All of this is as he remembers.

And then Victor stumbles onto a friend. "Joey?" he calls, and someone on Eileen's blanket hollers back.

Chemistry majors from Berkeley. They all introduce themselves, and the names fly out of Noah's brain as quickly as people say them, except for when Eileen steps forward. She's lankier than he remembered, tanned skin, hair lighter than it was later in their relationship. Her face is angular, even in her youth, and she conveys an intimidating certainty.

"Eileen," she says, holding her hand up in a wave. Like Klein had done on the other side of the window.

He falls out.

Back in, but they're drinking now. At the bar for tourists that abuts the overcrowded beach. Eileen brings him a frozen daiquiri and he looks down at the blue slush, bewildered.

"You asked for this," she says, laughing a little. "Are you that drunk already?"

He won't learn how to drink until graduate school. In college, he still wants things sweet and strong.

"Yes," Noah says finally.

Around them, people are pairing off. Mike is talking too loudly to a crowd that includes Diane, but Diane keeps looking around absentmindedly. One day, three years after graduation, Mike and Diane will sleep together after a wedding, and when Diane wakes up regretting it, Mike will come to Noah and Eileen's hotel room and sob, but after that, he will finally be able to let Diane go.

Victor and Esther are quietly pawing each other in a corner, talking softly between kissing, Victor's hand around Esther's waist, Esther heavy-lidded from drinking. Noah thinks this should be upsetting him, watching it, having to suppress a crush on his friend's girlfriend, a girl who is so smart it bowls him over—why should Victor get to have that? Victor is smart, but stupid in his life, not arranging it so as to become smarter. He is gifted naturally, and it annoys everyone around him. It's okay, Noah tells himself. Victor will marry Esther, and they will have a child, and then they will divorce, which Noah and Eileen will find out from a holiday letter in which they explain exactly why, how they married too young, how they needed to grow into the people they wanted to be without the hindrance of anyone else.

Not like us, Noah and Eileen will say when they get the letter. They throw it away. They're still child-free at that point, self-satisfied.

Around them at the bar, Eileen's Berkeley friends start to tell her they're heading out. Eileen declines rides, nods at Noah, and his fingertips tingle. She wants to stay with him. She wants to keep talking. Maybe they'll make out.

Fuck, he's drunk. Eileen's face slips a little in his vision, like part of it is melting away. He hasn't prepared for being drunk in a fold.

He's falling out, but before he does, he puts his hand on Eileen's chin and kisses her, her lips against his, his tongue meeting hers for two seconds, a line of desire burning through his throat—

Was that cheating? He felt ill, like later he would be very sick, but he shoved it down and restarted the machine.

This time, after they've had sex in the motel room, the one he pays cash for, the white obliteration of their orgasms still pulsing through their veins, they fall apart. She unsticks herself from him. She has so much experience and control, it's obvious to Noah, and it makes him want to do it again, immediately, so as to know more of her. He settles for burying his face in her hair, which smells like sunscreen.

But she starts talking right away. "I think you're not a biology major," she says, pulling the blanket up under her breasts.

"Chemistry, then?"

She laughs. "Gross."

"Esther's a chem major. It's notoriously difficult. At least at Stanford."

"Please," Eileen says. "Chem makes people jump off bridges at my school."

"So what am I, then? A religion major?"

Eileen turns on her side and props herself up on an elbow. The way Noah's self here in Florida can barely restrain himself from touching her and the way Noah decades from now in Marfa feels nothing but sadness and tenderness toward her are crashing against each other. Noah tries to tamp it down, the dichotomy. It will pull him out if he doesn't contain it.

"I think you're a physics major. Quantum mechanics."

"I don't even like physics," Noah says.

"But you are drawn toward big, unanswerable questions."

"Am I?"

"See what I mean? You want to get in on quantum physics. You can linger in the uncertainty. It's the only thing that looks at the invisible and the macro at once. Like you."

"How are you so sure you know what I'm like?"

She pokes him in the chest with a finger, a little too hard. "I know what you're made of."

No, this is not what he came here for. This is how it happened. This feels pleasant, satisfying, exactly as it happened, happening again.

Noah gathers himself as if about to scream. But all he says is:

"I have something to tell you. I've come from the future, about twenty-three years in the future. You and I stay together, for a long time. We get married, go to graduate school, I work for JPL, you get the best university job there is, super cushy, and for many years we're happy."

Eileen starts to laugh. "See, physics—"

But Noah cuts her off. He can't stop now. "We travel, have lots of sex, and then we have a little less sex, but we are still very happy. We buy a house in L.A., which we never think we will do, because we both love it up north so much, but we accumulate a life down there. Then we decide to have a child. Later than all our friends, who have all written us off as people who will be smug and well rested forever. We aren't sure that we've done the right thing, not until she's born. Her name is Serena. I don't know if I should tell you that. If it matters. She's perfect. I mean, she's colicky at first, doesn't sleep for, like, a year, even though we hire a sleep consultant."

Eileen's face. She isn't laughing anymore. She looks worried.

"And then, right before she turns four, she dies. She has this heart condition but it doesn't present in the way it normally does, maybe because of her age. Or maybe we missed it. But the doctors say it wasn't our fault. It comes on quick and then in the middle of the night she stops breathing. They say you're out of the danger zone of that happening after a year. They're wrong, though. I guess as a parent you're never out of the danger zone. Anyway, we divorce about a year later. Whatever we had, we'd remade it around Serena, and the structure of our relationship can't sustain the center dropping out. It's a bad divorce. I mean, there are worse divorces, but we aren't friends at the end of it. We can't be. I think—I'm sorry, I don't mean to say this to make you mad—but I think you heal from the grief better than me. But I get married again. To a really wonderful woman. You're happy, too, I think. I'm not sure, actually. I should ask you. But what I mean to say is that, I guess, does any of this make a difference? Do you hear me?"

At first Noah thinks Eileen is stunned. Her face doesn't move. She doesn't move. Outside he can hear time passing, the not-too-far surf crashing on a beach, the low din of people still out drinking at this hour, making bad choices. But then her face breaks. A horrible expression, terror and sadness and disbelief and Noah doesn't even know what else. She backs away from him on the bed and almost falls off. Then she turns over.

"Eileen?" he says quietly. "I'm so sorry."

A quick, low sob escapes her, or at least Noah thinks it does. But then she turns back to him, and her face is normal, placid, a little amused. She scoots closer to him. She lifts her hand, points her finger, and shoves it into his bare chest. Like nothing's happened. Like it never happened.

"I know what you're made of," she says. "Physics, that's it. That's what you'll do."

Eileen

She and Noah drove through a storm to find Talia Bolson. Eileen had already located her. It wasn't hard. She did some light googling and found Talia's husband, an English teacher who once taught at Berkeley High. Curtis Bolson. She found a couple of old addresses for them, called a few numbers, but the leads dried up around five years ago. But Eileen knew someone who knew someone at Berkeley High. Prem.

She texted him, unable to bring herself to call him just yet. He texted back right away, all business. Yes, he would ask his friend. And then, an hour later, *Don't run away.*

I'm not running away, she texted back.

I think you're too good at running away not to realize that's what you're doing.

Eileen didn't respond.

Prem texted again, *You have a life here.*

I know, she wrote. *But my old life is here, too.*

That wasn't really true, she knew. Her old life was nowhere, now that Serena was gone. Location not found.

A half hour later Prem responded with the forwarding address Berkeley High had for Curtis Bolson.

Thank you, she texted, and he didn't reply.

Alone in the guest suite, lights off, she tried to fall asleep, but Prem's diagnosis lingered: She was good at running away. Had she done that to Noah? She'd thought of leaving him as self-preservation. But had she made a mistake, leaving him, letting him swirl in the grief? Had she tried enough? Had she tried at all? To do what, even?

That was what it came down to, she thought as she began to fall asleep. It's impossible to grieve with someone. It's personal and isolating, grief. We're all alone in it, she thought.

The address was in El Paso. Where Eileen had just been. She and Noah could drive there this morning. When she knocked on his door and explained, he agreed to go along, even though he looked much worse than the day before. He admitted he'd thrown up a few times in the night and couldn't eat, but said ultimately he was fine. Effects of the time bath, he said.

He fell asleep in the car the first hour, and Eileen watched the storm get closer and closer. The clouds were black. Noah slept like a child next to her.

She remembered now, driving toward this storm, how they had been children when they met, after the Europa explosion. Noah was young and skinny with lots of nearly black hair. He kept glancing at the girl next to him, who Eileen would later know as Esther. How had she not seen this group before, so close to her blanket, this kid who seemed both eager and shy, both anxious and charming?

Her instincts were right. They usually were, but she didn't know it then. At the bar he'd proven himself to be smart but not showy, attentive but not overly so, tipsy but within bounds. She'd decided after the

first drink that she would sleep with him, and after they slept together, she briefly worried that it was more than a one-night stand.
She was serious about her studies, about biology, about getting the right
placements and internships and lab opportunities and grad schools,
and a guy like Noah at another school across the bay would screw all
that up.

In the end, it wasn't up to her. He showed up at her dorm, she let
him in. She thought of the disaster as a cleaving moment, after which
was the time of Noah.

Now, in the middle of the storm, Eileen was temporarily blinded,
and she slammed on the brakes. Noah startled.

"It's okay," she said, turning the windshield wipers as high as they
could go. "Trying to get through this."

They didn't speak for the duration of the storm, which was intense
but short, rain blurring the windshield, headlights weak in the sudden
midmorning darkness. Noah stayed awake, looking out at the road with
Eileen.

When they came out of it, she said, "We should tell Talia how we
met. She might get a kick out of that, and it'll open her up to talking
to us."

Eileen had been able to give Curtis a call, a heads-up, and say they
were old friends of his Berkeley High colleague and were in town and
had some questions about Talia's work with the Klein Michaels Foundation. It was a shot in the dark, since Eileen didn't even know how
Talia was connected to this, but it worked. Curtis was hesitant at first,
but Eileen insisted they'd only take up an hour of their time, and he
relented.

But Noah perked up when Eileen mentioned their origin story. "You
were thinking about the Europa disaster?"

"I was, yeah."

She could tell he was practically vibrating in his seat. He still didn't look well, and he hadn't eaten anything that she'd seen today, but this seemed to light some fire in him. "I have to tell you something."

Noah explained what he'd done the night before, that he'd gone back to operate the fold by himself. A tricky thing to do, he admitted, requiring him to move fast, which meant his temporal locks weren't as solid, which meant he kept falling out of the fold and having to re-initiate.

"That's why you're sick," Eileen said, putting it together. "How many times did you do it?"

He shrugged. "Doesn't matter. What I wanted to say was that I went back to that day. The Europa disaster. I met you again. We had the whole night."

She let a silence settle between them. He'd gone back and lived it. They'd fallen for each other, got drunk, slept together. She felt a blast of discomfort, like he'd taken advantage of her, but that feeling vanished when she looked over at his face. He wasn't lost in the reverie of the memory. He looked worried.

"What did you do?" Eileen asked.

"I tried to change things. I tried to tell you the truth, where I was from, about Janus and Klein and the life we lived. I told you about Serena."

"You told me about Serena?"

"In bed, after we were together. You thought I was joking at first, but then, I don't know. It was like you melted away, you couldn't handle it, and you went right back."

"Went right back to what?"

"To what actually happened. When you told me I should major in physics because I was after big, unanswerable questions, and physics was a place where I could linger in uncertainty. But it was like a glitch, whatever I was trying to do; the timeline wouldn't alter, wouldn't adjust."

The timeline wouldn't alter. He sounded crazy, Eileen knew.

"That's not what I told you. I said you should major in physics because there's a theory for everything. You were demanding answers after the explosion. You couldn't sit in the uncertainty. I felt like that's why you wanted to sleep with me, because it was an act that would, I don't know, produce a result."

"A result? Jesus, Eileen."

"You know what I mean."

He was quiet. A sign passed, thirty-six miles to El Paso.

"So I remembered it wrong," he said.

Eileen shrugged. "I don't know. Who's to say it's wrong? It's what was real to you."

"But if that's true, then what we're doing at Janus, at the lab, all of it is—"

"You know this about memory. It's faulty, inconsistent."

Noah nodded. She could see she'd poked a giant hole in whatever balloon had briefly inflated him with talk of the Europa disaster. He hadn't seen that the Janus Project was flawed from the beginning, because it relied on one person's mind, one person's memory. Some would say that people's minds were unreliable, but Eileen thought of the mind as simply unknowable, that private core in the center of all beings.

"That storm we just drove through?" she said. "It's not *a thing*. It's a collection of things. Of forces and pressure drops and built-up condensation and rising heat. It's a thing that is constantly happening and *becoming*. An accumulation of experiences."

Noah looked at her, impatience in his frown. "And?"

"That's what memories are like. Living things made up of your experience, plus my experience, plus Esther's experience. All of it happening at once, the truth of it somewhere in the middle, the objective truth not even important at all."

"What's important, then?"

"That you heard me say what you needed to hear. I heard myself say what I needed to hear. That's the truth."

They passed the next ten miles or so in silence. She wasn't sure if Noah was mad at her, but she was willing to sit in the discomfort of that possibility. And then, as they entered the land of big buildings and strip malls and traffic, he said, "Okay, then. That's the truth."

Curtis Bolson answered the door of their modest one-level home in a new development and immediately told them that he and his wife, Talia, had signed an NDA that prevented them from disclosing anything about Talia's work at Klein's lab. After a few minutes of Eileen's pleading, Curtis sighed and looked at Noah, seeming to register his pallor. He asked if Noah wanted something to drink, or to sit down. Noah nodded, and Curtis let them in through his incredibly normal house, beige and basic like it was temporary housing. And then in the back room, Eileen saw why Curtis had let them in.

By the window looking on an overgrown backyard sat a woman who looked about fifty, but whose skin had the same gray tint as Noah's did now, and who seemed frail and withered. When she looked at them, there was recognition. This was Talia, and she had been through the same thing as Noah, and that was the truth.

Maya

Noah liked to talk about entropy, and Maya liked to listen to him talk about it, and entropy was on her mind when she eventually did go home with Ren. It felt less like a decision than a destination, the end of the evening, the random landing place of disorder. Those points of disorder were: another dinner, this time at a Michelin-starred sushi counter, a too-big sake bottle drained too fast, an extended walk toward the train station, winding around a neighborhood they both suspected would not lead them to the train station, a decision not to take the train after all, but to walk onward in the cold, to see where the night took them, why not, they were both in Tokyo, a point of disorder itself, him here to reacquaint himself with his art, her here to separate from her marriage.

As they walked, Maya stayed linked through the crook of his arm the entire time, told herself it was for warmth, and it was, but that warmth included some other, more existential warmth.

Ren's apartment was at the top of a winding road that was thick with silence, hard to come by in the middle of Tokyo. The building was three stories tall, the inside sparkling clean, and the door to his apartment opened and closed with a gentle, expensive whoosh. In the entryway, she exchanged her boots for untouched gray house slippers and marveled. Where her parents' apartment was a more common build from the mid-century—small, functional rooms, a replicable layout—this one was shockingly modern, all clean lines and glass. Ah, she realized, money.

"A long way from that Portland apartment by the overpass," Maya said, approaching the windows that wrapped around the two walls of the living room.

"I liked that place," Ren said.

"How could you like that place? It was damp all the time. So loud. Dark."

He joined her at the window. "It was what we needed back then, don't you think? Suffering, scrounging, scraping by."

Maya nudged him. "Is that what you say in your interviews? That time with me was your blue period, giving rise to your, I don't know, Whitney Biennial period?"

"Your personal vendetta against the Whitney, man."

"Well, my boyfriend got in, got famous, and then got a new girlfriend."

"I didn't get a new girlfriend," Ren said, sitting down on the couch.

"You got rid of one."

"So we're negotiating the breakup again. I was wondering when this was going to happen."

They were still smiling, but there was a knife's edge to it.

"I don't need to negotiate," she said. "I know what happened."

He slid over and made room on the couch next to him. "Tell me what you remember. We'll see if it's what I remember."

She sat. He'd turned on a few lamps in the room and the way the honeyed light slanted across his face made her stomach drop. He was more handsome now than when they were young, and she wondered if the same was true for her, if she was more beautiful now, if she'd sharpened into the person she'd wanted to be back when they were together.

"Well, you announced that you were moving to New York because that's where you had to be to make it. The gallery representation was there, the buyers were there. And then you moved and you didn't ask me to come with you."

"You didn't ask to come with me."

"How embarrassing to have to ask, Ren. We lived together. In romantic squalor, remember? Then suddenly, you're moving and we're not living together anymore? We had the fight. I was confused. Then I visited you a couple times, and it got weirder and weirder, and then that last time, you had to break up with me on the street outside that tiki bar, but you said it like it had already happened, and I missed it somehow."

"It had already happened."

"When?"

"When I left Portland."

"But I'd already bought a plane ticket to visit you. You packed the moving truck and I had a plane ticket, a date."

"You bought that ticket without asking me."

"And when I came to visit you that first time, when I stayed with you, when we slept together, when we got ice cream in the morning, when we saw movies in the middle of the day, you were thinking I wasn't your girlfriend?"

"You were thinking you were?"

"Come on."

"Sometimes that's just goodbye. When you're young and dumb."

This felt silly. They were both in their midthirties, rehashing a fissure from their twenties that could all be boiled down to a misunderstanding—a foolish girl, an arrogant boy, impetuous, selfish decisions, not enough life experience. But Maya couldn't admit that. She supposed he couldn't either.

"What else is a girlfriend but someone you waste a whole day with like that?" she asked.

"That was just it, though. I didn't want to waste time with a girl-friend. Not then. I felt like I had no time to waste."

"So I was someone you wasted time with."

"That's not what I said."

Maya felt a familiar hurt and sank deeper into the couch. A bruise in her chest rebloomed.

She excused herself to go to the bathroom, which was also cut in sharp whites and grays and expensive tiles and copper and marble. A pristine white hand towel sat rolled on a small basket seemingly made to fit it, waiting for her. Their divergent lives seemed clear in that towel. In Maya's bathroom in Los Angeles, she'd had a pink hand towel with brown dots hanging from a rack, one her mother had sent her when she was in grad school, so kitschy Maya was beginning to like it. Often it hung there for weeks, bent and grayed with use. She wouldn't even know where to find a basket for a hand towel to rest on.

So this was where Ren's life was always going to go. She splashed her face with water and looked at herself in the mirror. No entropy. Only the way things always were.

When she left the bathroom, she passed through a dark hall, where a picture hanging on a wall caught her eye. It was a photo, one Maya immediately recognized as *Weight*. The same photo she had featured in the talk where she met Noah.

Back on the couch, she said, "You like that photograph? The Mat-suda?"

"It was a gift from Matsuda herself."

"I once gave a talk about that photograph. I used to think it was so sad."

"I think it's sort of bright and hopeful."

"Noah always said—" She stopped herself.

"Tell me," Ren prompted.

"He thought the photo was about sadness, but that it was dynamic in its sadness, which I guess is a way of being hopeful. That the sadness can change, because it's always in movement, always changing."

"Your 'results' man said all that?"

Maya smiled. "I like Matsuda's work, anyway. Sadness or not."

"You're in luck," Ren said. "She's here in town, actually. A big showing. We should go to the opening."

He went to the fridge, where he grabbed a couple of Asahi beers. He brought one back to her, and after a long swig he said, "I did get another girlfriend. She worked at the gallery that first represented me there. Which is so terrible, I know. Predictable. I wanted so badly to belong then, to New York, to the art scene. It seemed like what one did. She was young, a couple years out of college."

"Chantal," Maya said. Though it was her fourth or fifth drink of the night, the beer tasted exquisite, exactly what she didn't know she wanted. Even the beer was better in Ren's world.

"How did you know?"

"I met her that last time I was there. I could tell."

"It wasn't right after you, you know. There were some months."

He meant this as a salve but it didn't land with Maya. She was back on that Cobble Hill street, where it occurred to her that they were breaking up, or had already broken up. She meant what she'd said to him; all of that was in the past. But it felt so alive in her now, here.

"I'm not still mad or hurt," she said. "It's just that it was one of those breakups for me. A breakup that wounded. And you still have the ability to wound me."

He shifted on the couch, his leg now millimeters from hers.

"I know I hurt you. But that's not me anymore," he said. "You're mad at me in the past."

His voice was quiet. She understood in its timbre that they had already made the decision to cross the distance between their bodies. The distance between their past and their present, the memories, the emotion of it, had already been crossed. Or merged. So they did the same with their mouths.

And the instant his lips touched hers, she felt like her body dropped in through the couch cushions, falling through a portal into another place, the place they'd last been together, which would be Brooklyn, but no, the place they'd last been happy together, that weird apartment by the train tracks in Portland. Always dark in there, in her memory. She closed her eyes as they kissed, and didn't dare open them, not even when she felt his body slowly pushing hers backward, his hands on her arms first, moving up to her shoulders, then her neck, then her chin, holding her face, and then she was on her back on the couch and he was above her, and she could open her eyes then, because everything else was obliterated. They could have been anywhere—Ebisu, Portland, Cobble Hill.

She thought for a second of Noah, which was when she realized she hadn't fully banished him from her mind, not with entropy everywhere. There he was, at the perimeter of her consciousness, a rim of bright horizon. She imagined she must be the same kind of light in his brain. Then she was back with Ren, his compact body, smaller than Noah's, harder, a little more forceful, and exactly as she remembered. Even with the memories, everything now felt new.

In Ren's bedroom, which was as minimalist and luxe as every other room in his apartment, he didn't turn the lights on. She sat on the bed, her bare feet on the tatami mat beneath it, and he joined her. There was a momentum to this moment, and she knew if she didn't propel forward, the train would slow and then stop.

She put her hand on his chest, and her forehead on his lips, and they stayed like that in the dark for a minute. Then they lay down together. Maya fit in Ren's half-circle embrace, his arm and body tilted toward her, hers toward him. Everything *was* new. That was the thing. The possibilities were endless.

First, she saw only white.

The Tokyo sky, streaming in through Ren's bare morning windows. Maya's mouth was sticky, and then she recognized thirst, and then a gentle nausea, almost comforting. She rolled over, and Ren was already awake, reading his phone.

Without looking up, he asked, "Do you want to waste the day together today?"

She expected him to take her to some obscure museum or all the way to Yokohama, but once they were on the train she realized where they were headed. She smiled at him and he nodded, but they stayed silent, rocking back and forth with the train's movement.

"Shimokitazawa," Maya said as they crossed under the arch announcing the tucked-away neighborhood. "I haven't been here since I was a kid."

"It's my favorite place to waste a day," Ren said.

Her phone dinged and she glanced at it. A check-in from her mother. Maya had told her she slept on a friend's couch because the trains stopped running. She looked up at Ren walking in front of her, at the lusciousness of his shearling-lined denim jacket, and then texted her mother back: *Home tonight.*

Her parents were having an anniversary party on Saturday, and she knew they wanted her help, though only for the sake of her being involved, not for any real labor. But a block into Shimokitazawa, she felt like she could stay here for hours. The neighborhood was known for vintage stores, small craft cocktail bars, and European-style cafés, all of which Maya liked, but even more she liked the narrowness of the maze of interlocking streets, and the way walking around there felt like hiding, even in Central Tokyo.

Ren led her to a converted garage space with stalls of vintage vendors. He picked out a chore jacket for Maya and she cringed at the price tag. He ignored her shock, added wide-leg pants with a curved seam and a tissue-thin tank top with a picture of a 1980s Japanese city pop singer on it. When she came out of the dressing room in her new outfit, he was waiting in his new clothes: a beautiful paint-splattered canvas shirt, selvedge denim, old motorcycle boots. They looked in the mirror together.

"I like it," she said. "I feel young."

"You are young."

She glanced around the place. The other customers were barely in their twenties, wearing impossibly cool hats that Maya could never pull off, big goofy shoes, and patterns and textures that felt more than just Japanese or French, but somehow both galactic and retro.

"Not here," she said, adjusting her top. "You look good, too."

"I know," Ren said. This had been what was so attractive to her initially, his confidence and swagger. Because he also had an innate sweetness oozing out of every part of him, his confidence never seemed arrogant, only fearless.

"Let's leave in these clothes," he said, grabbing Maya a deadstock wool coat. "My treat."

"No way, that's way too much money."

"It's one percent of one sale to a TV producer who keeps his collec-

tion in Saint Lucia, where humidity warps the lines. And he's a regular." Ren put the coat over her shoulders. "Trust me, it's fine."

They left the store and Maya was giddy with feeling new. Somehow, without her saying it, he'd understood that she didn't want to
live in the past. So he'd given them an unexpected neighborhood and
new outfits.

They grabbed lunch at a place specializing in seasonal vegetable
soup, and Maya felt like eating it was seeding new energy inside her.
Ren made her pose for a photo next to a Spider-Man statue outside a
store, and then he bought a few artsy comic books inside. She found a
record shop upstairs from a Muji and they split up. She bought him an
Elvis record and he bought her a pack of cashmere socks with planets
on them. They were the only people in a six-seat bar where the cock-
tails were all inexplicably dental-themed. Hers came with bright blue
floss wrapped around the skewer and Ren's tasted like Listerine. They
felt loose enough for karaoke then, and found a spot with only four private rooms. They could hear the sounds of the Cranberries' "Dreams"
bleeding through from the neighboring room, so Maya selected the
same song, and they sang it back at the wall. They sang songs from their
youth. Maya sang a song in Japanese, to Ren's horror. Ren mangled
a Radiohead song, but Maya liked it. Afterward, they grabbed a booth
at a crowded jazz bar and didn't speak for a whole hour while they
listened to a wailing saxophone, the sort of live music Maya would normally not stand for. At the table, with a thumb of whiskey, she felt like
she was asleep in the best way, completely relaxed, in a dream.

She looked to Ren, who was listening to the music. Yes, this was
what she wanted. She had no idea what time it was. When they decided
to leave, the trumpet was still wailing, there was a line to get in, and it
was dark outside. "Oh, sorry!" Maya said to the line, and a few people
looked up at her, confused. "We lost track of time," she explained.

Most of the stores were closing, and they were full of alcohol and soup, so they walked down the serpentine streets toward what Maya thought was the Shimokitazawa train station.

"This was very easy," she said. "Wasting a day with you."

"We're very good at it, aren't we?"

"This must have been how we passed lots of time all those years ago."

"No," Ren says. "We worked hard, remember? We were always working on something or other. I think I'm listed as part of a short film on IMDb, but I have no memory of it."

"Anything that would pay."

"Anything that would make us feel like we *weren't* wasting time."

"You're right," Maya said. "It all felt so important then. But now, I don't know. It seems like we had all the time in the world."

Ren stopped in front of a closed but lit-up art gallery. Inside were prominently displayed pastoral watercolors, stuff for rich people to buy for their entryways.

"Do you think life would have been easier if we had done this type of thing?" he asked.

Maya laughed a little, but then she saw in the corner of the gallery a sculpture on a pedestal that looked like spilled wax. It was taupe and shiny and the gesture was upward, the spill frozen in midair. She pointed it out to Ren, and they stood there looking at it for a while. It was tucked away, like the gallery owner thought it would never sell. Maya and Ren discussed the possibilities for a while, and she said it reminded her of the Gutai movement, like one of Ren's earlier works, then she gathered the courage to ask if she could see his studio. He was always private about his studio, and hated to show works in progress. He'd told her he even once denied an Oscar-winning actor access to his in-progress commission.

"It's not set up for studio visits," he said faintly.

"Oh, you know I don't care."

"I know, but I care," he said.

"If I don't go now, I'll never go," Maya said, and though neither of them could explain why, they both knew this was true.

Ren relented. Maya saw then that there was a part of him that wanted her to ask to see it. She carried that knowledge with her on the short train ride there, holding it like a warm ball in her chest, that particular pleasure of taking a leap and being caught.

His studio was the first floor of a slim residential building near a big serene park. The two upper floors belonged to a wealthy restaurateur from New York who used it when he was in town, and who was a big fan and collector of Ren's work. The ceilings of the studio were fourteen feet high, and the space was huge but nearly empty. Maya spotted the plywood worktables that Ren always liked to build so he could work. It was chilly inside, and Ren pulled a blanket out of a cupboard for her to wrap around her shoulders. A few blank canvases were turned away and leaning against a wall, stacks of materials and tools sat piled on the floor, unopened. His brushes were clean, and his paints were packed away. A small closet served as his darkroom, fully stocked. Maya walked through the place, trailing the blanket behind her.

"I told you it was nothing," Ren said. "I'm not working on anything right now."

"I don't believe you," Maya said, squatting to turn one of the canvases around to face them. "You're always working, even when you're not. You've got to be tossing an idea around. Right?"

He didn't answer, but he approached the canvas, picked it up, and dropped it on the table he'd built. "These are cheap. Cotton. There's distortion over here, look."

He took her hand and put it palm down on the lower right corner of the canvas. "There," he said. "See how that depresses a little if you run your hand across it?"

Aja Gabel

This close, she could smell him, the soup and the gin and the vintage fabrics he was wearing. She ran her hand across the surface, and yes, she did feel it, for a moment, then it was gone.

The magnetism she felt between them now was everything, sexual, romantic, and simply attracting, attracting hands together, bodies toward the studio, attention toward the art. It felt dangerous to be around him, but in a productive way, because being together could be transportive, carrying her back to their Portland life, back to being confused about who they were and what they wanted to say and make. She'd been so afraid to be that way again, to ask questions with difficult answers. But it was what was required. It was required all the time, to ask yourself what you wanted to create, what you wanted to inscribe, what change your presence was making in the air, the space, the life.

"Can you shoot me?" Maya asked, still looking down at the canvas, knowing he would say yes.

"I can," he said.

They didn't talk much, but Ren worked fast, setting up lights and choosing the right camera. He didn't ask Maya what she wanted to do, so she decided. She decided not to be afraid, having never been the subject before, not even in school. She arranged the blanket around her feet and held the massive canvas in front of her face. He started shooting. She moved, small movements at first, and then drastic ones. She took the jacket off. She dragged the canvas behind her. She stood behind a light. She'd never felt so free while being watched. There was no explicit destination, no problem to solve. They were doing anything to see if they could make something. She hadn't felt like this in years.

Afterward, the smell from the developing agents made her unexpectedly woozy, and she fell asleep on an old couch in the corner, wrapped in the blanket, while he worked in the darkroom. She dreamt of the hybrid plant she'd bought back in Marfa. She dreamt it had grown huge and tall and vibrant, a dinosaur of a plant. The feeling of dirt in her hands as she started to dig around the stalk.

She awoke when Ren was done and joined him to look at the negatives he'd hung to dry. She felt like she was looking at a stranger, the lines of her body, the way he framed her up against objects in the studio, the way her body subconsciously imitated forms around her, how Ren saw the forms she was making. She pointed to a few she liked.

"But I'll have to see the full-size prints," she said. "Make them big."

"Oh," Ren said. "I have plans for this."

He insisted on driving her home, since the trains had stopped running. He had an expensive car and the ride was smooth, the air thick with luxurious silence. She leaned against the car window and started to drift off as they drove through Tokyo. At a stoplight she opened her eyes, and they were in a neighborhood she didn't recognize. Outside an office building stood a collection of balloons waving in a breeze, anchored by a clip. She parted her lips to tell Ren about them, but before she could get anything out, a single blue balloon came loose and started to dance upward. The light changed and Ren pulled forward. He asked her what she was craning her neck for, and she couldn't say, because the balloon had blended in with the dark sky, the distance between them and the balloon's pull ever widening.

Noah

The answer Talia gave them was not the one Noah wanted to hear. She told him and Eileen that what they were doing would kill them.

The first question they asked, delivered by Eileen after explaining who she and Noah were, was about Talia's involvement with Janus, with Klein Michaels. Eileen explained they'd found her card and a photo, and she showed the artifacts to Talia. Talia didn't register any recognition of the card or the photo, except to say yes, that was her name and her face.

"Her memory is not so great anymore," Curtis said, stepping in. He was never far from their conversation, hovering with water, a napkin, a blanket, anything Talia might need. "That's part of what goes. Ironically."

"What do you mean, what goes?" Noah asked. "Alzheimer's? Is she okay?"

Talia looked up at him sharply. She didn't say anything, but he felt it. No, of course she was not okay. None of this was okay. Eileen put her hand on Noah's arm and he sat back.

"You know who we are," Eileen said to Talia, who seemed to be growing more agitated. "Why don't you tell us who you are? However you want to."

Talia had been on her way to full professor at UC Berkeley, in physics. Her main research area had been in string theory, but shortly before Klein recruited her, she had become attracted to semiclassical quantum gravity. She was an algebra nerd through and through, Curtis said, and the emerging theory gave her more opportunity to work with what she loved, those numbers. Klein had reached out—well, really, Oliver first, and wasn't he a strange little guy?—because of the ways she might be able to prove what they were doing, with her work in semiclassical equations. Of course, once she got to Marfa, she should have known that they hadn't really needed her research expertise. What she had been researching had nothing to do with the *quantum process in cognition*. She uttered the phrase slowly and with derision.

When Talia grew tired, after a few sentences or so, or when she could not remember details, Curtis took over. In the beginning, he said, it was so exciting. To feel like you were out there at the edge of the world, at the edge of science, a poetic landscape, a place where cowboys and artists and scientists and thinkers of all kinds came to be quiet together. There was a whole team she was working with, all of whom believed they were part of an endeavor that would foundationally change science. But once Nils made clear what they wanted from her, to be the test subject, she became subsumed. Curtis had quit his job and was working on the novel he'd always wanted to write, and Talia was in the lab all hours of the night, prepping to fold, and then folding to various degrees of success.

Which was all right, Curtis said. He was used to her bouts of work taking her away from him. They had no children and enjoyed leading independent lives. But Talia herself seemed changed.

Here, Curtis became uncomfortable, and Talia resumed talking.

"Curtis is being polite," she said, interrupting. She had become scrambled. There was no better word for it. An inability to understand the lines between past and present. She hadn't been a very good test subject, and she hadn't made it very far into the missions they'd set, but she was also stressing her body by going on separate, secret folds.

"This is what you need to know," Talia said, taking a big breath. Right after she and Curtis got married, she went on a road trip up through Oregon and Washington with her adult niece. Talia knew she wouldn't have kids, but she loved her sister's child like her own, and the two were so close they often went on weekend trips together. Her name was Freya. Talia paused here. Her name *was*. They'd driven over a pass and into a sudden snowstorm somewhere in Oregon. Talia was driving and Freya was navigating, but visibility was low. Like she'd been temporarily blinded. She could have sworn the car had slowed to a crawl. But confusion mounted and soon Talia couldn't see up from down or left from right, and she'd only find this out afterward, but she drove clear off the road, into a deep ravine, where the car flipped four times before landing upside down on a gnarl of trees. The part of the car that took the brunt of the accident was the passenger side, where Freya died instantly.

For years Talia wondered what if. What if Freya had driven? What if they'd waited a day? What if they'd checked the Doppler more closely? What if they'd taken a different route? What if Talia had simply pulled over and waited for it all to pass? How many points along the way were there moments to make choices in which Freya could have lived, even if Talia had died?

Talia's sister never pursued legal action or restitution, but Talia often wished she had. Instead the punishment was a permanent estrangement. Not one born out of rage, but one born out of necessity. To see Talia would be to know again and again the randomness with which Freya had died. Talia accepted this. And then years passed, and Talia and Curtis moved to Berkeley, and they both got jobs and life seemed worth living again.

Curtis said they were happy. Talia was excelling at work, he was happy at the high school, they traveled, they had friends, they were engaged with their lives. But that all changed after Klein, after Janus. Curtis explained what had taken them months to find out: The core of the time bath, the one engaged by Nils's resonance program, delivered more radiation to the subject's brain than they were willing to admit. Each fold was equivalent to a week's worth of radiation blasted into the base of the skull. There were other problems, too. The nano-repeaters didn't filter out of the bloodstream as efficiently as claimed, and Talia's doctors found issues with her kidneys and also suspected the early stages of myeloma. And the effects of the Fold Cocktail took longer and longer to recover from, sometimes landing Talia in bed for days.

Perhaps worst of all, Curtis said, was that Klein and Nils were much closer to effecting causality than they let on. They were developing a port that directly connected the core to the subject's brain via implant, and once that was working, they believed they could effect causality in the folds. What they were doing in these folds, the ones without the working port, was testing out the methodology—could a subject withstand that much radiation? Could they not only withstand it, but function in a fold within it? And how many times? For how long? With how many trillions of nanorepeaters clogging the blood and the kidneys? And after how many doses of the Fold Cocktail?

Curtis had been the one to find all of this out. Talia was in no shape to question anything. But Curtis had worked with teenagers; he knew how to get skeptical and unruly people to trust him. Nils wasn't suspicious of Curtis, who was kind and unassuming, so Curtis was able to sneak onto phones and computers. And Nils didn't hide his data very well—the shared server was messy and unprotected. Curtis had also been the one to break all this news to the team of researchers, to cause their mass resignation. Klein threatened everyone with legal action that would leave them permanently destitute, good as dead. The cast of researchers, engineers, and scientists were now flung across the globe, living in silence under ironclad NDAs and monthly payments. No one person had had access to enough of the source code to re-create it to compete with Klein, so there was no clear path to retribution. Talia and Curtis were also offered a deal they couldn't refuse. If they moved to El Paso, left their life in Berkeley behind, and told no one as per their NDAs, Klein would pay for Talia's treatment and their living expenses. And what was Talia's treatment? At the moment mostly cognitive therapy, treatment for radiation exposure, and the beginnings of memory care. If Talia and Curtis stayed quiet, Klein said, he would mothball the program. They took his word and lived by the agreement.

But here Talia and Curtis were, violating the terms of their agreement. Why?

They had believed Klein would shut the project down, with no one working for him anymore. They'd believed it foolishly, Curtis admitted.

"And because," Talia said, looking directly at Noah's face, her eyes suddenly alive and searching, "I can see in this man what happened to me."

While Talia and Curtis spoke, Noah couldn't look at Eileen. He wasn't ready to witness what must have been crossing her face—the anger, the panic, the urgency to take action, to move, to flee. He felt none of that himself. He only felt recognition.

Yes, he recognized it all. So Talia also had a past trauma, one that

Nils and Klein knew she would use to fold repeatedly, so they could get more data than they were technically recording. They had it all, all the data, because they had Talia, and they had the machines, all records of every fold, even ones they weren't there for.

Noah tried to hide his face from Talia and Curtis. He didn't want to tell them he knew about Klein's plan for causality, that he'd considered being a part of it.

Curtis looked at Noah withdrawing and misinterpreted it. "Numbness is one of the side effects," Curtis said. "I've cried months and years over what they did to Talia, but her sadness, her loss, it's all muted now."

Talia only looked down at her lap. "We should have known they'd find someone else who was also at the Europa disaster."

Noah vibrated. "What do you mean?"

Talia looked at him with mild pity at all he didn't know. "Klein was a large investor in that project, his first big flop, the start of his public downfall. So that's his goal. To fold back there, to have you—or someone—prevent what happened."

Noah was confused. "But he's fine. He's a billionaire."

"He doesn't need money," Curtis said. "He needs to get rid of the shame of failure."

Noah rubbed his forehead, his gullibility coming back to him in embarrassing waves. "He said figuring out causality could help climate change."

Now Eileen put her hand on Noah's knee, a gesture that conveyed sympathy for his eagerness to believe.

He let out a deep, whole-body sigh. "I guess I could have figured if he wanted to help climate change, he wouldn't be a billionaire."

No one said anything to that.

"We'll have to trust you won't rat us out," Curtis said. "But chances are, they already know you're here. They know more than you think."

"We took precautions," Noah said. "I figured out the lights trick."

Curtis nodded. "A little simple for them, don't you think? Lights on, cameras recording. Lights off, free rein. I felt dumb for not figuring that out sooner."

"There's a lot I should have figured out sooner," Noah said.

He felt Eileen's hand on his knee. Still, he wouldn't look at her.

"I'm so sorry," she said. It seemed like she said it to everyone present.

Curtis insisted on feeding them simple sandwiches for lunch, and they talked of other things. What they missed about Northern California and how Eileen liked it there, the people they might have in common, places in Marfa that had changed, places that had stayed the same. Talia was mostly quiet, and she didn't eat. Noah forced himself to take small bites even though he wasn't hungry.

When they were ready to go, Noah said goodbye and thank you, and Talia held his hand a few seconds longer than he expected. "It doesn't look too late for you," she said. "Okay?"

"Okay," he said, but he didn't know what he was agreeing to do, exactly.

He got in the car while Eileen was saying her goodbyes. He felt suddenly ashamed. That he had taken this woman's time, their secret, and that Eileen, his ex-wife, was making nice with them in his stead. Why couldn't he take care of himself? Why couldn't he take care of Maya? Watching the way Curtis tended to Talia had made him feel tendrils of regret for how he'd let Maya go. From the moment they arrived in Marfa. Or from the moment she agreed to go. He'd known, always, somewhere in the back of his brain, the location currently blasted with radiation, that given the chance, he would fold to Serena. Wasn't he doing something just as bad, spending these days with Eileen, also a relic from his past? Where was he, really? In what reality, what present, with what desires and goals? He wanted Maya, and his life with her. But he also wanted Serena. And he would always want Eileen, in the way that they were forever bonded, both by what they'd lost and by what they'd made.

He wanted too much, because so much had been taken. But maybe he was looking at it wrong. Maybe he was simply unable to see what he had been given.

When Eileen got back in the car, her eyes had a sheen. As they pulled away from Talia and Curtis's block, she began to cry. Silently, but with a force, thick tears spilling over her cheeks, dripping off her chin. Occasionally she lifted a hand to wipe them away. She merged onto the highway. Noah thought of Talia's car accident, and apparently so did Eileen, because then she said, "I can see. I'll be careful."

"I'm not worried," he said, even though he was.

"They know you won't stop," she said.

Noah didn't say anything. He didn't know if he would stop. Or how. Or if he could.

"But we'll figure it out," Eileen said. "We always do."

She spoke with such certainty. A contrast to the shaky tenor of Talia's voice, and the sad mezzo of Curtis's. Eileen knew their future, that's what Noah felt. He only knew their past, certain that there were answers there. And here was Eileen, as she was all those years ago, at the Europa disaster, certain there were answers in the future.

Eileen

Noah didn't have to ask her; Eileen wanted to spend the night. Neither of them wanted to be alone. While he slept, she went back to the mudroom, as if drawn there by a magnet. The room felt different from the rest of the uncanny living space. Eileen felt it was arranged like the inside of someone's mind, Maya's mind. There were loose papers and sketch pads placed on the radiator, a fire hazard, and Eileen began to stack them, to move them. But she also wanted to look at them. Knowing too much about Maya could only hurt her, she'd thought. But here, in this room, among these colors and this view, Maya seemed to be trying to figure out a problem, to answer questions. Questions were always interesting to Eileen.

She found herself holding an unused postcard that had slipped out of a sketch pad. She turned it over. It was the photograph her student had ended her presentation with earlier that fall, the photo somehow correlating to the physics concept of coherence. Eileen was startled. What were the chances? She wanted to go wake Noah and ask him what he knew about this, but she also didn't have confidence he'd be coherent enough to answer.

She flipped the postcard back over. *Weight*, a photograph by Yuko Matsuda.

Coherence. Who or what was cohering? Eileen with Maya? Eileen with Noah? The photograph was stunning. Exuberant in its color, and the way it managed to combine the real body with the painted backdrop, giving each dimension through reflection. But the photo was also stunningly sad, the woman's naked backside at the center, the invisible face, a body about to jump or fall, the buoyancy of the balloons just out of reach. Eileen wondered what it said about you, which you noticed first, the happiness or the sadness, the possibility or the inevitability. She'd seen the exuberance first, the joy.

She placed the postcard on the easel and then opened the sketchbook. Maya's sketches, done in thick, dark pencil. Still life, very occasionally a partial face, often animals. Eileen touched them with her fingers, trying not to blur the images. This felt intimate, and she wondered briefly if she should put the sketchbook back, let it lie. But she kept turning pages, marveling at the half scenes, the repeated studies of a bird in flight, the careful tip of the animal Noah had told her was a pronghorn, the same animal on the painting on the easel.

And then Eileen found herself.

Her own face and body, younger, and pregnant. She and Noah had gone to the gardens at the Huntington Library, right as Eileen entered the third trimester, physically uncomfortable and filled to the brim with hormones. She cried and screamed at Noah some nights, for no reason. Such was being pregnant, given to the whims pulsing through your veins, powered by your uterus. And that day at the Huntington gardens had been better, but she remembered she had cried in the parking lot before they went in. She couldn't remember what had made her sad or angry, but she hadn't wanted Noah to touch her or comfort her. He couldn't understand, whatever it was, especially if she also didn't understand. And finally they left the car and walked in, and she'd slowly dried her tears, and the sun was low and the light was going golden, and she felt a little better with each step they took toward the palm garden.

She had been terrified to have a child. Not only to give birth to it, but to *have* it, to be responsible for it, forever. The times when she shed that terror were temporary, but bright. When they arrived at the place where Noah laid out a blanket and cracked open some nonalcoholic wine, she was fully in it. The optimism and hope. The gift of a child like a life raft, not a burden.

Take a picture, she'd said to him. They hadn't done a maternity photo shoot. There was hardly any evidence of her pregnancy. And she held her belly, looked at him, and he snapped. This was that. This sketch left certain things out, of course. The quality of light, the shadow made by the giant palms. But it got so many things right, specifically the way her young, plump, pregnant face looked at the camera, at Noah. The moment when, she guessed, love took over.

How had Maya seen this? Did Noah have this photo somewhere? Eileen touched the sketch, her fingers tracing the contours of what would be Serena. Then she closed the sketchbook.

In the morning, Eileen woke Noah with an embrace. She didn't want him to feel afraid, and she sensed he would, after their visit with Talia, after a night when he'd talked in his sleep, moaning nonsense words.

"Hi," he said finally, his body loosening under her arms.

Eileen knew what she had to do. But in the night she'd decided she couldn't extricate Noah from this situation without first seeing what it was he was tangled in. It was risky, yes, but she felt there was no other choice.

"Help me fold," she said.

"The experience will be messy and uneven," Noah said. "You haven't practiced."

"I've been learning from you."

"I don't know if that's enough to properly map a memory."

Eileen sighed. "I'm not saying you required excessive training. I'm saying I require less."

She knew that he knew this was true. She had always taken to things quicker, understood the pathways from here to there with a glance, and was unafraid facing tasks that Noah found daunting. He didn't push anymore.

He dressed quickly, and opened up Building D for her. After administering the Echo Injection and fitting her to the mapping helmet, he tried to tell her the best way to meditate on a memory, but she stopped him. "Just let me do this," she said. If she fell out of the fold early, then so be it. She was hurrying herself, and felt as though if she didn't do this now, she would never do it.

Once the memory was mapped, he prepped the time bath. She stripped down, thinking not of Noah watching her now, but of how he said he'd slept with her past self in his recent fold, and all the times in their marriage they'd seen each other naked, bodies no longer mysteries.

Eileen opened the time bath as Noah instructed and climbed gently in, as he had demonstrated. She kept her breath steady as the top closed over her. The pain was familiar and a little sweet, the grief an old friend, and she sank into it, while floating in the water. She opened her eyes only once, when Noah came in to give her the Fold Cocktail. Relax, he said. Don't fight it.

The transition was peaceful.

*   *   *   *   *   *

She feels a great weight in her chest. Noah said to remember to look up, and she lifts her head and looks up, and the world fills in around her heavy body. Serena's room, honeyed with dim bedtime light, five more minutes of play after bath and before crawling into bed. Eileen is seated on the floor, cross-legged, her body like lead, but as she looks around the room and finally lands on Serena, she lightens.

This is the night before Serena dies. The last bedtime. Serena wants to play with these miniature cats and she's putting them in the car that came with her dollhouse.

"Look, the cats are driving the car. Look, Mama."

Her voice like a thin sterling needle through the heart. Eileen gasps, and the world around her shakes a bit. Steady. Stay in this.

"I see, baby," she says. "I see the cats driving the car."

"It's funny," Serena says, and she then laughs, a real laugh.

So this is what Noah is dying for, Eileen thinks.

Here is Serena, wearing cat pajamas, playing with cats, this love for cats even though they have no cats because both Noah and Eileen are allergic. Eileen is present through these minutes of playtime, though Serena doesn't need her. The cats are having a conversation, about their day, about a girl who was nice at school, who shared a doughnut hole, about the rain, how it will rain tomorrow.

"Watch out," Serena says, the voice of the passenger cat. "There's a bump in the road. I don't like bumps."

Eileen chimes in here and there. "Yes, I will go slow," she says. She holds a mini cat outside the car, observing. This is real. This is her daughter. This is nothing, the normal last night.

"Time for bed," one cat says to another. Serena takes the cats out of the car and lays them down on the drawing table in a perfect line, all three of them, plus a baby cat no one is playing with.

"Me, too," Serena says.

"Yes, you, too. Into bed." Eileen stands, ushering Serena into her bed.

Serena pulls the covers up around herself, and Eileen tucks them under her small body. Serena is smiling up at her, but then her gaze shifts. Eileen follows the gaze: the ceiling, where Noah placed all those glow-in-the-dark stars in a cluster, according to Serena's direction.

"Good night, black hole," Serena says.

"Is that a black hole? Is that what Daddy told you?"

Serena nods. "Mmm-hm. Daddy says so many stars are heavy and they have lots of gravity. Lots of gravity makes a black hole."

"Does it, now?"

"What is inside it?"

"Inside a star? Hydrogen, mostly."

"No, inside a black hole."

"Oh, um . . ." Eileen tries to remember what happens when a star becomes a black hole. "I think there's an explosion, called a supernova. This is a question more for Daddy. And it emits . . . radiation?"

"No, Mama." Serena shakes her head. "Inside a black hole is future."

"Future?"

"Daddy said inside a black hole is future."

"The future. Okay."

"Why is it the future?"

Why, why, why. Yes, Serena was always asking why.

"I don't know, baby," Eileen says. "Let's ask Daddy in the morning."

"Okay."

She sits there by Serena's bed, stroking her hair, for a long time. This is impossible, she thinks. To go back, say goodbye. To go back and do anything, be any other way except the way you were. Life is not moldable this way. Everything we do here, Eileen thinks, is a revelation of what already is.

This makes sense to Eileen now, but later, when she is out of the time bath, it won't, not right away.

"You have to go, Mama," Serena says.

Eileen's heart breaks. She has spent years avoiding this break, but it breaks, pain cracking through her chest, stuck in her throat, a panic surging through her, no way out but through.

"Okay, baby," she says. "I love you so much."

"How much?"

"To the inside of a black hole."

"And back."

"And back."

Eileen stands, pulls herself away. She walks to the door and hovers her hand over the light switch.

"Dream good dreams," she says.

"Okay," Serena says.

Then Eileen flips the switch and, in darkness, walks out.

I'll dream of hydrogen, Mama.

Eileen fell out of the machine the same way Noah had, hot streaks shooting up through her knees. He was there, suddenly, covering her with a robe. She was crying. She wasn't making a sound, but her eyes had tears streaming out of them; she could feel their warmth, even as the rest of her body was coated in time bath liquid.

Noah didn't ask where she went, or why. She presumed he knew enough to know that it was hard to explain, occupying the space of a fold. Instead, he guided her to the shower in his place, and he fed her soup, and he pulled down the covers so she could lie in bed and try to sleep, though sleep wouldn't come. She heard him on the phone, murmuring, then Nils's name. He was postponing the fold they had scheduled for today. Eileen was sick, he was saying. He couldn't leave her here.

Leave me, she wanted to shout from the bedroom, but she couldn't find the strength. She stared at the window, covered by a gauzy beige curtain, faded beige light coming in. She rolled on her back and looked up at the skylight. The same yellowing light, like a fire somewhere far, pushing smoke and haze into Marfa.

Nothing like the blue sky in the photograph, *Weight*.

Nothing like the darkening teal sky behind her at the botanical garden, holding Serena in her belly.

Nothing like the hazy sky in the aftermath of the Europa disaster. Somewhere, a fire.

A star burns on hydrogen. Until there is no more.

And just before she fell asleep, Talia Bolson, at the doorway of the house, looking down while Eileen said goodbye to Curtis.

"What will you do now?" Curtis had asked.

"I'm not sure," Eileen said. "I'm going to try to get him out of it, unscathed. Or as unscathed as possible."

"There's damage they try to protect the subject from, with the steel casing," Talia said, suddenly clear and cognizant. "That's what they say. But if you look at it, the core, there are so many terrible things happening in it. And there's a hydrogen fuel cell right there, too. So terrible."

Curtis looked at his wife quizzically. "They're leaving, honey."

"They don't tell you that," Talia was saying, and she was starting to shake. "Bromine, fluorine, who knows what did this to me. They don't tell you."

Curtis went to her. "I'm so sorry," he said, to both Talia and Eileen.

Eileen backed away. "It's all right. Thank you so much."

Now, Eileen was almost asleep. In Noah's bed, enveloped by the tinted light. And before she slipped into a dreamless nothing, she felt gratitude, and not a creation of a new thought, but a revelation of what was already there, given to her: Talia had given her the key to blow up the time bath.

Maya

There was a tree in the center of the house, a Japanese maple with plum-colored leaves. The house was spare but warm, four stories high, each level wrapping around a center courtyard, where the tree lived. The furniture was low to the ground, the materials worn with age, and in that way they pointed to the tree in the middle, which revealed its abundant self with each story's ascension.

The house belonged to Maya's mother's wealthy friends, a couple who lived between this Tokyo suburb and Singapore and also somewhere in Switzerland for ski season. The couple was nice, but boring, which Maya's mother admitted. But her mother had always loved this house and was friends with this couple for their proximity to impeccable taste. Thus, her parents' forty-second wedding anniversary.

For a long time, Maya had equated this level of wealth with a certain inability to develop a personality, but walking into it now, she thought this display was personality enough. She texted Ren as much. He wrote back, *That's what the Art Basel crowd believes, too.*

A waiter handed her warmed sake in a wooden cup and she downed it. Her mother came over to her—swanned over, really. She looked beautiful in a red dress made of reclaimed kimono silk, fitted but draped perfectly, with exuberant bell sleeves. Her hair was swept up, her eyes were glimmering, and for more than a moment Maya saw her as Hitomi, someone alive and independent of her daughter.

These moments had become more frequent as Maya settled into her parents' apartment. Both she and her parents had begun to soften into this new reality, with Maya here. She wasn't a child in the home anymore, and she wasn't a stranger, either, as she'd often been during her brief visits over the years. Instead she'd become a comfortable guest, falling asleep on the couch in the middle of a movie, making dinner for them, finding a new restaurant to try, reading aloud from a book she found on the bookshelf, just so her parents could point out gaps in her kanji fluency. It had only been a few days, but with family, a few days were enough to project forward and backward a life.

And her parents seemed newly interested in her, lacking a filter to their questions that Maya had come to expect. She thought coming to them in her state, stripped of pretense, of Noah, let them receive her stripped and bare themselves. Her parents were people, she now saw. The thought relaxed her. Which made her see that she had been tense about coming to them, fearful, even, of what judgment they might pass on her, of what judgment they might see she had passed on herself. But because they had none, she had started to feel lighter herself. That was the gift of parents: The way they saw you, the way they loved you, it could transform the molecules of your emotions.

Maya's mother grabbed her hand and walked her over to where her father was standing with a group of their friends. He handed out champagne and they clinked glasses. Their arms grazed and her father gave her mother a peck on the cheek. That counted as PDA in this crowd.

"What are you smiling at, Maya?" her mother asked in English.

"I've never seen all this for a forty-second milestone," Maya said, gesturing to the pastry display, the hired bartenders, the jazz trio in the corner.

"You'll see," her father said. "After twenty-five years, each year deserves to be celebrated like this."

This prompted questions from her parents' friends about Noah: *Where is he, how long have you been married again, what does he do?* Maya put a smile on and answered honestly: *Texas for work, three years, physics.* As she answered, she could feel her parents' eyes on her. She hadn't gone into detail about what happened with her and Noah, and didn't even know where she would begin, but they hadn't pushed, either. They both knew at some point she would tell them. They'd accepted that there was time to repair whatever had happened, enough time.

With her parents' friends, Maya decided to fully commit to small talk, to see what she could find in it. It was the only way to survive a party like this. If she approached each interaction with depth, she would receive it back. Or she wouldn't. Regardless, it was the approach that Maya began to enjoy, as she moved from conversation to conversation, going in without expectations, without limits, only an open-ended curiosity.

It occurred to her this was something Ren would do. He would think of it like an art project, a piece of performance art. He would see where each interaction broke, and then follow the broken part of it, indulge in the awkwardness, try to pull the pretty from the ugly.

Then it occurred to her this was also something Noah would enjoy, but for a different reason. This wouldn't be art to him, but a data set. The question of what happens when you commit to small talk, and a plethora of possible answers, waiting to be sorted and categorized, analyzed, answers drawn.

With this, all these ways of living alive inside her, she started to have fun. A son of her mother's dermatologist was talking to her about how he was also a dermatologist. Why did he love it? Because people always came in believing there was something inherently wrong with their skin, and his job was to show them that they, like everyone, were born with perfect skin, and that there was a way back to that perfect skin.

"To take away all the damage of living?" Maya asked.

"Exactly," he said.

"But some people, some babies, they aren't born with perfect skin," Maya said. "Right?"

The dermatologist's son refused to be caught. "It's perfect for them, though."

She realized she had been absentmindedly touching her own face while he was talking.

Later, Maya's parents cut into a layered crepe cake, flavored with green tea and vanilla buttercream, and everyone clapped, and they gave a speech, about all the time that had passed and how they'd persevered through it. Maya felt her phone buzz in her pocket, and when she checked it, Ren, Justine, and Caroline had all texted her. Ren asked how she was doing. Justine wanted to check in on how the project was coming along and see if she could invite a journalist from El Paso to preview it. Caroline wanted to know if Maya had disappeared in the desert and if she should call the police.

Never call the police, Maya wrote. *I'm sorry.*

For what?

I did disappear. I'm in Tokyo.

omg.

I'm seeing my family. And an ex-boyfriend. Taking a break from Noah.

OMG.

Am I horrible? I don't feel horrible.

Never. You're doing the best thing, which is looking for something bigger.

A photo of Jasper comes through, holding up a drawing of black and brown ink, smeared and off-putting, Maya thought.

This is my world, Caroline wrote. *Small child, poopy drawing.*

I don't know, Maya wrote. *Jasper's a whole world. From the mind of poopy drawing, what will come next?*

She picked up another glass of sake, her third or fourth, she didn't keep track. She sat on the floor, looking through the glass at the maple tree running up the center of the house. Her mother joined her on the floor, bending her legs elegantly and politely under her. She held out a piece of crepe cake, which Maya took.

"This is such a weird idea," Maya said, cake in her mouth.

"The tree? I suppose it makes this whole house a separate eco-system."

"I miss our old place in Chiba," Maya said. She blurted it out before she could even consider how true it was, which must have meant it was very true. When she thought about that place, she felt ease.

"You do?" Her mother sounded genuinely shocked. "I thought you couldn't get out of there fast enough."

The house had been cozy and serene, a somewhat traditional minka home, with tatami rooms and shoji doors. Of course, there'd been an extension off it, with more contemporary rooms where they actually lived. Maya remembered it belonging to her father's family.

"Whatever happened?"

"To that house? You know we sold it."

"I know, but why?"

Her mother thought for a moment. "After you were gone, we wanted to live back in the city. We missed being around people. We had a life, you know. Before you."

Maya laughed. Of course they did. But when she tried to imagine it, staring at the tree, she couldn't see it. She'd thought about that night they met, the story they'd told many times, past midnight in Daikanyama, but what came after that, before Maya?

So she asked.

"What was that life?"

Now her mother reached over and cut a piece of cake for herself. "Well," she said. "We managed to rent that little place in Daikanyama and we lived there before I even met your obaasan. She didn't care for me being American, even though I was almost more fluent in kanji than your dad. And, it was a strange time. Your dad, he knew, I think, that he was going to have to follow in his own father's footsteps at the company, and there was this brief window, like a Rumspringa, where he could pretend that he wasn't going to do that. And me, I had that money from my grandparents, and so I also had this window where I could pretend to be free, too. So, that's what we did. If we wanted to go to the islands, we went. If we wanted to stay out until five a.m., we did, and we made best friends with everyone else who did, too. Can you believe that? Us, best friends with street kids? I suppose we were street kids, too."

Here she paused.

"I did have a pregnancy before you, Maya."

"What? You never told me that. When?"

"Oh, about one year before I got pregnant with you. It was an accident, that one, of course. I think we were in India. I thought I had food poisoning. That whole plane ride home, your father was sweating bullets. The pregnancy was the sign, you see, that we'd have to start living life. Or, we were living life, but we'd have to start living a different life, one that other people wanted us to. We weren't quite ready, which I didn't say to anyone for a long time, because when I miscarried, I was very sad, and then I was very guilty. Like our not being ready had caused it."

"But that's not—"

"Of course it wasn't the reason," she added, cutting Maya off. "Things aren't related in that way. But they are related in some way. Because then we had you, and we were less scared."

"And more resigned."

Her mother paused. "No, Maya. You always thought that. That we were resigned. But we weren't."

"I kept trying to leave and you never tried to keep me."

"But that's not what people are for, to keep. You will always be ours, but you also always wanted to wander. You had a lot of questions."

"I had questions?"

"Well, not exactly questions. But desires. Beyond what we could fulfill. Your dad wasn't really like that. But I was. That's why I came here, to Japan. That's why you left."

Maya felt bowled over by her mother's plain explanation of a truth that Maya was only now beginning to see. "I didn't remember it like that at all."

"You know, it is possible for two people to have two different memories and experiences of the same thing. We couldn't be resigned to you because we had no idea *what* you were. We couldn't have predicted what it was going to be like to have you, to raise you, to see you off, not a single bit of it. And we couldn't control it. It was its own matrix. The definition of being a parent, I guess."

Maya closed her eyes. An image of her mother kneeling in the tatami room in their old house, facing the wall, crying softly late at night. It had annoyed her back then, as a teenager. *But of course*, she thinks now. *Of course all of it was scary.*

"I should have asked you more," she said now.

Her mother touched Maya's forearm. "I should have, too. But that's the power of hindsight. It's hard to know in the hard moment exactly what to do."

Here, her father wandered in, and asked her mother not to abandon him to the lions. He was red-faced from all the drinks, and he emanated heat. Both of them looked at Maya, expectant, so she spoke. She told them everything. About how she'd taken a leave from a good museum job and that made her feel reckless and stupid, about how she felt unable to continue to ask questions about art if she couldn't even bring herself to make art, how embarrassed that made her feel. She told them about Noah, and how he had retreated into his work, and how that made her angry, because she felt like she had given up a lot for him.

"What have you given up?" her father asked, and Maya was so shocked at the question, the direct intimacy of it, that she could have cried. He'd never asked her anything like this before.

She had given up wildness. A way to see the world that was indeterminate. A way to exist that allowed for there to be no answer, or many answers. She loved Noah. She loved the way he saw the world. She felt most connected to him when they were joined in wonder, whatever it was they were in wonder about. But his loss, it couldn't coexist there, in that space where everything else had questions and answers. It was only impossible questions, unanswerable grief. She didn't want him to forget Serena. But she needed to stop participating in a belief system in which there would be a way to solve Serena's absence. Did her parents think she was a bad person for thinking these things?

No, they didn't.

"I understand," her mother said.

And the baby. They wanted to have a baby. Maya did. And she thought Noah did, too. But it wasn't a straight line, an easy decision, when there was still so much sadness in that space.

"There is always sadness," her mother said.

"Is there?" Maya asked. "Because if there always is . . ."

"Wherever there is living," her father said. "There is freedom once you realize that. Not every sadness is yours to solve."

He took her mother's hand. "Over there, they're doing tea ceremony."

"For us?"

It was a confusing choreography, but everyone was a little light and slippery with drink, and they had a beautiful chashitsu setup with a brazier set into the tatami. There were already guests sitting on their knees, and one of the bartenders was whisking the powder. Maya wanted to say to her parents, *Thank you for listening*, but that would be too much, and besides, she didn't need to say it. She knew they knew.

So she said, "I'm going to stay here. And then after a little while, I'm going home."

She meant she would stay on this side of the room, but she also meant Tokyo, and that it was time for her to go home to America soon. Her parents nodded, and walked to the tea ceremony, watched by guests like a bride and groom.

Maya watched for a little while, but her view was obscured, so she wandered away. She found a back staircase and slowly walked down it, keeping an eye on the tree in the middle of the house. She was descending through the floors like climbing down the tree. When she reached the bottom floor, she was in the back of the house, not the way she'd entered. She noticed a room with a door slightly ajar, and wondered if that's where they'd put everyone's coats. But when she pushed it open, the room was nearly empty, and inky dark. Windowless, with only a small desk in a corner, and a few cases of wine stacked against a wall. These people were so rich they had an empty room in a house in Tokyo, Maya thought, marveling.

She flipped the light switch, but nothing. It smelled new in here, like fresh wood floors, fresh paint, fresh furniture, no clutter from living. No sadness, she guessed. She stayed in the room, and closed the door behind her.

On the wall opposite the door, a projection.

It took her a moment to realize what she was seeing, that it wasn't a ghost suddenly animated in the room with her. The door behind her was made of rich amber maple, but it was unfinished as an aesthetic and had a small, perfect hole in it, where a bright light from the hall-way and ambient light from the rest of the house streamed in. Because the room was dark, the light through the hole acted as a camera ob-scura. Maya had never been in one before, but here she was, the bot-tom third of the tree trunk vividly projected onto the wall of this room, but upside down.

She tilted her head to try to see it upright, but to no avail. She walked toward the projection, her shadow blocking some parts of the image. She put her hand against it. There, beneath her hand, were the perfect irregular lines of the curved trunk, just before it split off into smaller branches, and just before those branches exploded in the last of the season's red leaves. All of that, the branches and leaves, the tree's upward trajectory, was down at her feet, the image slipping over the baseboard.

Incredible, she thought. An object she'd been looking at all night, brand-new, newly alive. The tree looked so real, like a photo, but also so different, more than a photo. She turned around to look at the closed door. All of this, coming from the small opening, coming from the light.

Noah

It was hard to tell what was sickness from the time bath and what was sickness from grief. Both ailments had similar symptoms. Malaise, general disinterest, muscle aches, a sour stomach, sudden bouts of incurable sadness, weeping without a source, dissociation that felt painful, not freeing. But watching Eileen's sleeping body—or rather, her tossing and turning, her restlessness—his sickness felt more real, and more acutely associated with what the time bath was doing to his body, the radiation, the stress on his nervous system, the havoc Nils must see in his biometrics, which he wasn't telling Noah about.

He dragged a chair from the kitchen into the bedroom and watched Eileen sleep, and he had the strange sensation he was watching himself sleep, his form in her form, a lump on the bed, until she finally rolled over to face him, awake.

"No," she said.

"No, what?"

"You shouldn't keep folding."

Noah looked down at his hands. They were starting to show age, he'd noticed. Fine, long hairs growing from the patch between his thumb and first finger, going paler with each passing year. Perpetually dry skin. They were shaking a little. He'd begun shaking after he started folding, a small tremor emanating from his heart, passing through his limbs.

"I know why," he said. "But, why?"

"You know why," is all Eileen said back.

Noah touched her hair, a shade darker than when they'd met, the same dark that Serena's would have been if she'd grown older. He was no longer nervous about touching Eileen. She was the same under his hands, the same as she was the night of the Europa disaster, the same as she was when they hugged the day she moved out of the house. Alive and familiar, even if sometimes she was warmer than others, or more brittle than others. All her modes were in him.

All his must be in her, too. He closed his eyes at the thought, at being known like that. At how lucky he was to be known like that, by more than just Eileen. By Serena. By Maya.

"Please," he said. "Come with me. One last fold."

He didn't expect Eileen to agree, but she had. It occurred to him that she would have agreed only if she truly believed all this would be over soon. She would make it so, destroy the project, or Nils and Klein, or the machine itself. He didn't know exactly how she'd do it, but the resolve had been in her since they'd left Talia, and he knew her resolve when he saw it.

There were two baths and a set of helmets for each. Nils had said the other bath, shoved against the wall, had been decommissioned, but Noah knew better. He knew the bath only had to be powered on and reset. And from the moment he first called Eileen to tell her what he'd experienced, he'd been thinking about a way to double fold, to connect the helmets such that the same memory could be written into both. It was a mechanical problem first, but he'd collected splitters and joints from the mess of the neighboring lab. The other problem—of two people folding into the same memory at once—was theoretical.

"I think it'll work," Noah said.

Eileen looked at him, then at the open time baths, then back at him. "You're crazy."

"If we both map the memory, I can run a program to resolve them both into an average."

"That's insane."

"Yeah," he said. "I know. But I've had a while to think about it. It's worth a try."

"And what happens if the memories don't average out?"

"I guess we fall out of the fold. I'm not sure."

Eileen crossed her arms over her chest and pressed her lips together. With that look, he knew she would comply.

"A vivid dream," she said, mostly to herself.

"No it's not," Noah insisted. He repeated the data they'd already gone over—he could bring up a synaptic map of average brain activity during dreams and compare it to her own markedly different map. He reminded her of valid research on superpositions and consciousness. And before he launched into a discussion of the irreconcilable properties of quantum physics and classical physics, an infamously unanswerable problem, and before he used the fact that it was unanswerable as a reason (*if you cannot explain why, then you cannot explain why not*), she stopped him.

"I mean that whatever we're going to do, the past remains unchangeable," she said.

"But you heard what Talia said, about Klein's plan for causality."

"But they aren't there yet."

"No, not yet." Noah paused. "But what about when they *are* there?"

Eileen narrowed her eyes. "That's what they want you for."

He hadn't explicitly told her as much, but it wasn't a question. She knew.

She said, "You won't do it."

Noah looked down with a flush of shame and anger. Her knowing his secret desires, telling him what to do. "You're afraid," he said quietly. It was an attempt to hurt her.

But all she said was, "Yes."

"So that night, then," Noah said. "The night she died."

"You woke up before me," Eileen said.

"I know."

"What if I don't want to see?"

He took her hand, which was icy cold. "I'll be there."

They put on the mapping helmets and sat, and for twenty minutes, separately, they remembered. After twenty minutes were up, he got out and went back to the controls.

"Are you ready?" he asked into the mic.

"I never was," she said. "So I guess yes."

He ran the resonance program and hurried back to the bath. They quickly undressed. He cut the lights, then while Eileen climbed into her bath, he self-administered the Fold Cocktail. He opened Eileen's bath to do the same. She looked peaceful, floating there. Her eyes opened softly, and he shook his head slightly to tell her not to talk. He gave her the shot, and got back in his bath.

He waited for the memory to come back, and while he waited, he thought he heard Eileen saying *no*, or *Noah*, or *now*. His body felt slick and raw, and he tried to forget his body and listen to Eileen, but he slipped—he slips—

* * * * * *

—into their bedroom. The old bedroom in the Los Feliz house. A sound slices right through him—not Eileen, but animal, brief, high

271

tenor, no words. Not a moan, but a cry. Later, he won't be sure he actually heard it, but now he's sure. It snaps him up from bed. The room gray with light, Eileen beside him, sleeping. He wants to wake her—how can she be sleeping? But she is. She was and she is.

He gets out of bed: 3:17 a.m. The heaviness of his body dissipates quickly now, the quickest it has ever faded, and before he knows it he's in the hallway, his hand on Serena's door, which is cold to the touch. He pushes it open. Everything is as he remembers it. The dollhouse askew on the small desk, a family of miniature cats strewn out on the floor beneath it.

He walks to her bed and kneels down. This is her body under his hands, warm still, warm, she is alive. Her eyes are closed and her mouth is open and her pillow is wet with drool, but she gurgles and raises her arms for him. When she holds him and he holds her, there is a memory, inside this living memory. Her first full sentence to him, when she was nineteen months old, rings in his ears: "Daddy, need my monkey." The expression of her need had filled him like helium. And now her clinging to him with what little life she has left.

This folding doesn't feel like a transition, but a completion. His body is now matching his mind, filling that burned-out hole he's carried around for so many years. He is reunited with his grief.

A sound comes out of him. A deep scream, the body's primal power.

He picks Serena up, wraps her legs around his waist, and runs. He didn't do this before. Before, he only made it to the living room, screamed for Eileen, and she called an ambulance.

Now, though. Now he can't help himself. He can't stop himself from helping himself, helping Serena. He runs down the stairs, out the door, down the driveway, to the car. The keys. Shit, the keys. Serena is limp now, and he places her in the back seat, where her red cheek smooshes against the leather.

"I'll be right back, baby," he says, and sprints back into the house, but when he gets inside, heart pumping, it's Eileen standing in the living room in her T-shirt, looking like a ghost in the gray light.

"What's going on?" she says, frantic. "What's happening? Where are you going?"

Eileen

She thought the door had been closed, but it is open.

Noah's left it open.

Instantly she is overwhelmed by a smell—the bed's smell, a mix of Noah's deodorant and her bergamot candle she always burned before sleep. They discontinued that candle two years later, so she'd forgotten the particular scent. Now she almost doesn't want to get up from the bed, comforted by inhaling the aroma of her old life.

But then Noah's voice, and Eileen tries to get up, to push away the covers, but it feels as if she is underwater. She tries not to remember that she is actually in water, because Noah warned it's not helpful to live in that other timeline when you're trying to live in this one. So, with all the strength she has, the same guttural, moaning effort she used when she pushed in labor for two hours, she gets out of bed. Or rather, she falls out of bed.

Then Noah's voice is there again, through that open doorway, a glimpse of his face. He's screaming. She's never heard him scream this way before. She pushes herself up from the rug, and now, suddenly, she's light. She's so light that she's afraid she doesn't exist.

Noah is holding Serena in his arms. But it's wrong. It looks wrong. She's too limp. Eileen tries to speak, but it feels impossible. She realizes that it's because she didn't wake this early, not when this all actually happened. Back then, she didn't wake until Noah had Serena in the living room and was screaming Eileen's name.

But here, now she is awake. Noah runs with Serena. Down to the living room and then, to Eileen's shock, out the door. Eileen finds the words when he is in the driveway, heading back into the house, and she pulls them up from her lungs to ask him the question. *What's happening?*

Then she's running, past Noah, outside, to the car, where Serena's body is limp in the back seat, to her daughter, and she holds her. She can feel Noah behind her, and then suddenly he is holding Serena, too. They hold on to her together, and that's how Eileen knows Serena is still alive. Serena is warm, and Eileen can feel the child's small hot breath against her neck. The smell here in the middle of the three of them is so specific it's almost indescribable. It has curvatures and color. Earthy, round, wet, close. The last waft of air in a dark cave after everyone has left. A sob grows in Eileen's throat.

Somewhere a clock ticks: 3:19.

Noah

The question of when Serena died. The medical examiner had put time of death at three a.m., but Noah knows Serena was alive when he woke. The cry he'd heard, the butterfly of her damaged heart against his chest when he'd held her. He'd tried to convince the doctor he was wrong, and the doctor let him speak, but the whole time he wore a look of sympathy, listening to the hysterical rantings of a man who'd just lost his child. The doctor knew nothing would change anything.

But what if something could? What if Noah could change it? Time of death was flexible. How much would he give for a few more minutes? Would he give an entire lifetime? Would he give Eileen? Would he give his career? Would he give a woman he hasn't met yet, Maya, who brings color back to his life when everything is sadness?

These are the questions Noah asked himself back then. The answer always yes, anything, I'll give anything for more time, more of it.

Now, though. Now what?

Eileen

"Serena, baby, I'm right here," Eileen is saying. Now she is in the back seat, holding Serena in her lap, but Serena is too heavy. Eileen can't tell if she's breathing. Serena won't open her eyes.

Noah is already in the driver's seat, starting the car. They're all still in their pajamas. The sky is going gunmetal, a hazy day getting ready to break. The door to the house is still wide open, and inside is endless dark.

The car pulls backward, but Eileen is having trouble taking her eyes off the open mouth of the house.

This feels wrong, she can't say.

This is what they should have done.

No, this is just something they could have done.

Something they are doing.

"Noah, stop." Her voice comes out meek at first, her throat still damp and closed from the fold transition.

But he throws the car in drive and they continue down their street.

"Noah, stop," she says, louder this time. On her lap, their daughter is heavier. Eileen can't look down. But she knows. Neither Serena nor she is here anymore.

Noah

He hasn't driven in a fold before, and the dizziness is overwhelming, but the overwhelm grounds him. This is the difference, this is movement, this is purpose, this will change things.

He doesn't know how long Eileen has been speaking before he hears her, but when he does hear her, it feels as if she has been speaking for minutes.

"Noah, stop."

If he stops. If he stops, nothing will happen. But something has to happen. So he doesn't stop. He continues, makes a turn at the stop sign, then another turn at the next stop sign, and he's on the boulevard, and Children's Hospital is three minutes away, and this will all work, or at least it will be different. He only wants things to be different.

But as he drives, as the dizziness clouds in his forehead, as his hands tremble on the steering wheel, as his vision waves with nausea, he hears an act so specific it's almost as if he can see it. Eileen's face against Serena's, her lips on their daughter's cheek still wet with sweat, the close sound of silent weeping, one body shaking against another. He can hear it, so he can see it, and it's like he's looking both ways at once, forward at the road and backward into the back seat, where this is happening.

Eileen's grief, like an open door. He should walk through it.

Eileen

This is all she knows how to do. Eliminate the space between her body and Serena's, her sobs and Serena's silence. She has longed on a cellular level to hold her daughter again. Serena was once inside her, and now Eileen holds on to her body as if she might return there, to her womb.

She doesn't look up, and her eyes are squeezed closed, but she can feel Noah looking. She tries not to think of him too hard. Not to think of what Noah needs right now. This is what she needs, and she hopes that in that way, in being honest about that, Noah will see what he needs.

Which is to stop.

—They tumbled out of it together, choking on the liquid, on all the pain in their veins. The next thing she knew, she was on the floor in Marfa, on all fours, black liquid slicking off her, coughing for air. She stared at the floor while she found her breath and thought of what she wanted to show Noah now.

He fell next to her, his knees cracked on the floor, and she looked at him. The same searching eyes, the same hope etched into the curve of his shoulders, the way they curved toward her, the way they always curved toward whoever he thought held the answer.

"Noah," she said. "I thought the door was closed. But the door was open."

Noah and Eileen

What had happened was this.

At 3:17 a.m., Noah wakes with a start. A cry from his daughter, the kind of cry that tells a parent something is wrong, not a normal night-time shriek brought on by a weird turn in the bed. Noah glances at the digital numbers on his bedside clock and then bolts to the hallway, where he pauses at Serena's door to listen for the cry again. It doesn't come. So he turns the knob in his hand and enters, and he knows immediately. The way she's lying in the bed, her face up to the ceiling, unconscious.

"No," he says, and then noises.

Noah sees the cluster of stars above Serena's bed, and as he starts to cry, the light blurs, and it becomes one big burst of aqua light. He runs to his daughter, scoops her up, and carries her down the stairs, to the living room, where he collapses, because he suddenly isn't sure if she is alive. He screams and screams for Eileen. She will know what to do.

Eileen snaps her eyes open in bed. "What what what?" she mumbles, turning over and finding Noah not there. Then she looks at the door, which is open. Later, she will recall that the door was closed, that Noah closed it, and in a way, later he will close it on her, and they will be severed in their grief.

But she will be wrong. The door was open. It is open.

Eileen runs through that open door. Noah's protests grow louder, *no no no no*. In the living room, he is holding her. Eileen sees this, the way his face is breaking apart, the way she isn't moving, and she doesn't go toward her daughter. Instead, she moves to solve the problem. To the phone. To 911. To an ambulance on the way. This is what Eileen does for Noah. She finds answers.

Noah is left alone with this impossible moment, which he will later recall as his being abandoned by Eileen, which, in a way, Eileen will later do, in order to survive.

The ambulance is here. Eileen has gathered the things. Clothes for Serena, clothes for her, shoes for her husband. She must remain calm, because Noah cannot. She must know there are answers, because Noah does not.

Both of them begin to understand that it is over when the EMTs rush through their home with their dirty boots and take their daughter and put her on a stretcher. This is not what's supposed to happen, ever. Something bad has happened, and it is irreversible, and that icy feeling grows in their abdomens.

Regardless, they follow, wishing the whole time there were other choices to make, other choices they made, a way to stop time, to hold it, to reverse it. They climb into the ambulance even though Eileen knows only one of them is allowed inside. The EMTs seem to take pity on them then. Eileen and Noah sit on either side of the stretcher. Eileen takes one of Serena's small hands and Noah takes the other, and they both look at their daughter, who is having all manner of contraptions attached to her face, until she becomes unrecognizable, or unseeable, and so Eileen and Noah look at each other. It's over sometime in this journey. It ends while they're looking at each other.

What Noah knows is that when they arrive at the hospital, he tries to hurry the EMTs, puts his anger and rage on them. What Eileen knows is that in the exam room, she tears through the mess of doctors and grabs her baby off the table and holds her to her body, as if she can fuse her back to life, hug her so tightly that she becomes a part of Eileen's body again. She imagines opening up, breathing her back in. The desire is overwhelming. So is the knowledge that her baby is gone. She doesn't feel any life inside her arms. She won't feel any life in her arms for a long time.

Soon the doctors take Serena from Eileen's arms—*We have to take her, ma'am, we have to examine*—and pronounce her dead, but we aren't there yet. Serena hasn't been taken from her yet, pulled from her, Eileen emptied. Noah stands there and looks on, a witness. He won't take Serena from her, either. For now, they're staying in that moment, one that isn't impossible, one in which possibility itself is the entire thing, the possibility given by a child, a life lived, however short, forever entangled.

Eileen

"Noah," Eileen said. "Again, but let me."

She got out of the bath to map a new memory.

"Remember," she said. "When she was born."

"Yes," Noah said. He was whispering.

"Okay, then."

She remembered. Neurons firing, but something else, too, something no one and nothing could take a picture of or map. A blooming in a place no machine could access, a whiff of what it was to be alive, a substance as visible but uncontainable as light.

Then they got back in their baths. Eileen was trembling.

A wave ran through her, starting at the crown of her head, pulsing down her neck, a feeling between dizziness and weightlessness, pleasurable until—

*   *   *   *   *

—it is not pleasurable. The pain radiates through her body with heat, both general and with a sharpness. She imagined contractions to be more like cramps, but this is a molten rod electrifying her entire body. There is nothing to do but moan.

She hears herself before she is conscious of making the sound. Then she opens her eyes at the end of the moan, and there they are, the dim room, the bright lights on her groin, Noah standing, holding one of her legs up, staring like a wild deer into the light.

The doctor, the doctor's name, Dr. Harrison, yes, that's her name, and there are two nurses hovering, one holding her leg, another somewhere else, waiting for the baby that is descending. Others beyond the periphery. She can't make out what anyone is saying, but there's a din of urgency, and the brightness of the lights on their expectant faces lets her know she should push now. She should push.

She pushes. Pushing obliterates the pain, the red bolt inside her, or at least counters it. And it takes everything from her, the effort. When she stops pushing, she feels like she has passed out, the world gone dark and quiet. It's Noah's hand on her calf, squeezing it, that brings her back. She opens her eyes, and there he is, present, looking at her.

"Hey," he says.

She can't respond except to push. The time between the contractions now shortened, incalculable, not so much a measurement of time as a period of gathering in the wake, like the ebb and flow of the ocean on the shore, hard to tell the moment when one ends and the other begins. This is it, now, she knows, the push when her mind stops making decisions and her body takes over. Her body pushes. She screams along with the surge. Everybody seems to be yelling, smiling.

There's the head.

She reaches down, touches the curve of a new skull, a body emerging from her body, and then she collapses back, another final contraction roiling up inside her. This will be the last one. Why did she come here? The pain almost too much to bear, her stubborn refusal to get an epidural, the taste of sick in her mouth, her body slick from sweat. The scream starts in her cervix, and blooms in both directions. Her body opens like a door. Briefly. Enough time for a human to slip out.

"Oh my god," she says. The first time she has spoken. Both in this fold and as a mother, as this new person. She feels different. A force of energy released from her, and another energy rushing in to fill the space. A baby cries, her baby.

In seconds, the baby, purple, wrinkly, confused, is on her chest. Noah is there. Something else is happening, the doctor delivering the placenta, she isn't sure, a nurse cleaning a mess. Eileen can't pay attention to any of that, she has no attention for anything but the baby on her body, the baby that was once in her body. And on the other side of the baby, his hand holding the baby's head, Noah. Suddenly it seems clear to her, what a family is. The volcanic fire that was running through her body, that produced this baby into the world, it transformed and is now a thin, tensile, indestructible fiber running between the three of them. Forever.

She can feel that now, the forever.

They don't try to change anything. They remain as long as they can.

The fold made them sick. Noah more so, but Eileen felt nauseated and weak, and after they showered, they both collapsed in bed, in Noah's place. Lights off. They hadn't spoken much since they came out of the fold. Noah fielded a call from Nils, agreed to a fold the following day, lied and told him everything else was going well.

Eileen lay on her side, her body a crescent in the direction of Noah. He lay on his back, looking up at the day disappearing through the skylight. It was hard to sleep, despite the weakness. Her brain buzzed with adrenaline. It had been so real.

She felt a question brewing in Noah, so she didn't speak, waited for him to ask it. Eventually, he did.

"What did you mean, the door was open?"

Of course, she hadn't explained it. He hadn't even known she'd carried that with her, a part of the grief, the idea that he'd closed the door on her while her daughter died.

"Serena," she said. "I thought, when you got up to go check on her, you closed the door behind you, leaving me in the room to sleep. I always thought if I had heard you sooner, if you hadn't closed the door, I could have come. I could have helped."

"You couldn't have," Noah said.

"I know," Eileen said. "But the closed door was this small idea that I could. A possibility."

He reached for her hand. She let him hold it.

"But in that fold, you left the door open. Maybe you only left the door open now. And before, my memory was right and the door was closed. I don't know. Maybe the idea that I could have done something is still there."

He didn't let go of her hand, but he turned on his side, to face her.

"The objective truth isn't important. What's important is that I left the door open now, and you walked through it."

Eileen smiled. He was parroting back to her what she'd said to him, about his fold to the Europa disaster. "That's the truth," she said.

She knew then, without asking, that Noah understood what she was trying to show him, in her fold. That he'd been looking for the wrong thing, a way to reverse the irreversible, instead of finding the permanence. What happened when Serena was born, it was always happening, their family. Her death was not something they could affect. Her life was something they always would have.

Later, when Noah fell asleep, Eileen finally got up and went back to Maya's painting room. She looked again through Maya's sketchbooks, flipping past her own face, a vulture, pronghorn, cubes, an empty landscape. She walked to the window and looked out at the black desert. At her feet was a small succulent in a pot, two plants held together with a rubber band. The plant on top had begun to flower a tiny white tissue of a leaf.

Eileen looked back at the dark, trying to see. She suspected if she let her eyes unfocus just enough, let reality blur in the right way, she could see whatever she wanted. But it was hard to let go. It was hard to help someone else let go. She needed someone else who could see what she couldn't, and what Noah wouldn't.

Eileen reached for her phone, tucked in her pocket. She had to call Maya.

Maya

Maya's parents wanted to go to the Yuko Matsuda retrospective with her. There'd been a change between them since the anniversary party. They seemed even more relaxed, not braced against whatever they imagined Maya might bring up. *That's how families work*, Maya thought, *all the terror, the making of the mind, the stuff of memories turned into potential threats*. Luckily, they had this chance to slough off all that old stuff and be new and simple again. That was also how families worked, she knew, endless remakings.

She grabbed donburi at the supermarket for them to eat quickly before heading off to the gallery, but when she got back home, she found her father tucked inside a small storage closet that was usually closed off by a love seat. In fact, she'd never been inside the closet before. But there she found him, looking too large seated on the floor, a box open before him with photos spilling out. His eyes were glazed, and he said, "Dust allergies," when he saw her standing in the doorway.

"Come," he said, scooting an inch for her to sit next to him.

She did, and immediately bumped her head on the sloped wall where the building's outdoor stairs ran. Above her head, a neighbor made their way upstairs, their feet clomping inches from her throbbing head. Her father gestured to photos piled into plastic sandwich bags, labeled with Sharpie on washi tape.

To sit, she had to cram herself shoulder-to-shoulder with him. She couldn't remember the last time she'd been so close to her father. Maybe that afternoon at Haneda Airport when she was seventeen, when her parents saw her off to the American college she'd insisted on, and her mother had been crying, which had made Maya cry, and so she looked to her father, who was stoic but offered her his arms, and she'd plunged into them. They weren't huggers, her family. It wasn't common in Japan, to cross the physical distance so casually. Though they'd spent time in the States earlier in her life, the practice alarmed her when she got to college, but then she got used to it, and when she went back home for the winter holidays, she embraced her father in a way that shocked him, and he recoiled, and she never forgot it. That's when the distance between them hardened.

"Here," her father said. He balanced a photo on her knee.

She picked it up. It was from her first trip to Japan with Noah, when they were dating, when her parents met him. Noah had wanted to come so badly, and she'd been apprehensive, but then they'd had the best time. It wasn't to do with her parents—her mother seemed to like him fine and her father seemed generally unimpressed but mildly amused by Noah's eagerness to please. Their good time had more to do with how, in this place far away from where they'd met, they seemed to see each other more clearly. She'd always felt like a child in her parents' home, even in the apartment she'd never actually lived in, but with Noah, she was more, an adult with the man she would probably marry, a native playing visitor, a no-longer-prodigal, gone-away daughter. Seeing the city through his eyes, too, made everything new and alive.

In the photo her father handed to her, she and Noah were standing between her parents, outside Meiji Jingu shrine.

"I remember Noah asked that drunk guy to take it," Maya said, smiling.

"The man did a good job," her father said. "We are in the center of the photo, everyone smiling."

He was right, they did look happy, all of them. Sure, that was partly due to all of them looking several years younger, and the slant of late afternoon sun, and the generous blur of the photographer's shaky hand. But it was also the simplicity of their pleasure, being outside, Noah seeing something new, the shrine and park that were practically in her family's blood. They'd taken their time wandering through the yellowing ginkgo trees of the outer garden, marveling at the decorative sake barrels, and Noah let her father tell a long and boring story about how they always waited here on New Year's Eve to say a prayer and eat soba. Then at the shrine itself they'd seen a Shinto wedding processional, the bride in the white hood obscuring everything but her red lips, and she could tell that Noah thought it was magic. He asked her mother if she'd worn one during her wedding, and her mother laughed and laughed, and that set off a laughing chain, because Maya had never seen her mother laugh with such abandon. They'd had to retreat from the wedding scene because Maya and her mother were laughing so hard, and it was when they'd finally calmed down, joy in their pores, that Noah asked the drunk man to take a photo.

"I like him," her father said now. "Noah is a good man."

Maya nodded. "I like him, too."

"You go back to him," her father said, not as an instruction or a question, but as a fact.

She looked at her father's face as he peered over the top of his glasses to study more pictures. She wanted to ask him a million questions. Why did he move his family around so much when she was little? Didn't he ever wonder how it affected her? Why did he seem to love the American parts of his wife so much but ignore them in his daughter? Why, when she came back from college that first year, did he refuse to speak to her in English? Why didn't he ever come to California to visit her?

"Ah, here it is," he said, holding out a photo. It was a grainy film photo, thick and curling at the edges. In it, Maya was about four, wearing a polka-dot swimsuit tied in big bows at her shoulders. She was on the beach, squinting through heavy bangs, clasping her hands, legs shy and chunky, her smile all teeth.

"Okinawa," her father said, as if he'd read her mind. "Your first time going in the ocean. People would stop us to say how cute you were. And not only Westerners. Japanese people, too. So that's how we knew, because all Japanese babies are cute, but you were extra cute."

"To think of all the money I could have made modeling."

At this her father laughed. "Models are quiet. You, you were never quiet."

"I wasn't, I know," Maya said. She looked demure in the photo, but devilish, too. "Why did you want to remember *this*?"

Her father cleared his throat. She saw he was nervous. "The anniversary party," he said. "Talking to you about Noah. You know, when children are this age, there is so much responsibility. We had to make sure you didn't sunburn, you didn't drown, that you were well fed, well hydrated. Now it's different, caring for you. There's not the same need. I'm sorry if I didn't know how to do that part, the later part."

Maya shook her head. It was okay, it was.

"I think you must forgive Noah, whatever you need to forgive him for, Maya-chan. Nothing distorts time the way having a child does. And losing one, I would imagine."

"All right," she said. "I know."

Then they heard the latch on the front door open and close, her mother taking off her shoes and padding down the hallway, calling out, "Tadaima!" Maya and her father looked at each other conspiratorially, and stayed quiet. After some grunting around the moved furniture, her mother appeared in the closet doorway.

"What on earth."

"Okaeri," Maya said, and scooted a couple of inches for her mother to squeeze herself in.

"Is this how we're getting ready to go to an art show?"

"Look," Maya said, handing her mother the photo from Okinawa.

"Ah," her mother said. "So cute. Even Japanese people would stop us to say so. But this day, you were such a little brat."

Maya couldn't help it, but she started to giggle. As she shook, her head hit the sloped ceiling, and she braced herself against the wall, jostling her parents out of the way. They bumped against walls, knocking over memories. No one quite fit, but they stayed in there anyway.

At first, Maya spotted Ren through the art. Yuko Matsuda's newer work hung from the ceiling, Lucite panes joined together with what the labels called "collage" in between them, but Maya thought they were much more than the randomness that the word implied. Matsuda had taken images from her photo archives and paired them with newer photos, but she'd cut both into pieces, so they were scattered between the panes like an almost-done puzzle, incomplete on both sides of the panel. She'd mixed in dried flowers and bits of other paper media—maps, newspaper, drawings. The panels were hung from sockets that allowed the cables to rotate if touched or blown by air, which they did as the gallery filled up. The otherwise static images became moving images. Seeing one panel side in its entirety was nearly impossible. Maya had to keep moving to take a panel in, to follow the slowly rotating images.

She first saw Ren through one of the swaying panels, his face appearing behind two sides of smashed dried flower. She led her parents through the maze of panels toward him. They found him standing next to Yuko Matsuda herself. Matsuda was a small woman, about fifteen years older than Ren and Maya. She wore oversize, androgynous clothes—a big denim button-down and linen pants—and architectural glasses, with her hair slicked back. Maya immediately wanted to be her and was also terrified of her.

"Tanaka-san!" Ren said, and bowed to Maya's mother before she pulled him into a hug. He smiled at Maya over her mother's shoulder.

Her father warmly accepted the bow and returned with his own—decidedly not a hugger—and Ren introduced them all to Yuko. He described Maya as "a critic and artist living in Los Angeles," which sent a thrill down her spine. Was that who she was? Yuko took her hand and said in English that she was pleased to meet her.

"Congratulations," Maya said, returning Yuko's English. "What an incredible way to present your life's work so far. It's so . . ." Maya trailed off, unsure how to describe what she was feeling in a way that wouldn't seem like she was diminishing what Yuko was doing. But she saw then that Yuko was listening intently, waiting for her to finish her sentence, and that she should tell the truth, exactly as she saw it.

"It's so difficult to take in, which I would imagine is part of the point here. That it's impossible to consume a life's work the way you might consume a movie or a book. And that it keeps shifting, the way it's presented. Not static. It's a difficult experience for the viewer— hard to even make your way through it, physically, to see where you're going to bump into something, or walk toward something that isn't actually there."

Yuko smiled at her. "It's nice to hear someone say what they really think. So many people come up to me saying lots of bullshit, what they think I want to hear. You're right. It's difficult. *Muzukashi-desu.* It was hard to live it, and to make it. Now it should be hard to walk through it."

Maya laughed. "There's a certain ostentatiousness to the very idea of a retrospective, isn't there?"

"Exactly," Yuko said. "Also, I am not dead yet, am I? Retroactively perceive me all you want once I'm dead. But for now, I've still got life."

"But then why do this at all?" Maya's mother asked.

"*Shouganai*. Because one must," Yuko said. "One must look back. And one must also get paid."

Her mother laughed then. Ren caught Maya's eye and nodded toward the back room.

"Please excuse us, Matsuda-san," Ren said. "I have something to show Maya."

Maya's mother raised her eyebrows.

"Calm down, it's just art," Maya said.

"It always is," Yuko said, and took her mom by the elbow to lead her toward a table full of champagne.

In the back room of the gallery, amid dollies and wooden platforms and empty pedestals, Ren brought Maya to a corner where he'd set up his work, covered with a tarp. He loved a dramatic reveal. His inclination toward the dramatic was part of what had attracted her to him in the first place, a tendency toward the sharpest angles, the slightest warmth of friction between ideas or people or places. It's partly what sprang her to life.

"You finished it," Maya said. "That was fast."

"I wouldn't say finished. But it's in a place I think is interesting." He nodded at the tarp. "You do it."

She yanked at the corner and the tarp fell away, revealing what Ren had made, what they had made. The photo was mounted but not framed. Maya's eyes went straight to her face. In the photo she was looking down to her left, so her face was mostly in profile, and she remembered feeling tired and a little drunk, but in the photo she looked focused and full, about to disclose a secret. Those clothes Ren got her at the vintage shop looked lived-in, perfectly draped on her, the tissue-thin tank top the color of her skin, the curved seam of the pants mirroring the way her left arm bowed out at her side, like she was about to pirouette. The light Ren had set up blasted the wall she was standing in front of, completely blown out so it appeared as if she were standing in white space. The blanket she'd abandoned was pooled in the opposite corner of the photo, so precisely rendered it looked like a circle of navy water. But none of this was the center of the photo. The center of the photo was the canvas Maya was pulling behind her, that imperfect blank one Ren had her run her hands across, but it was no longer blank. She bent down to get a better look. With tiny brushstrokes, Ren had painted on the photo. No, he'd painted over a photo he'd printed onto this canvas.

"What I did was I printed out this photo we took that night, and then I resized and placed the old picture of us from Portland over the canvas. Then I took the photo again. Then I painted over the canvas part." Ren explained this to her, sensing her confusion.

That's why it looked so distorted, and so vibrant. A photo of two photos, one of them painted over.

The old photo resized on the canvas: a damp gray night in Portland in that apartment near the bridge, water dripping sideways from the street above them onto their window even though it wasn't actively raining anymore. Just the silent drips, and the aftermath of their fight. It was near the end of the relationship, after he'd floated the idea of moving to New York, after he'd been selected for the Biennial. That night they ate the cheapest burritos they could find, and he mentioned he'd found a studio in Cobble Hill.

"A studio for your work?" Maya had asked.

"A live-work place," he said. "Like, I'd live there and work out of there until I find a studio space for my art."

This was the problem then. Whenever he spoke about New York, he never once spoke about "we." She was so angry he ruined the burrito for her. She had been starving, and now she wanted nothing to do with it. She put the unfinished food down on the counter, where it would stay until morning. The fight that erupted then was the worst they'd ever had, having an effect like an earthquake, a strong jolt along a fault line, resulting in a permanent breakage. She screamed at him, and he hated to be screamed at. He iced her out. She felt abandoned. He didn't know how to leave her. She didn't want him to leave. As she cried, she remembered when they first met, how perfectly they'd fit together, their desires and their pasts and their imagined future. She thought this fight, his imminent departure, was making all that came before false. He'd been a coward. She'd been a coward. They'd both been afraid to look at what was really happening, their lives diverging, the logical end of a molten partnership.

Now she knew, of course, that it had to happen that way. That he'd had to leave and she'd had to be alone. That he'd become what he became, and she'd move toward scholarship, which she loved, and which he'd never have tolerated in their relationship. Back then, he'd thought an academic perspective would ruin whatever he had going on, that what he was doing resisted intellectual analysis. But for her, it was the way toward the art. It was only after he left that she could admit that to herself.

The fight eventually lost steam, and while they hadn't made up, they'd reached a détente. She crawled into bed, as close to the edge as she could manage. The memory of the swell of anger was still gurgling in her chest. He set up a camera on a long stand so it nearly hovered above the bed. He didn't ask, but she knew what he was doing, and she didn't protest. He got into bed, but didn't touch her. He stayed on his side. He on his back, and she circled on her side. The kitchen light was on, but it was dark near their bed, so the effect was shadowy and golden. She heard a click of the remote in his hand, the shutter going. This would be their last photo together.

That's what he'd put over the canvas. And then he'd painted over that, making their faces blank beige orbs, but drawing each finger of her hand wrapped around her wrist, and the contours of his closed fist around the shutter trigger. The light was better in his painting, more dramatically shadowed, both of them in golden dark, and a raindrop-filled slant of light between them on the bed. Maya saw the textures of the paint he'd used, the thick, wobbly lines where he'd corrected a stroke. In the spot where there'd been a depression on the stretched canvas, he'd swirled blue, like the blue of the blanket on the floor. In the center of the swirl was a black dot, almost like a hole in the picture, a portal to somewhere else.

She stood up. Nostalgia sliced through her, and not a nostalgia to *return* to that damp bedroom, but a visceral memory, the feeling of dampness, a chill, a separation, a silence. The clarity of having been there, the knowledge that it was gone.

"Natsukashii," she said to Ren. The Japanese phrase for an evocative memory, of the particular, of a life that existed only in a single moment in time. The word had a positive connotation, though. Nostalgia without the sadness, without the loss.

He nodded. "That's what I'll call it."

Maya's mother and father were enjoying themselves without her. She watched them, leaning against the bar, drinking champagne. By now the crowd was thinned out, but her parents were still enjoying. The way her father put his hand lightly on the small of her mother's back captivated Maya. He wasn't guiding her—her mother was always the one to lead. But he was putting a hand there as a way to sustain his presence. Not revolutionary, she knew. But it was the careful architecture of their relationship now so clear for her. Her father moved the family from place to place for his job, but her mother was the one who kept them together, making an apartment a home, bridging her Japanese husband and her American daughter. Maya had left for America because she didn't want to be a side of the bridge anymore. Children who have no siblings bear this pressure.

Maybe her parents' life hadn't gone exactly how they'd imagined it, that life of travel and adventure they'd seen promised in each other the night they'd met, thrilled by their differences. Nothing was that simple, though. Children, a job, those loose tethers across countries and cultures. But looking at them now, Maya saw that ultimately it didn't matter. What they'd been for each other when they met, they still were, even if the context of their life changed. Her father a stanchion, her mother with her face turned toward translucent art.

Maya looked down at the show pamphlet in her hand. "Yuko Matsuda: Disappearing." When she looked up, she couldn't find her parents. She walked through the maze of panels for a bit, and then at the end of a path came to a video installation that was running on a loop on one wall. There were a few of these, old works Matsuda had reinterpreted in video form, and Maya hadn't paid them much attention. She didn't care much for video installation as a form. It always felt cold and distanced, which, she knew, was sometimes the point. But she'd much rather watch performance art in person than a video rendering of art.

But since no one was standing in front of it, she did. And it took several seconds before she realized this was *Weight* reimagined. It was the static photograph, the one she'd been lecturing about when she met Noah, the one in Ren's apartment, but here there was artificially imposed movement strobing across it. She leaned down and read the label: "Made with volumetric video capture, often used in augmented reality."

"Sounds expensive," Maya said under her breath.

"It was." Maya startled. Yuko appeared next to her, eyes heavy from the evening.

In the photograph, the woman, visible from the back, was holding the balloons, but then her form shot out, jumping off the edge of the building. The woman, obviously Yuko herself, wasn't holding the balloons anymore, and she fell, but because the photo didn't move, her body never descended. Maya could only tell the body was falling by the way her clothes and hair moved upward.

"I used this photo for a lecture I was doing when I met my husband," Maya said. "But this version is way cooler."

"Yes, the original is a bit depressing, isn't it?" Yuko said.

"That's what my husband says. That the woman always looked like she was going to jump, and obviously the balloons couldn't help her."

"Oh, that's not what I meant," Yuko said. "It's a bit depressing because of the lack of a decision in the photograph. Don't you want to scream at her, *Do something*? That's why I made her do something in this."

"She's jumping, though," Maya said. "Isn't that depressing?"

Yuko didn't respond right away. She tilted her head. "I don't know. That's Setagaya, you know. The skyline doesn't even look like that anymore."

Maya saw she was right. A few tall administrative buildings were missing from the corner of the frame, ones recently erected, in the time that Maya was away from the country. So the woman leapt, but she was held by the past.

Later, Maya stepped outside the gallery for some air. It was the beginning of a cold drizzle. She stood under the awning and looked in the gallery from the outside like she was a ghost. Ren was still around, even though he'd insisted he had to go home at least twice. Where no one else noticed her, he saw her standing on the other side of the window and walked up to her from the inside. He spoke, pointing to an invisible watch on his wrist, pointing down the street, but she only heard a deep muted tone. *Are you leaving?*

She smiled. She looked down the street in the direction he'd pointed. She looked back at Ren. His face was hopeful, eyebrows raised, mouth open. Hopeful she'd leave, or hopeful she'd heal, or hopeful she didn't hate him, or hopeful she loved him.

Maya nodded. "I'm leaving," she said, loudly.

He heard, or he understood, anyway. He bowed his head slightly, then looked back up at her.

Home, she mouthed. She meant to where Noah was, not to her parents' apartment.

He understood that, too. He put his hand up and waved it once.

Maya backed up onto the sidewalk, out from under the awning. She thought of the Brooklyn street where Ren had left her all those years ago, crying, the buzz and smell of people and alcohol and bad decisions. Here the street was quiet, the corners dark and orderly, the sound of drizzle turning to big, fat raindrops hitting the cement.

Maya's phone vibrated in her pocket. She looked at it and saw a number she didn't recognize.

"Hello?"

"Hi. Maya?"

Her voice was thinner than Maya thought it would be, or perhaps Eileen was tired and slightly afraid. Eileen said she'd gotten Maya's number off Noah's phone. Maya listened and Eileen explained about Noah, about Nils, about Talia Bolson, about the unchangeable past pushing like a spike through their present. Eileen was finding out, Maya could sense, that Marfa and its lie of an endless sky made you think anything was possible, which was not a freeing idea at all. That actual freedom was knowing that each moment that slipped away was permanent if you lived it the right way, that moving forward was accumulation and not erasure. Maya was the one who could help Noah see that. Eileen asked her to come, and Maya said she'd already decided to and how strange it was that they'd both decided the same thing—Maya had to go home—at the same time, like entangled particles, like knowledge traveling faster than the speed of light, like people of the same family, context, past, future, now.

IV

Light

Noah

The evening Noah met Maya, he'd been out on what his therapist called one of his "grief walks." Annabel, his therapist, was seventy-two years old and she'd lost a child, an adult child, when she was in her fifties. Noah knew Annabel would have retired by now but stayed in business because of him. After Noah's divorce went through, his brother, Colin, seemed to feel duty bound to be there for him while also being completely unable to process emotions, resulting in incessant calls about going to therapy. Noah sought out Annabel mostly so Colin would stop calling. He came to like her, though. She never annoyed him with inane questions or meaningless platitudes. He told her he'd taken to going on long walks during the transition from dusk to dark. He liked to leave his house in that sad part of the day and return when it was dark. He'd become bored of his neighborhood, so he drove out to UCLA to walk around the campus there. No one stared at him like he was crazy for walking. When he walked, he did so for hours, noticed everything, took nothing in. A way to be around the world but not in it, Annabel said. That was okay, she said. The world would be there when he was ready.

He hadn't meant to go looking in classrooms. He was looking for a bathroom. But the door to the room Maya was presenting in was ajar, and the tone of her voice made him pause. She was speaking as if to a friend, impassioned but articulate, small jumps and skips in her alto that drew him closer. He slipped in and took a seat. Her professors sitting in the front didn't even turn around. He saw Maya clock him. Her eyes fluttered and she paused for a second. And he saw then that she was beautiful, with thick dark hair, dark eyes, a spattering of freckles across her cheeks. She smiled, and he sank into his chair. It had been a while since he'd felt a woman was beautiful. He saw lots of beautiful women (it was Los Angeles, after all) but he hadn't *felt* it, had his heart seize a little like this. Not even with Lily, the woman he'd briefly dated from the app; they were both using each other for company. Lily did make him nervous, but he was only nervous that she'd want to talk for real. Luckily, she never did.

Then he saw the photograph projected behind Maya, *Weight*. What was remarkable about it was that the longer he looked at the photo, and the more Maya talked, the more the photo changed. He noticed new things each time he examined it. The way the balloons were so shiny they must have been slicked with oil, that the cityscape looked like a painting, that the woman at the center was nude. The woman blended in, until she didn't. And then he saw her posture, and he recognized the emotion, a slight turning in, sadness pulling at her center like a black hole. He had that posture now.

After Maya finished, he waited a few minutes to talk to her. He felt like those moments were important, the pause before life expanded. He could sense the change coming, and though it was a positive feeling he was headed toward, he lingered. There was something sad about leaving your sadness behind.

He told her he appreciated the way the photograph made sadness feel like it had life. He appreciated the way she'd made him see that. She was charming, and spoke so fluently about image and meaning, it made him nervous. He was out of practice, talking about real things.

But the longer he stood there, the more he knew that he couldn't let her slip away. A dangerous current to that feeling, nudging toward desperation. Whatever Maya had here, this life, he wanted that.

So when the motion-sensor lights flicked off, he opened his eyes wider to the dark and asked her out. Over tacos she asked him what he liked most about physics, and he said, "Black holes," even though he'd never told anyone that was what he liked about physics. He didn't even know if it was really true, but right then it felt true. In a black hole, time and space are elastic—time is space, space is time. Explaining that to Maya was akin to what he felt being with her: that sitting at the table with her then, there, also indicated the future, the two of them entwined, the way he wouldn't let her go, the way she'd attach to him like a magnet, the long arc of whatever life they lived together, for however long, in whatever form.

"Black holes disrupt our understanding of past and future," Noah said. "I like that."

"I guess I always think of them as being about destruction," Maya said. "The death of a star."

"But they're about both, destruction and construction, rebirth," he said. "If a black hole exists, so does its inverse, a white hole."

"A white hole?" Maya leaned in. She was smiling. Her long hair fell over one shoulder.

"If a black hole consumes, a white hole ejects. Even stranger, if a black hole contains the future, a white hole is the expression of the future."

"You lost me," Maya said. "But that's okay."

Noah shrugged. "It's all hypothetical, anyway."

They smiled at each other across empty taco plates, the buzz of cars on the street fading in their comfortable silence. This was what it was to know you'd met someone you were supposed to meet; the beginning of everything. An event that contained the full weight of all possibilities, but happiness for one.

. . .

He had that feeling in his heart and mind when he sat on the couch in the house, waiting for Maya to walk through the door. Eileen had told him Maya was coming back, that she'd called Maya and asked her to. Noah had nodded; it made sense, though he couldn't articulate exactly why. He needed her, and also Eileen, future and past.

When Maya came in, Noah knew the feeling they'd had that first night was still there, under the years and mistakes they'd lived. She looked tired but deeply familiar, like a portal to his real life walking into the living room. She took her coat off and sat next to him on the couch. She leaned into him, and he held her weight.

"How was it?" he asked.

Maya sighed. "It was like time travel" was all she said.

He knew about Ren, the existence of Ren, the possibility of Ren. He wondered how much of each other they'd seen, what they'd done, if they'd touched, what she'd thought about touching him. Noah leaned down and inhaled Maya's hair and scalp, a smell like waking up late on a Sunday, sunlight from the window baking the comforter.

"Thank you for coming back," he said. "I need you."

"I'm ready to be back," she said. "I wanted to be back. That's all I wanted."

Then she saw the plant. She leaned forward and picked it up from the coffee table. Her hybrid succulent, green on bottom, magenta on top.

"Eileen found it," Noah said. "In the back by your paintings. She brought it out here. The light's better here, I think."

Maya turned it in her hands and examined it like it was rare gold.

"What?" he asked.

"It grew together. Like the woman said it would. There's no more rubber band."

"Oh, cool."

"It happened so fast," she said, still marveling. Then, "Eileen found it?" Her name like electricity between them.

"Yeah, I think she liked your paintings, so she was hanging out back there. Have you met her yet? She's in the guest suite."

Maya leaned back on him, placing the small plant carefully on her lap. "Not yet," she said.

He held her. She was with him; she would not go anywhere. "There's time," he said.

Nils seemed to be in a good mood, despite Noah's hunch that this summoning was bad. Oliver opened the door (in a suit, this one tweed) and guided them into the sunken living room, where they sat on the floor and waited for tea. When Oliver reemerged holding a tray with the tea, Klein came with him, wearing workout clothes, a light sheen on his forehead.

"Nils, my friend. Noah," he greeted them. "Please, stay seated. Let's drink."

Oliver poured the tea in silence, while Klein appeared to study Noah. Then Klein picked up his mug and began a toast: "To the past, the future, and the men who make it."

Noah held up his mug and drank. It was bitter.

"It's come to my attention—our attention—that you've been going rogue," Klein said. "We have access to fold records as they immediately upload to the cloud, despite deletion. It's not that we're upset. We expect curiosity. It's part of why we brought you on. You have a life's biography that breeds the curiosity we need in a test subject, a drive to find out whatever is possible to know."

"No one said I couldn't use the machine on my own," Noah said.

Klein nodded and smiled at Nils. "Of course. It was implied you wouldn't, but yes. But if you were sure what you were doing was aboveboard, then why did you walk around campus turning off light switches?"

His entire tone was bemusement, which made the conversation more chilling. Noah struggled to match his tone. "If you weren't worried about secrecy, then why install hidden cameras all over the campus?"

"Ah," Klein said, smiling. "We live in an age of continuous monitoring and exceptional optimization. Knowledge is key to all of that, of course. But you're smart to have figured it out so quickly. The others, it took time."

"The others?" Noah looked at Nils.

"We know you went to see Talia," Nils said, almost quietly, so as not to disturb Klein holding court.

"Don't worry," Klein said as a wave of panic crossed Noah's face. "There's no law against that. She'll be fine. Curtis will be fine. We take care of our own, as I'm sure you know from meeting with her. But Noah, what happened with Talia, well, it was unfortunate. We thought it best not to tell you so you didn't catastrophize, so you didn't have that reality in your head as you tried to enter other realities."

"You should have told me. I should have known everything."

"Oh, but you can't know everything. We don't even know everything," Klein said.

"Talia and I are the same. A presence at the Europa launch. Tragedies in our past that you knew would compel us to use the time bath in ways detrimental to our health."

"Well, now we know the health effects. But if you take a look at the documents you signed, you'll see that any short- or long-term health consequences are entirely your legal responsibility, as we cannot control what your past compels you to do."

"But you hired us because of our pasts. You made my house here look like my past house, for Christ's sake."

"I brought you on because of your entire profile, which includes many elements, a general unrest with the state of physics being one of them. And you'll also do well to consider the generosity with which we welcomed you here, and your wife, and then your ex-wife. It's the first time someone's brought in an ex."

"So you're saying I'm being let go."

Klein nodded at Nils. This part was Nils's job.

"Correct," Nils said. "But we would like you to complete the mission. You were quite close the last time. One more fold should do it. And don't worry about the health effects of one more fold. Talia worked many more folds than you. It took her a while to catch on, whereas you moved quite quickly."

"I do think you'll be fine, all things considered," Klein said. "Health-wise, that is. You're experiencing acute effects right now, but your biometrics continue to remain strong in folds."

"If you keep doing this, people will die."

"If we don't do this, people will die, too," Klein said. "People dying, it's the human cost of extra-human exploration. When we figure out what we need to figure out, everything will be different, everything will have been worth it."

"But you won't figure it out. You don't know exactly how causality works yet. You can't erase your public embarrassment no matter how much money or how many people you throw at this."

"I'm not in the business of being insulted."

"So you want one more fold out of me, and then I'm free?"

"One more for us. What you do for you, it's up to you."

"Why would you let me continue to use the time bath outside of sanctioned missions?"

Klein finished his tea and wiped sweat from his brow. "Because, Noah. Everything is data."

Eileen

Eileen was thinking about Prem. She was lying on her bed, thinking about him and how she'd left him. She hadn't formally left the relationship, but he'd asked her not to go, and she'd gone. That constituted leaving someone behind, even if he didn't live with her, even if they weren't that serious. As she lay there, she heard footsteps and a suitcase being wheeled on the gravel outside, the sound of Maya arriving at the lab. Good, she thought. Stability was locking into place with Maya's arrival. As if before, everything had been thrown up in the air and Eileen and Noah were swimming through antigravity, and now Maya's presence made everything settle. Maya was the one they had been missing.

But Prem, Prem. She'd been thinking he was simple, but now that seemed unfair. He wasn't simple, but rather unencumbered. She'd only fooled herself into thinking she was also unencumbered, but when it came to opening up to Prem, to telling him what it had been like to have Serena and to lose her, she'd suddenly seen everything she had been carrying around, all the memories like a pack of half-inflated balloons tied around her waist. Easy to forget, but impossible to move freely. He was just trying to see her, that was all.

When her phone lit up with his name, at first she was confused. Had she called him? Had her thinking about him willed his call?

His voice was warm and gentle, like he'd just finished laughing, exactly as she remembered it, despite how badly they'd spoken to each other when she left. As they talked, she watched the sun go down and the gray night fill in. He'd almost finished grading finals. A few of his students had already heard about their transfers to four-year colleges. He was proud of them. It had gotten cold and crisp, but no rain yet. An atmospheric river was coming, a wet system set to sit over their county. He'd checked on her plants. Once, he ran into the colleague covering her classes, who was also checking on her plants. She had multiple people who checked on her plants while she was gone, even if she hadn't asked them to.

"I'm sorry," he said, as though he was walking himself to the confession. "I wanted to say that. I'm sorry for being insensitive to your loss, to Serena. To whatever you needed to do to be with the loss."

Tears immediately filled Eileen's eyes. It was a gift to be understood, even just once in life. But twice, it made her throat burn with gratitude.

"I'm a liar," she said, her voice breaking.

"Oh, no, you're not."

"I mean to myself. This idea that I'd packed up the memory of her and moved on. She's everywhere," Eileen managed to say. Her face was wet now, her small sobs silent. But she knew Prem could tell that she was breaking.

"For what it's worth, I never believed that. Even if you insisted."

"Good," she said.

She thought of the door, how she'd become a door in the fold back to Serena's birth. The way her body itself had transformed into a portal between prelife and life. She'd thought the door of her body had opened only briefly. But now she understood that once it opened, it was open forever, the channel between forming and being. She didn't just have access to it—she *was* the channel. And after Serena died, she lived like the door had been slammed shut, when in fact an element of the pain was that the portal was always open, if it had once been.

On the phone with Prem, she closed her eyes and tried to tell him some version of this, that you couldn't unmake yourself, that she'd come here to try to tell that to her ex-husband, but that also she'd had to tell herself.

Later, Noah texted her to come over. *Maya wants to meet you.* Eileen put a coat on and walked the short distance to their house. She knocked, and Maya opened the door immediately, probably having heard her walk up, or even watched it. Eileen laughed a little, and so did Maya, and they stood there on opposite sides of the doorway for a moment, looking at each other. Maya looked like she did in the pictures Eileen had seen online, blessed with supple skin that would always look young, chocolate hair that was just the right amount of wavy, and effortlessly cool even in her soft, drapey sweats. She had an eye for fabrics and cuts, it was obvious. Eileen felt strangely comforted, knowing she herself had no such eye.

Maya held out her hand. "Please, come in."

Eileen grabbed it with both of her hands, and Maya pulled her across the threshold.

There was Noah, behind Maya, standing at the kitchen table, looking down at the floor. Then, slowly but with purpose, he dragged his head up, and looked at both of them holding hands.

"So what this won't be is weird," Eileen said. "Okay? Noah, you're not the center of us. We talked without you."

"Oh, I already told him this isn't some weird fantasy come true."

Noah sighed. "That'd be a real sick fantasy."

310

Talking on the phone was one thing, but standing together, physically in the same space, was another. Eileen could feel Maya's eyes lingering, studying her, and Eileen resisted the impulse herself. A small surge of jealousy shot through her gut, seeing the way Noah moved almost imperceptibly toward Maya. Then the surge faded. No matter what, her past was still alive in her.

Noah produced a bottle of wine and Maya opened it. They sat at the table and drank. Eileen took the lead catching Maya up on everything, all they'd discovered, the various folds, Klein, the monitoring system in the lights, Talia, the way Noah's health had deteriorated. He still looked unwell. She saw all the light switch panels in their place had been taken off. Then Noah told Eileen about his meeting with Klein and Nils, how they wanted him to complete the mission, how they'd locked him in with an NDA and vague threats pertaining to Klein's endless supply of money.

"So they'll continue to do it, with someone else as test subject," Eileen said.

"Absolutely," Noah said. "That was clear."

She stood up and began walking toward the back of the house. She gestured for them to follow. Once outside deep in the brush, she spoke again, quietly.

"Then what we'll have to do is destroy it," she said.

"I'm in," Maya said, right as Noah said, confused, "How?"

"Talia told me how. Sort of. The bath has a powerful hydrogen fuel cell inside it, something like sixty percent concentrated hydrogen is what Nils said. It runs throughout the entire body of the bath. I think, from looking at it, it's poorly ventilated. I saw that it was also pretty easy to crack open, with the right tools."

"Cracking it open would only slowly poison me, in the time bath," Noah said.

"Not if you introduced fluorine gas into the closed system."

"Where am I going to get fluorine gas?"

"It's in the core. Along with about three other highly reactive gases, in case there's not enough fluorine."

Maya wasn't quite following, but Noah stared at Eileen, mouth slightly agape, as if to ask, *How did you figure all this out?*

Eileen shrugged. "If you listen to what people are saying and look around with a scientific curiosity . . ."

Noah smiled. "Okay, okay, Dr. Merrick. I've been a little busy." He seemed to understand the plan without her explaining the rest. "But if we destroyed the machine, they would build another one."

Eileen nodded. "Yes, they probably would. It would take them a while to gather all those elements and materials, though."

"A destructive event might be enough—bad enough PR to delay them or stop the project entirely," Maya said. "I could make sure someone's here. A journalist from El Paso previewing my work. Justine mentioned that."

"They'd come after me," Noah said.

"They'd be a joke," Eileen said.

"And they have enough money to make me a joke, too," he replied.

"Men like that aren't driven by revenge. That's what the money's for. They're driven by recognition," Maya said.

She brought a blanket and another bottle of wine outside, and over two more glasses, they convinced Noah it was the right, safe, responsible thing to do, the only way to end a journey that had already caused enough damage. And they went over the steps, how it would happen. And then they settled into simply talking, about Eileen's class, her students, the way she'd originally seen *Weight*. Maya told them about meeting Yuko Matsuda, how she'd changed the photograph, how she'd made the image move, have consequence, even if the woman's leap from the building's edge was never finished. She told Eileen about the dying pronghorn, the way no one could figure it out, or wanted to figure it out. Eileen wondered if it had to do with the refuse from the lab leaking into their water supply. Maya seemed interested, and Eileen said she would ask around.

Noah was content, listening to them talk, but he didn't say much. Toward the end of the bottle of wine, Eileen asked him if he was all right.

"I'm okay," he said. "I don't have anything to report. Not like you two. I have only these folds, and they're so awful, and also wonderful, but confusing. Impotent, too. There's nothing to say about them."

"Oh," Eileen said, sympathetic now to the way Noah's brain had been co-opted by the Janus Project. She felt sure he'd get it back, but she saw how fuzzy he was.

"Take me," Maya said, cutting the silence between all of them. "I know you took Eileen on folds. It's okay. But take me. I want to see."

"To see what?"

"Serena. Let me meet her."

Noah held his hand over his mouth, but beneath his fingers, his face broke apart. Eileen felt it in her chest, the surge of pain, thinking about Serena alive, and the surge of love, like a harp string plucked, vibrating. Maya wanted to know Serena, a ghost that had been for so long just between her and Noah. That's how a memory stayed alive, how a person lived beyond their death. You had to tell the story.

Maya

Noah and Maya slept in each other's arms, which they hadn't done since the early stages of dating, when they'd pass out from a mixture of drunkenness and desire. But she wanted to be close to him. She saw he was sick, and that he wanted her, and she felt a strange but exacting want building in her as well. She wanted to know him again, and here he was.

But he woke her early, as the sun was rising. He wanted to show her now, he said. He wanted to take her to Serena, and he wanted her mind clear and unencumbered, still almost asleep, if possible. Maya dressed quickly and followed him into Building D. She tried to shake off the feeling—the knowledge—that they were being watched or monitored. She wanted to be with Noah, wherever he needed her to be.

She waited while he mapped his memory. He looked like he disappeared, everything slack, his brain somewhere else. He gave her the shot, so tenderly she barely felt it. She was looking at the disappearing spot where the needle had gone in when he said, "Look at me."

He held her hands. "It's going to feel weird, I think, having someone else's memory lit up in your brain. I don't actually know if it will work. But you can make yourself more amenable by not resisting. Let it feel familiar, like it comes from you, even though you know it doesn't. Focus on how it feels, not what it is. Does that make sense?"

Maya nodded. Nothing had made more sense. It was the sort of art sentiment she had long been trying to explain to Noah. That when you looked at art and took it in, your job wasn't to digest what it actually objectively looked like, but what it subjectively manifested inside you. There could be no wrong way to do that, to feel an image.

They undressed quietly. Maya didn't want to disturb the placid electricity between them. He helped her climb into the bath, and then he carefully got in his. A small wave of panic throttled her throat from the claustrophobia, the sense of imminent drowning, but she heard his voice through the helmet: *Breathe.*

She hadn't heard his voice like this before: a quaver, but a depth, too, as though they were descending so deep there was insufficient air. She felt, of course, grief—that was the waver cutting through everything. She felt also his love, but not as she'd previously been afraid of feeling it. Before, she had been afraid that witnessing his grief would be to witness his love moving away from her, toward the past, in the direction of something she could never provide. Now she felt his love going both ways at once, toward the past and toward her, the future, merging them. And as she began to see the contours of Serena's ponytail, blond, bobbing in a dimmed bedroom, a sensation like falling rose up in her, and she opened her mouth to let out a yelp, but before she could produce a sound—

· · •· •· ·

—she is standing in Serena's bedroom. Noah is standing next to her. His eyes widen, seeing her. *Go, go.* He ushers her into the closet, behind a folding slatted door. She presses herself up against a stack of plastic bins, at the top of which is a sharp princess castle, poking into her back. That's when she realizes she's not wearing clothes. She hadn't had anything to fold into, because she hadn't been here. Her being here defies everything a fold is meant to accomplish, a completed line of time. She'd never been in this time. But here she was.

"Dry hands!"

Maya hears Eileen's voice from the hallway. It's buoyant, younger. Then Serena bounds into the room, wiping her hands on a blue princess dress she's wearing. "I did it," Serena says. "I went potty."

"Excellent," Noah says, clapping his hands together.

Maya watches all this through the slats, an image broken up into several images, her brain making them into one. She can hear her breath loud in her ears. Then she sees Noah, and more than seeing, she feels him. This is Noah as a father. He's easy with Serena, physical, letting her crash into him and accepting her body with gentleness, but also with a full embrace. Maya hasn't seen him like this before, not exactly like this. She's seen him hug and play with Caroline's kid, but this is different. This is knowing a body and every possible force and direction it can take.

And Serena, she's harder to take in through the slats. She moves a lot, bobbing and weaving between sentences and ideas and the furniture and her toys. Her thin ponytail follows Noah around the room as he gathers up something. Stars. They're peeling stars from sticky sheets, glow-in-the-dark stars to put up on the walls.

Daddy, she calls him. Maya stops breathing for a moment, to hear him be called this, alive as a father again.

"Daddy, on the ceiling," Serena says. "Not on the walls. Stars go on the sky."

Noah peels a star from the wall above her bed. "Okay, then," he says. "Show me. Wait, Eileen! I need a ladder!"

Serena hides from Eileen when she enters the room with the small ladder. "Where's Serena?" Eileen asks. She is sturdier than the Eileen Maya knows, almost broader, a smile taking up her entire face.

"Dunno," Noah says, shrugging. "She got sucked up into the stars, I think."

Serena giggles from behind a rocking chair, where she's crouched.

"Okay. Say hi to her for me when you get her!"

Eileen leaves them to it, and Serena holds the ladder legs while Noah climbs atop it.

"You're in charge of the stars," Noah says. He touches the ceiling with his fingertips. Then he winks down at Serena.

Winks. Maya has only seen him wink a few times. At Caroline's son, now that she thinks of it. Kids, beguiled by a wink. Serena eats it up.

One by one Serena hands him a sticky star, placing it on his fingertips, which he then hovers under the ceiling so she can direct him exactly where she wants it. "Not there, too far away," Serena says. "Not there. Closer."

It's always closer, closer, she wants the stars close together.

"But some stars are really far apart from each other," Noah says.

"How far?"

"Light-years."

"What's light-years?"

"Distances so far that even light, which is super fast, takes a long time to travel."

Serena considers this. Maya thinks he hasn't done a great job of explaining it. "Closer," Serena says.

It takes ten, fifteen minutes. Maya's breath is making the wooden slats moist. Finally, Noah says, "Done." He climbs down from the stool and turns the light off in Serena's room. Maya can't see the ceiling, but she can see the yellow-green light coming off the stars, all from one section, a cluster Serena has instructed him to make. It glows bright above her head.

Serena reaches for Noah's hand, and he holds it. Then he looks back at the closet door, at Maya breathing between the slats, and Maya can't quite see his face in the dark, but she can feel it, his eyes looking for her, saying, *See this, this is Serena.*

I see her.

"That's all hydrogen," Serena says, mispronouncing the word as "hydra-don."

"You're right," Noah says.

"If there's too much, it will be a black hole. That's what you said. We should change it."

"Why?"

"Black holes are bad. They break light."

"But that's not necessarily bad, being a lightbreaker."

"Lightbreaker." Serena laughs at the new word.

"Yeah, maybe a black hole traps and breaks light, but then after it breaks, it's something so different and new we can't even understand it."

"Like a dinosaur."

"Like a unicorn."

"Like magic."

Noah picks Serena up and holds her on top of the ladder, so she can be closer to the glowing. "Maybe we came from a black hole. Maybe that's where we go."

"When?"

"When . . . we go somewhere else."

"Why would we go to a black hole?"

"Because," Noah says. He holds on to her waist so she doesn't fall. "Because inside a black hole is both time and space, which means inside the black hole, waaaaay inside, is the past, and the future. Something we can't know yet."

"Light-years," Serena says.

"Or bigger than light-years. Maybe on the other side is a whole world of light."

"I'll go there. I want to go there, a black hole," Serena says. "I'm a lightbreaker."

"Okay."

Here, Maya's knee falters, and she bangs into the closet door. Ouch. When she looks up, Serena's staring at the closet, and Noah has stepped away from her, and Maya tries to stay still, but Serena says, "Who's there?" And Maya inhales a little and that's enough for the walls of the closet to start moving, circling around her, and with a creeping nausea she—

—fell out. She pushed the top of the time bath open and coughed her way out of the machine, sputtering liquid on the floor. Noah got out next to her, and he said, "You'll feel fine in a minute or two," but she knew she wouldn't; she knew she was going to throw up. She looked at him and he saw it, and he pointed her toward a utility sink in the corner, where she ran and retched. Last night's wine, bile. Immediately she felt better.

Noah came to her with a robe and wrapped her up. Then he put his arms around her, and she sank into them. Her husband, a man who proposed in an art exhibit because he knew she'd like it, a man who wept at cacti, who walked into random art talks, who wanted so badly to believe. She wanted to say, *Thank you for taking me to Serena*, because she sensed it would be his last visit to her. But it didn't seem like enough to say only that.

So she said, "When I was a kid, I always thought of light-years as this magical railway made of light, like light just hurtling through space, so when someone said it was light-years away, I didn't think it was impossibly far but, I don't know, hopeful. Like a light highway running toward something, anything it could meet. It seemed, I guess, like love."

Noah nodded into her shoulder. He understood. Yes, that was right.

Maya worked uninterrupted for two days. First she called Justine and persuaded her to call the journalist, to have her come see the work, to promise it all had nothing to do with death. Maya wasn't lying. When she worked, she didn't feel death. She wasn't intending to communicate that. She wanted, instead, to make something alive, super alive. When she first finished the painting that Justine had loved, she thought the dynamism had to come through a color story. But now she saw that wasn't quite right. The dynamism was instead going to be about perspective.

This is what she did. She found the video she'd taken at the Marfa Lights the night she saw the pronghorn in the dark. It was grainy, but she lightened it a bit, and it was possible to see the figure of the animal looking at the camera, light reflecting in its eyes, and then it leapt away, bounding through the scrub, and that was how you knew the landscape, the distance to the horizon. She then projected that video upside down onto the canvas she'd painted of the pronghorn in the backyard, as though it were coming through a camera obscura. The gray darkness of the video blurred the painting a bit, but the vibrant color of the painting worked against the blurring. Then the movement of the video worked against the color, like the two modes were talking to each other.

But that wasn't quite right, either. So, with the lightest hand, she took a pencil and sketched a ghost of the upside-down video projection onto the canvas, but slightly out of alignment with the video. As though the video were itself moving in the wind. She sketched so lightly that she wasn't even sure anyone would see it if she didn't point it out, or if they didn't stare at the canvas for a very long time. A true ghost image. This ghost image she thought would have an effect even if not specifically perceived: an indication that between the world of color and the world of movement there was more, an imprint of what happens when you let something be both alive and disappeared.

Maya only realized she was sweating from the precision of sketching when she heard Eileen come in. She and Noah were talking about the plan, what they'd do during his final mission, and then they made their way through the kitchen back to Maya's painting room, as she now thought of it. The whole canvas was set up how she wanted it, and though there were some minor adjustments she wanted to make to the light sketch, she was happy with it.

"Oh," Eileen said, taking it in. Noah had already seen the stages of this, a process he'd never been a part of before, but that Maya welcomed him into. He silently looked, and then at the very end he would tell her what he liked about what he saw, lightly, gently.

"It's . . ." Eileen shook her head, trying for words. "Gorgeous? I don't know. The movement in it is eerie. Dizzying. In a good way."

"Right," Noah said. "You know, it totally reminds me of the Robert Irwin installation, right, Maya? Eileen, you should go there. We could take you, before we leave. You walk through it and . . ."

As they spoke, Maya perched on the sill. They talked easily, fluently, a vestige of the years they'd known each other. She liked seeing Noah like this, open. It reminded her of when they first met.

Maya told him that later, in bed, in the dark, staring at the open skylight above them.

"Seeing you with her is like getting to watch you be totally yourself," she said.

"I'm myself when I'm with you, too."

"I know, but I don't get to watch it then. I'm part of it."

He propped himself up on his side, facing her. He breathed like he was going to tell her a secret. For a moment her heart beat faster. But before she could imagine the possible bad futures, he spoke.

"When we get home, I think we should start trying to have a baby. For real."

She didn't know if it was because of how much focus she had exerted on the painting or if it was residual cognitive effects from the nanorepeaters and the folding, but a series of images passed through her mind, calmly and evenly, like a psychic flipping over tarot cards. The photo of her as a child on the beach in Okinawa; her young mother meeting her father on a quiet street in the middle of the night decades ago; Noah's ghostlike face becoming more substantial in the back of the auditorium while she talked about dynamic sadness in photography; Ren making something ugly beautiful in his studio in Tokyo; Noah making dinner in their kitchen while she read a book on the couch, knowing he had to stay alive for her; and now a strange pulsing aliveness in her, pulling her forward and forward, into each new second ticking by.

"I want that," she said.

This was it, a feeling about her connection to Noah sealing, a seed finally fused with soil, ready to start the journey back toward the sun. Trying to have a child was sharing a belief in an unknowable future. Faith in possibility. For now, that was enough.

"Oh," he said, curling himself around her, his mouth in her hair. "I hope, I hope, I hope."

Noah, Maya, Eileen

On the morning of his final fold, Noah felt more centered and calm than ever. Nils noticed. He put a hand on Noah's shoulder and said, "Despite everything, brother, I'm proud of you."

Noah wasn't sure what "everything" referred to exactly, but he nodded. "Thank you."

"Are you so steady now because you know the end is near?"

"Something like that," Noah said.

"I'll leave you to it, then," Nils said.

He began the recording session, which was Noah's cue to initiate memory reading. He closed his eyes and disappeared into the moment.

* * *

In the house, Maya arranged her canvas just so, everything not quite perfect but perfectly presentable. In studio visits, people liked to see some level of disarray, a wild artist's mind at work. She kept her sketchbooks flipped open and discarded canvases propped up against the wall. She covered her paints so they wouldn't dry out, but she didn't clean up the flecks everywhere, or the palettes where she'd made colors. She dressed in a big blue caftan with a black turtleneck under it. In the bedroom, everything was already packed away in suitcases, ready to go in the morning, and Maya made sure to close the bedroom door. No need to spark any questions.

The journalist's name was Belinda. Justine said Belinda had a chip on her shoulder. She said she wasn't sure exactly what the chip was about, possibly to do with being turned down for job after job in New York, being stuck in El Paso, and being uncredited for all the work she'd done reporting on Marfa's art scene, how it was always *Vanity Fair* writers who got big splashy praise for writing about how Marfa had become an art destination. That sounded like explanation enough to Maya, but she also knew a New York–bred gallery girl like Justine wouldn't understand what it meant to not get everything you wanted in exactly the way you wanted it.

When Justine came in, wearing what Maya thought was a tad too much makeup, she swooned.

"The work is gorgeous, and I knew you could do it without making it about death," Justine said.

"I mean, it's not *not* about death."

Justine put a finger to her lips. "The best work goes unexplained by the artist, at least at first. Let's let Belinda take it in and interpret."

Fine, Maya thought. She'd be happy if Belinda interpreted it as being about life, too.

* * *

Eileen hadn't left Marfa, but she thought it best to be away from campus that day. Besides, she had a contact at a research facility twenty minutes outside of town who might have a hunch about the pronghorn deaths. These researchers were studying the water table and aquifer changes, but a colleague from her college had texted her that she knew a scientist there named Simon who was also an animal lover and would likely welcome any questions she had about wildlife.

The facility was modest but new, all glass and shiny wood, boasting an influx of recent funding, but Eileen was clear about why she was there. Simon took her on a walk through the grounds, down a hill where, despite the night freezes, some tiny yellow flowers were blooming.

"I care for them," Simon admitted. He was half-British and spoke with a lilt, one of those researchers who were used to being stuck in lonely outposts for weeks or months at a time. "But it's about to get too cold for this batch. That's all right, I have more."

Eileen explained what Maya had told her, that the already limited population of Trans-Pecos pronghorn were showing up dead from mysterious causes that no one seemed to want to get to the bottom of, and some of the animals had even been observed to show indications of dementia and suicidal behaviors. Of course, Simon's first question was about who was in charge of necropsies.

"No one seems all that interested in necropsies. I believe the bodies are simply disposed of."

Simon raised his eyebrows. "Someone's always interested in necropsies, unless there's a liability issue."

"I do think some of the incidents have occurred on Klein Michaels's land."

Simon gave a little laugh. "Ah, you should have said you were from the Michaels Lab."

"You're familiar?"

"His foundation funds us, too."

Eileen's stomach sank. A dead end, she supposed. She'd wanted so badly to find an answer for Maya, to do justice for the animals in her beautiful painting. She stopped walking and looked back at the main building, inside which a few more strange men were conducting their research, gathering their data, spitting out their results. None of this— research, data, questions, hypotheses—was the same as answers.

"This is cutleaf daisy," Simon said, pointing to his yellow flowers. "It's what the pronghorn mostly eat. They also eat other kinds of scrub. But I've seen them trying to eat this. Scrub is where they get much of their water in their diet, actually."

"Hm," Eileen said. How much of this guy's botany lesson was a polite amount to listen to? When could she leave?

"I've noticed that the cutleaf don't grow as well during certain times. It's almost cyclical, when I observe damaged ones."

"Damaged?" *Damaged*, Eileen thought, *implies responsibility*.

"I haven't studied this, of course."

"No, of course."

"Not my area."

"But hypothetically."

"Hypothetically, if wastewater were being dumped that was, say, slightly radioactive, or contained some other poison, on a schedule, then the way certain plants expressed this poison might be detectable in the animals that consume the plants."

"I see," Eileen said. The flowers really were a vibrant, sunshine yellow.

"I don't study prion diseases."

"All right."

"But it almost sounds like you're describing mad cow disease but for pronghorn. You'd need a wildlife biologist to do the right tests. Why the pronghorn's specific DNA is susceptible to this, if no humans have gotten sick from it. Lots of assumptions, you know."

"Yeah," Eileen said. "Hypothetically, a lot of assumptions."

Simon leaned down and picked a daisy for her. "Here," he said. "This one's the real deal."

Just before Nils returned to begin the fold, Noah emerged from memory reading and thought of entropy. The year after he met Eileen and changed his major to physics, he took a class called Mechanics and Relativity. The professor opened every class with a different description of entropy. Mostly it was a joke, entropy about defining entropy, but sometimes it was poetic, and allowed Noah a new way to envision the concept. One of his favorite class openings was when the professor described entropy in terms of time. Entropy in the past was low, and that's how we told ourselves stories about what happened, he said. Memory arranged itself because entropy had settled. But in the future, the potential of entropy is high, until it isn't.

Noah raised his hand, as bold as he was naive in those days. "But doesn't defining it that way imply that we have some control over arranging the entropy in the future?"

"First of all, there isn't entropy *in* the future. Entropy *is* the future. And second of all, yes, it does imply that, to an extent. You arrange the chaos of time simply by living time. Control, I don't know. But change, yes. It's the only change possible, the future."

Noah had felt embarrassed by this teacher's twofold answer, embarrassed to have thought he'd found a flaw in the logic. That had been part of what spurred him toward mathematical models. Models closed up any logical loopholes. But that hadn't been why he'd gotten into physics in the first place. He'd gotten into it to go sit in those logical loopholes, to see what came when all that you knew didn't add up.

Now, as he nodded at Nils behind the glass and prepared to enter the time bath, he understood that the professor hadn't been embarrassing Noah, but rather modeling exactly the kind of thinking Noah should feel comfortable embodying if he was going to go further in the field. Maybe Eileen's version of what she'd told him after the Europa disaster was the correct one—that he had a need for answers, not a penchant for uncertainty. Or both versions were correct, and Noah had wanted both things: the sureness of answers *and* the richness of uncertainty. Past and future. The gravity of order, the lift of possibility. Maybe that's what everyone wanted, everything.

He entered the time bath as he'd done so many times before. Nils was talking, but Noah wasn't there anymore. In his mind he was both places: the past, where he needed to do one last thing, and the future, where what he needed to do were first things, all of them.

· ·°· ·°· °·,

Immediately, Maya felt for Belinda. Yes, she did seem beleaguered, but also slightly frustrated. Maya liked when people started from that place, though. The only way to go was up. Her painting could give Belinda some bounce in her step.

"Traffic," Belinda said. "Which is strange, because, you know, middle of nowhere and all. Mostly it was getting out of El Paso. Something I've been trying to do for years."

Belinda laughed too loudly at her own joke. Maya matched her laughter, but Justine only raised her eyebrows.

"We're so excited to preview some of what Maya will show and talk about at the Koppelman Gallery," Justine said. "And we're so lucky to have an artist associated with the Klein Michaels Foundation and lab to cement the connection between the ephemeral and the tangible."

"Which one is ephemeral and which one is tangible?" Belinda asked.

Maya looked at Justine because she, too, was unsure.

Justine snorted. "Art is ephemeral and science is tangible, don't you think?" But the moment it came out of her mouth, it was obvious that she questioned it.

Belinda shrugged, and scribbled something in her notebook.

Eileen got back in the car with answers but no solution. Science had long taught her the difference between the two. Answers were results, but a solution made the various results in the problem cohere. Yes, of course Michaels was poisoning the groundwater with whatever waste the lab was producing, probably the same (or at least adjacent) poisoning that had happened to Talia Bolson, that could slowly etch its way into Noah's brain. But what to do about it? Klein Michaels, the project, the idea of time travel, of repairing past losses, all of it seemed too powerful to fight. Yes, they could and would destroy the machine, but what they really ought to do was destroy the way loss wounds people, propels them toward insane, corrosive ideas.

But then Eileen thought about Alice, her student who'd represented scientific breakthroughs by tracking art and culture. She'd said, "Science ignores people." She'd said, "Thank you for seeing more, Dr. Merrick." Maybe that was all this was, the Janus Project, a way to see more. What Noah had to have in response—what they all had to have—was the ability to know the difference between seeing more and doing more. Doing more was always in the future, a state not returned to but reached for.

The day in the fold seems, once again, impossibly bright. Things are brighter in memory. Noah is calmer than he has ever been in a fold. He strolls down the path that leads behind Klein's residence, and spots the lockbox. He kneels in front of it. It's 9:07. He closes his eyes. He wants to remember this, his last fold. A light breeze through his hair, sending a chill down his scalp, a bird taking off from a tree, sending the dead leaves shuddering. Small rodents rushing through the underbrush. A warmth coming up through the earth, warming his knees, even as winter approaches.

He opens his eyes. The perfect mirror of the back of Klein's home. Klein is there, watching him, or not. He knows now it doesn't matter. They made it clear he doesn't matter to them, and it was a relief to hear that, so they could matter less to him.

He isn't aware the minutes have passed by until the box suddenly ticks and the lock makes a mechanical sound, releasing. Carefully, Noah lifts the lid with both hands. Inside is a folded piece of paper. He picks it up and opens it, reads it. It isn't easy to memorize, but he reads the lines, whispering them to himself until he feels they are imprinted. Then he places the paper back in the box and stands.

He turns away from the glass to face the open field. For a moment, he scans, wanting to see evidence of life—a pronghorn, a deer, a gopher, a bird, a butterfly, a bee, a dandelion disappearing in the air. But then he stops himself, stops the searching. He's already seen it, what he needs to see, though he can't articulate it yet.

It's only when he willingly falls out of the fold—for the first time willingly—that he knows what he's found. In that gummy split-second space between past and present, he thinks, *What a gift*. Not the fold, though there has been goodness in those. But the return, that's the gift. The ability to return, the desire to return, the way life streams painfully back into him as he opens his eyes to the world of light.

"It's beautiful," Belinda said, and Maya immediately believed her. She believed her because Maya also thought it was beautiful. Belinda walked back and forth in front of the canvas, sometimes blocking the projection, but trying to take it in from many angles.

"Will you make more? How many for the show?" Belinda asked.

"I'm not sure," Maya said. "I'll make more, but I'm not sure how many."

She wasn't lying. But she wasn't making them for the show. There would be no show. They'd leave; their time in Marfa was up. Whatever Maya was going to do with art or curation or criticism or teaching or her degree was back home, with Noah, with the life they'd made there.

* * * * * *

Eileen pulled into the lab campus and sat in her parked car with the engine off. It would be any moment now. Afterward, she would leave and go home. She wanted to go home, but she also wanted to stay in this moment, the moment before the rest of her life. Serena existed a little bit more here. Which reminded her of something she wanted to tell Noah.

* * * * * *

Noah told Nils what the note said.

> *Time present and time past*
> *Are both perhaps present in time future,*
> *And time future contained in time past.*
> *If all time is eternally present*
> *All time is unredeemable.*

Nils smiled, and so did Noah, and then Nils asked, "Are you laughing? At my choice of poetry?"

"A little on the nose," Noah said.

"I'll have you know that every time we fold I write something different on that piece of paper, just in case. I happened to be reading Eliot last night is all."

"I like it," Noah said. He did. It tumbled over his tongue, didn't quite make sense, not until he'd repeated it many times. He liked having to work for it.

"Read it sometime. *Four Quartets*. And that's it for me, brother. You shut it down and meet back in my office for a debrief, sound good?"

Noah nodded, wrapping himself in a robe. "It sounds perfect."

He listened to Nils's metallic footsteps heading toward the exit to Building D, and then the heavy door close behind him. Noah moved quickly. It would only be minutes before Nils checked on whatever hidden camera Noah assumed was pointed at him in this room.

He found the small screwdriver he'd tucked into the pocket of his robe, and set about draining the bath just enough to be able to access the panel and the valves inside it. But as he did the mechanical work, his mind circled something else, the word *unredeemable. All time is unredeemable if all time is eternally present.* He'd once met a scholar of loop theory, a visiting professor from Europe who hosted a cocktail hour. Noah had been sitting nearby when the scientist was holding court about the Big Bang, how he preferred a new term gaining popularity, the "Big Bounce," wherein instead of the universe having sprung from nothing, it had contained in its singular point the remnants of a previous universe that had compacted down. And so it went on like this, a universe springing from a universe, then eventually shrinking back down, only to birth another universe, and on and on, in a loop— loop quantum gravity—all the information of the entirety of everything bouncing between existing and not existing. Noah had his questions, but what was attractive about that paradigm was that it meant nothing was wasted, no energy disappeared into blackness. Instead the energy was changed, morphed, evolved, devolved.

He thought of the Big Bounce when he thought of that phrase, "If all time is eternally present, all time is unredeemable." He'd bought into this promise that Klein and Nils had implicitly made, that the past was redeemable somehow, and that in redeeming the past, one was able to redeem a more perfect future. In that first meeting with Klein, he'd told Noah that anything was possible. Klein was right, but not in this way, not in the way that meant changing the past was possible. He was right that anything was possible because everything was already possible, was contained in the present: the past, that wild, dynamic future. Possibility wasn't unlocking some locked-up past, but seeing what new universe sprang forward in each second, each day, each turn—stopping into a room in a building because a woman's voice in a classroom was laced with trembling passion; becoming a regular at a bar where he could be a secret for a few months; loving a woman, a child, another woman; none of it going away, ever, only surging into the next, and the next.

* * *

Now, Eileen thought. Now is when he would be introducing the hydrogen from the fuel cell into the core, which contained highly unstable gases. Noah would have less than a minute to jog out of range, but once he was on the other side of the heavy door to Building D, he'd be safe. They all would be safe, but the time baths would be incinerated. Was it symbolic? She wondered. She didn't think it mattered. The line between what was symbolically destructive and what was actually destructive had thinned to almost nothing these past weeks and months. What one understood to be true and what was actually true, those distinctions weren't what people were about, when it came down to it.

What was true: Fluorine was highly reactive. She'd wait to witness that.

* * *

Belinda did something Maya hadn't ever seen anyone do on a studio visit: She touched the painting. Maya understood why. The way the projection worked, the painting appeared to be living. Maya was moved, actually, that Belinda touched the painting. Maya had made Belinda doubt herself, or rather, she'd made her believe.

But Justine gasped, a small gasp, when Belinda's fingertips touched the canvas, and Belinda drew back sharply. She turned to glare at Justine, with a look that Maya was worried meant Belinda would storm out, but just then, a boom cracked through the air. Maya was surprised at the duration of the sound, the lifetime of it, that she could feel the origin, small but deep, and then listen as it bloomed over a matter of milliseconds into something louder and almost metal in nature, everything in the time bath lab collapsing in on itself, or bending outward. The destruction over time, that was what was surprising to Maya. It took time to let go of something; she felt the length of it.

Belinda and Justine ducked, and even Maya did a little, backing into the shuddering windowpane. But then she ran through the kitchen and the dining area and the small living room to the front door, where she needed to see that Noah had gotten out of the building, and when she got to the door, she opened it right as Noah opened it on the other side, the two of them together, swinging that door away.

She was relieved, and she hugged him. He was warm, sweaty under his shirt. Behind him was Nils, scrambling out of his office, and then Klein, who stepped through his front door, which Oliver opened, and then coming from the parking lot walkway, Eileen, all of them staring at the courtyard, at the closed door to Building D.

And behind Maya came Belinda, who walked the farthest into the courtyard, who stared—scowled—at everyone, and then took out her small notepad and started writing.

Later, what felt like much later but was only the next afternoon, the three of them stood in the living room that already felt empty, even though it had all the same furniture in it from when Noah and Maya had arrived. The emptiness came from what they were finally about to do: leave.

Nils and Klein hadn't spoken to any of them since the explosion, but Oliver had come by, demanding to know what Noah had done. Noah explained that as he was turning the machine off, a piece of the core broke off, and that they really shouldn't have designed such unstable, reactive gases to live next to each other, especially if corrosion inside the core could cause a spark. He was lucky to have made it out in time. Oliver clearly didn't believe him, but Belinda had already filed her story in the paper, which included a tidbit Eileen had anonymously told her, a casual theory about what could be killing the already endangered pronghorn population. Belinda's story was set to be picked up by the papers in California first, and then likely New York. The Marfa police had even come by, then Texas Highway Patrol, and Oliver didn't want Noah or Eileen or Maya to talk to any of them. Noah told him they'd already packed their bags and would be on their way.

Inside Noah's bag, buried in scraps between the pages of an old copy of *The Man Who Fell to Earth*, were the crumpled remains of the hard copy design schematics Nils had casually tossed in his wastebasket. They weren't the final time bath designs, but they would be enough for JPL to build on. And waiting in Noah's email was a list of the names and last known addresses of as many former employees of Klein as Talia and Curtis could remember. No single employee had enough of the source code to do anything worthwhile, but if Noah convinced them all to work together, they could bring a large chunk to JPL, who in turn had promised to use the full force of their legal team to protect them against Klein. In the meantime, Noah would help JPL take from Klein the one thing he couldn't buy: the power of being the only person to hold this technology, and the danger of wielding that power.

And now they were on their way. Their suitcases stood next to them, little soldiers marshaling a plan to its conclusion. But none of what they'd done or were doing felt like a plan. None of them could have predicted what had happened, the ways their lives intersected. There was a feeling, though, that they'd continue to web around each other in the years to come.

"You do what she says," Eileen said to Noah, nodding at Maya.

"Always," Noah said. "Thank you for coming."

"I'll always come when you call. You too, Maya."

"Okay," Maya said, accepting that. "You're family." Eileen *was* family. Whatever child Maya had with Noah would be related to Eileen's child, gone or not.

But then Eileen stood awkwardly, her knees turned in. Neither Maya nor Noah was used to seeing Eileen this way. She was usually sure of herself and graceful.

"I wanted to say something. I wanted to say, mostly to Noah—"

"Should I go?" Maya asked. "I can load the car."

"No, no," Eileen said. "Stay. Because it's about you, too. But I wanted to tell Noah, I guess, tell him—you—that you made Serena exist more. Since I've been here, she exists more. I can hear her and feel her. So, thank you for that."

Noah looked down at the ground, and then when he looked back up, his face bore a curious look made of layers: hope trying to emerge from sadness.

"All I wanted was to see her," he said quietly. "And I did."

When he said that, he grabbed Maya's hand. She had seen Serena, too. That mattered.

"That made me think," said Eileen. "Family is an idea you have to keep at. We have to keep at it." She looked at Maya. "Don't stop."

For a while, no one knew how long, they didn't say much of anything. They let time pass. In that passing time, in a brief moment, so brief it was impossible to hold or name, the future became clear: In eighteen months, Maya will give birth to a boy named Sol, and when Eileen comes to meet him, Maya will say, quietly, "Serena's half brother." And Eileen, by that time, will be living with Prem in Vancouver, having fallen in love with both him and teaching. She will thrive living in a place that isn't solely a refuge from the ruins of her former life. And Noah will no longer be in ruins. He'll be building something new, no longer a shell or a shield himself. He will be a man in the world, vulnerable, with raw, beating hearts outside him, knowing the worst, hoping for the best.

But all that is later.

Finally, when they were ready, they left.

Maya and Noah drive out of Marfa the way they came in, but a little lighter, with fewer expectations. Her painting is tucked carefully in the back seat. The sky is clear and the temperature is crisp. She tells Noah the story of finding her father under the stairs, looking at photographs, and it's too sentimental for Noah to make sense of, not with what he knows about his father-in-law, and he laughs as she tells the story. They're still laughing as they pass the sign indicating that they've exited Marfa, and they don't even notice it.

At the same time, Eileen makes a stop. Maya told her about the Robert Irwin installation and that she had to see it before she left. Noah advised her, "Start on the dark side." Eileen laughed. That was very Noah. But when she gets there, she does start on the dark side, simply because it makes the most sense. Enter at the dark origins.

This will be the last thing she does here, she knows. Prem is expecting her. She's good with that, being expected. But walking through the dark side of the building makes her slow down. It isn't exactly dark. It's more dim, copper in its dimness, which means it's hard to see clearly where she's headed, but she's never blind to anything. And then she turns the corner, into the transition part of the building, where the darkness gives way. She picks up her pace and rushes through these scrim doors, excited to see where this will lead, and then she reaches another corner, and there, it's all light. Midafternoon, warm, steady, creamy light. Loss and pain, you never get over it, she thinks. It's the wrong way to think of loss. There is no *over it*. There is only the day you turn the corner, when something new is born.

So this art is about living, she thinks.

This happens just as Noah and Maya finish laughing, as the way they love each other newly now changes their very cells, and they tingle with it, the change—not the expectation of what it will mean, but the anticipation of what it could mean, how they can arrange future time in their heads, the lie and the truth of time travel existing right there, in their minds, the two of them and Eileen, moving forward toward light that hasn't happened yet.

Acknowledgments

Gratitude for this book belongs to:

My agent and editors: Andrea Morrison, Alison Fairbrother, and Laura Perciasepe.

The Riverhead team, including Glory Anne Plata, Hannah Lopez, Viviann Do, Sara Wood, Meighan Cavanaugh, and Kym Surridge.

The residences where I wrote parts of this: the Catto Shaw residency at Aspen Words and the Virginia Center for the Creative Arts residency in Auvillar, France.

Those who read or discussed drafts of this book with me: Sierra Bellows, Chloe Benjamin, Erin Saldin, Maggie Shipstead, Emma Rathbone, and Myung Joh Wesner. The writing orgy: Emma Borges-Scott, Jade Chang, Angela Flournoy, Jean Chen Ho, and Xuan Juliana Wang.

The advocates Faisal Kanaan, Merideth Bajana, and Jason Richman.

The prose of Yiyun Li and Rob Delaney, who wrote about their own child loss in luminous books, helping me understand the unfathomable.

The books of Carlo Rovelli, which made the awe of physics accessible.

The conversations with scientists Jacob Reimer, Tien-Tien Yu, and

Acknowledgments

Tiffany Watkins, who told me what was not scientifically possible and (hopefully) forgave me when I wrote it anyway.

The music of Francis and the Lights and Christine and the Queens, for giving sadness, joy, love, grief, and nostalgia a soundtrack.

The writing of Ted Chiang, which helped me see where humanity meets science.

The films of Brit Marling, which opened up a gateway of wonder.

The caretakers who spent time with my children while I worked: Lidia Ortiz and Iliana Pineda.

The mothers: Anne Gabel and Alice Kordosh.

And David, Thomas, and Kenzo, my beginning of time.

RAISING READERS
Books Build Bright Futures

Dear Reader,

We'd love your attention for one more page to tell you about the crisis in children's reading, and what we can all do.

Studies have shown that reading for fun is the **single biggest predictor of a child's future life chances** – more than family circumstance, parents' educational background or income. It improves academic results, mental health, wealth, communication skills, ambition and happiness.[1]

The number of children reading for fun is in rapid decline. Young people have a lot of competition for their time. In 2024, 1 in 10 children and young people in the UK aged 5 to 18 did not own a single book at home.[2]

Hachette works extensively with schools, libraries and literacy charities, but here are some ways we can all raise more readers:

- Reading to children for just 10 minutes a day makes a difference
- Don't give up if children aren't regular readers – there will be books for them!
- Visit bookshops and libraries to get recommendations
- Encourage them to listen to audiobooks
- Support school libraries
- Give books as gifts

There's a lot more information about how to encourage children to read on our website: **www.RaisingReaders.co.uk**

Thank you for reading.

hachette
UK

---

[1] OECD, '21st-Century Readers: Developing Literacy Skills in a Digital World', 2021, https://www.oecd.org/en/publications/21st-century-readers_a83d84cb-en.html

[2] National Literacy Trust, 'Book Ownership in 2024', November 2024, https://literacytrust.org.uk/research-services/research-reports/book-ownership-in-2024